Then the storm was on him, and the world shrank to a fury of heat and sand.

Blisters rose on exposed skin, scrubbed bloody by flying grit. Asheris closed his eyes against the scouring wind before it scraped them out.

Simooms killed humans and livestock easily, but the jinn had no fear of them. Before he was bound in flesh, Asheris had danced with such storms across the Sea of Glass. They were kin. So why was his stomach filled with cold, even as the heat bore him to his knees?

He opened *otherwise* eyes and nearly wept. Past the veil of the Fata, what rolled over Ta'ashlan was not a cloud of dun and copper dust, but a seething inky blackness. Not the absence of color but the antithesis of it. The obliteration of it. The music of the Fata, nearly silent in the cities of men, rose harsh and discordant all around.

The ghost wind. His heart pounded a nauseous rhythm. The black wind that haunted the Sea of Glass. He had never seen it in either of his lifetimes, but in both he'd heard stories. It devoured anything in its path, it was said, men and spirits alike. It poisoned wells and stunted trees, stripped unlucky creatures to bone, and bone to dust. It would take him apart layer by layer.

Asheris drew his cloak over his face and waited for the nothing to devour the world.

By Amanda Downum

The Necromancer Chronicles

The Drowning City
The Bone Palace
The Kingdoms of Dust

THE KINGDOMS OF DUST

THE NECROMANCER CHRONICLES
BOOK THREE

AMANDA DOWNUM

www.orbitbooks.net

This book is a work of fiction. Names, characters, places, and incidents are the product of the author's imagination or are used fictitiously. Any resemblance to actual events, locales, or persons, living or dead, is coincidental.

Orbit
Hachette Book Group
237 Park Avenue, New York, NY 10017
www.HachetteBookGroup.com

First Edition: March 2012

Orbit is an imprint of Hachette Book Group, Inc.
The Orbit name and logo are trademarks of Little, Brown Book Group Limited.

10 9 8 7 6 5 4 3 2 1

Printed in the United States of America

To Jodi, of course.

The abyss becomes me
I wear this chaos well

VNV Nation—“Genesis”

Death is a dialogue
Between the spirit and the dust.

Emily Dickinson

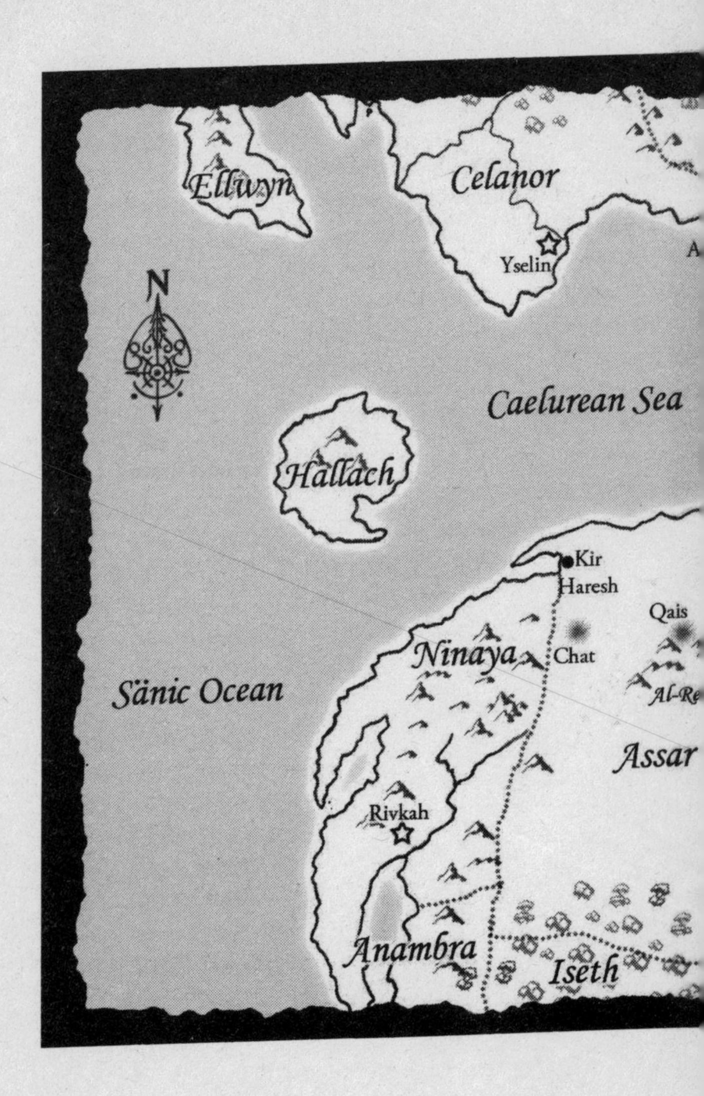
Ellwyn
Celanor
Yselin
N
Caelurean Sea
Hallach
Kir
Haresh
Qais
Ninaya
Chat
Sänic Ocean
Assar
Rivkah
Anambra
Iseth

Ashke
Ros
The Steppes
Selafai
Sarkany
R. Mori
R. Herodis
Iskar
Kehribar
Erisin
Inle
Skarra
Sherazad
Khitoum
Hajar
Ta'ashlan
R. Ash
R. Nilufer
Khejuan
R. Mir
Symir
Sivahra
Khebari
Strait
Archeon Ocean

THE KINGDOMS OF DUST

PART I

Storm and Shadow

CHAPTER 1

1233 Sal Emperaturi

The Çirağan Serai was called a palace, but it was one of the few buildings in Kehribar that had never been one. At the height of the Ataskar Empire every bey and sultan and merchant prince had built a fortress or a manor house, and after its fall they had slowly been repurposed into brothels and hostels and gambling halls. The Çirağan had only ever been a prison.

The dour stone fortress crowned the westernmost of the city's five hills. Once it had faced a courthouse—a hope of justice, or a mockery of it—but over decades of revolution and power shifts the court had been burned, abandoned, and eventually razed, leaving the prison alone in a wide, desolate yard. The closest neighborhoods on Hapishane Hill were poor and mostly empty, populated with squatters and stray dogs and patrolled by the city guard. The Çirağan wasn't isolated as many prisons were, but the guards were known for their brutal efficiency.

Thieves in dim wharf taverns told of cunning escapes, of eluding traps and outwitting wardens; all their stories were lies.

Few visitors passed the Çirağan's black gates. Men condemned to its cells were forgotten by their families and friends, mourned for dead. Soldiers came, and inquisitors, and the rare penitent priest, all on strict, well-supervised schedules.

But tonight, as summer rain washed the city and midnight bells tolled the hour, a carriage rattled and juddered up the uneven streets of Hapishane Hill. The driver's pockets were heavy with silver kurush and his thoughts heavy with the shadow of sorcery, dulling his memory of the night. The faces of his passengers had already faded in his mind.

Inside the coach, Isyllt Iskaldur leaned against the window, wincing at every pothole that jarred her spine and watching the night. Rain softened square buildings and spindle-sharp spires, bled orange halos from scattered city lights—the color of the amber for which the city was famed. Watchfires burned on distant walls, golden pinpricks against the dark.

The lights, the streets, the scents embedded in the carriage cushions were all foreign. Even the rain tasted different, the alchemy of wind and water subtly altered as it blew off the Zaratan Sea. By day she could distract herself but at night homesickness stole over her. Even nights like this, when she had work to do.

Another bone-jarring bounce, and Isyllt's companion cursed. Isyllt kept her invective to herself for fear of biting her tongue off mid-jolt.

"Are you sure you don't want me to go with you?"

asked the girl when the road smoothed again. She called herself Moth, though it wasn't her name. Neither was she precisely a girl, but it was a convenient façade.

"I've made the arrangements," Isyllt said. "Best to keep this quiet and quick." Wisdom for any jailbreak, even one arranged through bribery and veiled threats instead of swords and black powder bombs. All the same, her tone was chillier than she intended.

"Just because you do stupid things," Moth replied with equal sharpness, "doesn't mean I have to like it."

Isyllt smiled ruefully, tugging the curtain shut against the damp. Walking alone into an Iskari prison was unarguably stupid, though nothing close to the stupidest thing she'd ever done. "I promise to come out again."

Moth's lips pursed, but she let the matter pass. They'd quarreled more than once about Isyllt's recklessness and distraction, but since arriving in Kehribar the girl had found distractions of her own. She went out every night, winding farther and farther through the city. Just as reckless, perhaps, but Moth had grown up a street rat. Six months ago she'd been Dahlia, a whore's androgyne child with a prostitute's life awaiting her. Now she was an apprentice mage and shed more of her old life with every new place they traveled. She was due her freedom.

Six months ago Isyllt had been a Crown Investigator, student to the spymaster of Selafai. Now she was jobless, her master dead, her home abandoned to ghosts and memories. What was she due?

The carriage slowed, knocking Isyllt's shoulder against the bench. She snorted humorlessly—due a cut throat or a knife in the back, if she couldn't shake this maudlin abstraction. She might be no longer employed as a spy, but she wasn't yet out of the game.

The driver tapped on the connecting panel. Wet wood squealed open. "We're here, effendi," the man called. "The Çirağan Serai."

"Thank you." Her Skarrish was atrocious, but money eased translation.

"When do I get to meet this friend of yours?" Moth asked as Isyllt opened the door.

"Give us a few hours." Were they still friends? They hadn't spoken in years; he might have no desire to see her. It didn't matter—she wasn't about to leave him in the Çirağan.

Moth leaned close. Light warmed the curves of her face, still soft with youth. Less so now than mere months ago. "Be careful."

Isyllt couldn't say the same in return—prickly adolescent pride wouldn't allow it. *I always am*, she nearly said, but they both knew that was a lie. She tugged her scarf higher, hiding her mouth and chin. "Send the carriage back for me."

Her boots splashed in a puddle as she stepped down and the wet summer night settled over her. The rain had slacked into haze. She rapped on the door and the carriage rumbled into the mist and dark, leaving her alone in front of the bulk of the prison.

Her nape prickled; only the attention of the guards on the watchtowers, perhaps, but she thought not. A shadow had haunted her steps for decads, one she'd had no luck shaking. Fifteen years of good service—as spying, theft, and murder were euphemistically called—had won her enemies, and now she was far from home, far from her friends and allies, with no king to protect her. No one to avenge her.

Isyllt touched the diamond ring on her right hand, the briefest indulgence of nerves, but it didn't reassure her. Not long ago the stone had been filled with bound souls, ghosts whom Erisín deemed too dangerous to go free. Trapped in her ring, they had served as a power source to augment her own magic, a resource she relied on all too often. In her desire to sever ties, she had released them before she left Selafai.

Like so many sentimental gestures, it seemed quite stupid now. But hadn't sentiment brought her here? If only doubt were as easy to banish as ghosts. She squared her shoulders and strode toward the black iron gates. She had work to do.

He was dreaming when the guards came for him.

Through the blue shade of fir trees he runs, eyes slitted against the wind, snow crunching underfoot. The scent of pine and winter fills his nose, clean and sharp. He would take joy in running, but for the shadows close on his heels. Beasts that run like men, men that run like beasts, night-shining eyes and snapping teeth, near enough that he feels their laughter and hot breath. Nearer with every step. Does he run on two legs or four? The uncertainty makes him falter, and the hunters have him. Fangs close in on his flesh, dragging him down, and the snow melts under a wash of blood.

Booted footsteps banished the nightmare, returning him to the dank filth of his cell, the weight of stone and iron and old earth enclosing him. The sharp pain in his limbs was only cramp, the moisture slicking his skin fevered sweat. Adam was glad to wake; delirium was crueler than any torture his jailors could devise.

At first he thought it was the daily meal that roused him, but the footsteps were too loud and too numerous and only one rat pressed its cold nose against his neck—they came by the dozens when food arrived. The lock clicked, and the door that hadn't opened since his cellmate died scraped inward. The unexpectedness of it stunned him as badly as the onslaught of light and sound. Torchlight wedged glass knives behind his eyes, prizing open the seams of his skull.

He lay still as rough hands seized him, though the touch of skin made his flesh crawl. The iron they closed around his wrists was easier to bear. Vermin scurried through rotten straw as the guards hauled him up. He was glad to be rid of the roaches, but he'd miss the rats.

Was he going to the headsman after all? The thought made him stand straighter, though gummy tears blinded him and he ached from the weight of chains. Had they forgotten him while bureaucrats shuffled paperwork? He chuckled, which became a deep, tearing cough. The guards flinched at the sound. Three of them—one for the torch and two for him. Once he might have tried those odds, but it would be suicide now. Or just pathetic.

They led him past a row of iron doors, a row of tombs. Deep beneath the earth, these cells, the bowels of the Çirağan. A place to bury murderers and violent madmen and unlucky mercenaries like him. Screams and curses rose up as the guards' boots rang on stone, taunts and pleas for attention, protestations of innocence. After the silence of his cell, each shout was another spike driven into his skull. His captors smelled of garlic and paprika, sweat and leather and oiled steel—dizzying after the unchanging stench he'd grown accustomed to.

They didn't speak, and that was a small mercy. It was effort enough to move his legs. To die like this would be a miserable joke—the gods' favorite kind.

Down the hall and up a flight of stairs the guards dragged him. They hauled him up the last few steps when he faltered, bruising his arms and stubbing his toes. The slighter one cursed and Adam nearly laughed—all the weight must have wasted off his bones by now.

He dreaded more stairs, but instead they unlocked a door—bronze-bound wood instead of rusting iron—and shoved him inside. He fell with a rattle of chains, scraping hands and knees on the cold stone floor. The room spun and his empty stomach cramped.

The guards spoke and a woman answered—the timbre of her voice sent prickles of familiarity across his neck. Tall and thin, dressed in dark colors. A veil hid half her face.

"Leave us." Her voice was cold, her Skarrish heavily accented.

"Are you certain, effendi? He is dangerous." The acrid scent of nerves wafted from the man. They couldn't fear him, not like this.

"Does he look like a threat?" Adam wanted to snarl at the dry dismissal in her voice; he wanted to laugh.

"As you wish." The door slammed shut as the guards retreated.

He knelt, head down, letting his eyes adjust to the candlelight. The sight of his hands sickened him: bone-thin and broken-nailed, ragged and embedded with grime. Soft where they had been hard with sword calluses. The manacles hung loose around the knobs of his wrists. Matted plates of hair fell in his face; he was crawling with lice, and glad for once he couldn't grow a beard.

"I know I'm pretty," he said when the silence stretched, "but did you have me brought up here just to stare?" He coughed again and spat thick phlegm. He wanted to stand, or at least square his shoulders, but the shakes didn't allow so much pride.

The woman laughed and stepped closer. Her scent cut through his own stench: clean skin, cool and bittersweet, threaded with poppy oil and cloying myrrh. Recognition quickened his pulse.

"Isyllt?"

"Quietly," she said, in Selafaïn this time. "I'm not using that name here. You look like you crawled through all nine hells, and a sewer besides."

"Or a war and an Iskari prison. What are you doing here?"

"Rescuing you."

The light was unkind when she drew aside her scarf—she'd lost weight where she had none to spare, and bruises darkened her cold grey eyes. With her pale skin she looked like one of the *bardi beyaz*—the white jackal women who prowled cemeteries and sang for those about to die. Small wonder the guards feared her.

He hadn't seen Isyllt Iskaldur in years—in all his dreams of rescue, freedom had never worn her face. But now she knelt before him and unlocked his shackles.

"I'm not dead, am I?" He could imagine her gaunt, aquiline features on the Lady of Ravens all too easily.

She laughed, but her smile fell away. "Not yet. We'll see how long you survive my company. Saints and shadows," she swore, looking closer. "You're sick."

He tried to shrug—it became a convulsion. "Prison fever. It comes and goes."

"You need a doctor," she said with a scowl.

"I need a bath."

"That too."

The room blurred as he rose. Isyllt reached to steady him and he flinched from her hand, from the shock of human contact. He shrugged apologetically, leaning against the wall.

She shook her head with wry understanding. "All right. Bath first. You're too filthy to die."

Adam wanted to watch the prison's black walls fall away, but as they passed beneath the gate the red tide of delirium washed over him again. He saw nothing of their route down Hapishane Hill and into another decaying neighborhood on the outskirts of the city. Chills and fever rode him in turns, Isyllt's voice a pale thread weaving through them. He clung to it. Monsters circled, hungry and waiting, but the scent of her magic kept them at bay.

After the carriage came a confusion of light and voices and falling, hands clutching him at every turn. An echoing building that smelled of moss and wet stone.

"Are you mad, effendi?" A boy's voice, high with shock. "You've brought plague into the house."

"It's prison fever," Isyllt answered. "Burn his clothes and kill the vermin and you'll be fine."

An argument followed in bad Skarrish and equally broken Assari. Coins rattled. Isyllt must have won, because the next time the darkness rolled back they were still in the damp place. Adam lay on his back on a hard, thin bench. Water rippled nearby. Either he'd get his bath, or she planned to drown him and put him out of his misery.

"Wake up," Isyllt said, her voice close above him. With his eyes shut the pain in his skull was bearable. Cold metal brushed his chest and he flinched so violently he rolled off the bench and onto the tiled floor, bruising hand and hip. Isyllt swore and crouched beside him, a pale and dark blur through a film of tears. Lamplight shattered off the folding knife in her hand.

"Your clothes are coming off one way or another," she said, implacable. "I don't think you're in any condition to do it yourself."

He held up one shaking hand, counted six, seven, eight fingers before his eyes focused again. "Maybe not."

They were in a private bath, low and dim. Intricate tiles covered the room, chipped now and furred with moss. Pieces had fallen from the mosaicked ceiling, leaving robed figures blind and faceless. The water swirling in the pool was clean, though, and that was all the decadence Adam needed.

"Where are we?"

"A safe house. Just to get you cleaned up—I'm not taking you back to my rooms with fleas. A physician will be here soon."

She stripped away rotten cloth as she spoke, and soon Adam crouched naked on the slick tiles. Red fever-rash splotched his chest and stomach beneath caked filth; the sickly sweet smell of pus wafted from infected scrapes. Isyllt didn't recoil, but he read the disgust on her face.

"How did you end up in the Çirağan?" she asked as he lowered himself into the water. Tepid, but it shocked his fevered skin. "Buying you out wasn't cheap."

He ducked his head before answering. The plunge sharpened febrile wits. "A border skirmish between Sarkany and Iskar." He coughed, spat green phlegm. The current carried it away, swirling toward a drain on the far side along with grey ribbons of dirt. "The Sarkens hired me. They lost. Their soldiers were ransomed back—we mercenaries were their blood-price. How long? It was spring when they led us in—"

"Last spring. It's Merkare now."

He felt the words like a blow to the chest. Midsummer, the solstice already passed. A year of his life, gone. "How did you find me?"

"Kiril's agents." The spymaster of Selafai. Isyllt's master, and the man she loved. Their falling-out had haunted her during the mission she and Adam had shared three years ago—from the flatness of her voice, not much had changed. "I'm sorry it took so long."

"Why send you? He must have people in Iskar."

Instead of answering, she nudged a tray across the floor with the toe of her boot: soap and oils, combs and scissors. Attar of roses, sandalwood, cassia—the profusion of scents made him sneeze. He finally found a dented cake of salted mint that didn't make his eyes water.

"Your hair," Isyllt said, crouching beside the pool. "The nits we can kill, but the tangles—" She shook her head.

"Easier to cut it off." Lather stung his eyes as he ground the soap into his skin. A grey skim of suds drifted across the water.

A smile teased the corner of her mouth. "But a pity." Her own hair, black as his but finer, slithered free of its pins to trace the square angle of her jaw.

Adam shrugged. "It'll grow back."

Isyllt flinched, so soft he barely caught it. She picked up the scissors.

The physician arrived soon after, an old Skarrish man with a limp and teeth stained by betel nut juice; the peppery bitterness of the leaves soaked his skin and wafted sour with every breath. If being roused before dawn to treat foreign spies was unusual for him, he gave no sign. He poked and prodded Adam, tested his reflexes and confirmed the diagnosis of prison fever, as well as weakness from long captivity. For the former he prescribed willow bark, blue mold, and garlic, and for the latter wine boiled with iron nails and milk fortified with beef blood.

"But first," he told them both, "rest and clean water, and plenty of both."

Rest was the last thing Adam wanted. From the frown creasing Isyllt's brow, she felt the same way.

"What's wrong?" Adam asked when they were alone again, waiting in a threadbare foyer for their carriage. The lightness of his head unnerved him. The slice over his left ear had already scabbed; he'd only flinched from the blades once.

"Someone's following me," Isyllt said, tugging her veil up to muffle the words. It couldn't disguise the tension in her limbs, the haunted, hollow look around her eyes. "It might be the caliph's people—I've been careful, but they'll find me sooner or later. But someone was watching me in Thesme, too." Her eyes narrowed. "Maybe all the way from Erisín, but I was too distracted to notice."

That wasn't all, but wheels clattered to a stop outside

before he could press the matter. He scanned the lamp-pierced darkness as the door shut behind them. A quiet, crumbling neighborhood, cleaner than many, but still layered with smells: animal droppings and human waste; the sour sweetness of rubbish; garlic and spices from nearby kitchens. Overlaying it all was the tang of rain on warm stone—he hadn't realized how much he'd missed that particular smell.

His back itched as he climbed into the carriage. His hand ached for a sword-hilt, never mind the strength to use it. Isyllt's blade was a quiet bulge beneath her coat and he'd seen what her necromancy could do, but he'd hate to let one skinny spy do all the work in a fight.

The driver—befuddled but much richer after his unusual night—delivered them to a narrow house on Mulberry Lane. Two-storied and square-angled like so many in the city, with walls of stained ochre plaster and a yard choked with grass and weeds. The windows were dark. Isyllt stroked a finger across the courtyard gate, and the wrinkle between her brows told Adam she was spell-casting.

They stood in the darkness of the overgrown yard, listening to the rustle of wet mulberry leaves and the steady drip from the eaves. Cats fought and courted in an alley, and somewhere a woman sang to a crying child.

"What's wrong?" Adam asked again, watching Isyllt through swaying leaf shadows. He thought she would put him off once more, but slowly she turned.

"Kiril's dead."

He let out a sharp breath. The spymaster had been in poor health, but the tension in her neck didn't speak of sickbeds and the perils of age. Adam had lost many friends and comrades over the years without a chance to say good-bye; it still stung. The old man had been his mentor once, and later an employer and something like a friend. He reached for Isyllt without flinching, offering comfort, but she didn't move save to shiver at his touch.

"When?" He withdrew his hand, frowning. He remembered cool pragmatism, but not the icy brittleness that held her now.

"Six months ago. I...don't work for the Crown anymore." She looked up, her eyes shining in the dark. "Will you stay?"

Flat and casual, but he could guess how much the asking cost her. He was sick and weak, with no money and nowhere to go, not to mention she had saved him from slow death. None of that could touch the hurt buried deep in her voice.

He remembered his dreams of snow in the mountains, the clean pine chill of the high forests. The nightmares of demons chasing him. The demons would chase him anywhere. The mountains would wait no matter how long he stayed away.

"I'll stay."

She nodded, and he watched her rebuild herself—spine, shoulders, the self-assured tilt of her head he remembered. She scanned the night one last time and led him into the empty house.

CHAPTER 2

The city slept, stifled by the midday sun.

Throughout Ta'ashlan shops closed their shutters against the glare and merchants retired to uneasy sleep while dogs and beggars curled in the shade. Dust settled in empty streets, undisturbed by feet or wheels. Even the temples of the Unconquered Sun fell silent. This hour was fit only for rest and restless dreams. Jinn dreams, men called them.

Jinn had nothing to do with it, as Asheris al Seth knew well.

He stood in the scant shade of a crumbling mudbrick wall, one eye on the house in front of him and one on the street. A hot breeze stirred eddies of sand, rattled chimes, and fluttered laundry strung on lines, but couldn't cool the air. Heat-shimmer rose from the rooftops; the sky was a hard ceramic blue, kiln-baked. The street was strewn with crumbled lily petals and scraps of wilted crepe left from the Festival of Inundation that had ended three days ago. The flooding of the Ash and Nilufer offered surety for the next harvest, but did nothing to lessen summer's grip.

In richer neighborhoods foolhardy tourists might venture out of doors, along with the water sellers and fan peddlers who catered to them, but in the slums of Marqasith Court the residents took what respite they could from the withering heat. There was no one to watch him—his outstretched *otherwise* senses told him so.

Other senses, those that had nothing to do with magic and everything to do with survival, told him he'd been followed here. Was followed still.

Paranoia, Asheris told himself. His own anticipation run wild. Even if someone were watching, he wore illusion layered with wool and linen. Other mages would be hard-pressed to see his true face; kamnuran would overlook him altogether.

He clenched tingling hands at his sides. The longer he stood here like a fool, the greater the chance that he would be seen. He'd searched too long to lose his quarry now.

The building was one of hundreds like it crowded in the neighborhood: red and ochre brick, walls tilting on their foundations, the roof repaired with palm thatch. Broken shutters dangled from blind windows. The tiny lawn was sere and brown, only one small lemon tree clinging to life. Unlike its neighbors, which might shelter three or more families in such a space, this house held only one heartbeat.

An unlooked-for convenience. Asheris wasn't sure he trusted it.

The door was unbolted. Skeins of wards draped the threshold, tangled and untidy. He remembered Jirair's craft as intricate and convoluted, lovely in its complexity—his throat tightened under the ghost of the collar he no longer wore. These spells were too knotted to pick apart, so he simply smothered them beneath his own. Jirair wouldn't need them again.

Inside, the little house reeked of urine and rot and opium. The front rooms were curtained and shuttered, and the drone of flies carried through dim, fetid air.

For three and a half years he'd searched for Jirair Zadani, the last of a cadre of the old emperor's mages to escape him. One last piece of vengeance. Jirair had stayed just beyond his reach, running from city to city, hiding in all manner of unlikely places, vanishing for months at a time. Asheris had grown so used to the chase that he nearly hadn't noticed when Jirair slunk back into Ta'ashlan, settling in Marqasith Court. Who would expect an imperial mage in a tenement slum, after all?

He knew better. He himself survived in good part because no one expected to find a demon in the imperial palace.

Once Jirair was dead, no one else should ever think to.

The ground floor was empty save for filth-soaked mattresses lumped in corners and food moldering in the kitchen. Asheris drew a corner of his scarf across his mouth to lessen the reek of waste and decay and pungent sweetness. He could go longer without breath than any man, but breathing was a dangerous habit to fall out of.

A black cloud of flies followed him toward the stairs. Over their buzzing he heard slow breathing from the next floor, unchanging in its rhythm. The stench changed as he climbed, trading rot for stale sweat and unwashed flesh. The opium sweetness thickened, crawling into his mouth and nose; the heat worsened.

In the upstairs room, sunlight slanted through a broken shutter, thick with lazy spirals of dust. The molten light touched the side of a thin pallet, limned the bones of the bare foot hanging off the edge. Metal and porcelain gleamed on the tiles beside the bed—a discarded pipe. Just past the sun's reach, Jirair curled against the wall. Asheris waited for a shout, an attack, an attempt to flee, but the mage lay still, with only the glitter of heavy-lidded eyes to show he was conscious at all.

He remembered Jirair handsome and laughing, shining with health and power. Now his brown skin was dry and sallow, stretched over fine bones, his eyes bruised and sunken in their orbits. His hair was hacked unevenly to his scalp—a remedy for lice, or heat, or care. A fly crawled over the ridges of his instep, and he made no move to shake it off. The spark of hate Asheris had nursed so long stuttered as he looked at the crumpled form on the bed.

"Oh, Jirair." The whisper sank in the stifling air, lost beneath the low drone of insects. "What's happened to you?"

Jirair stirred as Asheris knelt beside him, golden-brown eyes widening for a heartbeat. One hand rose—in greeting or warding Asheris wasn't sure. Rings slid around gaunt fingers, the weight of their bezels pulling them down. Diamonds flashed beneath caked filth.

Asheris's jaw tightened, anger burning bright once more. He remembered those hands well: cradling a cup of drugged wine, offered to a man with a slow smile; lighting sweet incense to beguile a jinni; graceful beringed fingers spreading to show a collar of golden wire, a filigreed prison to cage two souls. The diamonds in those rings were empty now.

"It took you longer than I thought it would," Jirair

murmured, not lifting his head from the sweat-darkened pillow.

"Time doesn't mean as much to me anymore," Asheris lied. Immortal he might be, but he could count the days to vengeance as well as any man. His neck itched. Would he be free of the phantom collar when the last of its crafters was dead? He wished he could believe that.

Jirair smiled, a flash of white between cracked lips. His hand twitched toward the pipe. "Or to me, now. But I'm glad you're here. The poppy doesn't stop the dreams anymore."

"Dreams?" It wasn't his place to unburden a man's conscience before death, but curiosity pricked him. He hadn't realized this would be a mercy killing.

"Of the black place. The hungry place." Jirair's eyes squeezed shut, creases like dry riverbeds fanning over his brow. "The storm is coming. The ghost wind, the poison wind. Kill me before it comes, please—I can't bear to see that darkness again."

"What are you talking about?" Nightmares. The ravings of an opium addict. But Jirair had been a clever and canny mage once, more sensitive than many to the shifting weather of the Fata.

"The Undoing." His voice was fading, or the insects worsening. "The quiet men showed me. I thought they would protect me from you, but they're worse. Worse than anything Imran ever did."

"Protect you from me." A hard knot tightened inside his chest. "You told them about me?"

Jirair shook his head, stubble scraping the pillow. "I didn't have to. They already knew." Skeletal hands closed on Asheris's wrist. "Kill me now. The storm is nearly here."

"Who—" The buzzing drowned his voice as well. Not insects. The building sound came from outside. From all around. The room dimmed as a shadow passed over the sun.

"No!" Jirair shouted as Asheris leapt up. "Don't leave me for it! Kill me first! Please—" But Asheris was already hurtling down the stairs, through the swarm of flies and out the door.

The street lay in sepia twilight. The sun was gone, blotted out by the cloud of sand sweeping over the city with a hollow rush. Shouts rose from nearby buildings, swallowed by the storm's roar. The wind that tugged at Asheris's robes was the breath of a furnace. His lips cracked under its touch, sinuses parching; his eyes felt as though they'd boil in their sockets. A simoom, the poison wind that Jirair had named.

He heard Jirair cry out and fall silent. Then the storm was on him, and the world shrank to a fury of heat and sand. Blisters rose on exposed skin, scrubbed bloody by flying grit. Asheris closed his eyes against the scouring wind before it scraped them out.

Simooms killed humans and livestock easily, but the jinn had no fear of them. Before he was bound in flesh, Asheris had danced with such storms across the Sea of Glass. They were kin. So why was his stomach filled with cold, even as the heat bore him to his knees?

He opened *otherwise* eyes and nearly wept. Past the veil of the Fata, what rolled over Ta'ashlan was not a cloud of dun and copper dust, but a seething inky blackness. Not the absence of color but the antithesis of it. The obliteration of it. The music of the Fata, nearly silent in the cities of men, rose harsh and discordant all around.

The ghost wind. His heart pounded a nauseous rhythm. The black wind that haunted the Sea of Glass. He had never seen it in either of his lifetimes, but in both he'd heard stories. It devoured anything in its path, it was said, men and spirits alike. It poisoned wells and stunted trees, stripped unlucky creatures to bone, and bone to dust. It would take him apart layer by layer.

Asheris drew his cloak over his face and waited for the nothing to devour the world.

Simooms rarely lasted for more than a quarter of an hour, however, and even the ghost wind proved no exception. It felt like an eternity, but the wind eased, the roar faded, and finally the dust settled as the sun returned.

Roof tiles and shutter slats and laundry from the lines lay strewn across the street. The lemon tree had lost its fruits; they lay scorched on the summer-sere ground. The high thin wail of a child broke the stillness, followed by a man's keening cry.

Sand sluiced off Asheris's robes as he rose, glittering with tiny green-black fragments. Glass carried from the deep desert—blood welled in tiny cuts across his hands. His cloak hung in tatters. More blood trickled from his nose, coating his tongue with copper as he swallowed.

A mortal might have died of heatstroke. Being a demon had its uses.

Speaking of mortals— He remembered Jirair's cry, cut abruptly short, and turned back to the house. His abused sinuses hardly cared about the stink now.

The floor crunched beneath his sandals. Dead flies lay in drifts across the tiles, and more died in a slowing iridescent thrash of legs and wings. Only a handful remained to buzz around him.

Halfway up the stairs, he recognized the depth of silence; he couldn't hear Jirair breathing. His chest tightened with a curious loss. He'd come to kill the man, but felt now as though he'd failed him. To die alone and in fear...

Asheris froze at the top of the steps. Jirair had died in fear, yes—the stench of panic was unmistakable over voided bowels—but not alone. The mage sprawled supine across the floor, the mattress kicked aside. One hand clutched at his throat, the other lay outstretched. His face was no longer sunken and pale, but purple and swollen. Brown eyes bulged, bloodshot, drug-shrunken pupils locked tight in death.

Dragged from his bed and garroted. Blood seeped from the wire-slice around his neck. The house was empty to Asheris's outstretched senses. No tracks, no opened windows.

He quashed the uneasy dread that grew where his anger had been, forcing himself to absorb the details instead. Habit kept him away from the body, to keep from contaminating the scene. Which was foolish, he realized a heartbeat later. No other investigator would study this room. No mortician would inspect the body. Jirair would be another addict murdered for his opium, just as Asheris would have left him.

He knelt beside the corpse. He sensed no thaumaturgical residue, but the killer couldn't have come and gone so tracelessly without magic.

Jirair's hands, claw-curled and stiffening, were bare; the murderer had taken his rings.

Sunset bells rang long that night, the temple songs loud and fervent. Gratitude, perhaps, that the day had ended with sun instead of storm, or that the singers lived to see it end at all. Hymns could always be heard throughout the city, but tonight the sound rose like a wall, a thousand voices blending into one.

Asheris couldn't join them, no matter how politic his presence at the empress's side would be. Every paean to the Unconquered Sun was also a ward, reinforcing the boundary between the Fata and the world of flesh, driving out spirits. And demons. He was strong enough to resist, but the words would close his throat if he tried to speak them. So while the empress stood on a westward balcony and gave thanks for another day, he paced a circuit through her private study and drank the good wine.

The room had no windows, but Asheris felt the light fade, and with it the last peals of bells and voices. A moment later Samar al Seth stepped inside, leaving a veiled and silent Indigo Guard in the corridor. She sighed as the door closed behind her and stripped off her white mourning scarf. Her undressed hair sprang up in a bronze-black cloud, breaking into locks against her shoulders.

"Well," she said, leaning against the door, "that was unexpected." The tightness of her shoulders gave lie to her careless tone.

Asheris moved to the sideboard to pour wine from the flagon resting in a basin of ice. Condensation dripped down his fingers, cold and sharp. Samar stripped to tunic and trousers, draping her formal robes over the back of a chair—plain linen, in respect for the dead, thick with embroidery instead of gold or stones. She kicked her sandals toward her desk, flexing long brown toes in the carpet. Every motion was ingrained with the grace of a woman raised from birth to be in the public eye; even her private carelessness was measured and elegant.

Asheris handed her a goblet, chilled metal a sharp contrast to the day's heat still clinging to her skin. "Unexpected, but not unprecedented."

From behind a carven sandalwood panel he heard a soft click and mouse-quiet footsteps. A heavy mouse with a limp. He filled a third cup as the panel opened silently, and Siddir Bashari stepped into the room.

Courtiers of the Lion Throne wouldn't be surprised to find Siddir attending the empress at odd hours. He was a favorite of the court: handsome, charming, kin to amirs and senators and shipping magnates, heir to and free with his family's considerable wealth. Samar doted on him as she would a favorite cat—her weakness for pretty eyes was well known. What might shock the court, however, was how often Siddir came to the empress through the palace's web of concealed passages, and how often he brought grim news instead of flattery and smiles.

Siddir bowed to Samar, sacrificing grace and flourish to keep his balance on his injured leg. The wound—a hunting accident, he called it, and that was true if he didn't specify the nature of the quarry—had been healing well, but now lines of pain were drawn fresh across his face. Asheris's own cuts and blisters had healed before he returned to the palace, but his skin remained tender and an aching weariness lingered in his bones. Anyone who'd been exposed to the black wind felt it still. Even the empress, safely ensconced in the palace, had a bruised and hollow look around her eyes.

"What news?" Samar asked, gesturing him to a seat a heartbeat after Siddir began lowering himself onto the couch. Siddir had been her friend and agent too long to stand on ceremony; the debts and secrets between her and Asheris also precluded formality.

They were two of the three mortals to whom he'd entrusted his secret. If not for Jirair's words, he might have thought them the only ones who knew at all. Better, he thought wryly, to be disabused of that notion sooner rather than later.

"One hundred and forty-two dead." Siddir drained half his cup in one swallow. White mourning ribbons fluttered from his sleeves. "That have been found so far. I've heard reports of chaos in the madhouses, and two mages and a priest had to be subdued after they started raving." His frown deepened. "The temple apiaries are devastated."

Asheris winced, remembering drifts of dead flies.

Samar sank into a chair, the weary slump of her shoulders quickly hidden. "What were you saying about precedent?" she asked Asheris. "My grandfather and nurses would tell us stories about the ghost wind when we were small, and about the saints who fought it. I thought they were only stories."

"The lives and battles of saints I can't speak for. The ghost wind, however, was most recently documented in 1157, seen west of the Ash. University mages made the record, so I'm inclined to trust it. Before that I've found records from 1007 and 806. Anything earlier is suspect, considering the archive fire of 799 and Nizam the Second's attempts at revising history. I can find no other instance of the storm striking Ta'ashlan—they usually seem to fade after crossing the Ash."

Siddir's hazel eyes narrowed. "There's a trend to those numbers I don't find at all reassuring."

"Do the archives know what causes these storms?" Samar asked.

"No. But scholars have noticed something." Asheris pulled a pouch from his pocket and upended it into his other hand. Red and tawny sand trickled into his palm, glittering with green glass. "The storm comes from the Sea of Glass. The cause must be there. I want to investigate."

Sculpted brows drew together. "Is there precedent for that?"

He poured the sand back into its pouch and scrubbed his palm on his thigh. "At least two expeditions have gone into the desert searching for the ghost wind. One found nothing—the other was never found."

"Even more reassuring," Siddir muttered.

"I think I would survive," he said dryly, though in truth he wasn't certain what the ghost wind could do. He'd survived blades and bullets, entropic magic and a volcano's eruption, but wasn't ready to believe himself unkillable. "Let me gather mages. The university loves a good fact-finding mission."

Samar leaned back, staring at her wine cup in silence for a time. "No," she said at last. "I need you here." She waved a hand when Asheris opened his mouth, moisture shining on her fingertips. "It's a mystery worth solving, yes. But even if your trend continues, it will be decades before the storm returns. I have warlords carving up the borderlands, governors banging on the gates, and my brother's partisans courting my niece's favor. Help me solve these problems—then you can search the desert for storms."

She didn't name the other reason, not even with the twitch of a hand toward her stomach, but Asheris knew.

Ever since her coronation, the senate had pressed Samar to marry again and bear an heir. Amirs and senators paraded eligible sons and brothers and cousins in front of her, but she had yet to find a suitable candidate. Her affairs had been few and far between, and always discreet.

But not always foolproof. A decad ago she had confided to him: She was pregnant, and the father was no one she had any intention of marrying. She had another month, perhaps four decads, to make a decision before her condition became obvious.

Argument would be pointless; he saw that in the set of her shoulders and mouth. Canny pragmatism had kept her alive to claim the throne, but she was kamnur—*dim*, mages called the ungifted—to the bone. If she had truly seen the storm, her priorities might be different. "And if the storm doesn't wait?" he asked anyway.

Gold-flecked eyes narrowed. "Then I'll pray it takes our enemies with it, and saves us the trouble."

"What can I do?" Siddir asked later, lying in the darkness of Asheris's bedroom. They nearly always met in Asheris's rooms—the servants were more respectful of mages' privacy.

"I don't know." Asheris stood by the window, letting the breeze from the garden dry the sweat that filmed his skin. He'd learned to take comfort in mortal embraces, but tonight the touch of flesh only reminded him of death. The taste of semen clung in the back of his throat, salt and decay. Even the green scent of the gardens smelled of rot.

"I could go to the desert, if you think it would help," Siddir said after a moment of silence. "It's easier for me to slip my leash."

"It's too dangerous for kamnuran. If the storm returns—" His jaw tightened at the thought of Siddir's brown skin peeling off muscle and bone.

"I'm in no condition to outrun it," Siddir finished, his voice threaded with frustration.

"You can help me find these so-called quiet men." Asheris had told Siddir about his final conversation with Jirair, but hadn't yet shared it with Samar. His place in the Court of Lions depended on secrecy—it would be better if the empress didn't come to consider him a liability.

He stared at the window, frustration knotting his fists. Siddir, however clever and resourceful, was no mage. And no matter how brilliant Ta'ashlan's theoreticians and battle mages, they were hampered by lack of exposure to the Fata. In a land where death was taboo, the study of undoing was in short supply. He needed—

Asheris turned, cutting off Siddir's reply. "No, there is something you can do. A way to slip your leash. If you're willing."

"Whatever you need, I can do."

"I need an entropomancer. I need Isyllt Iskaldur."

CHAPTER 3

Across the desert, past the rush of the River Ash and the burning wastes of Al-Reshara, an old woman sat beside her mirror in an empty house, waiting for news. Nerium Kerah didn't study her reflection as she might have decades ago. She had known her share of vanity, but now she felt all her years and battles in her back and hips and spotted, blue-veined hands; she had no need to see them in her face.

Light slanted through the windows, hot and honey-gold, undimmed by the storm that raged far across the empire. If she looked east she might see the stain of its passing across the desert, but that view was of no more interest to her than her reflection. She'd seen the devastation of the ghost wind before.

This was the first time she had caused it.

Nerium shook her head. She was weary enough without regrets. With nearly a hundred years of service behind her, she had seen what the storm wrought—other members of Quietus had not. Perhaps now they would understand what would happen when the old seals, the old ways, finally failed. And fail they would, of that she had no doubt. Other members of the Silent Council deluded themselves that the darkness they bound in diamond prisons would stay bound forever. Or at least another thousand years—it was difficult to maintain personal investment in something that might happen centuries after one was dead. Even she couldn't imagine she would see the turning of the next millennium. Not in this decrepit flesh.

"Mother."

The voice came from the dark glass, husky and breathless, edged with fear. Nerium winced to hear her daughter afraid, but she counted to ten before she responded, keeping her face and voice calm.

"Is it done?" She brushed the surface of the mirror, and her own tired face gave way to another. Like watching time roll away: the loose flesh of her throat and jaw firmed; close-cropped hair darkened; the lines on her face smoothed. Then the illusion vanished, and the woman in the mirror was herself again. Nerium tried to recall the name her daughter was using now, but it escaped her.

"Yes, it's done." Annoyance replaced fear in her voice, but the younger woman's eyes were wide and dark and shadowed, olive cheeks pale and splotched. "What happened? The storm—"

"Isn't it obvious? The seals failed. We've lost a diamond, years before schedule, and another is close to failing. We're sealing the breach, but the system won't last." The words were dull with repetition by now. With any luck, she'd only have to present this lecture one more time.

"I have Zadani's rings—"

Nerium shook her head. "Only a stopgap measure. We

don't have enough stones to keep this up, no matter what Ahmar claims. She would scheme and delay us all into oblivion. But we won't let that happen."

Her daughter's head tilted at that *we*, not bothering to hide her weariness. "What do you need?" She kept her voice pitched low and her eyes flickered to one side.

"You on a ship to Kehribar within three days." Dark eyes rolled, and Nerium nearly mimicked the gesture. "I don't ask the impossible." Sending her best agent to clean up a colleague's mess had irked her, but it meant her daughter was placed to leave Assar quickly.

"No, only the intensely annoying. What's in Kehribar?"

"An entropomancer. Isyllt Iskaldur. Bring her to me. Offer her anything she wants. Find the right leverage."

"She's under surveillance already, isn't she? Why do I need to bring her in?"

"Her watcher is one of Ahmar's pets. I need someone I can trust." Her daughter glanced aside again, tracking some distant sound. Behind her Nerium could make out red hangings and candles. "Where are you?"

"At church." She grinned at Nerium's frown; the temples of Ta'ashlan were also full of Ahmar's pets. "Shall I ask for absolution while I'm here? Wash the blood from my hands?"

"There isn't any, is there?"

She snorted. "Of course not. I used a wire."

"Find Iskaldur. Keep me informed." Nerium touched the mirror again, and the connection broke. Her own grey and weary face took its place once more in the glass.

Her knees cracked as she rose to dress and her robes weighed heavily on her shoulders. The day stifled, and she would have been just as happy to go to her fellow councillors in a nightdress, but Quietus was fond of formality and comforting rituals.

The light didn't change, but Nerium felt a shadow gathering behind her. A smell like char and bone and the musk of insects drifted through the room.

"She looks tired," the shadow said with a voice of rasping sand. "You work the poor child too hard. But you were always careless with your toys, weren't you?"

She turned, because it was weakness not to look. The creature in the corner was darkness and smoke, roiling like storm clouds within a tall, gaunt outline. His head was a vulture's, bald and beaked and snake-necked. Ragged wings lay folded down his back, and two pairs of arms crossed his sunken chest.

"My daughter is none of your concern."

"I've always felt a kinship with her. We failed experiments should stick together." Sunlight glinted on dust motes inside him as he moved forward.

"She isn't a failure." From the mocking tilt of his head, Kash knew it for a lie.

"Merely a disappointment, then."

"I don't have time to play with you today, Kash."

"No, nor strength. You're so tired." He drifted behind her, resting insubstantial taloned hands on her shoulders. "You'll wear yourself to rags if you don't rest." His wicked beak brushed her cheek. "And when you fall I'll be there to eat your eyes."

She shook her head. His taunts had long since lost their power to unsettle her. "Not today, Kash."

"No? What if I tell the others what you've done? I don't think they'd appreciate your games."

"You don't want me to face council justice. You want revenge."

"Maybe I'll take whatever I can get. I'm used to scraps and carrion, after all."

"You'll get your chance. But not today."

She turned, his cold shadowy form still pressed against her, and laid her hand against his beak. Under her fingers it was solid as any living bone and chitin. She spoke a word of silence. Kash recoiled, but the spell had already taken. His beak opened in a silent hiss.

Once she would have trusted him to keep her secrets. Once he had trusted her to keep her promises.

With a word of banishment he was gone, and she was alone again.

Her knees and neck ached as Nerium left her rooms, the familiar pains worse than they had been two days ago—the ghost wind's handiwork. Qais had been spared the worst of the storm, protected by layers of spells, but its shadow lingered.

The mages' dormitory was silent; even the tall brass-studded doors swung shut behind her with only a whisper to mark her exit. The Chanterie, the red sandstone hall was called, and had been for centuries. Nerium didn't know the cause, but assumed it was a bitter joke; this was not a place for music.

The courtyard too was quiet, buried under drifts of copper sand. Wide pools lay stagnant, overgrown with weeds and filmed with droning midges. Green water shone gold in the westering sun. Qais wasn't as deserted as it appeared—farmers and craftsmen and soldiers lived here, servants who should have been tending the pools—

but she could go days without hearing anyone. She couldn't remember when she'd last seen children playing in the desolate streets.

Nerium frowned. She was hardly sentimental about children, but their presence here served a function—fresh life to ward off the constant shadow of decay. Swept streets and clean fountains also served: order combated entropy, and mastery over one's environment had thaumaturgical benefits as well as aesthetic ones. She would have to speak to the staff—too much was at stake in Qais to let the city fall into disrepair.

The city was a replica of lost Irim, carefully constructed after its doom. As much red sandstone as the survivors could carry away from the ruin had been reused—the rest had been carved from the same cliffs in Hajar. Gardeners bled myrrh trees as they had in Irim, though the Smoke Road that had carried wealth and incense across the desert was long abandoned.

Qais was meant to be a monument to all that had been salvaged from Irim, a memorial for all that was lost. To Nerium it was a sepulchre, another corpse of a long-dead kingdom. The survivors of Irim—the founders of Quietus—could have moved on, but had instead chosen to shackle themselves to the past.

She shook her head. None of her morbid thoughts was untrue, but the black veil of despair that hung over her was another effect of the storm. With the seals' renewal it would pass. When the moribund bindings now in place were replaced with fresh ones, she might in turn see new life brought to Qais. Or better yet, let the desert claim it once and for all.

She followed a broad, paved lane lined by crouching

criosphinxes till she reached the hypostyle, a forest of fat sandstone pillars holding aloft the ceiling of sky. When she pushed aside the ghost wind's depression, she could appreciate the stillness of the hypostyle, its latticed shadows and carven flagstones, whose lotus patterns appeared and disappeared with the drifting sand. She tried to hold to that stillness as she emerged from the columns and crossed the broad courtyard to the observatory temple, but it was no use.

The Aal, the peoples of Irim and Qais and the greater desert, had been sky-watchers, filling volumes with sidereal patterns and movements. They strove to speak to the stars themselves. This desire for knowledge, surviving records indicated, had brought doom to Irim.

The observatory was a broad building, terraced in a series of receding slabs—nothing like the gilded domes and graceful minarets of modern Assari temples. A wide staircase dominated the front, but couldn't long draw the eye away from the round tower rising above it. From such a tower the scholars of Irim had sung to the stars.

By the time Nerium climbed the last of the steps, the sky was a wash of carnelian streaked with high, violet clouds. The Reshara desert spread to the northeast, red sand melting into the gloaming sky. Shadowed in the east, as Nerium had thought, by more than dusk; she turned her gaze back to the red stone steps.

Khalil Ramadi waited for her at the top, robed in grey and leaning on his cane. His white hair was long and neatly braided as ever, but thinner each year. Gold flashed in sagging earlobes, the last echo of the flamboyant warrior-mage he'd once been. His brown skin had been creased and weathered for decades, but now pain deepened the furrows around his eyes and pressed his mouth to a bloodless line.

"I'd hoped not to see the storm twice," he said, offering his hand as she climbed the final step. His fingers were crooked and gnarled, trembling in hers. The band of his smoky diamond ring—twin to her own—pressed into paper-thin flesh; she doubted he could ever take it off.

"We may see it yet again if Ahmar continues to ignore the truth."

Shoulders once broad and strong hunched further. He had been a tall man—now his curved spine pressed against his robes and bent him as low as she. "I stand with you," he said quietly as they limped toward the tower door. "But there isn't much fight left in me."

Relics, all of us, she thought bitterly. Fit only to be locked away in dust and darkness.

"You deserve rest," she said. "We all do." If her plan worked, they would have it.

They entered the observatory tower, but followed the spiral staircase downward instead of up. Quietus had no use for the sky—their concerns were bound in earth. Nerium conjured witchlight as they descended, careful not to show the strain it took to hold the glow steady. Architects were much too fond of stairs.

The snail-shell spiral ended at a red door. Rock salt, rose-colored slabs veined with crimson and porphyry, banded with steel to hold it to the hinges. The metal showed signs of recent scouring, but rust still blossomed. Salt for protection, to help contain the darkness that slept inside. As much use as a sticking plaster on a severed limb, as far as Nerium could tell, but it was very pretty.

The room beyond the red door was round and domed,

like the observation tower above it, and like the tower roughly twelve cubits across—three times the height of a man. In the center lay a black pit six cubits in diameter. Such a small space to hold so much power. So much destruction. Nerium drew a breath, bracing herself as she stepped across the threshold. Behind her, she heard Khalil do the same.

Her witchlight flared as they entered the room, reflected in diamonds set in the curved ceiling. Hundreds of stones, bought and stolen and smuggled over centuries, a fortune to ransom kingdoms. The mages who built the prison had chosen to re-create the night sky—crystalline constellations glittered coldly in black marble, unchanging, locked forever in a night centuries past. Like the salt door, it made no difference that she could see, besides beauty. The power of the stones was real; Nerium nearly staggered under the weight of magic in the room.

A man and a woman waited for them. The woman, Shirin Asfaron, was Quietus's historian and the third member of the Silent Council who dwelled permanently in Qais. A thin, reedy woman, she had taken on the same yellowed shade of parchment as the records with which she surrounded herself. She inclined her head to Nerium, and witchlight shone against her sweat-slick brow. Her hands trembled at her sides, and the cords of her neck stood taut. She was younger than she looked, but years of living in Qais had taken their toll. She wasn't as resistant to the constantly leaking entropy of the oubliette as Nerium.

The man, Siavush al Naranj, didn't turn. He faced the wall, muttering a constant chant of spells under his breath as he replaced a diamond in its stone setting. He was the youngest of them all, Ahmar's prized pupil, and very clever at bindings—vinculation, as university mages called it.

Ahmar and Siavush claimed holding Qais was an honor, a mark of great strength and trust. That was not untrue, but they were also the youngest and strongest of the circle and meant to remain so. So they lived far from the specter of Irim, guarding Quietus's interests and their own ambitions, shaking their heads at the fate of their poor fading comrades. Trying to ignore the reality of their oaths.

The object of those oaths lay in the blackness in the center of the room, whispering softly even now. Al-Jodâ'im. The Undoing. The doom of Irim.

In all of Quietus's years of study, no trace had been found of a greater destructive force, not even the ancient cataclysm that sank fabled Archis. In their desire to commune with the stars, the scholars of Irim called something down from the heavens, and nearly destroyed all of Khemia.

The touch of Al-Jodâ'im crumbled stone and withered flesh. Men and spirits alike disintegrated in its shadow. Crops failed and earth grew lifeless. Plagues sprang up where it passed, spreading lesions and tumors and twisting organs against themselves. In the dark times after Irim, the storms men called the ghost wind had swept across the desert, killing hundreds and stunting the land.

Out of that chaos Quietus had risen, dozens of mages who risked—and often gave—their lives to seal the hungry darkness where it could do no more harm. But Al-Jodâ'im were stronger than any spirits human mages had ever dealt with. A diamond might bind a ghost forever, but even the strongest of mage stones eventually failed under the entropic touch of the Undoing. So a new generation of mages had taken up the burden of Quietus, and then another, for over a thousand years. They pledged service till their deaths, and to uphold the seals above all else. They pledged secrecy too, lest the greed and curiosity of man cause more disasters like Irim. They had been ruled by ennearchs and heptarchs and triads, and even a few autocratic witch-kings.

And now there were five of them. Though only four gathered today.

"Is Ahmar joining us?" asked Nerium when Siavush was nearly finished. She kept her voice light despite her lingering unease. If he'd found signs of her tampering, he surely would have said something by now.

Shirin shrugged. "I've heard nothing."

Siavush stopped chanting and finally turned from the wall. His face too was drawn and damp, his warm copper skin lusterless with fatigue. He held himself straight against the strain, but the glitter of his rings betrayed shaking hands. "She's busy dealing with the destruction in Ta'ashlan. I speak for her."

"I'm glad to know how seriously she takes this," Nerium said dryly. "But of course, I already knew that."

Siavush frowned. His weight shifted as if he meant to step forward, but thought better of it. No one wanted to stand close to the lip of the pit. "We all take our mission and oaths seriously. A lapse in the seals is nothing trivial. But it's remedied now." He waved to the newly replaced diamond. "The seals will hold, with vigilance. Ahmar will replenish our diamonds."

Nerium wanted to turn away from the faith in his

voice, the affection he still felt for his teacher. Those too would wither with time, but the reminder of her long-faded youth stung.

"With vigilance." She snorted. "With the vigilance of Qais, you mean, while you and Ahmar sip iced wine in the comfort of the cities."

"I'm hardly sipping wine here, am I?"

"No," she acknowledged, smoothing her tone. "Your sense of duty is not in question. But all of our burdens could be lessened if we stopped binding ourselves to this carious corpse of a place, and to an expensive and antiquated method of vinculation."

"There is little profit in changing methods that still work," Siavush said, "and a great deal to risk if something goes wrong. One broken seal is enough to loose the ghost wind—imagine what could happen if we removed them all. Ahmar and I—"

"You've made your feelings clear. As has Ahmar, with her absence from this meeting. If not for my oaths, I would be happy to let you fail. Luckily for the rest of the world, I won't."

Siavush's face pinched. "What have you done, Nerium?"

"I've acted, as we should have long ago. I've summoned an entropomancer, a vinculator. The best candidate I've found in thirty years to help us deal with our burden."

"That stormcrow spy? You risk everything we work for. We won't allow it."

Nerium smiled, sharp and cold. "The majority is mine, Siavush." She glanced at Khalil and Shirin, who each nodded slowly.

"Nerium is right," Khalil said, knuckles whitening on his cane. "Something has to change."

"Enough argument." Shirin's voice cracked. "Let's finish what we came to do, and get out of this tomb."

Nerium nodded. "Yes. Let's." She often wondered if the founders of Quietus called themselves the Silent ironically, or if the quarreling had come later.

Siavush frowned, but finally nodded. The four of them positioned themselves evenly around the black pit. They didn't hold hands, but their magic commingled and flowed into a circuit.

Her blood beat hard in her ears; under its rhythm, a different music swelled. As she turned her attention to the oubliette, the whisper grew, became a song. Polyphonic, discordant, inhuman, but its meaning was clear nonetheless—loss and loneliness, exile and longing. It scraped and shivered over her skin, ached in the roots of her teeth—it would take them apart, if they let it, layer by layer, muscle and bone, until all that was left was dust.

They hadn't let it yet.

Sleep was the only mercy they could grant Al-Jodâ'im, bound as they had been for centuries. Her tampering had disturbed their rest years before they might have woken on their own. But since her colleagues refused to consider the evidence otherwise, she had no choice but to force the issue. She quashed a pang of guilt before it could infect the working.

Each of them focused their power differently: Siavush chanted under his breath, incantations and litanies of strength; Khalil recited sword-forms, though he hadn't practiced them in decades; Shirin ran mathematical equations in her mind. Nerium sang. Her voice was not what it once was—that had been lost, with her beauty, to time—but rhythm and pitch she still had.

Disparate as they were, their rotes served the same function: strength, order, precision, and perhaps even love. All the things that stood against the chaos and destruction that were Al-Jodâ'im, and the despair they had learned to wield as a weapon against their captors. All these they wrought into chains to bind the darkness, as their order had for centuries.

They left the temple in silence when their work was done, limping, trembling, cold with sweat. No amount of pride could disguise the cost of these spells. But the crushing air of hopelessness had eased—the night air was still, soothing. The seals would hold.

For now.

They paused in the courtyard before the hypostyle, and Nerium couldn't resist needling Siavush one last time. "Zadani is dead, by the way."

"Good," he said, his voice clipped. While no one argued that Quietus needed fresh blood soon, Siavush's choice of the imperial mage had proven a poor one. Next time, she'd let him clean up the mess himself. "It's time I returned to my work, then."

Shirin's lips pinched. Nerium marked it too, how he placed his second life outside Qais over his sworn service. She didn't bother scolding him, though; she was finished with that.

"Would you prefer the short route or the long?"

His eyes narrowed at her solicitude. "The short, if you please."

A journey across the desert took decads, a month with

slow camels, fraught with the danger of storms and wells gone dry. Quietus had faster methods of travel, though not always more pleasant.

"Kash!"

He balked at her summons; a hundred years of servitude had not broken him to the bit. She respected his defiance, but it was often inconvenient. She tightened the leash of her will and called again. The air curled away from him as he manifested, like skin from a wound. Black wings flared, blotting the stars. Shirin flinched, and Khalil turned his head.

To the rest of Quietus, Kash was a necessary evil, a tool to be used quickly and set aside. To Nerium he was her grandfather's legacy. Any oathsworn member of Quietus could call him, but her family were usually the only ones willing to do so. He had become their inheritance, an unholy bequest. Once he had been even more, but that had ended badly.

"Kash, escort Lord al Naranj back to Ta'ashlan, if you please."

Kash had been a jinni, captured and exposed to Al-Jodâ'im's touch in an experiment to discover the effect of entropy on immortal spirits. It turned his fire to smoke and ash, left him dark and bitter and twisted, but it also wedded him to the void, an avatar of the great nothingness. A way to harness its power.

Kash hissed soundlessly, still held by her silence. She read calculation in his eyes—wondering, no doubt, if she was weak enough to challenge. Not today. He acquiesced with a mocking bow and the air parted once more behind him, a doorway into emptiness.

"Ahmar won't be happy about what you've done," Siavush said, turning reluctantly to Kash.

Nerium smiled at the threat. He was so very young. "She's welcome to discuss the matter with me. I'm always here, after all."

Kash might hate her, but he scorned the other mages more. The rift sealed behind Siavush before he could have the last word.

CHAPTER 4

A decad and a half passed in the ochre house, while Adam ate and slept and paced the length of the weed-tangled yard. When the sun rose high over the dusty streets of Kehribar he sat beneath the mulberry tree and breathed in the scent of earth and stone and sap, the tapestry of smell the city wove. The fever eased—drowned, he imagined, by all the tisane Isyllt poured down him—but his strength was slow to return.

Isyllt's young apprentice courted him as if he were a feral dog, watching him from doorways and leaving plates of food where he'd find them. He felt like a carnival curiosity, but tried to smile. He'd imagined a younger version of Isyllt when she first told him she'd taken a student—thin and pale and sharp-edged—but Moth bronzed in the summer sun, and baby fat still softened her limbs.

She spent her nights in the city, carousing with companions she never named, bringing home food and wine and trinkets. She slept through the mornings and studied sorcery in the afternoons, playing tricks with pink witch-lights and scrying in bowls of water. There was a tension between her and Isyllt that neither spoke of; each treated the other as if she were made of eggshell.

Isyllt talked of politics and recent events. She told him of the unrest in Erisín and the sorceress responsible for the death of Selafai's king, and Kiril's death as well. She received letters—some slipped beneath the warded gate, others sealed and delivered through the post. A lassitude Adam recognized as grief held her, giving way in turns to restless energy that left her waspish and pacing.

Perhaps it was only her paranoia catching, but after a few nights Adam's neck began to itch. Someone was watching them, and neither his senses nor Isyllt's magic could tell them who.

When he slept, he dreamed of stone walls.

Isyllt woke before dawn, the sound of rain on the eaves rescuing her from her dreams. Not a nightmare this time, the ones that left her clawing at the sheets and choking on cries. The quiet dreams were worse. Dreams of Erisín, of Kiril. Waking left her bruised and hollow.

A streetlamp cast rippling rain-shadows against the horn-paned window. Her eyes ached, but it was no use sleeping again. The dreams would only wait for her.

The tiles were cool and sticky beneath her feet as she crept downstairs. Moth curled on the couch, twitching with dreams. Adam sprawled in the bowl chair across the room. Both of them snored.

Moth was scarcely recognizable as the threadbare street child Isyllt had met six months ago. Some of it was the work of better meals and clothes, growth and sun, but not all. Taking a new name had shed a chrysalis—she emerged brighter, fiercer, lit from inside with a reckless spark.

Was this what it was like to be a parent? To look away for a moment and find a child changed? To see the irrevocable passage of time on someone else's face? The thought made her wince. She'd always imagined she'd make a terrible mother, and the past few months had done little to disabuse her of that notion.

Adam had changed too, and not for the better. She'd known when she walked into the Çirağan that a year in its depths would mark him, but the reality was worse than she'd imagined. His color was better after days of sun and food, but nothing like the burnished olive she remembered. His long face was as gaunt as her own, eyes and cheeks and temples hollow. The hinge of his jaw worked in his sleep, and she could count the rings in his larynx when he swallowed. She'd never thought to see him so weak, his strength and predator's grace stolen.

Her throat tightened as she studied him, but her pity was selfish. She wanted him to be strong to remind her of better times. The last thing she needed was a mirror.

His twitching stilled and his breath changed. His fingers brushed the hilt of the knife that never left his side and fell away. "You're staring again." Dark lashes fluttered and his eyes opened. Green-gold as a wolf's, and as wary.

Her mouth twisted sideways; she was stretched too thin to tease. "I can't sleep, and you need to eat."

"You're one to talk." He rose slowly, carefully, wincing as his joints cracked. They spoke softly—not that a riot in the street would have woken Moth.

Isyllt heated water in the battered brass samovar that had come with the house, measuring tea for her and tisane for Adam—ginger and willow bark smothered in honey and lemon. His cough was better after days away from the prison's stale air, but he still tired too easily.

They sat outside, sheltered by the eaves in the house's tiny rear garden. Rain fell in shining ribbons, shaking the overgrown jasmine vines on their sagging trellis. Adam drank his tisane in determined gulps while Isyllt stared at her tea.

"What are you going to do?" Adam asked at last, setting his cup aside.

She swallowed tea and wished for wine; she'd been expecting this question. Her breath steamed as she exhaled. "I don't know." She turned her cup round and round again. She hadn't gloved her left hand yet; the scarred palm and curled fingers made her feel naked and she fought the urge to tuck the hand into her lap. Adam had bandaged the wound for her, so many years ago. "There's always Assar. I've kept in touch with Asheris al Seth."

Adam's eyes narrowed. "The man who tried to kill you. Twice." His gaze settled on her left arm—not the injured hand, but the bracelet of scar tissue that ringed her wrist. A burn, ridged and glossy, in the shape of a man's hand.

"That wasn't his fault. We're friends now." She arched her eyebrows, daring him to argue.

"So you'd defend the empire instead of undermining it?"

They'd sailed together to Assari-held Sivahra to foment revolution and fund nationalist rebels. While doing so they'd discovered imperial embezzlement and smuggled diamonds. That discovery helped the emperor's opponents in the Imperial Senate, and led to Rahal al Seth's death in a suspicious accident and his sister Samar gaining the throne. Quite a success, as far as Isyllt's masters had been concerned. It had only cost her most of a hand, and Adam a partner.

Isyllt shrugged. "I haven't had any better offers. I just wish I knew who was following me so doggedly."

"Could it be Selafai? The king might not want you working for a rival."

"No. I wouldn't either, if I were him. But I don't think Nikos has it in him. Not yet." She'd saved Nikos Alexios from the machinations of a vengeful sorceress. She'd let that same sorceress murder his father. Though not fond of his father, Nikos had dismissed her from her position—keeping traitors on the payroll set a bad precedent.

The thought of returning to government service made her tired. She could find work, she had no doubt, with another crown or in private employ. Secrets were a valuable commodity, and she had a collection. But she was scraped hollow and sick of looking over her shoulder. Perhaps a university position, safe and boring...

"Come north with me," Adam said. "To Vallorn."

She blinked, a knot tightening in her chest. She was Vallish by birth, though raised and trained in Selafai, but she hadn't seen Vallorn since she was seven, nor spoken its tongue since her mother died four years after that. Adam likely spoke it better than she by now.

"There's nothing for me there." The argument rang hollow. There was nothing for her anywhere—she still had to choose.

Adam shrugged. "So not Vallorn. Veresh, then, or Riven. I want to see the mountains again."

Memories rose, long faded—towering pines and sharp-toothed peaks, white with snow even in summer.

The dregs of her tea couldn't ease the dryness in her throat.

"We can't stay here," he continued.

"No." Selafai and Iskar had no open hostilities, but Kiril and the caliph's spymasters had maneuvered against each other more than once. Kehribar wasn't somewhere she could let down her guard. If any such place existed.

"Rest," she said, collecting her teacup. "We can't go anywhere till you're stronger. I'll think on it."

He reached across the table as she rose, stopping before he touched her hand. She felt the heat of his skin. "Thank you." It was the first time he'd said it.

She shrugged it aside and tried to smile. There was nothing to say, so she retreated into the house, leaving him to the thinning rain.

In the fading darkness on the rooftops of Mulberry Lane, the woman who called herself Melantha crouched heel to haunch on wet tiles and watched the necromancer vanish into the ochre house.

Low clouds rode the city, the orange glow of streetlamps bleeding through the haze. Her wet silks chilled whenever the wind shifted. The damp was welcome after summer in Assar, the sharp scent of rain on clay pleasant after days of brine and unwashed sailors. The weather kept people's heads down, and she'd happily trade that for the hazard of slick tiles.

Her eyes narrowed as Iskaldur's gaunt companion rose and followed the necromancer inside. Something about him nagged her—the shape of his shoulders, the tilt of his head—but she couldn't place it. It had been years since she was last in Iskar, and her mission had been brief. Corylus might know—he'd worked with her then too. She didn't think she'd ask him.

Corylus had long since retired for the evening; crowds were his specialty, where darkness was hers. She might go down now and talk to Iskaldur, if she had any idea of what to say.

Quietus had set a shadow on the necromancer when she first left Erisín, while the council argued over what to do with her. Iskaldur had thwarted their plans before, if unwittingly—now the council wondered if she could be of use to them, or only more trouble. The consensus leaned toward trouble, but Nerium was fond of taking matters into her own hands. There'd been no chance of wooing the Selafaïn spy away from her old master, but now that he was dead—

She wasn't sure how open Iskaldur was to courtship. Find the right leverage, her mother said, but Melantha was best at the sort of leverage that came from a knife-point. She might restrain Iskaldur alone, but wasn't eager to fight three people at once. Never mind her mother's hurry, she would have to wait till a moment presented itself.

She rose from her crouch and stretched. Let Iskaldur have a few hours of privacy; she looked as though she could use the rest.

From rooftop to rooftop Melantha ran, a darker shadow in the waning night. Night was her time, her senses heightened in the darkness. No one looked up as she leapt across alleys and balanced on garden walls. Her feet never touched the ground on her way back to the Corylus's rented room. She might have stepped into the shadows, moving more quickly through the nothing-place her magic opened to her, but the rhythm of breath and muscle relaxed her, silenced the voices in her head. Too many days confined to a ship had left her stiff and restless, haunted by dreams. She rarely slept easily, but after the storm in Ta'ashlan the nightmares had worsened.

Corylus had taken quarters in a nondescript building in a nondescript neighborhood. A glimpse through shadow told her the room was empty, so she stepped from one darkness to another, bypassing the door. Inside was narrow and dim, worn but clean—as plain and unremarkable as everything else about him.

Of all the agents Quietus could have sent, it would have to be him. She wished she could blame malice on the part of either Ahmar or her mother, but knew it for bad luck. And her own mistakes.

They had been partners on and off for years, till ambition became a strain between them. His ambition—the inner circle of Quietus was not where Melantha wanted to spend the rest of her life. Once she might have waited for him in bed; now she turned the room's single chair to keep her back to the wall.

She didn't have long to wait. A stair creaked. Tumblers clicked with the turn of a key. She heard the pause as he realized he wasn't alone, then Corylus stepped into the room.

He wore brown, his color as black was hers—the kind of brown that blended into a crowd and out of watchers' memory. She'd known him before he took up the mantle of anonymity that made him such an effective agent, but still his features faded in her memory to a blur of brown hair and hazel eyes, a soft, colorless voice too often sharpened with sarcasm.

"How was your night, dear?" she asked. An old joke, but the words felt flat on her tongue.

You never should have slept with him, said the voice in her head that sounded like her mother. Melantha hated it when she was right.

"Oh, the usual." He draped his cloak across the foot of the bed. A stripe of light fell through the narrow balcony window, splashing his hair and cheek with yellow. "This is a surprise."

"Lady Kerah sent me." The formality sounded ridiculous; everyone knew Nerium was her mother. "I'm to retrieve Iskaldur."

His face creased in a frown. "*Retrieve* her? That's not what I've been told."

"My orders come from Nerium, not Ahmar. I'm to bring the necromancer back to Qais."

"Nerium has lost her mind. Iskaldur is dangerous. Reckless."

Melantha shrugged. "She's grieving."

Corylus snorted. "What do you know about grief, Mel? You're your mother's daughter."

She couldn't argue that—her mother had trained her too well for regrets, let alone more hazardous emotions. But she'd heard the details behind the necromancer's departure from Erisín, and glimpsed the pain beneath Iskaldur's cool mask tonight. Melantha knew a little about leaving old lives behind.

"I am," she said instead. "And I have my orders."

"Look at what happened in Symir, and that mess in Erisín. Trouble follows her like flies to carrion. Bringing her to Assar is only a risk for us. Ahmar will never allow it."

Melantha rose, spreading her hands. "Perhaps that's true. But Ahmar isn't here, and neither is my mother. Let them sort this out between them."

The jaundiced glow of the streetlamp faded as they spoke, replaced by the leaden gloom of dawn. Rain dripped steadily past the window.

"You're right," Corylus said at last, his voice smoothing. The tension eased in his spine. "No sense in you finding another room now. We can have breakfast sent up. Or a bottle of wine."

She let him draw her close and kiss her neck. He still wanted it all—a partner and a lover, but one he could throw to the jackals the moment it would advance his career. Not that she wouldn't do the same.

"What's wrong?" he asked, his breath tickling her nape as he kneaded the taut muscles in her shoulders.

"Too long on that damned boat." She conjured a smile; he could read her duplicity as well as she could his. She wasn't going to sleep anyway. "Send for the wine."

CHAPTER 5

Two days later, Isyllt took Adam shopping.

They left Moth sleeping on the low couch, curled and twitching with kitten dreams, and walked two blocks from the quiet of Mulberry Lane to find a carriage. As the stink and clamor of the city rose to meet them, Adam's heart raced like it had before his first battle. The carriage slowed as they neared the Great Bazaar, and the coach shook from the crowds pressing around them. Adam scrubbed his palms on his thighs.

Isyllt's lips thinned, and she craned her head out the window to shout at the driver. The din swallowed most of it, but Adam heard *Istara Carsisi*. A smaller market in an older, less-trafficked neighborhood. The driver yelled to the horses and cursed pedestrians, and the carriage began to turn.

"You didn't have to do that," Adam said as Isyllt settled back in her seat. "I can take it."

"It would be embarrassing if you cut someone's head off in the market, and I can't afford to buy you out of the Çirağan again. Besides, if our shadow follows us today, I want to be able to see him."

The blue domes of the Istara rose above the rooftops as they approached, smaller and fewer than those of the Great Bazaar. Banners flapped in the breeze, reflecting the nationalities of the merchants inside: the crown and stars of the Ataskar Empire, altered and reused by Skarra and Iskar alike; Assar's three-headed lion on crimson; the silver tree on blue of Vallorn; Selafai's white tower and crescent on grey; and a dozen others besides. Even the knotwork horse of the Steppes clans, gold on sky-blue.

Colors dazzled as he stepped out of the carriage—gleaming spires, tangling flags, buildings painted ochre and orange, pinks and reds and blues. Sunlight sparked off brass chimes and windowpanes. Dogs barked and snarled after food carts, and goats bleated on their way to the slaughterhouse. Adam was full of sympathy as he followed Isyllt through the wide arch. At least the market had a roof to protect him from the yawning mouth of sky.

Light streamed through high windows, swirling with dust from the packed earthen floors. Sweat and spices and the heat of bodies thickened the air, enough to make him sneeze. Every draft carried a new scent—fruit, bread, oiled leather, wool, incense—a map to guide him through the labyrinthine aisles.

Isyllt didn't haggle well, but still managed to collect bread and persimmons for a good price. She wore a glove over her black diamond ring, but her pallor and sharp cheeks and sharper smile served just as well. Few merchants found it worthwhile to antagonize a witch over pennies. The cheesemonger, however, was less impressed, and charged her three clipped silver kurush for a round of wine-soaked cheese.

She bought clothes and boots for Adam as well. Everything practical, but he saw her gaze and fingers stray to southern styles more than once. She was considering Asheris's offer more seriously than she would admit.

By the time they left the clothiers' row Adam's neck had begun to itch. Even small markets in Kehribar were crowded, and too many people had brushed or bumped or shoved him already, but the watched sensation didn't change.

The next aisle belonged to the metalworkers, booth after booth of gold and silver, bronze and steel, polished and gleaming. The bitter smell of oil and metal soothed him; the sight of sword racks soothed him even more.

"Have you seen our friend yet?" Isyllt whispered in Selafaïn, leaning close as a lover as he studied a row of blades. Her breath chilled the sweaty stubble above his ear.

A flicker of movement in mirror-bright steel, and he knew. "The brown man." Brown skin, brown clothes, brown mien. The kind of man who left a gap in a watcher's memory, but Adam had seen the same gap too many times to discount him.

"Damn." She turned her head with a laugh and leaned in again, her lips brushing his ear. "Then there are two of them."

They didn't leave the bazaar after Adam found a sword, but retired to one of the inner balconies to drink coffee and study the crowd. The upper level was still hot, but a breeze wafted through the windows, drying the sweat on his scalp and neck.

"Who's your second shadow?" Adam asked, running his hand over the pommel at his hip. Three merchants had nearly come to blows over his choice, all swearing the quality of their goods on a lengthening line of dead ancestors. Each told the truth, but no matter how well crafted the yatagans and kilijes, how lovely their curves, the balance of chopping blades wasn't right in his hand. He'd refused them all until the last vendor unearthed a western longsword in the bottom of a trunk.

Isyllt lifted her coffee cup. "The woman in black," she said, hiding her lips behind the rim. "By the glassmaker's table."

A slender woman, neither short nor tall, wearing loose robes and a veil hiding her hair and the bottom half of her face. Another nondescript darkness in the press of shoppers, but something in her stance nagged at him, the bend of her wrist as she lifted a glass. Try as he might, he couldn't pin the memory down.

Adam raised his own cup but didn't drink. The liquid was thick enough to stand a spoon in, rich with cardamom and so sour it was almost salty. His hands tingled from the few sips he'd taken. "Lose her? Follow her?" The brown man had vanished when they sat down, but the woman lingered.

"There's no need to rush." Isyllt pulled a persimmon from her satchel and a small folding knife from her pocket. Juice ran down the blade as she carved the orange fruit into slices. She only used the thumb and forefinger of her left hand—the other three fingers curled toward her palm, hidden in a black glove. "She buys things to keep from being noticed. The longer we sit here, the more she spends."

Adam laughed and took the slice she offered. The sweetness shocked him, nearly as potent as the coffee. "Cruel."

Sure enough, the woman handed the merchant a handful of coins in exchange for a glass perfume bottle. He read annoyance in the set of her shoulders as she turned away, losing herself in the current of the crowd.

Isyllt wiped her knife clean and tucked it away. "Do you two want to be alone?"

When he frowned, she tilted her head toward the sword angled across his lap. His left hand hadn't left the hilt, absently tracing the grain of the wyrmskin wrappings. An eastern touch on a western blade—the great serpents were rare, and never seen west of the Zaratan Sea. The chunk of amber set in the cross-guard was another, an unblinking orange eye.

Adam snorted and took his hand away. "It's been a long time."

That earned him a sideways glance and the slow lift of her eyebrows. He blushed, and cursed the sallow pallor of his skin that let her see it.

Her gaze sharpened and turned back to the market floor. "Now," she said, taking a last sip of coffee and grimacing at the dregs. "She's distracted again. Let's go."

They moved casually, twisting through the press toward the doors. "I want to catch her," Isyllt said. "Are you up for a fight?"

His hand tightened on the sword. His palms were soft, and his shoulder ached from the weight of the satchel he carried. "No." The word was bitter, or maybe that was just the coffee on his tongue.

"I don't know that I am either."

They shared a wry glance. Three years ago, that might not have stopped either of them.

Sweat sprang up on Adam's brow as they stepped

into the hammerfall of sunlight, thickened with billowing dust. Isyllt squinted into the glare and shook her head. "We're getting old."

"Speak for yourself," he said. But the lost year was another pushing him closer to forty. Grey flecked the stubble on his scalp for the first time. Not quite doddering yet, but an age when a mercenary had to plan for the future—or rush headlong toward it.

They ignored the waiting carriages and ducked around the side of the building, where the alleys were crowded with more merchants selling fruit and crafts and fabrics from baskets and handcarts. Adam's knees and hips and shoulders ached from dodging the crowd, and the light and noise fed the headache growing behind his eyes. He breathed deep and forced the discomfort away, keeping pace with Isyllt's long-legged stride. The world wouldn't wait for him to catch his breath.

Adam watched the entrance while Isyllt pretended to peruse a stand billowing with silk shawls. The bazaar had smaller doors for merchants and security, but if their shadow meant to follow them she would come this way. Heartbeats slipped into moments, and she didn't appear. Had she lost track of them? Given up? Wrapped herself in sorcery and slipped away unseen?

Isyllt's own tactic backfired—she eventually paid the shawl-seller for a black-and-silver scarf and shoved it into her bag. "Where did she go?"

"I don't—" Adam broke off as his shoulder blades began to prickle. He spun, to hell with stealth, and caught the brown man watching them from the far end of the alley. The man vanished between stalls as soon as their eyes met.

"Shadows," Isyllt swore, and hurried after him.

They found the alley their tail had taken, a narrow dusty lane shadowed by buildings. Isyllt scanned the rooftops and kept going.

"You know this is a trap," Adam said. His breath came rough and painful, but the rush of a chase gave him new strength.

"Of course." She tugged off her right glove and the cabochon diamond shone dully.

Another turn, and this time they caught their quarry ducking around a bend. Adam had the man's scent now, and it was as bland and forgettable as the rest of him. They dodged sleeping beggars and a startled dog and turned again. They were gaining.

The next twist led to a dead end. Adam cursed as they stared at a grimy brick wall. The man might have climbed it, but there was no sign of him on the roofs.

Isyllt nudged him till they stood side by side in the alley mouth. "Look."

Tracks in the dirt. Dust recently disturbed settled slowly. Adam breathed in, and that bland brown scent filled his nose. Close.

"Why are you following me?" Isyllt asked softly, speaking to the wall.

No. Adam tilted his head and saw the shadow against the bricks. The outline that didn't quite blend. Sorcery, cunning as a chameleon's changing skin. His sword hissed free of its scabbard; the sound made his blood sing. Instinct, at least, hadn't atrophied.

Isyllt held out a hand. Pale light flickered in her diamond. "I want answers, not blood."

The shadow wavered and resolved into the brown man.

He drew a long dagger from beneath his cloak. The blade was painted matte. "And if I wanted your blood, I would have spilled it by now. Let me pass."

Isyllt had spoken in Selafaïn and he answered in the same tongue. The words were muffled by the dun scarf across his mouth; Adam couldn't guess his native language.

She didn't budge. "Why are you following me?"

His eyes creased. "Can't you guess?"

"I'm tired of guessing. Enlighten me."

He stepped forward, slow and cautious, hands wide and nonthreatening. "If you must know—"

A flare of nostrils, a shift of weight. A heartbeat's warning.

The man moved like water, his blade a black blur. Adam lunged, swung. Too slow. Too weak. At least he was a distraction; the brown man twisted mid-strike, only inches from Isyllt, to block Adam's blow. Steel rang. A twist, and the hilt wrenched from his fingers. In one smooth move the man drove his knee home, and Adam fell retching.

Through watering eyes he watched Isyllt collide with the assassin, black hair flying as her scarf fell away. She hadn't drawn her knife, but she could kill with a touch.

So why, heartbeats later, were they still scrabbling in the dust? Adam pushed himself up, groping across packed earth for his sword.

Isyllt's hands were around the man's neck, his face already a mess of scratches. Blood smeared hers. She held on like a terrier, but he wedged a boot into her gut and flung her back.

"Bitch," the man choked, a note of admiration in his

voice. He rolled to his feet, still graceful despite his purpling throat. "I would have made this easier—"

He choked and stumbled sideways, a scarlet bubble bursting on his lips. A dark stain spread down his shoulder. Adam knocked Isyllt aside as the man's knife thumped against the dust. The man followed a heartbeat later, knees buckling. As his bloody hand fell away, Adam saw the weighted dart that pierced his throat. Red mist sprayed from his nose and mouth as he tried to breathe.

Black cloth swirled on the rooftop and was gone.

They waited, breath held, pressed against the cool plaster while the brown man kicked and gurgled his last, his dun scarf soaked red. His dullness faded as he did—the smell of blood and shit filled the narrow alley, as strong as any death.

For a long moment Isyllt lay still, Adam's arm pressing her into the dust. As the shock of battle faded, her pulse pounded in scrapes and bruises. The chill in her diamond numbed her right hand.

It was only when Adam pulled away that she realized the chill was greater than a simple death would cause. Her eyes narrowed, looking *otherwise*, and she saw the pale, smoke-tattered shape of a fresh ghost lingering beside the corpse.

"*Kastanos!*"

A Selafaïn word that meant only "dark-haired"—hardly a name to conjure with, but it was the best she could do in her haste. All the same, the ghost paused, swaying toward her. As she focused on him, she felt a shivering connection between them, frail as a spider's web.

Names were best for binding souls—knowledge took the place of consent—but other things formed a connection that a clever vinculator could exploit. This man had followed her for decads, chosen to risk his life to murder her. He had tied himself to her through his actions, and she'd be damned if she'd let him escape a second time. Her right hand rose, clenched in the ephemeral gossamer ice of his soul. Her ring blazed white and blinding.

He fought. Even in the confusion of death his will was strong. But she had years of training and the strength of anger. Her grip held and the diamond opened, swallowing the brown man into its crystalline depths. Her arm ached to the shoulder with cold.

When she could feel her fingers again, Isyllt searched the cooling corpse while Adam kept watch. She had already contaminated the scene, but she tugged her right glove on before touching him again. It helped hide her shaking, and the nails she'd broken in the dead man's flesh.

The dart was a wicked thing, barbed and weighted with lead—made to kill mages. Copper and silver and other metals could be used in spells; lead held no magic, and weakened any that came near it. If the assassin was a mage herself, she was either very careful or very foolish.

Isyllt wished she could blame her own failure on the lead.

She should have killed him. She'd wanted to, answers or no; her hands still tingled with nerves and rage. She could stop a man's heart with a touch, or worse. The last mage who'd tried to kill her had crumbled to dust in her arms. But when she called for the magic, the nothing that lived inside her, all that answered was a choking helplessness.

The feel of his soul stirring in the depths of her ring soothed her pride a little.

With his spells faded the dead man's face was clear, though still ordinary—rounded features and heavy-lidded hazel eyes. A small scar nicked his upper lip, and thoughtful lines creased his dusty skin. He might have been handsome with the right smile. His brown-on-brown coloring had the look of no particular nation, but he could have come from any of the mongrel port cities. He carried nothing but a purse half full of small coins and a partially eaten lunch tucked into one pocket—no incriminating letters or signets or foreign coins.

His hands and forearms were clenched solid with death-spasm, fingers curled as if they still gripped a knife. A familiar bulge under his left glove caught her attention, and she cut the thin leather away. A topaz glittered on his smallest finger, sand-colored and square-cut in a plain gold band. A lesser mage stone, not as sought-after as rubies or sapphires or soul-binding diamonds, but a useful gem all the same.

"Valuable?" Adam asked.

"Worth a few lir." She'd received a parting payment from the king and much of Kiril's estate, but six months of travel had eaten into her resources. Still, stealing mage stones was never wise, and she'd have to break his finger to get the band off. Anything she might discover from the stone she could more easily learn by questioning his ghost. She emptied his purse and slipped the coins into her own pockets.

"Are you all right?" she asked belatedly as Adam helped her to her feet.

"Just my pride." He winced with every step, giving lie to the words. "No worse than your face."

She hadn't stopped to notice, but her lip and cheek stung and the taste of copper filled her mouth. She touched her upper lip and winced; her fingers came away smeared red.

"We should go," Adam said. "You've been framed for murder before."

Her mouth twisted. "I remember."

She would find no sympathy among the caliph's agents, nor a comfortable house arrest. And neither her king nor Kiril was waiting to ransom her safely home. Pressure swelled in her chest, a sharp hitch of panic.

I can't do this alone.

She quashed the thought. She had no choice. Every wirewalker learned to work without a net one day. Or died broken.

The sky glowed orange and violet when they returned to Mulberry Lane, and the last light slanted warm and heavy across the rooftops. The aftermath of violence left Isyllt stretched taut and brittle. They had to leave town, but whether that meant the docks or the northern road she couldn't decide. First she had to retrieve Moth and their luggage.

Her unease grew as they neared the ochre house. The street was much too quiet for the hour. Adam paused with her, nostrils flaring. "Trouble."

She stopped in her tracks at the gate, boots scuffing heavily on paving stones; a man sat on the doorstep. Lean and hawk-nosed, dressed in professionally nondescript clothing. She might have run, but other ordinary-looking men drifted from shadowed nooks along the street. The caliph's Security Ministry. The euphemism on the streets was "the friends of the family," or more simply the Friends.

"Hello, Lady Iskaldur." The man rose, the westering sun gleaming on his shaven scalp. "Or is it Kara Asli?"

The name under which she'd entered the city and rented the house. Isyllt sighed; so much for that set of papers. "Either way," she said, "you have me at a disadvantage."

The man bowed low. "My name is Ahmet Sahin. I would be delighted if you would come with me."

CHAPTER 6

She ought to feel something.

Melantha stared down at Corylus's slack face and waited to feel regret, sadness, even anger. Nothing came. They had been . . . perhaps not friends, but she had enjoyed his company once. Now a fly crawled across one half-open hazel eye and she felt nothing but confusion.

He should have known better. He should have listened to her.

She hadn't meant to do it—to stop him from killing Iskaldur, yes, but not like that. Then the necromancer's companion moved from sun to shadow and she'd seen the copper-green flash of his eyes, and the sense of familiarity that had nagged her all day snapped into place.

Adam.

It shouldn't have mattered. She'd been another person when she knew him, and that woman was dead. He would bear no love for her memory. But when Corylus attacked him, she'd moved like a person possessed.

The thought chilled her. She was warded against spirits

and specters, but what defenses did she have against the ghosts of people she had been?

She couldn't leave Corylus here, no matter what she did or didn't feel. The dust of Iskaldur's footsteps had barely settled when she came down from the roofs, but she didn't have long. Already a brindled dog circled at the mouth of the alley, licking its muzzle hopefully.

"Sorry," she muttered, bending down to grab Corylus's ankles. She wasn't sure if she meant it for the dog or for him. The smell of cold blood and waste rose up as she tugged him, and her nose wrinkled. His left hand bounced in the dirt, claw-curled. Her breath came hard through clenched teeth by the time she dragged the corpse into the deeper shadows at the back of the alley. Mages and scholars speculated on the weight of the soul, but as far as she could tell the lack thereof had never made a body lighter. Especially when she was the one disposing of it.

Melantha dropped Corylus and laid a hand against the warm bricks, catching her breath and gathering her magic. This would be easier at night, or at the height of the noon—the brighter the light, the darker the shadow—but the fading afternoon would suffice.

Many mages learned simple skiamancy or skiagraphy—viewing through shadows, or casting them into illusions. Even making them solid for heartbeats at a time. Melantha knew better tricks.

Darkness gathered beneath her hand, pooling like tar. Rough brick smoothed to glass, and slicker still. Soon what had been a wall felt like oil, a patch of black that rippled at her touch. Sweat chilled on her scalp and neck.

She hooked her fingers in the crawling shadow and yanked. Darkness tore like the husk of rotten fruit, with a sick wet sound she felt in her chest. She braced against the dizziness that always came. Shadows were natural, even the black of a moonless night. This was something more, unreal in its intensity. A gift from her mother, double-edged like all the rest.

She tensed as the fabric of the world parted for her. She hadn't opened shadows so deeply since she'd murdered Zadani. The ghost wind had been waiting for her even in the dark paths that day, had nearly swallowed her before she could escape. Today, however, she faced only empty silence.

Melantha took a deep breath and grabbed Corylus by the ankles once more. He would have no burial or burning, even if he had kin or friends to perform the rites. Nothing she took into the abyss came out again, once she let it go. Every time she crossed the threshold she feared she'd trip over memories, tokens, corpses—all the things she left behind. It hadn't happened yet, but how much could the dark hold?

Quietus wouldn't mind the absent corpse—they weren't sentimental—but she'd have to explain it to Nerium. She hoped her mother was right and Iskaldur was worth this much trouble. Closing her eyes, she heaved herself backward, hauling the corpse with her.

Like falling into a pool whose depth she couldn't measure. She floated in lightless cold, with no sense of up or down. The urge to struggle was overwhelming, the urge to open her mouth and scream, but practice had taught her better. There was no air for her in the dark, and the thought of taking the blackness into her lungs terrified her. She could only move through shadow for the span of a held breath.

Her hands tightened on Corylus. Soft boot leather, flesh and muscle and bone beneath. The dark drank the last of his warmth greedily. She ought to have something to say, but there was nothing.

She let go.

An hour later, she found Iskaldur's apprentice in a tavern called The Three-legged Dog.

The building was low and dim, wedged into one of Kehribar's oldest and least reputable neighborhoods. The air smelled permanently of spilled beer and scorched onions, burning olive oil and sweat. Lamp-smoke blackened the beams and the horn windows, enfolding the common room in a permanent gloom no matter the hour. Not the sort of place for tourists, but the girl who called herself Moth sprawled comfortably across a booth in the back, laughing with a boy her own age.

Melantha smiled behind her scarf.

She had learned a little about Moth from her mother's notes and more from Corylus—too much wine left him gossipy. Before the girl took up with Iskaldur, there had been little to tell. Her name in Erisín had been Dahlia, the mark of a prostitute and a mother's cruelty. According to Corylus, she had been a thin sparrow of a girl, lost in Iskaldur's shadow. That changed in Thesme, when a pimp thought the name gave him leave to lay hands on her. Iskaldur left the man in a pool of his own guts, but the next day Dahlia had cut off her long dark hair and taken a new name.

Melantha understood such transformations all too well. She quashed a feeling of kinship; nostalgia was as dangerous as regret.

Her quarry paid her no attention as she paid for a beer and slipped into a dark corner. The drink was only cover, but the house brew turned out to be rich and malty and bittersweet, good enough to overlook the dubious cleanliness of the mug. In between sips, she shuffled shadows till she found a clear view of Moth and her boy.

Moth's lips were swollen from kissing, and the fevered sparkle in her eyes couldn't be entirely the work of the half-empty bottle of raki on the table. Trouble of the adventurous sort—her companion looked like the type. A thief or a hustler, cocky with youth and careless with success. Not that Melantha would know anything about that.

She might not have time for this; she might have too much time. She'd searched for Iskaldur in time to watch Adam and the necromancer taken into custody by Kehribar's secret police. Either they would talk their way out, or Melantha would have to devise a cunning rescue. She hoped Iskaldur was a fast talker.

Distracted by quarry and quandary, she nearly missed the mutter that rippled through the room. The afternoon crowd thinned like smoke in a draft; one of the bartenders vanished as well. Melantha had seen enough raids to recognize this one. Sure enough, a shift of shadows showed city guards in the street outside.

Light and heat spilled in as the door swung open, and conversation died. Five men stepped inside, swords and pistols at their belts, the sigil of the watch on their breasts. Moth's companion sobered at the sight of them, his interest in the laces of her shirt abandoned. As the guard captain stepped to the bar, the boy slumped against his bench, melting out of his seat and under the table, motioning Moth to follow as he slunk toward the rear door.

They almost made it, but the guards turned as the door swung open. A shout rose up as they gave chase. Melantha grinned; she was always better at acting than planning, anyway.

The shadows of the booth turned cold and liquid, swallowing her. It had taken her this long to shake the chill from her bones, too. At least this time all she needed was shallow darkness.

She writhed quicksilver from shadow to shadow, through walls and over obstacles, keeping pace with the fleeing children. The Friends would have sent their own agents, not city guards—this was a separate trouble. Heavy footsteps drew near as Moth and the boy reached the back door—the alley beyond was clear, for the moment.

In the heartbeat's pause while the thief wrestled with the barred door, she struck. Reaching through the shadow that lay like a skin over the walls, she seized Moth's arm. The girl yelped once before the dark stole her voice. Back and up Melantha swam, dragging Moth behind. Only a few yards separated them from a shuttered room on the second story, but they were both chilled and breathless when they emerged.

"Easy," she whispered, one gloved hand over Moth's mouth. "Stay quiet and the guards will be gone soon. And sorry. It's always vertiginous, the first time."

Sure enough, the girl's shoulders convulsed. When Melantha let go, she fell to one knee and fought not to retch. She didn't scream, though.

"Who are you?" she asked at last, voice rough with suppressed coughing.

"The patron saint of clumsy thieves. Can you make

a light?" The single stripe of daylight burning between the curtains was enough for her, and she could feel the contents of the room through the dark besides, but there was no point in telling Moth that. She wrapped her scarf across her face.

Sparks blossomed, rose-pink and shimmering. By their glow Moth found a candle, and witchlight kindled to real flame as it touched the wick. The light reflected in her eyes, and along the blade of the little knife in her hand.

"No need for that," Melantha said, hiding a grin. "Who did you rob?"

"A lapidary in Yashkis."

The upscale market district, and in daylight, no less. Melantha whistled. "Your friend must have wanted badly to impress you."

Moth swallowed and glanced at the floor. "Jemal—"

"He'll be fine. I'm sure he's done this before."

The girl's face was flat and still, but the ripple of light along her knife betrayed her nerves. "What do you want?"

"To give you a warning: Your mistress is in danger. This isn't the time to be playing tag with the city guard."

Moth's eyes narrowed. "You're the one who's been following us."

"I'm not the only one. Iskaldur was taken by the Friends. Mulberry Lane is being watched, so tread lightly. Their headquarters is in Golga Court—tread even softer there."

"You're a spy. Why should I believe you?"

"Your mistress is a spy, too."

Pride lifted the girl's chin. "That's why I know better."

Melantha nearly winced. If Iskaldur was half the

stormcrow Corylus made her out to be, Moth would never be safe at her side.

Do you suppose your company is any safer? No, of course she didn't.

"Believe what you like, but be careful. Your mistress is no use to either of us in prison. Here—" She reached into the leather bag slung across her back and pulled out a small well-wrapped bundle. A quick touch told her the glass was still intact. "A present for Iskaldur, when you see her again."

Moth took the wrapped bottle with a frown. "What about you?"

"You might see me again, too." With Melantha's wink, a coil of shadow snuffed the candle. The sound of Moth's cursing followed her as she vanished.

Dusk settled slowly around the Susturma Serai. A true palace once, its former grandeur lingered in delicately carven arches and intricate tilework, clung to the lintels with flakes of gilt. Its halls still remembered the footsteps of lords and princes and perfumed courtiers, but for the past twenty years it had been home to Iskar's secret police.

Distant bells tolled the setting sun, but silence filled the little room where Isyllt, Adam, and Iskar's spymaster sat. Tea cooled on a table while they watched one another. Sahin's guards waited outside, having taken Adam's sword and Isyllt's blade and kit. They had eyed her ring as well. Better for everyone that they'd chosen not to touch it.

She knew Sahin the same way she knew much of Kehribar—Kiril's wealth of notes and records. She'd thought he would be older; the skin around his long black eyes was smooth, mustache untouched by grey, but she'd heard his name for nearly fifteen years.

"My agents tell me you've been in Kehribar for over a decad," Sahin said. "So I'm lucky to have only one alleged corpse so far." His eyes glinted when she raised her eyebrows. "I had reports of Symir."

Isyllt's mouth twisted sideways, tugging at scabs. Maybe it was for the best she'd lost her position with the Crown—she was ruined for foreign assignments. "An *alleged* corpse?"

"We were told of a disturbance near the Istara Carsisi, and of a foreign witch's involvement. When we arrived, we found only a bloodstain in an alley and a confusion of footprints."

Isyllt spread her hands. Every gesture snagged her glove on a broken nail, sending a thrill of pain up her arm. "As your search revealed, I have no corpses in my pockets." She kept her movements calm and relaxed when her heart wanted to speed. "I can hardly be the only foreign witch in Kehribar."

"No." Sahin sipped his tea. "What happened to your face?"

Her smile split her lip again. "I'm no good at haggling."

He chuckled. "You'll forgive me if I find it all too easy to believe you're involved. Several parties have expressed interest in you already."

"What sort of interest?"

"Some would like you dead. Others would simply see your friend returned to the Çirağan, and you in a lead-lined cell below him."

"I only came to Kehribar to find my friend," she said, voice mild. Adam tensed; could they fight their way through a palace of armed killers? "Having done so, I'm happy to leave. I didn't come here to cause trouble, Sahin Bey. I'm no longer in the business."

He smiled, a more honest expression than she'd yet seen. "I retired once, several years ago. It lasted two months. One does not leave our business so easily."

Two soft taps sounded against the door before Isyllt could reply, followed by another two.

A fine line appeared and smoothed between Sahin's brows. "Excuse me."

She blew a sharp breath through her nose as the door closed behind him. Adam's knuckles were white on the arms of his chair. A year ago she might have tried their odds against the Friends. Now the thought made her palms sweat.

A murmur of voices rose from the hall, faded again. Heartbeats thudded by till she lost count. Her mouth was dry, and she drained half the cold tea in her cup. Her arm ached with the effort of making the movement seem relaxed. Even the new weight in her diamond didn't reassure her as it should.

Isyllt imagined half an hour or more passed before she heard footsteps in the hall again. The door opened, and lamplight warmed the curve of Sahin's skull. His face was calm, but his shoulders and jaw were tighter than they had been when he left. His smile was tighter still.

"It seems that not everyone wants you buried."

Another set of footsteps approached—uneven steps, accompanied by the click of a cane. Sahin stepped aside for a hooded man. The light from the hall cast his face in shadow.

"My lord?" Sahin asked when the man stayed silent. He spoke in Assari, and Isyllt's skin prickled.

"Excuse me." One brown hand rose to throw back his hood. "I was waiting for an explosion."

Adam swore under his breath a heartbeat before Isyllt laughed. A name rose to her lips and she swallowed it. "My lord. Imagine meeting you here."

She had met Siddir Bashari in Sivahra, where he'd worn the guise of an insouciant nobleman, all silk and oiled curls. He wore plain linen now, and his dark hair was cropped short. He'd grown a beard, but the laughing hazel eyes were the same. An Assari spy shouldn't be a comforting sight, but her smile made her cheeks ache. On the heels of her relief, a cold weight settled in her stomach. It felt like a snare closing.

Sahin watched them, sharp-eyed as the falcon that was his namesake. Assar had made incursions northward for centuries, first rebuffed by the Steppes horselords and later driven back by the navies of the Ataskar Caliphate. Subsequent generations had made peace, but kingdoms had long memories. Sahin might yield to an Assari agent, but he would never enjoy it.

"Lady Iskaldur." Siddir offered a hand and she rose to take it, relief overpowering her misgivings for the moment. "A mutual friend sent me to find you. Will you come?"

Her smile sharpened. "I find myself with few options."

He bowed, as gracious as if he hadn't just backed her into a corner. "Thank you."

* * *

"Convenient timing," she said as they descended the steps of the Susturma Serai into the sticky night. Her kit was a reassuring weight at her hip. "Or did you orchestrate this all?" The scales of relief and distrust shifted every time she glanced at him; they would balance eventually, she supposed. They had to, in their work.

She snorted in soft disgust; how easily this became her work again.

Siddir's eyes widened, all innocence. No grown man should have eyes like that. "We only arrived in port this morning. It's both our good luck that one of my contacts heard of a northern sorceress being apprehended by the Friends this afternoon."

"Very convenient."

"Let's call it *fortuitous*. And let's be on our way." The ferrule of his cane clicked against the stones. "Too much serendipity gives me a rash."

Hours later, Isyllt stood on the quay with Moth and Adam, watching the *Marid* prepare to sail. The perfume bottle warmed in her hand, blown glass swirled with blue and violet ribbons, delicate as a soap bubble. The woman in black's taunting gift. Isyllt wanted to fling it against the boards, or into the sea, but it was too lovely a thing to waste in pettiness.

"You don't have to come with me," she said, soft beneath the slow lapping of the tide and the sailors' shouts.

Moth snorted contempt for the idea, but her eyes lingered wistfully on the skyline. It was Adam's silence, however, that weighed on her. When it stretched too long Isyllt broke and turned to face him. Green eyes narrowed as he studied her in turn. Moth glanced at each of them and edged quietly away to talk to a young sailor.

The sea breathed over them, cool and damp and bitter with brine. Adam's face was lost in shadow, save for the glint of his night-shining eyes. She read the tension in his shoulders, in the tightness of his hand on his sword-hilt.

"Will you come?" she asked at last, swallowing her pride. "I can pay you for a month of your time, longer if Asheris pays me."

"I've wondered," he said, the words coming slowly, "how the last three years might have been different if I hadn't gone with you to Symir."

Her jaw tightened, the name he didn't speak leaving a bitter residue on her tongue. Xinai Lin. His partner and lover, who'd sailed with them to Symir and abandoned him there to rejoin her rebel family. Adam had left her behind at the end, choosing Isyllt and the mission over a chance at reconciliation.

"I know I'm not the safest person to be around..." She tried to make it a joke, but it was all too true.

Adam chuckled. "Stormcrow. At least I'm not likely to be bored."

Hope sparked. She drew in a deep breath and let it out. "There's another thing. Something I haven't told you."

"Only one thing?"

"I didn't just leave the Crown's service." She hadn't explained this to anyone. The words were slow to come. "I broke my oath of service. My magic was bound to that oath—my power broke too. It's better than it was, but sometimes I have...relapses."

He frowned. "When were you going to mention this? Before or after we were killed?"

She forced her arms by her sides when they wanted to wrap across her chest. She deserved the acid in his voice. "I thought you should know, just in case."

"Any other secrets you want to share?"

"None that might get you killed. I think."

He turned his head, jaw working like he meant to spit. "Spies," he muttered instead, the word a curse.

She couldn't argue with that.

"Lady Iskaldur." She turned to see Siddir gesture toward the gangplank. "We're ready." Moth had already shouldered her bags, shifting her weight impatiently. The night was nearly spent, the eastern sky glowing with false dawn.

Adam sighed and hefted his own meager pack. "We can both try not to get each other killed."

Isyllt felt every hour of the short summer night as she stowed her luggage, but the cabin's narrow cot offered no comfort. Instead she returned to the deck, leaning against the starboard railing to watch the orange lights of Kehribar dim behind them. The eastern sky pearled with the coming dawn, and the mountains in the north faded from indigo to a whisper of grey.

She didn't hear footsteps over the creak of ropes and canvas and rush of waves against the hull, but she felt the break in the wind as someone drew near, smelled amber and olibanum and bitter oranges through the ocean's tang. Her shoulders tightened—even months after she'd tracked and killed the sorceress Phaedra Severos, certain scents brought back the weight of memory. She still couldn't drink cinnamon tea. The wind changed, and all that remained was the bouquet of brine and decay.

She forced herself to relax as Siddir leaned against the rail beside her. "What happened to your leg?" She'd thought it an affectation at first, but though he'd abandoned his cane he still favored his left leg.

He grimaced. "Blown cover and a bad aim. The bullet was meant for my skull."

"How long have you been looking for me?" she asked, sifting through the rest of her questions.

"My ship sailed from Sherazad fifteen days ago. We knew you left Thesme heading east. Kehribar was a lucky guess."

Or a thorough web of contacts. Isyllt knew which one she'd put money on.

"Asheris might have sent a letter instead of a press-gang. I would have come if he'd asked." She wasn't sure that was true, but it sounded pleasantly indignant.

"I'm sorry." If she hadn't known better, she might have thought him truly contrite. "He felt the situation was too important to trust to the vagaries of the post." He slitted his eyes against the wind. More grey threaded his hair than four years should account for. She didn't think he was more than a handful of years older than she, forty at most, but their work could age a person. After the assassin and Sahin and a sleepless night, she felt twice thirty.

"What is the situation?"

He waved a hand. "Oh, the usual—trouble on the borders, unrest in the senate, pressures from the church."

"You don't need me for any of those."

"No. There are...thaumaturgical problems also. I would prefer to let Asheris explain."

She watched grey water foam against the hull. "How is

he?" She had neglected their correspondence since Kiril's death.

From the corner of her eye she saw Siddir smile. "Well." He dipped on shoulder in a shrug. "Or as well as he can be, I suppose. He makes the best of his situation."

Isyllt turned to study him, leaning her hip on the rail. He nodded in answer to her unspoken question. "I know. He told me."

She cocked an eyebrow. Asheris's secret, that he was a jinni bound in human flesh—a demon, as such meldings were commonly called—was a dangerous one. She had learned it by chance in Symir, and nearly died for it. "Who else knows?"

"Only the empress."

The old emperor and his mages had been responsible for the binding. Their deaths had been one of the first things Asheris had done with his freedom. She'd been surprised to hear that he'd gone to work for the new empress, but only for a moment. As Sahin had said, leaving their line of work wasn't easy, no matter what one's intentions.

"Thank you," Siddir said. "For freeing him. He isn't the man he was, but I have a friend back all the same. For that I am in your debt." He fell silent for a time, picking at the varnished rail with one fingernail. "I was very sorry to hear about Lord Orfion."

The words were nearly lost beneath the sound of the sea; she wished they had been. She nodded, the most gracious acceptance she could manage. Siddir turned away, leaving her alone with the salt and rising dawn.

CHAPTER 7

Across the wine-dark stretch of the Caelurean Sea, the sun rose on Assar. Over the peaks of the Teeth of Heaven, across the flooded stretch of the River Nilufer, and finally to the domes of Ta'ashlan. As the first rays gilded the temple spires, bells and voices rose to greet the rising light. Paeans to the Unconquered Sun, gratitude for another day. Rich and golden as temple honey, but Asheris took no comfort in the sound. Every note and chime was a reminder that this was not and could never be his home.

Prayers sang out in the palace as well, and servants hurried to their chores, but in the royal apartments shadows and quiet still held sway. The royal family might sleep till noon undisturbed, if they wished. Asheris didn't think the empress had slept at all.

The curtains were still drawn in Samar's private breakfast room, though light and song slivered through them. A brass lamp burned in one corner, casting filigreed shadows across the walls.

"I appreciate your adherence to the letter of my command," Samar said dryly, not glancing up as she poured coffee, "but sending my best agent to retrieve a foreign spy hardly follows the spirit. A spy who helped turn Symir into smoking ash."

"That wasn't precisely her fault. Besides, we could use a necromancer on staff."

"It would keep the court on their toes." She looked up, hazel-gold eyes narrowing. Bruised and tired without the armor of cosmetics; her sleep had been troubled long before the ghost wind blew. "But when I say I need your attention on more immediate matters"—a manicured nail tapped sharply on the parchments stacked on the breakfast table—"I mean it."

"The storm may not return for decades," Asheris said. He sat cross-legged on the far side of the low table, but had not yet touched the food. He wasn't sure just how angry Samar was. "But return it will, I'm certain. And if it is a problem we can solve, wouldn't you rather have one less trouble waiting for you? One less waiting for your heirs?"

He regretted the words as soon as he spoke, and prepared to have a cup thrown at him. Her only reaction was the thinning of her lips. Then her shoulders sagged, and she cast a rare unguarded glance over her shoulder, toward the wall that separated her suite from her niece's. The room was dim, but inhuman eyes saw well in the dark, saw all the doubts and fears she could never bring before the sun.

Samar had been married once. No one at court spoke of it, but all knew the story. When her elder brother Rahal gained the throne, he'd been jealous and insecure in his power. Their eldest brother had already died under questionable circumstances, and no doubt Rahal feared the same fate awaited him.

The accident that befell Samar and her family was equally questionable, though no one could prove the emperor's involvement. It was also unsuccessful, sparing Samar and claiming instead her husband and young daughter.

When Rahal died and Samar took the throne, the senate agreed she should be empress in truth and not merely regent to her brother's daughter. But the Princess Indihar was still her best choice for an heir. The discomfort of the situation wasn't lost on empress or princess, or anyone else in the court. With the birth of Samar's child, Indihar stood to lose her inheritance again.

"All I want is peace," Samar murmured, brow creasing. "For the empire, between my family. Why does that seem so impossible?"

Asheris kept his eyes on his empty plate until she turned her gaze to him. Then he shrugged. "Perhaps the nature of empire is inimical to peace."

There had been no open war in their lives—his mortal life, at least—but conflict always seethed somewhere in Assar. Skirmishes with the tribes of Iseth, or Ninayan ships, or rebels in Sivahra. Bandits like their current plague of warlords harrying the borders. Princes and chieftains who flew the lion banner but kept their former colors bright in their hearts and nursed old grudges. And the constant dynastic infighting that left so many rulers and heirs with troubled sleep.

"If not the nature of empire, then the nature of the world." Samar smiled wryly. "When did we become so cynical?" She sighed and poured a second cup of coffee.

Plates and papers competed for space on the breakfast table: bread and hummus, honeyed figs and goat cheese, labneh drizzled with mint and olive oil next to reports from border garrisons and sepats. The newest of the troubles that robbed her of sleep.

They ate in silence for a time, ignoring the papers and their news. Asheris appreciated the taste of food again, as he hadn't for days after the storm. Though as honey melted over his tongue he couldn't help but think of the ravaged temple apiaries.

"Hamad and his bandits have taken Mamarr Elizar," Samar finally said, dipping her last triangle of bread into the labneh. "At least three caravans have been lost since. We've warned the merchants in the city to seek other routes for the time being, but we can only buy their complacency and silence so long." She raised her coffee cup in a sardonic toast. "So enjoy this while it lasts."

Asheris's mouth twisted, but he raised his cup in answer and drained a long bitter swallow. The southeastern province Zelassa, reached by the Elizar pass, was rich not only in coffee plantations but also sugarcane, qat leaves, and grains. With warlords holding the pass through the Teeth of Heaven, markets in Ta'ashlan would soon feel the lack. Not enough to threaten famine, but shortages would mean rising prices and rising tempers.

"We still have coffee plantations in Sivahra," he said. "And cane."

"Yes. I imagine qat grows there well enough, too. That comes with the costs and dangers of shipping, though, and many caravan merchants are too set in their ways to buy ships. My finance ministers are fond of telling me so."

Asheris sipped lemon water to rinse away the bitter taste of coffee. "Many things must adapt or die."

Samar chuckled. "I do so love you when you're ruthless. In the meantime, I suppose we could orchestrate a fondness for northern delicacies. Skarrish lokum, perhaps, though it sticks in my teeth." Her amusement was short-lived. "I should have killed Hamad and his cronies when I had the chance," she said, soft and vehement. "Why was I such a fool?"

Asheris shrugged. "Mercy was a welcome change after Rahal. It went over well at the time."

"And now they've come back to plague me."

Samael Hamad, once a general in the imperial army, had acted as an intermediary for the former emperor, fencing smuggled diamonds from Sivahra without the knowledge of the senate. Rahal, an expansionist like his forefathers, had used the money to fund his armies. One of Samar's first acts upon taking the throne was to strip Hamad and his co-conspirators of rank and lands and exile them.

Who exactly had bought those diamonds was a question that had long troubled Asheris.

"Back, and well funded." Hamad had been popular with his soldiers; nearly half of his legion had defected with his exile, joining their commander in outlawry. Asheris and Siddir had kept an eye on them, but mostly the warlord had laid low, robbing caravans now and then and vanishing into the desert wastes.

Until last year, when the bandits' incursions had redoubled, fiercer and more cunning than ever, and better supplied than many imperial legions. Hamad attacked garrisons and prison caravans, recruiting any who would join him and slaughtering the rest. Merchants whom they didn't kill they taxed. They seized salt mines and poppy fields, sometimes stripping them bare and riding on, sometimes ransoming them back to their overseers. Survivors from razed villages drifted into neighboring sepats in greater numbers, and the provincial governors demanded action. Samar had kept news of the troubles out of the streets of Ta'ashlan, but that elision couldn't last.

Hamad, familiar with imperial tactics and with his enemies, had evaded or defeated all the troops sent after him. Age and experience couldn't explain why no one could scry him out, though—neither Asheris nor any of the army's battle mages. Survivors' stories had grown in the telling to include chained beasts aiding the slaughters, or chained monsters. Having heard reports of the carnage from reliable soldiers, he was hesitant to dismiss the tales out of hand. Siddir had attempted to infiltrate a bandit camp to learn more, but his cover had been quickly blown, and he escaped with only an injured leg to show for his efforts.

Samar reached for a fig but set it down again, frowning as if at a sour taste. "This ghost wind. Do you suppose it would swallow up Hamad and his playmates if I asked nicely?"

She asked it jokingly, eyebrows raised, but her eyes were canny and cool. She would do it if she could.

"You'd do as well asking the khamsin or the simoom," he said, matching her light tone. "We understand them better."

She stood, pacing a restless circuit around the room before stopping beside a curtained window. "And this necromancer of yours? This entropomancer. Will she understand the storm?"

He read an invitation in the tilt of her head and rose to join her. "She might. And if not, I've merely recruited an agent from Selafai. I'm sure you could find a use for such." Siddir's message had come an hour ago, whispered to a flame across the sea: He was coming home, with Isyllt.

"Can you control her? I would rather not see a repeat of Symir."

He drew a breath, tasting the fragrance of rosemary and shea butter in Samar's hair. Pregnancy had altered her scent, made it richer and sharper, more pungently female. She had taken to wearing perfumes outside her own rooms.

"I believe I can trust her," he said slowly. "She needs work and safety—we can provide those." It was a familiar bargain to both of them; he had given Samar the throne, she gave him shelter and purpose.

"Safety?" She snorted indelicately. "You know better than that."

Asheris shrugged. "I am in her debt."

The corners of her eyes creased, flecks of amber and tourmaline glinting in her irises. "As I am in yours." She stroked her knuckles across his cheek, a warmth of affection behind the teasing gesture. The touch lingered. Were he mortal, she might solve her problems by naming him consort. Just as well, then, that his nature made him anathema. His appreciation of women was in the main aesthetic.

Her hand fell. "We are all tangled in webs of alliance and debt, my friend. Never think I don't value all you've done for me." She tugged the curtain back, and morning sunlight clove the space between them. "But I won't allow Assar to be threatened by foreign sorcerers any more than warlords or your desert storms. Bring Iskaldur here, and offer her all you wish, but keep hold of her leash."

Asheris spent the rest of the morning pacing his chambers. He had found only a few more records of the ghost wind since his search began, most redundant or too muddled to be of use. His hunt for rumors of Jirair's quiet men had fared no better.

He hadn't yet taken his questions to the university mages, starting instead with the city's black-market sorcerers. Sand witches and unlicensed vinculators, people who bound little spirits for sale, who would bind your enemy's soul in a bottle for the right price. He had found answers there, of a sort.

"A myth," one old woman said, waving a gnarled hand in dismissal. "Stories to frighten foolish thieves and wizards. 'Keep your head down or the quiet men will find you.' It's all nonsense."

"Don't say that name!" hissed the next man, a shriveled, pallid sorcerer who might not have left his basement room in years from the look of him. "They have eyes everywhere. They know." His own eyes had narrowed then, and he spat a warding spell. "This is a test, isn't it? Get out."

The last man Asheris spoke to had been saner, thankfully, but no more helpful. "Certainly I've heard of these quiet men." The aging thief-keeper smiled and winked. "My wife's cousin's boy did a job for them once. They paid him enough to retire, but whatever he saw that night turned his hair white."

Asheris had asked no more since, lest he draw attention to his inquiry. Whatever these quiet men truly were, though, he had to believe they existed. And that they knew his secrets.

When the noon prayers rose across the city, pricking him like thorns, he abandoned his fruitless paper chase and fled to the garden. The palace temple had changed incense; it drifted through the halls and arcades, filling his head with cinnamon and clove and bitter patchouli. Not an unpleasant scent, but cloying in its strength. He was grateful to reach the open air of the garden.

The royal gardens were lush and green despite the baking summer heat. Fig trees and pomegranates shaded manicured lawns, along with willows and sprawling tamarisk shrubs. Fountains fed fish-stocked ponds, and exotic lizards and small furred beasts from every end of the empire prowled the grounds. The last tame lioness had died months ago and not yet been replaced. Asheris was just as glad—watching wild things grow fat and slow in gilded collars struck too close to home.

He had thought to be alone in the rising heat; Samar sometimes entertained her courtiers beside the pools, but today she was closeted with advisors. But as he followed the winding, marjoram- and laurel-lined paths toward the center of the garden, he spotted a flash of red through a trellis. Curiosity drew him on, but he paused as he recognized the figure seated beside the pond.

The sanguine sweep of skirts belonged to Ahmar Asalar, keeper of the temple apiaries and personal secretary to the high priestess of the Unconquered Sun. Not someone he expected to find lounging in the gardens. Samar had said nothing of a meeting with her. He would have retreated to learn more, but the Asalar's companion glanced up at his footfalls. He walked on, unstumbling, and came face-to-face with the priestess.

"Lord al Seth." The Asalar smiled, as sleek and lovely as ever despite the heat. She was a tall, long-limbed woman with grace that rivaled Samar's. The gilt-edged scarlet of her formal robes was too strong for her complexion, but her bright eyes and arching dark brows kept her from being washed out. More than faith brought crowds to the temple yard when Ahmar offered the honey alms.

"Your Radiance. An unexpected pleasure." He bowed over her offered hand; incense clung to her skin and robes as well. The combination of perfume and the sun's heat left him light-headed.

Ahmar's hands bore the marks of her office: ink-stained nails and knuckles swollen with bee stings, as well as the blood-black ruby and honey-colored topaz in her rings. Ash streaked her fingers, smudged his skin in turn. At her touch he felt strength and quiet power—sanctity, the church would say, the Sun's blessing. Asheris suspected it was merely a talent for magic turned inward with meditation. He also felt the usual frisson of being in the presence of the church; if the priests knew his true nature he would be banished or worse, and all who sheltered him cast out as heretics.

Another scarlet figure stood behind her, this one veiled and armed. The Khajirite Order—red pilgrims, they were more often called—was the strong sword-arm of the church. They guarded powerful clergy and poor faithful alike, and protected distant villages from the threat of demons or hungry spirits. And, more rarely, they gathered to serve the Illumined Chair's will, a fierce red army that gave even imperial generals pause. This pilgrim stood silently with her hands clasped, but the sword-hilt at her shoulder and ivory-hilted jabiya in her belt spoke eloquently enough.

For one Khajiri to attend the Asalar was nothing unusual, except that Ahmar had visited the palace many times with far less deadly accompaniment.

"I came to speak to the empress," Ahmar said, "but found her otherwise engaged. So now I wait."

"Is there anything I can do to help, Your Radiance?"

"I'm afraid not, unless you wish to add your voice to our cause."

For over a year, the church had petitioned the empress for a grant of land. Such gifts weren't uncommon—the church owned farmland and forests and salt mines, the profits of which allowed it to thrive. This time, however, the Illumined Chair wanted part of the southern border, in the jungles of Iseth. Rich land, and well positioned to bring in new followers, which in turn meant fresh funds.

It would also mean more imperial troops needed to protect the new temples, and fresh unpleasantness with the native tribes. Samar had promised a halt to expansion when she took the throne, less money spent on war and fewer soldiers dying far from home. After three generations of emperors eager to expand their realm it was a welcome change, especially to poor families whose children swelled the army's ranks.

Asheris had no desire to see the Unconquered Sun drive any more spirits from their homes. If the church's power grew, the Fata would wither as dry and lifeless as the Sea of Glass.

"Mine is not a voice Her Majesty would give weight to in such matters," he said. The taste of smoke and spices coated his tongue, and his pulse beat hard in his temples.

"False modesty doesn't become you," Ahmar said with a narrow smile. "All know you're the empress's closest advisor."

Pet mage was what he was more often called. He walked a careful wire in the Court of Lions, making friends and alliances so as not to draw dangerous rumors, but not letting anyone close enough to threaten his secrets. Some knew the sort of work he had performed for the last emperor in Sivahra, but many younger members of the court assumed Samar kept him close for the same reasons she did Siddir: pretty eyes and flattery. Asheris tried not to disabuse them of the notion.

It's only the truth, is it not? A kept pet. Just because Samar doesn't make you wear a collar doesn't mean your wings aren't clipped.

He shook his head against the bitter voice. Ahmar cocked an eyebrow. "Excuse me," he said. "The sun—" He was a desert creature, more than any mortal could be, but today the heat seemed unusually fierce.

"Yes. It is scorching, isn't it? Perhaps we should find some shade." She rose, shaking her robes smooth, and started down the garden path. Asheris fell in beside her, while the silent Khajiri walked several paces behind.

"Have the temple apiaries recovered from the storm?" he asked, gathering his sunstruck wits.

Ahmar's expression darkened. "Not yet. It was a terrible thing. We lost so many hives. But we have new queens—we'll rebuild."

Innocent enough, but the words disquieted him. The

high priestess was old and frail, and as close to holiness as Asheris had ever seen a mortal come. She was shrewd as well, but he'd never known her to dabble in secular matters. Not all priests were so unworldly in their designs. When Mehridad died, Ahmar would be among the candidates for the Illumined Chair. Her election would not make for a placid relationship between church and state.

"I'm told you've taken an interest in this ghost wind," Ahmar said, her eyes narrowing.

"I saw the worst of the storm. It was...memorable. I want to learn its cause."

"Yes. I imagine so." She slowed as they neared the gated arch that led back to the palace proper. "I hear you've sent for a specialist in such matters."

Asheris's eyebrows climbed and he slid his hands into opposite sleeves to hide his tension. It was no surprise to learn the church had agents in the palace, but he and Siddir had been very circumspect in their plans. "Your hearing is keen, Your Radiance. Yes. An old colleague of mine from Selafai. She has experience in these things."

"A necromancer." Her dusky lips pursed in distaste.

"Who else would one call, for a ghost? Or a ghost wind."

"The church also has its experts." She tilted her head toward her Khajiri shadow.

Knowing how to destroy something wasn't the same as understanding it. He kept his sharp reply to himself, but she read it in his face.

"I have only respect for the learning of the university mages, Lord al Seth, and for your judgment. But still I'll risk a word of advice." Her dark eyes pinned him, calm and cool. "The Fata is treacherous, as is necromancy and any traffic with spirits. Carelessness therewith is how abominations are made. Be judicious with your involvement."

She knows, he thought, and his blood chilled. How could she, though? And if she did, why not act? The church would never countenance a demon in the city, let alone one standing near the throne.

If she knew what he was, that knowledge was a knife at his throat, and at Samar's.

"I should return to the temple," Ahmar said, pausing at the gate. "As you've reminded me, the apiaries need my attention more than matters of land. My discussion with Her Highness can wait a few more days. A pleasure as always, Lord al Seth." She offered her hand and he bowed over it once more; his lips were numb as he pressed them to her ring. "I'm sure we'll speak again soon."

"I'm certain, Your Radiance," he murmured.

He resisted the urge to scrub sweat and ash off his hands. The Asalar and her guard vanished into the shadow of the palace, leaving him alone in the heat and haze of clinging incense.

CHAPTER 8

Afternoon brought Asheris no peace. The sun's heat lingered in his flesh, and neither shade nor chilled wine nor flavored ices could soothe it. His limbs felt clumsy and wrong; the thought of food revolted him, as did the sensation of blood pumping through flesh. He hadn't felt like this since Jirair and the emperor's mages first laid the binding on him. The sight of himself in the mirror—wingless, soft, dull as spent cinders—made him want to scream. Only the knowledge that he would hear a human cry and not a raptor's shriek kept him silent.

He should speak to Samar. The Asalar's threat couldn't go unanswered. He had sworn the empress an oath when he accepted her offer of employment. Not the sort that could break a mage's power if forsworn, but honor meant something to men and jinn alike, and he had no desire to surrender his for cowardice.

But he couldn't face another conversation with mortals. Another hour spent pretending to be tame.

Pretending? mocked the bitter voice inside him.

When the midnight bells faded and the fever in his

brain hadn't cooled, Asheris wrapped himself in a threadbare burnous and spells of invisibility and left the palace through a servant's gate. A visit to a night bazaar fetched him what he needed; a satchel swung heavy at his hip when he left.

He might be mad, but not yet foolish: He took a circuitous route through the city, twisting and doubling back till he was satisfied he wasn't followed. Only then did he turn west, toward the outskirts of Ta'ashlan.

He would never have permitted himself an errand like this before the ghost wind struck. Should word of it reach the court, not even his position as the empress's pet would protect him from the scandal. Although if Ahmar truly knew his secret…

What could they do against the Asalar, the second most powerful figurehead of the church? Assassins could find their way inside temples as easily as palaces, but a bloody schism between the Lion Throne and the Illumined Chair was the last thing Samar needed her reign remembered by.

Why did he care? The scheming of men had made him a demon, cast out of the glass towers of Mazikeen and anathema to the people he now lived among. The last emperor's greed had enslaved him—why serve his replacement? Because she offered him scraps and a place to sleep?

Such kindness turned wolves to dogs.

He passed under the arch of the aqueduct gate, noting the drowsing guard with grim amusement. The smell of wet seeped through the stone. This was the final ring of walls. Beyond, houses and farms and shops swept out from the city, tattered as the hem of a beggar's robe. Especially tattered here to the west—no one wanted a view of Qarafis. The dead city.

In the shadow of the outer wall he halted, stretching out his senses to be sure no one had crept up during his moment of distraction. He felt the dull spark of the sleeping guard, and hundreds of others clustered in nearby buildings—some brighter with health or magic, some flickering like fireflies as death drew near. He had grown used to the stench of the city, but now it rolled over him with the strength of a khamsin: warm flesh, washed and unwashed; the piss and excrement of men and beasts; spices and cooking grease; seared meat and plants; the pungency of hay and horse-flesh from a nearby stable.

Asheris shook his head against a sneeze and turned away. The breeze from the west smelled of old stone and old death, the distant sweetness of the River Ash. Clean and soothing after the miasma of the living city.

The necropolis began far from the last houses, a walled cemetery half a river-measure in length. Beyond the walls of Qarafis, scrubby hills rolled toward the Ash, and beyond that lay the burning expanse of Al-Reshara. And farther still, the shining towers of Mazikeen.

The city of glass was barred to him. The city of the dead was not.

Qarafis housed more than old bones and jackals. Mortals lived in the northern tip of the sprawl of tombs. Morticians—funeral workers and those mages for whom the cold call of necromancy was too strong to ignore. They dwelled in repurposed tombs, raised livestock and crops between mausoleums; only here, with only each other and the dead for company, could they put aside the veils and wrappings that they wore among the living.

Would Isyllt retire here when the empress had no further use for her? Perhaps he would join her, when his unchanging youth could no longer be disguised.

The gates of Qarafis stood open even in the dead of night. Death, after all, could not be bound or barred. The twisted branches of a salt cedar tangled in one half of the tall iron gate.

Tombs clustered close inside, curving domes and beehives beside octagonal mausoleums and small square crypts, punctuated by the sharp spikes of obelisks. One broad avenue led into the center of the necropolis—the other paths were narrow and winding, treacherous with broken stones and tangled weeds. The moon was setting and a veil of dust dimmed the stars. Even to inhuman eyes, the cemetery was a collection of shadows and jumbled black shapes. A cat cried nearby, and the shrill warble of a jackal rose in the distance.

Asheris had often wondered why a people who feared the touch of death so much kept graveyards at all, instead of merely burning their dead. Of course, he also wondered why they bothered to fear death, when all mortals were born to it.

After several stubbed toes and unspoken curses, he reached the living quarter. The last milky moonlight bled away and the crypt-houses were dark and silent. Mortals didn't travel after moonset if they could help it, without even the reflected light of the sun to keep hungry spirits away. If any Fata'im lingered in Qarafis, this was their hour.

In the sea of darkness, one lamp burned.

The lit house stood away from the others, surrounded by the widest yard. Lamplight fell from one small window, as did the smell of blood. Not human blood, as many rumors suggested, but his nape prickled all the same.

Asheris-the-man had heard stories about Raisa the butcher well before he gained a second soul, but discounted them as petty superstition. Afterward, Asheris-the-demon had wondered about the stories, but was too insecure in his mortal guise to follow up on them. The last thing he needed was to be caught speaking with a woman said to be inhuman.

The door of the narrow house stood open to the night, propped with a polished stone. Someone hummed inside. The humming stopped when Asheris rapped on the door frame, and a woman's voice invited him in.

A curtain divided the long room. The front was clean and homey, if cramped. Rugs and cushions softened the floor, and a narrow couch lay against one wall. Dry herbs and polished chimes hung from the ceiling; the cracked plaster had been painted recently, a rich blue. Niches in the walls once meant for coffins were now stuffed with books and lamps and jars of beans and honey.

The curtain parted and a woman stepped through, bringing the smell of blood with her. A veil covered her face, though her sleeves were rolled up and her hands streaked with red. Gore smeared her apron, but her white robes beneath it were immaculate. Her skin was a pale brown, like tea with too much milk, her long eyes an indeterminate shade of sandy taupe, framed by thick sooty lashes.

"Well." Her eyes narrowed as she inspected him; creases spread at their corners, but her arms were sinewy and firm. He couldn't guess her age. "When the jackals told me a stranger was coming, I wasn't sure what to expect. You're not here to rob me, are you?" Her voice was low and smoky and veined with amusement.

"I'm not, mistress." He bowed low, and his satchel slid forward off his hip. "In fact, I brought gifts, to lessen my imposition at such an hour."

"Mistress? Gifts? Perhaps you have the wrong crypt. You do realize I'm an untouchable and a carnifex, not a perfumed courtier?"

"If you're Raisa, then I have the right address. No one's station is an excuse for rudeness. Though you must forgive me if I don't kiss your hands."

She looked down at her bloody hands and laughed; her nails were long and very thick. Asheris fought down an anticipatory shiver—if the stories were true, her human guise was one of the best he'd ever seen.

Soft parcels dented under his fingers as he knelt to unpack his bag. The bitter richness of organ meat perfumed the air. Sweetbreads—lamb's heart and calf's cheek and beef tongue. A carven box held incense, sandalwood and labdanum and sticky dragon's blood. Blood and smoke, traditional gifts to the Fata'im.

"Lovely," Raisa said, "but don't you know that human meat is sweeter?" Her eyes glinted.

"So I've heard, but I'm afraid this was the best I could manage. They count the humans, you see, in case one goes missing."

Raisa's white-veiled head tilted with her laugh. The Fata rippled with the sound, a quicksilver flicker. Asheris's heart climbed in his chest.

"Sit," she bade him when her shoulders stilled. "I'll put these on ice."

She returned clean-handed and without the apron, carrying a bottle of wine and two goblets on a tray. Nothing rattled as she sank into a cross-legged seat. "You've brought me fine gifts, but not yet given your name. Would you think me greedy for asking it?"

"No, mistress. But will you permit me to close the door? My business tonight is not for stray ears."

Golden-grey eyes regarded him for a moment. "As you wish. We in Qarafis understand discretion."

The room warmed quickly with the door shut. Raisa turned down the lamp flame and lit a candle instead. From that in turn she lit a cone of incense and dropped it in a brazier. Smoke rose in lazy coils, musky resin mingling with the scent of blood and wine.

The smell reminded him of Ahmar's cold smile. Of Jirair's smile so many years ago. His throat closed beneath the ghost of a collar as he knelt before Raisa.

"My name is Asheris al Seth," he said, marking the quirk of her eyebrow. He was in this too far to back out now. "And I make one final gift to you, and pray you keep it."

Bowing his head, Asheris uncased his wings. Their light rose to fill the narrow house, pinions brushing plaster walls. He waited for a scream, a curse, anything to prove him wrong, to prove him doomed.

Instead Raisa let out a long breath. "Oh, *serafi*," she whispered. "What have you done?"

Serafi. Burning one. Most jinn would say he was no longer worthy of such an epithet, but his heart-of-fire flickered all the same.

"It was not of my choosing." He blinked prickling human eyes. "Now I merely make the best of it."

"We tell stories of you in Carathis," she breathed.

"The lost jinni. I thought you were only a parable against mortal treachery." Her veil rippled with an in-drawn breath and she rocked back on her heels. "Or are you a lure for it?"

Asheris spread his hands. "No trap, I swear it. On the Tree of Sirité I swear." The jinn oath came clumsy to his tongue, but Raisa relaxed to hear it. "I only want answers, and the pleasure of your company." He tried to reclaim his easy tone; she was the first spirit he'd seen since he returned from Symir, the first to speak to him in far longer. He would have lain his head in her lap and wept, if either of their dignities could have borne it.

"Then sit and drink. But put those away," she said, gesturing to his wings, "before you set the rugs on fire."

"Yes, mistress." Preternatural feathers furled and vanished once more into flesh, but he felt them still, like the phantom of severed limbs.

She snorted. "Call me Raisa."

She poured wine, the line of her wrist as elegant as any courtier's. Though jinn often made jokes about the grace and breeding of ghuls, Asheris remembered a delegation from the Bone Queen sent to Mazikeen. He had danced with a ghul maiden at the ball in their honor, and she had been as graceful as any jinni on her clawed toes.

The wine was a good one, a rich Chassut red. Raisa frowned at her cup before she drank, and finally reached for the pin that held her veil in place. "Since you've been so forthcoming with me, *serafi*, I'll return the favor." She drew the cloth aside, revealing the face of a beautiful woman of middle years, black-lipped like a dog. Her smile bared delicate fangs. Unlike his perfect human prison, a spirit's guise would always have a flaw. "It's such a relief not to drink under that accursed thing. Red wine stains worse than blood."

"Asheris, please." He paused. "How have you lived here so long? And why?"

"The fear and isolation help. My neighbors may suspect something, but they're inclined to overlook any peculiarities. They certainly won't invite the Unconquered Sun in to look for heretics. As to why—" She smiled over the rim of her goblet. "Would you like a sad, romantic story? Perhaps I loved the Bone Queen's daughter, above my station. For my hubris I was exiled, to make my way on the surface alone. Or maybe I'm a spy."

Asheris returned the smile, but the idea of ghul scouts advancing on Ta'ashlan sent a chill snaking down his back. He didn't press the question.

They drank in silence for a time, until Raisa set down her cup. "You said you wanted answers. What are you hunting, besides the truth of me?"

"The ghost wind. And the mages called the quiet men."

Black lips pursed. "Dangerous prey. Both of them."

"What do you know of either?"

"Rumor and speculation. Legends and ancient history. And perhaps a bit of truth. My people are curious, after all, and less…insular than yours." She shrugged apologetically, but it was true.

"A bit of truth is more than I have. Will you tell me?"

She touched her tongue to her upper lip in a pensive gesture. "Why not?" she said at last. "We have hours yet till dawn." She refilled both their cups and sat back on the cushions.

"Centuries ago, long before the birth of Queen Assar, Al-Reshara was called the kingdom of Aaliban…"

* * *

Raisa filled the night with stories, till Asheris thought his head would split from their weight. Some were familiar tales, told to fledgling jinn in their rookeries, but with a foreign slant. Others were entirely strange. Some might indeed have been true, and those terrified him more than any retold haunting or cataclysm. The wine ran out long before her words.

When the night faded and dawn was a growing pressure in the east, she finally fell silent. "That's not all, but perhaps enough for one night."

"Thank you." His voice was rough, as though he'd been the one talking. His brain burned, the stifling fog of humanity stripped away.

"Thank you, for the gifts and the company. Perhaps I'm lonelier out here than I've realized." She smiled, then lifted her veil again. "But I don't think we should make a habit of it. My position is perilous enough—yours is wirewalking."

"You're right, but I wish it were otherwise."

"There are safer places for such as us. Nahasheen would welcome you."

Asheris blinked. "The Tower of Whispers? I thought it was a myth."

"Silly jinni. What do you they teach you in Mazikeen? No, Nahasheen is very real, and the teachings of Eblis are followed there."

Nearly all his knowledge of the Eblite heresy had come from his human life. Eblis was called a man or a spirit or a demon depending on the book, but most accounts agreed that he had preached the commonality of flesh and Fata, peace between the worlds. The church had driven his followers out of Assar, but legend held they traveled west across the burning sands, to build a fortress in the mountains on the Ninayan border. A perilous path to follow chasing a rumor.

Raisa led him to the door. The morning breeze was a shock after the warmth of the blue room. "I'm no haruspex, to read your future in blood, but I know a dark road when I see one. Walk it carefully." She laid a hand on his cheek like a benediction. "I'll ask the jackals to look after you."

He turned his head to kiss the hollow of her palm. Her smile reached her eyes, but they were sad as well. She closed the door, leaving him alone in the ashen gloom of the necropolis.

CHAPTER 9

Isyllt had thought all her tears behind her, but she cried again the first night at sea. Perhaps it was the irrevocable sense of loss she felt as the shores of Erebos faded into the distance, as though she would never see any of the places she'd called home again. Perhaps it was the sea rocking her like long-faded memories of her mother's arms. Perhaps salt called to salt.

She woke the next morning and scrubbed the brine from her cheeks. She was no sibyl to hear her future in the sighing of the waves. There was no point in looking back.

Moth's bags sat on the other side of the closet-size cabin they shared, but the girl's bunk looked untouched. Isyllt was no stranger to sleepless nights, but they became less and less appealing with each passing year.

The sun was high and fierce and the wind carved the water into glittering whitecaps. The deck tilted rhythmically, tarred boards warm under her bare feet. The roar of the sea rose around her, punctuated by creaking ropes and the shouts of sailors. Salt and sun weathered everyone alike, but from their voices she thought the crew were mostly Assari. The last time she'd sailed had been to and from Symir, and most of those voyages were a blur—on the journey south she'd been distracted with grief over her break with Kiril; on the trip home she'd been sick with fever and her freshly crippled hand. This voyage might be a happier one, but she wasn't willing to bet on that yet.

Laughter and raised voices drew her to the main deck, where she found a ring of sailors gathered before the mast. Inside, Adam and Siddir circled with knives drawn. Moth stood on the sideline, gesturing to one of the sailors—wagering, Isyllt suspected.

Adam was still too thin, ribs corrugating his sides and the knobs of his spine sharp through his skin, but his color was healthy again. Black stubble covered his scalp, not yet long enough to lock. More reassuring was the grace he'd regained. He crouched lightly on the balls of his feet, teeth bared, waiting for Siddir to attack.

Siddir smiled in return, close-lipped and cat-smug. He moved like a cat, too, languid and intent, one hand rising and falling in lazy feints. But despite his slow, controlled movements, he couldn't disguise his stiff left leg.

He wasn't trying to, Isyllt realized a moment later—he was using it to lure Adam close. A feinting stumble drew the mercenary in, only for Siddir to catch his wrist left-handed. A sailor's shoulder blocked Isyllt's view; when she craned her neck to see around him, Adam was on his knees, his right arm twisted behind him. A small red blossom unfolded on Siddir's shoulder.

Moth groaned, and the sailor beside her laughed.

Isyllt's face felt stiff and strange. It took a moment to

realize she was grinning. She slipped back to her cabin before Adam or Siddir noticed her, to fetch a knife. Not her bone-hilted kukri—she wouldn't risk losing that over the side—but a long curved blade of plainer make. She relied on magic in a fight far too often.

She returned to find Siddir on his back, Adam's knee on his chest and knife at his throat. "You cheated," Siddir said with a laugh.

"I didn't think spies knew the meaning of the word." Adam rocked back and pulled the other man up. Sweat sheened his face and his breath came sharply, but there was a light in his eyes Isyllt hadn't seen since she walked into the Çirağan.

Siddir grinned. "It's only cheating when the other side does it. Two falls out of three."

"Wait." They both turned as Isyllt spoke. The crowd fell back to let her through. "Let me have a dance."

The second day of their voyage, Isyllt remembered her diamond's new occupant. Siddir stopped her when she would have brought the ghost out and questioned him, however.

"Transporting foreign sorcerers is one thing, especially if you keep that ring out of sight, but the crew will never countenance necromancy on the ship. Summon a ghost here and we'll find ourselves swimming home."

Adam spent the days resting and practicing by turn, with Isyllt, Bashari, and Moth, and occasionally with the sailors. He lost as many rounds as he won, but his muscles firmed again and his hands peeled and toughened as salt and sun baked the lingering illness from his bones.

He'd joked with Xinai, years ago, about becoming pirates. Before she'd chosen revolution and the ghosts of her past over their partnership. The roll of the sea had called to him then, sun and wind and brilliant endless blue. A freedom he'd never felt on land. Now the ship was just another cage to pace.

As he measured the length of the weather deck one morning he felt eyes on him, and turned to find Moth perched on a coil of rope in the shadow of the forecastle. Still awake, he thought, not up early. She seemed completely nocturnal.

He stopped his circuit, shade sliding cool across his face. Moth blinked as he crouched beside her.

"Your eyes— I thought it was a mage trick at first, but it's not."

"No trick. I'm no mage." He stretched his legs in front of him and waited for the inevitable question.

"How, then?" At least she didn't ask *What are you?* Many weren't so circumspect.

When he was Moth's age, he'd lied as often as not, just to see the asker flinch. *I drink demon's blood. My father was a wolf.* The truth had grown rote with time.

"My mother was Tier Danaan. Do you know what that means?"

Moth cocked her head. "I've heard stories. I didn't think they were real."

Adam chuckled humorlessly. "The stories likely aren't. They're not blue, or giants, or shapeshifters, or any sort of demon that I know." Thought having met a few, he understood why Valls and Celanorans thought they were.

"So what are they?"

"I don't know. Witches, maybe. They live in the high

forests in the Aillerons and rarely venture south. They live with beasts—that much is true—and speak to them. The way mages speak to spirits or the dead, perhaps. I've never understood it."

Moth watched him expectantly and he sighed. "Only my mother was Tier. I've always guessed my father was eastern, but I don't know. However I came about, I didn't pass muster when I was born. She left me with a Tzadani caravan when I was only a month or so old. They named me and raised me."

"And?" Moth prompted when he fell silent.

"Isn't that enough? Bandits attacked the caravan when I was twelve. Slaughtered nearly everyone. Some of the children—including me—they kept to sell. I escaped." His voice was flat; the memories had lost the worst of their sting after twenty-six years. Except when nightmares found them. "I ended up in Selafai and eventually became a mercenary."

"Did you ever find your mother again?"

"No." He closed his eyes against rising images: white tattooed faces; shining yellow eyes; the smell of pine and snow and hot animal musk. Those memories could stay buried. "Blood only matters in the spilling. I made my own family after that." And lost them again, one by one.

"Oh." Moth hunched forward, elbows on her knees. Her teeth dented her lower lip. "I wish my mother would have given me to the Tzadanim," she said at last. "That might have been easier."

She picked at the coiled rope, releasing the scent of hemp and brine. "I'm androgyne. Not exactly a boy or a girl." She eyed him sideways, looking for a reaction.

Adam nodded. "I guessed as much. You don't smell like a girl, exactly."

She looked away, olive cheeks flushing scarlet. "In Erisín I would have joined the hijra when I turned sixteen." Another sideways glance. "Do you know what *that* means?"

"Only stories."

She snorted. "Whatever else is or isn't true, it means I'd become a prostitute." She shrugged, not quite succeeding at nonchalance. "I grew up in the Garden. I've seen flowers there get rich and retire. And I've seen them dead in an alley with their throats slit." Her jaw tightened. "It's not a worse life than any other, maybe, but I didn't want it chosen for me."

"So you found Isyllt." Children with no families found their own; children with no opportunities made them. Sometimes those opportunities turned them into killers and spies, but there was always a worse fate.

Moth nodded, but her mouth flattened. "But now—" Her voice dropped. "I don't think she wants me here. I'm a burden."

Adam frowned. "It isn't you. Her burdens are all in her head. She doesn't know how to share them and it makes her prickly and skittish." How many people had he driven away or fled from because of his own ghosts? "At least you're not old and decrepit like me."

"You're not old!" Moth said, too quickly.

"Your eyes go wide when you lie. You should watch that."

She blushed again.

"Don't worry. Spend enough time with spies and you'll learn."

* * *

The restless boredom broke on the twelfth day with the sight of birds. The thirteenth brought the distant smudge of the Assari coast. Adam spent much of that afternoon on the forecastle, rolling a borrowed spyglass between his palms and trying to determine what particular smudge he was looking at. He'd seen plenty of maps of Khemia, but had never set foot on the southern continent.

He smelled Isyllt and heard the familiar rhythm of her steps before he felt her warmth beside him. "What can you see?" she asked, leaning against the rail to his right.

"I'm not sure. I think that blur"—he pointed—"is Sherazad." The westernmost of Assar's large ports.

Isyllt grinned, an unguarded happiness he hadn't seen during their stay in Kehribar. Her nose was sun-reddened and pale freckles dusted her cheeks and shoulders. "I hope so. I've always wanted to see the library there."

They stood in silence, sailors' voices faint beneath the rush of waves. The pale glitter of Isyllt's eyes warned him before she moved. She reached up—slow and careful, letting him see the motion—and stroked the side of his head. The rasp of stubble shivered to the roots of his teeth.

"It is a pity."

He caught her left hand, turning it palm-up to study the scars. She tensed, but permitted the touch. An assassin's blade had pierced her palm three years ago, severing tendon and cracking bone. He'd helped her bind the wound. "So is this. My hair will grow back."

She glanced away. The sun caught the edge of her irises as her eyes narrowed, paling them like light through old ice; the tips of her lashes gleamed auburn. Too gaunt and cold to be beautiful, but she had the sharp elegance of a blade. Like any weapon, he hated to see her edges blunted.

She came to him that night, salt and wine clinging to her skin. Past midnight, but Adam lay awake on his cot, restless with the rhythm of the sea. Memories had chewed the corners of his mind since they left Kehribar, slipping away like quicksilver when he tried to pin them down. The familiar knock ended another round of chasing his tail.

Isyllt came inside when he called but lingered in the doorway, steadying herself against the ship's sway. Through the warped glass of the porthole the moon silvered the waves, just enough light to show the pallor of her face in the gloom. Desire sharpened her scent, sharpened his pulse in turn.

It had nearly happened once before, as another ship had carried them away from the ruins of Symir. The same silence in the dark, the same awareness that might have led to more. But she'd been sick and injured, and Xinai had been a fresh wound, and nothing had come of it.

"Do you want me to go?" she said at last, her voice rough.

It was grief that brought her here, grief and loneliness. She didn't need him to tell her that. The darkness left him longing for things he couldn't name.

"No."

Her hands were cold, her lips flecked with brine. Her weight against him was warm, though, and it had been longer than a year since a woman kissed him. Her tongue moved against his, bitter with wine. Tentative at first, then demanding; her teeth caught his lip and he tasted the bright heat of blood. His hands knotted in her hair, pulling her closer. She made a soft noise against his mouth and he felt it in the pit of his stomach. His hands moved under her shirt, tracing the ridges of her shoulder blades, the smooth slope of her back and the furrows of her ribs. Her hands were callused, but the rest of her skin was silken over bone and too-lean flesh.

Her nails left welts down his back and his teeth carved crescents in her shoulders. Both of them bruised knees and elbows against the wall. Her hipbones were as sharp as he'd imagined.

Afterward, they lay tangled together, not speaking. His breath, not fully recovered from the fever and cough, rasped loud in the tiny cabin. Isyllt's hair fell free of its knot, and oily, salt-stiff strands wrapped his fingers and tickled his cheek. She traced idle patterns across his stomach and chest, following the lines of old scars. Her touch tingled—her magic reading all the brushes with death written on his skin.

"What is it?" she asked eventually. Her fingers brushed his jaw and he realized his teeth were clenched.

"Xinai." It was, he thought a heartbeat later, a stupid thing to say. Isyllt snorted. "Not just her." He rolled onto his side, tucking his left arm under him awkwardly. If either of them had been a healthy weight, they wouldn't fit together on the bed. "Something about the assassin in Kehribar was familiar, but I can't place it."

"Do you know many women who kill with plumbatae?"

His chuckle pressed his chest to hers. "No. I do seem to have a fondness for dangerous women, though."

Isyllt, Xinai, Sorcha: the only women in the past

twelve years who had been more than an evening's distraction, and all of them deadly. And Brenna—laughing, black-eyed Brenna, who had been worse than dangerous. Treacherous. The thought of her still made his hands ache. For years he'd thought of her only as a thief and a traitor; now he realized she had probably been a spy.

Isyllt pried open the fist he hadn't noticed making. "You could try meeting nice women. It might be more restful."

"I wouldn't know where to look." He moved closer and ran his palm over her flank. She laughed and lay back on the thin mattress. Laughter became a muffled curse as her elbow cracked against the wall again. Skinny and a spy, but she was warm and close and he trusted her enough to fall asleep in her arms. He lowered his mouth to hers.

He dreamed of black hair enfolding him like raven wings. Teasing smiles and laughing eyes. Not Isyllt—the scent was different, the texture of skin. He couldn't see her face, and every time he reached she slipped away.

He woke reaching still, tangled in the bedclothes. Dawn rose over the water, and Isyllt was gone.

CHAPTER 10

Nerium woke from unquiet dreams to the sound of screaming. She was halfway to the window, nightdress tangled sweaty around her legs, before she realized the sound didn't come from a human throat. Instead it was the shrill reverberation of her wards.

Startled panic turned to dread. She ran barefoot from the Chanterie and into the street, ignoring the knife-edged pain in her joints and lungs. Darkness blotted the stars and thickened the air; the few streetlamps guttered in the choking shadow. All around her the wind rose, flinging grit into her eyes. Sand scoured her feet as she ran toward the temple; slivers of glass tore her skin. Light blossomed in windows, dimming again as the watchers flung their shutters closed. No one emerged—Nerium couldn't blame them.

Once she could have run the length and breadth of Qais. Now her breath gave out halfway through the hypostyle, and she leaned against a column to get it back. Each gasp felt like briars ripping through her lungs and tightening around her heart. And what was the point of haste, anyway? The damage was done, the storm freed. What point in anything but returning to bed and letting it devour the world?

She pinched her arm, hard and savage. The sudden pain cleared the dulling miasma from her head. She was sworn to stop Al-Jodâ'im. Death might free her from the vow, but age and misery did not.

Besides, she thought, forcing her aching feet on, she ran quite well for a woman of one hundred and two.

As she reached the last row of columns, a grotesque shape appeared out of the haze, nearly startling her out of life she could ill afford to spare. It was only Khalil, bent double over his cane. Behind him was Salah, captain of Qais's guards; his dark face was grey with strain, but he braved the storm.

Nerium led the way up the stairs, buffeted by the scouring wind. Stepping inside the shelter of the temple should have been a relief—instead her stomach cramped at the misery welling up the stairs.

She descended into darkness absolute. Her witchlight died as soon as she summoned it and she wasted no strength on another. One hand on the wall, the other outstretched for balance, she climbed blind, one groping toe-curled step at a time. She miscounted somewhere down the spiral, and bloodied her knees missing the final stair. Sticky warmth trickled down her left shin, and she wanted to cry like a child.

The salt door was cool to the touch, the latch rough and clogged with fresh corrosion. Hinges shrieked as she tugged it open and their cry mingled with the cacophony pouring from the oubliette. She knew she should wait for

Khalil but she couldn't hear him over the wail, nor stand long before its onslaught.

Two strides into the chamber she realized her mistake: She was walking straight into the oubliette. Her legs folded like a discarded puppet and she sat down hard on the floor. Where was Khalil? Where was Shirin? She didn't dare take her attention away from Al-Jodâ'im long enough to search for them.

"Kash!"

He fought the summons—not his usual reluctance, but a real struggle. Under other circumstance she might have indulged him, but she couldn't afford the distraction now. The clouded diamond on her left hand flared. Her grandfather's diamond. She granted Kash what freedom she could, but part of him was always bound to the stone. She tightened the leash, reeling him back into his faceted cage. Leaving her alone once more to face the fury of Al-Jodâ'im.

Nerium began to sing.

Evening has fallen like the first evening

Nightjar has spoken like the first bird

Her voice cracked at first, and the howling storm warped all her notes out of true. But she kept on, and her throat relaxed and warmed, and the pain in her lungs subsided to make room for words.

Praise for the singing, praise for the gloaming

Praise for the light fading soft from the world

One of the church's sunset hymns, one of the hundreds of songs that some ancient member of Quietus had helped to write. A hundred little wards set to music and spread across the continent, to weaken the night, weaken the Fata, and strengthen the seals against the darkness.

Nerium had never involved herself in ecclesiastical matters, but some of the hymns were pretty. She had sung this one to her daughter in the cradle—it always calmed her, even through the worst colic.

And part of that child lived forever in the oubliette.

Nerium sat in the darkness, singing and weeping, for what felt like an eternity. If there was a hell of punishment, of atonement, this would be hers. The thought that even death might not bring peace terrified her.

It wasn't until someone called her name that she realized she could hear again. The howling had subsided once more into a sleepy dirge and magelight glowed against the darkness. Blinking back tears, she saw Shirin pacing the circumference of the pit, tracing numbers on the dusty stone.

"Lady Kerah." Salah knelt beside her, chafing her cold hand in his broad callused palms. "Are you all right?"

Her laugh was a harsh, ugly sound. Her legs were numb, and when she straightened them her scabbed knees cracked and bled fresh. Her left hip ached from landing on the stones. She'd lost vocal discipline—her throat felt scraped raw.

"I'm alive," she croaked. "That will have to suffice."

Salah smiled crookedly. "It will. Can you stand?"

She could, with help. Across the oubliette, Shirin met her eyes and gave a strained nod. The diamonds in the walls sparked with rainbow fire as her light bobbed above her shoulder.

Salah hesitated as he helped Nerium through the door. "Lady, I hate to burden you further after all you've done tonight—"

She closed her eyes. "What is it?"

"Lord Ramadi. He tried to help you, but he fell." His voice lowered. "I think it's his heart."

Looking up, she saw Khalil slumped on the spiral stairs, one fist pressed against his chest. His breath came loud and harsh and his face had drained a sickly grey. His cane lay discarded and useless at the bottom of the stair. Nerium threw off Salah's supporting arm and stumbled up the steps to his side.

"What happened?" She tried to keep her voice brisk, but her own heart filled her throat and choked her. His brow was cold beneath her hand.

"Forgive me," he whispered. "I tried to help." He took her hand, turning his cheek against her palm. "I never meant for you to face them alone."

"It's all right. It's over now and I'm fine. Shirin will finish the work."

"Good. I'm glad you're still strong. I have no strength left."

"Don't be silly. You just need to rest." The words were ashes in her mouth. She felt the weakness creeping through his limbs, the strain in his heart. Such injuries would never truly heal.

"It's over, Nerium."

"Not here it isn't. Not like this. Captain"—she turned to Salah—"can you carry him?"

"Of course, Lady."

"Let me rest," Khalil said, reaching for her hand.

"Yes." She pressed dry lips against his fingers and wondered if her own heart was failing as well. "You can rest. You've earned it. But not here."

She couldn't watch Salah carry him up the stairs, couldn't bear to see a man once so tall and strong cradled like a child. She had understood, in a clinical way, that to extend her own life would be to outlast things she knew. That knowledge was a bitter balm now.

When Khalil was laid in his own bed, Nerium sent Salah for willow bark and hot water. The captain didn't hesitate, but she saw the resignation in his face.

"You don't have to fuss over me, Nerium," Khalil said when Salah had come and gone again. He set the dregs of his tisane on the bedside table. It couldn't undo the damage already done to the muscle, but at least it might ease the strain, and the pain.

"Yes, I do," Nerium replied, soothing his blankets.

"Let me rest. Give me mercy."

She couldn't hide her flinch. "Would you ask that of me? I've never known you to run from a fight."

"The fight is over. We're losing the war. You've said so yourself."

"I'll find a way. I'd hoped you'd be with me when I did."

He smiled. "Still a beautiful liar. But we've both always known you'd leave me behind."

Nerium closed her eyes. She was lying, though not in the way he thought. She needed the other Silent for her plan to work, but she'd known for some time that they wouldn't be aware when it happened. Khalil and Shirin might make the sacrifice willingly, but Ahmar and Siavush never would. It didn't matter—their vows were consent enough.

"I'm sorry." She hadn't realized she meant to say it until the words fell from her lips. "I'm sorry I left you."

He waved the apology away. "You did what you had to. We've all made sacrifices for the order." His bony fingers closed around hers. "I never stopped loving you, though. Even *they* couldn't destroy that."

"I know." Qais hadn't withered her love, either. At least not at the beginning.

She'd left on assignment nearly forty years ago, the last great absence she took from the empty city. Fear had prevented her from telling Khalil, her lover for many years, that she was pregnant. Her magic extended her life and her fertility, but she still worried that she wouldn't carry the babe to term. And then she did, but despite her hopes for a successor, a mage to take her place on the Silent Council, her daughter had been born kamnur. No training had ever woken more than a spark of sensitivity. From that disappointment grew bitterness, and by the time she returned to Qais, she couldn't bear to return Khalil's love.

She still couldn't bear it, but she'd learned to push past the limits of her endurance. She bent to kiss him, tasting honey and bitter medicine and even bitterer mortality.

"Sleep," she whispered against his lips, filling the word with power. His eyes closed as she leaned back, his breath deepening. She held his hand for a long moment before folding it across his breast. The diamond winked in the dim light, a cold reminder of what she had to do.

She'd always had a talent for healing, a rarity among Quietus. It kept her from becoming a skilled entropomancer, but that sacrifice was worth it. For decades she'd studied medicine and anatomy, taking bodies apart layer by layer to understand their function.

No amount of skill would let her work miracles—Khalil was over eighty years old, and had spent much of his strength withstanding Al-Jodâ'im—but it let her find the weak place in his heart and wrap it in threads of magic fine as spider silk. Not true healing, but preservation, the sort of spells the necromancers of Selafai learned to keep corpses fresh.

She cocooned him in stasis and sleep. The greater working was still to come; she would return with amber and honey and myrrh, and make of her friend and lover a vessel strong enough to withstand the void. This would serve for now, until she recovered her strength.

A sound drew her from the fugue of magic and fatigue. Nerium turned, stiff neck crackling, to find Shirin standing in the doorway.

"How is he?" the librarian asked, her voice low.

"Resting." Nerium rose with a wince and closed the shutters. The sky beyond was bruised with incipient dawn. The bed hangings stirred with the last breeze, ghostly in the gloom, then hung still.

"It's his heart," she said softly, joining Shirin. "I did what I can, but—" She lifted her hands in a gesture of futility. "It's best if he sleeps for now."

Shirin nodded slowly and let Nerium steer her out of the room. For an instant Nerium thought she read suspicion in the other woman's eyes, but Shirin blinked and it was gone. A trick of the light. The pricking of her conscience.

"Another stone failed—a smaller one beside the one we just replaced. I redid the bindings. Not as strong with only the two of us, of course, but they'll hold." *For a while.* Shirin didn't need to speak the coda aloud—they both knew. "I'm sorry," she added after a moment. "I was too slow in answering the alarm. I tried, but…"

"I understand." Nerium laid a hand on the woman's

shoulder, and wondered if the tension she felt there was a flinch or merely lingering strain. Blaming Shirin for Khalil's collapse might have soothed her own guilty nerves, but it would be a lie. And anyway, Shirin would have the chance to redeem herself soon enough.

Dawn broke across the desert and Qais and its prisoners returned to uneasy sleep. The wind that had escaped the oubliette, however, did not die. Instead it churned eastward, gathering strength as it spun.

In the Fata, it drained color from the desert, leaving a grey trail behind. Little spirits fled its passing. In glass-walled Mazikeen the jinn felt it and shivered. Even in distant Carathis the ghuls hunkered deep in their tunnels and their queen shuddered on her bone chair. In the necropolis outside of Ta'ashlan, a veiled mortician pulled her robes tight around and whispered prayers to dead gods.

In the lands of flesh, animals also fled, but not all were fast enough. The ghost wind stripped their flesh, leaving polished bone behind. An unlucky band of nomads lost their last camel to the wind's kiss, stranding them deep in the erg. The nearest well collapsed and dried as the storm rolled past.

The wind bore toward Ta'ashlan, as its last incarnation had, but as it neared the River Ash its attention shifted north. The main storm faltered and faded, spending the last of its momentum to birth a dozen smaller whirlwinds. Fish and river birds died as they sped past, and flooded fields fouled. Waterwheels broke their axles, leaving distant crops to wither in the heat.

But even the power of destruction burned out in time.

The small storms sputtered in turn, until only one remained. That one, driven by more than wind and sand, fueled by desperation and curiosity and slow-simmering inhuman anger, gyred north along the river, toward Sherazad and the sea.

PART II

The Conquering Sun

CHAPTER 11

The *Marid* sailed into Sherazad as the sun reached its zenith in a cloudless sky. Isyllt and Moth stood on the forecastle, passing a spyglass between them as the walls and towers of the city drew closer. The heat was fierce and promised to worsen; the sun pressed a heavy hand against the back of Isyllt's head and shattered like glass knives on the waves.

"It's so flat," Moth said, frowning as she peered through the lens.

They were both used to Erisín's high walls, its cliffs and hills. Isyllt had faded memories of the mountains and towering pines of Vallorn, too. Sherazad was built around the delta of the River Ash, amid the sweep of flat beach and ochre desert. The rocky outcroppings flanking the city sprawl were much too small to hold up the vast blue dome of sky. Isyllt found herself longing for walls.

The city obliged her. The *Marid* slowed, turning toward a channel of glittering buoys, and Isyllt lowered the glass from the distant sky as stone eclipsed her view.

Waves broke and frothed around a rocky islet, and the tower seemed to spring straight from the sea.

No, Isyllt realized, looking up. Not a tower.

A statue rose from the water, high and higher still, taller than any Isyllt had ever seen. A woman, her right arm outstretched and lifting a great glass-walled lantern, her left cradling a book to her chest. Her robes were carved of creamy stone, her face and hands cast in bronze. Time and salt had smoothed the folds of her gown and pitted her hem and hood, but her arching nose and amused smile remained, if green-tinged now with age. Her eyes seemed to follow the ship as it neared the harbor; Isyllt startled as they flashed in the sun. Lifting the spyglass, she saw that the statue's dark metal irises were set with mirrors.

Moth's eyes widened; Isyllt whistled admiringly.

"The Prophet Aaliyah," Siddir said, the click of his cane announcing him. "Lightbringer, and first saint of the Unconquered Sun. It's said her lantern shines on every corner of the empire. While I can't vouch for the hyperbole of that, ships can see the light for miles at sea." Despite the wry humor in the words, his gaze was unusually serious as he stared up at the Prophet's face. Then he grinned. "Also, she distracts ships from more immediate concerns."

Following his pointing hand, Isyllt saw the towers along the seawall behind Aaliyah, battlements and narrow windows studded with cannon. Drops of red scattered against grey stone—soldiers manning the defenses.

Isyllt chuckled appreciatively, but her stomach was heavy with anticipation as they sailed under the saint's outstretched arm. The city resolved from a dusty blur into buildings: pale brick and plaster, painted domes and gilded spires; square shops and houses stacked like children's blocks; the curve of a commemorative arch; green trees vivid against dusty stone. The wind gusted hot and salty, drawing a copper veil of sand along the coast. The sound of noontide bells drifted across the water.

Siddir grinned and gestured grandly toward Sherazad and the land beyond. "Welcome to Assar."

"Where's the river?" Moth asked as they followed the porters off the skiff.

Isyllt had been wondering the same thing. The skiff had taken them from the *Marid* into a canal, one of a dozen neatly bricked waterways pouring into the harbor—nothing like what she'd expected of the Ash. The River Ash and its twin the Nilufer were described as the widest and longest in the known world.

"The channels here are half of it," Siddir said, offering the girl a hand up the stone steps. "The rest splits south of the city and flows west into the Lantern Marsh." He gestured vaguely west. "The distributary was drained and channeled when Sherazad outgrew her first walls."

He answered lightly enough, but his eyes were restive and wary again. His happiness at landfall had been short-lived.

"Keep your gloves on," he told Isyllt as they waited for their carriage. "You'll have to take the white veil eventually, but for now I don't want the attention."

Isyllt flexed her hand in her pocket, the band of her ring pressing flesh. Erisín was built on bones, level after level of catacombs mazing beneath the streets, many of them ancient before the founding of Selafai. Without the necromancers of the Arcanost and the priests of Erishal to keep ghosts quiet, the dead would rule the living. In Assar death was proscribed; tombs stood outside the city walls, visited only on holy days, and anyone who touched a corpse performed ritual cleansing. Those who dealt with death for a living became untouchable. *Hadath*. Sivahra, though an imperial territory, had been distant enough to avoid such inconveniences—here she wouldn't escape them.

She glanced at Adam and met his narrowed gaze. He understood the situation—if he and Moth remained in her employ, they would become pariahs as well. A servant might make do with only a white armband and obsessive hand washing. A lover…

The arrival of their carriage saved her from that thought. She drew her scarf over her head, blaming the sudden warmth in her cheeks on the sun.

They settled in the Azure Lily, an expensive inn whose namesake flowers carpeted courtyard pools and floated in bowls in all the rooms. The motif continued to the tiles of the deep bathtub; at least the soap wasn't lotus-scented.

After a bath, they lingered over an afternoon meal. Isyllt and Moth wanted to explore the city, but Siddir kept them inside.

"Only mad dogs and foreigners go out in this heat," he said, sipping chilled wine.

That point she had to concede. Shade and the breeze off the fountains cooled the courtyard where they took their meal, but she could still feel the relentless sun. The streets had been noisy when they arrived, but now the din of voices and wheels and animals died and a dusty stupor settled over the city. Behind a screen, an oud played sleepy songs. Potted ferns and carven screens granted them the illusion of privacy from the few other patrons lounging in the heat.

Isyllt had nearly succumbed to the wine and warmth and growing urge to nap when bells shattered the stillness. Not the temple bells they'd heard as they arrived, but a wild tintinnabulation. Siddir's chair scraped back as he startled; around the courtyard, other patrons rose as well.

"What is it?" Isyllt asked, hands braced on her own chair.

"Weather bells. We would have seen a storm at sea. That means—" His throat worked as he swallowed, and his face greyed. "Not again."

A cry rose up from the street. Some guests hurried for shelter, but others—Moth and Isyllt among them—ran to see what was happening.

"Get inside," Siddir said, grabbing at her arm, but Isyllt twisted away. The bells continued and shouts carried from blocks away. People leaned out windows, and Isyllt wished for a higher vantage point.

"What is it?" Adam asked.

"Al-shebaraya," Siddir said, brushing a warding gesture over his eyes.

Isyllt had never heard the word before but she could parse the Assari roots: the ghost wind. A question rose on her lips, and died as the light dimmed.

A cloud rose over the rooftops, darkening the sky. No, not a cloud—a sand pillar. A whirling tower of dust as tall as a cathedral spire, bearing down on Sherazad. It twisted through the streets, dodging buildings with a dancer's grace, till it turned onto the broad avenue in front of the Azure Lily.

The hollow rush drowned the shouts of onlookers. Hot wind streamed past Isyllt, ripping her hair free of its braid to blind her. Her scalp prickled at the wind's touch and the hair on her arms stood on end. Her magic stirred, too—not the chill of death, but something deeper, darker. The space beneath her heart grew heavy, the hollow place that held her entropomancy. The sudden pressure forced the air from her lungs.

She heard her name as if from a great distance, felt the weight of a hand on her shoulder, but she couldn't tell who called her. The world receded, streaming away till she was alone with the roaring wind. It, too, was calling her, the sound of her name rising and falling on the hissing dust.

What would happen if she answered?

A blow to the side of her head settled the question. She staggered sideways and the siren call of the wind vanished under the ringing in her right ear. A weight bounced off her shoulder onto the ground. A fish.

Another followed, then another, falling like silver hail. Minnows and small perch and whiskered bottom-feeders, landing all around her a nauseous *splat-splat-splat*. Most were dead when they struck the ground, but some still writhed, gills gaping, rainbows sliding down their scales as they choked on air.

She might have stood there dumbfounded, staring at fish till the dust storm swallowed her, but Adam grabbed her arm and pulled her into the shelter of the courtyard.

The storm died before it reached the inn, disintegrating in a fine haze of dust and a last splatter of fish. They stood in breathless silence while the echo of the wind faded.

"I think," Siddir said at last, "I preferred it when explosions followed you."

Moth made a choked noise. Tears streaked her face. Isyllt reached for her, but the girl flinched away. She hugged her arms across her chest and wept, watching fish thrash and die in the dirt.

They went to their rooms at sunset, exhausted from travel and the enervating touch of the storm. Isyllt paused beside Adam's door as he turned the key. His green eyes were inscrutable as ever, but in his posture she read the same hesitance and curiosity that tugged at her. Her magic stirred as it always did when he was near; death loved a killer. It was a complication, though, and she had less love for those.

A scuffing footstep broke the deepening silence. Down the hall, Moth lingered at the door of the room she and Isyllt shared. She tilted her head before vanishing inside. Not quite a summons, but eloquent all the same.

Isyllt's cheeks prickled. "I should—"

Adam nodded. "Yes." He smiled wryly. "Good night."

Isyllt sighed as the door shut behind him. Complications.

"You wanted to talk to me?" she said as she latched her own door. Curtains fluttered in the breeze—a normal breeze now, cooling fast as night came on and fragrant with city smells. Dust lay in serpentine drifts beneath the casement. No one had kindled a lamp, and blue dusk filled the room.

Moth sat cross-legged on the far bed—if reed mats and cushions could properly be called a bed—walking a silver coin across her knuckles. She looked up when Isyllt spoke and arched her eyebrows. She'd washed her face, but her eyes were still red-rimmed and puffy.

"Does Siddir know?" she asked. "He might be jealous—he looks at Adam the way you do."

Isyllt flushed, though it was ridiculous to think that Moth—or anyone else on the ship—hadn't noticed. "Siddir has enough to keep him busy. And yes, I'm sure he knows. He's trained to observe." She leaned beside the doorway. "Did you only want to tease me?"

The lightness in Moth's tone vanished. "We haven't talked much lately."

Isyllt opened her mouth and shut it again. "You're right." She moved into the room, forcing her arms to her sides. Moth might not have a spy's training, but she could spot a defensive posture.

"It would be easier if I thought it was just Adam." Silver flashed as the coin continued its circuit over and under her hand. "But it's older than that. Before we reached Kehribar."

Isyllt drew back the netting and sank onto the foot of her own mat. Sand grated unpleasantly in the folds of her clothes. The bedding was softer than she'd imagined, certainly no worse than her bunk on the *Marid*, but she'd miss northern feather mattresses. Even the cushions were embroidered with blue lotuses.

"After Thesme—" The words stuck in her throat.

Moth's coin flashed as it fell. It rolled across the tiles with a silver chime, rattled and lay still. The girl tensed, leaning forward, but didn't rise. "You dealt with the man in Thesme. It won't happen again. And if it does, I'll be the one to deal with it."

Isyllt blinked. The would-be panderer she'd killed wasn't what she'd meant. What troubled her was the night her walls had broken and she'd sobbed herself to sleep while Moth stroked her hair. It had left her hollow and vulnerable, and she'd been careful to rebuild her defenses. The dead man was easier to talk about.

"I promised Mekaran I'd take care of you." Moth's old guardian had been less than happy about letting his ward leave Erisín with a necromancer. Isyllt had just killed a sorceress who'd preyed on the Garden, however—that and Moth's insistence had worn down his arguments.

Moth snorted. "I was taking care of myself before Meka took me in." She looked up, blue-grey eyes narrow. "Do you regret apprenticing me?"

Shadows deepened before Isyllt answered. "Sometimes," she admitted. "Not because you don't have potential," she said quickly, seeing the hurt in the girl's face, the walls rising to cover it. "But because I did it for the wrong reasons."

"Pity?" Moth's voice was cold enough to frost the windows.

"Yes. But not for you—for me."

That silenced whatever scathing comment the girl had been about to make. "Oh."

"I was lonely and scared." Isyllt's neck ached as she forced herself to look Moth in the face—a pale oval in the twilit gloom. "Sick with grief and terrified at the thought of leaving behind everything, everyone. But I couldn't stay in Erisín, either. With you I wouldn't be alone, but I thought—" Her jaw tightened, but she forced the words out. "I thought you wouldn't remind me of Kiril. I thought you'd be safe."

"Did it work?"

"No. Everything reminds me of him."

The thump of hooves rose from the street, followed by the glow of a kindled streetlamp. The light lined Moth's head and shoulders in amber and cast her face in shadow.

"What would have been the right reason?" the girl asked, as the lamplighter's cart rattled away.

"I don't know. Kiril—" Would she ever be able to say his name without flinching? "He wanted to use me. I always knew that. He saw a mage with no family, nowhere to go, and he knew he could turn me into a tool. And I wanted it, wanted to be something useful. Something dangerous." Not to be scared and alone anymore—she nearly laughed at how well that had turned out. "And then I fell in love with him, and everything was...complicated."

"I don't love you."

Isyllt laughed. The words stung, but it was a clean cut. "Good." Witchlight answered her silent call, and the iridescent glow drove the shadows into the corners. She tugged off her boots, shedding more sand onto the floor. Her chest still ached from the wind's touch. She was so tired. Tired of ships and rented rooms, tired of not knowing what lay ahead. Tired of missing things dead and gone, and not knowing what to say to the people who were left.

Tired.

She stripped to her underclothes and lay back on gritty cushions. The witchlight died, leaving only the dim glow from the street. Isyllt watched shadows shift across the ceiling and listened to the sounds of a foreign city until her eyes sagged and the noises dimmed. By the time she heard the soft scrape of the window opening and Moth slipping out, she was too tired to care.

She stood in an empty street, the ground littered with dying fish. The sky was orange in the aftermath of the storm, the roar of the wind still echoing in her ears. Or maybe it was only the sound of her pulse. A fish writhed at her feet, gills straining, iridescent scales dull with dust. She could end its suffering with a touch, but she didn't move. Couldn't move.

"Isyllt."

She wondered at first how the fish knew her name, but that voice—like the slow rasp of sand across stone—could never come from the poor choking perch. A shadow fell across hers, and she felt the presence behind her.

"Isyllt Iskaldur," the shadow said. "Isyllt Ilsesdottir."

She tried to turn, but the dream held her fast. Long hands closed on her shoulders; even from the corner of her eye, she could see they weren't human.

"How do you know that name?" She only gave it to a handful of people after her mother died, all in Erisín, and most of them dead.

The shadow chuckled. "I know what the void knows, and the void knows you."

"Who are you?"

The shadow pressed close, cold against her back, and a feathered cloak enfolded her. "We might become enemies, but I would rather be your ally. We have so much in common—including a problem. Quietus wants you. They'll offer you sweet promises and lies, but never believe them. They mean to use you, as they use everything."

Another gaunt grey hand snaked around her, pressing

taloned fingers against her left breast. Nothing sexual in the touch, but a terrible intimacy all the same. The shadow reached through skin and bone to grasp her heart. She shuddered and went limp, but the grip on her arms held her upright while the third hand ripped open her chest.

No crunch or crimson spray. Instead of a handful of greasy muscle, her heart slid out slick and glistening. Cold and black and hollow, as translucent as glass. As a diamond.

"They'll offer you whatever you want, but don't listen. All their gifts are poison."

The hands released her and Isyllt fell, heartless and hollow, to lie in the dirt beside a dying fish.

And woke gasping, to bells and the grey light of dawn. Her good hand pressed against her chest, nails carving crescents into her skin.

CHAPTER 12

Breakfast brought word that Asheris was on his way to meet them, having been delayed on the road by yesterday's storm. Isyllt had expected Siddir to be cheered by the news, but if anything his mood worsened.

Isyllt's mood was little better. She'd slept only fitfully after the temple songs faded, and the unease of the dream lingered, aching in her chest. Moth, returned from her wandering, had slept through the bells and slept still. Morning was nearly gone.

"You brought me to the city of stories," Isyllt said, jabbing a honey spoon toward Siddir. "Show me some of them." Academics at the Arcanost would risk much for a visit to Sherazad's famous library; thinking of the Arcanost only soured her mood more.

"It wouldn't be prudent." Siddir sat with his back to a sandstone pillar, watching the street. The sun was high and the morning's crowds had already thinned—fewer crowds than yesterday. A flock of pigeons braved the heat to scavenge crumbs from a baker's cart. "The storm has the city unsettled. And I wasn't sure yesterday"—

he raised his glass to cover the words—"but I am today. We're being watched."

Isyllt's mouth twisted. She fished a frozen mint leaf from her tea; ice crunched between her teeth and her next breath chilled her throat. A costly luxury—if Asheris had no work for her as a spy, she might earn a living making ice for inns and taverns. "Someone was following me in Kehribar. At least from Thesme, maybe all the way from Erisín. I could find out who, if you weren't so squeamish."

Siddir's brows pulled together, then relaxed into a less angry frown. "Perhaps you're right. All the same, I find it difficult to flout my upbringing. Asheris won't share my squeamishness, I'm sure."

Asheris had shown few qualms about Isyllt or her magic in Symir. Certainly none about touching her. Unexpected warmth rose in her cheeks and she covered it with a cold swallow of tea.

"Make our shadows work a little," she said, "if they're so intent on watching us. We can draw them out if we leave the inn."

Adam snorted, and Isyllt shot him a narrow glance. It *had* worked in Kehribar, if not as cleanly as she might have hoped.

"I was sent to bring you to Assar, not get you killed as soon as we arrive."

Hooves and wheels carried through the still air, cutting off Isyllt's reply. Pigeons fluttered and hopped aside as a carriage rolled to a stop in front of the gates. Siddir half rose, paused, them completed the motion, straightening his robes with careful nonchalance. Isyllt nearly laughed, but she had pushed back her chair, too, and her hands tingled on the arms.

They reached the courtyard gate as the carriage door opened and a man stepped down. Dust puffed beneath his sandals. Dark hands rose to throw back the hood of his sand-colored burnous; sunlight gleamed on the smooth mahogany curve of his scalp. Asheris al Seth looked up and smiled.

Isyllt couldn't stop her answering grin. Even when they'd been enemies, friendship had come easily to her. To both of them, she liked to think, never mind her scars. She stepped forward, wincing at the heat and glare.

"Lord al Seth."

"Lady Iskaldur." Kohl lined his amber eyes, made them as striking as a cat's; it clumped in creases when he smiled. She'd almost forgotten how magnetic that smile was.

She expected to feel the warm rush of his magic when their hands clasped; instead sparks stung her through cotton gloves, and a shock like lightning seared her nerves. His eyes flared—not with nightshine like Adam's, but a fierce fiery light that was nothing beast or human.

"I'm sorry," he said as she flinched, tucking his hands into the sleeves of his robe. His smile vanished.

"What's happened?" His control had always been better than this, even after she'd broken the sorcerous chains that had bound him to the old emperor's service.

Siddir joined them, his eyes tracking along the street. "Let's save the pleasantries for the shade."

Isyllt squinted past Asheris's shoulder. Without yesterday's veil of dust, the city glittered. Everywhere she turned sunlight flashed on glass, on brass, on polished tile and gilded spires. Leaves rustled gently above a garden wall. A glint of metal—

Siddir was faster; he tackled her into the dust with a shout as a shot shattered the air. The carriage horses screamed and stamped. Pigeons scattered in a storm of grey feathers.

A rifle, she thought as she struck the dirt. Metal flashed again and she glimpsed the sniper, a shadow vanishing in the foliage of the garden. A shutter flew open in a nearby house and someone shouted; feathers drifted slowly down.

Adam joined her and Siddir as they rolled behind the cover of the inn's outer wall. Asheris followed, cursing softly—a crimson stain spread across his shoulder, seeping through wool and feathering across pale linen below. He touched the wound and stared at his fingers, eyebrows rising in disbelief. Black swallowed amber as his eyes widened, then yellow flames rose to drown them both.

He was the only one among them who couldn't be killed by a bullet. That did nothing to temper the rage that burned like naphtha in Isyllt's veins. She lunged to her feet, drawing veils of magic around her as she ran for the wall. Rustling leaves marked the would-be assassin's retreat.

Siddir and Asheris shouted, but she ignored them. She'd had enough of shadows and threats. Heavier footsteps matched hers—Adam racing after.

Anger gave her momentum, but it helped that the garden wall was low. One hard jump and she caught the decorative crenellations. Cotton gloves snagged and tore as she hauled herself up; something stretched unpleasantly in her left shoulder.

She dropped into cool green shade on the other side, smelled loam and sap and honeysuckle. Adam landed beside her an instant later, eyes flashing from light to shadow.

"I thought we were trying *not* to get ourselves killed." His nostrils flared. "This way." He pointed to the left, where a narrow gate led to an alley beside the house.

She tripped over the rifle, abandoned in a tangle of vines at the bottom of a trellis. Isyllt wasted a heartbeat to ward and obfuscate it; they'd need it later if they had to trace the person who fired it.

Down the alley and into a curving street. Every breath seared her lungs, and her legs already ached from the sudden exertion. Her shoulder throbbed. On her own she would have lost her quarry, but Adam had the scent now and neither of them slowed.

A flicker of movement ahead of them, a brown cloak and rising dust. She half expected to see the woman in black, but this assassin was a man. The few passersby drew back, wide-eyed, as the three runners barreled down the street.

Another alley, another hard turn that nearly spilled Isyllt into an open gutter. She drew power from her diamond, dulled the pain in her muscles, and ran harder. She'd regret this tomorrow, but now she was closing on the sniper.

The man turned again, this time into a market. If he meant to find a crowd to hide in he was out of luck; only a few sleepy vendors looked up from their stalls. Children and dogs drowsed in the shade along one wall, blinking sleepily at the sudden clamor. Brass gleamed on tables; silk scarves rippled in the lazy breeze.

"Thief!" Isyllt shouted. The word ripped out of her chest. "Reward!"

At once half a dozen children were on their feet, racing after the man. Lean copper-colored dogs gave chase, barks echoing between the walls. The children, not already exhausted, easily kept pace with the sniper, pointing wherever he turned and shouting encouragement to Isyllt.

The man grabbed a barrel from a vendor's table and flung it after him. Polished marbles scattered in all directions, flashing as they struck walls and stalls and unlucky children. The urchins fell back, still laughing, but now giving their prey safe distance. The merchant shrieked invective.

Marbles bruised Isyllt's feet through the soles of her boots, bruised her hands as she fell and caught herself. A thud and a curse told her Adam hadn't been as lucky. Her desire to take the sniper alive diminished with every step.

The man ducked under an arch and Isyllt followed him into a shaded door-lined corridor. The sudden gloom blinded her; her eyes ached as she forced them to adjust. Behind her, she heard Adam warning the children away.

Caught in the chase, Isyllt didn't realize until she stepped through a broken door into a dark room that she had just cornered her quarry, and herself. She drew up three strides in, deafened by her pulse, gulping air heavy with must and spices and a harsh reek of alcohol. Her ring chilled in the presence of death.

A draft breathed across her sweaty cheek and she spun, taking the blow across her shoulder and back instead of the back of her skull. Her vision washed red and grey as she crumpled, the wind knocked from her lungs.

She rolled, caught a booted foot aimed for her face. She didn't have the leverage to bring the man down, but a shove sent him hopping backward, off-balance. He clutched at a shuttered window and wood creaked and swung open. Daylight spilled through grimy glass, showing a cluttered, shelf-lined room and the wreckage of the wooden chair that had just broken against her back. A storm of dust motes spiraled through the slanting light.

"Who are you?" Isyllt gasped, pushing to her feet. Her left arm didn't work. Numb, she prayed, not broken.

He didn't answer and she reached for her knife. The man was faster—he lunged, head down like a bull, and rammed her backward into a shelf. Wood cracked. Glass shattered, raining down around them. Cold fluid soaked Isyllt's back and sluiced over her hair. She tried to catch her breath and regretted it instantly.

Fumes burned her nose and throat, sharp and pungent and reeking of death. Harsh wine and decaying flesh. Glass shards struck her scalp, followed by something heavy and rubbery that bounced down her chest and slid into her lap. She reached for it, touched what felt like wet clay and soggy leather. *Not another fish—*

She held a dead snake. A cobra. She flung it away and found three others beside her in the spreading puddle of wine and broken glass.

Her attacker stumbled back, a hand over his mouth, brown skin greying as the stench rolled over him. Isyllt glanced up to see dozens of pickled cobras staring from glass bottles. Snake wine. Other dried skins and animal parts hung from the ceiling, and jars of herbs and more dubious things lined the far wall. They had broken into an apothecary's shop.

Death sighed around her, heady as the wine fumes. Isyllt wasn't sure she could stand; she didn't need to.

Her magic reached through glass and wine to touch the floating serpents. Dead flesh stirred, writhed, scales sliding against the curves of their prison. The man reached for her and recoiled when he saw the snakes move.

Some had sat too long—their flesh was too soft to use. A dozen were still intact, though, and those answered her summons. Isyllt covered her bleeding face with her hands, her ring glowing through her ruined glove. Magic called; death answered.

A dozen cobras moved as one, shattering their bottles. Wine and glass sprayed the room. The snakes sprang for Isyllt's attacker with fangs unfolded. He screamed high and sharp as they uncoiled, long slick bodies whipping through the air. She wasn't sure if their venom could survive death and pickling, but it didn't seem to matter. After several bites, he curled on the floor, weeping and trying to bat the undead snakes away.

A shadow fell across the door and several snakes turned. Luckily for Adam, Isyllt turned too, and recognized him before they could strike.

"Don't worry," she called. "They won't hurt you." The cobras lowered their bellies to the floor, hoods furling against their necks. Purple tongues tasted the air; their eyes were empty sockets.

"Blood and iron," he swore, muffled by the fold of his cloak held over his face. "What is that?"

"Snake wine. And our sniper friend. Help me up, please." She hated to ask, but her left arm still didn't want to move, and as her heart slowed she began to feel the blow her back had taken. Wine stung her eyes and a dozen cuts on her face and scalp. The liquid dripping down her face stained her robes rusty pink.

Adam looked at her and grimaced. For a moment she thought he would refuse. Then he limped carefully through the snakes and took her outstretched hand. She whimpered as he pulled her to her feet.

"What happened?" he asked, touching her face and frowning.

"He hit me with a chair. And a shelf. Then a jar of snakes fell on me. Then I turned the snakes on him."

"Right." He looked past her, to the unbroken jars watching them from the wall. "People drink that?"

"It's medicinal. Let's see how it worked for our friend."

The assassin curled on the floor, keening inside a ring of snakes. At Isyllt's command the serpents slithered back, leaving room to crouch beside him. Adam went first, his knife ready, but there was no fight left in the man.

"Let me see," she said gently.

He had been bitten on the cheek, the shoulder, the arm and thigh. A fang had pierced the webbing of his right hand. Already the bites were black in the center, the skin around them inflamed and peeling. The beginning of necrosis. The alchemy of necromancy and cobra venom was an ugly one.

Isyllt tugged off her right glove and laid her hand on his brow as if checking for fever. He was clammy and sweating, eyes black with pain and fear. Questing tendrils of magic spread from her touch, searching for death echoes in his wounds. In each one she found them. Any one of these bites would kill in a day or two if untreated; with so many it was a matter of hours.

"H-help me," he stammered, muscles standing out in his jaw.

"I'm sorry." She kept her voice soft. Hard to stay angry with the dying, even though her back throbbed and seized with every movement. "I can end the pain."

"Please—" His hand groped for hers. Or perhaps it was simply convulsion. She took it anyway.

"What's your name?"

"Reda." His face was sun-browned despite its current pallor, weathered. The hand in hers was callused and strong. He was younger than she'd first thought; fear made him younger still.

"Tell us what we need to know, Reda. Why were you trying to kill me?"

"Orders. Kill the foreign witch, keep al Seth off-balance. Weaken al Seth, weaken the empress."

"Whose orders?"

"H-ha-ha—" She feared he'd bite his tongue off before he could finish, but finally the seizure eased. "Hamad. General Hamad. But it was the red woman's bidding."

Isyllt glanced at Adam. He lifted one shoulder in a shrug.

She looked down at the dying man, trying to think of other questions. He wouldn't live long enough to interrogate—the veins around his wounds were black, the skin already sloughing. She wasn't that cruel.

"Mercy," she said, rocking back on her heels.

"Mercy," Reda whispered. "Thank you."

Adam reached for his knife, but Isyllt shook her head. It would be easier to let him, but some things shouldn't be delegated. She slid a slim, straight blade from her boot. Adam read her intent and pulled Reda closer, pillowing the man's head on his thigh. "Close your eyes," he murmured.

Reda sighed and did so. Isyllt nodded thanks—a second mercy, not to see the dagger's needle point hovering over his eye. She only needed one arm for this.

Reda's short, sharp cry covered the pop of skin and sphere, the crunch of the delicate bones behind the eye. Isyllt felt them all. She twisted the blade. He convulsed and fell still. Blood and milky vitreum dripped down his cheek as she eased the knife free.

She felt the cold exhalation as life and soul escaped the body. Her ring sparked, and she reached for Reda's ghost out of habit, ready to wind it into her diamond. She let her hand fall. Where did the dead go in Assar? She knew next to nothing about their otherworlds.

"You're not binding him?" Adam said. When she shook her head, he leaned close to check her pupils. "He must have hit you harder than I thought."

The gathered crowd of children and vendors fell back as Isyllt limped into the light. She shoved her right hand into her pocket before anyone could see her ring. A few spectators leaned toward the doorway, trying to see what had happened.

"*Hadath*," Isyllt said wearily, shaking her head. Unclean. She felt it, with the stench that clung to her. Merchants and urchins fell back, making warding signs against death.

"Our reward, meliket?" asked one of the braver urchin girls.

"Of course." She fumbled with her purse and passed it to Adam; he had two working hands. "And an extra silver falcon to anyone who will take a message to the Azure Lily."

* * *

When Isyllt staggered back to her room over an hour later, she found the chamber ransacked and Moth missing. Adam's nostrils flared as he followed her inside; the scent he caught peeled his lips back from his teeth and drew a snarl from his throat.

A note pinned to a cushion waited for her, a pale blot in the deepening shadows.

The girl is safe, it read, in a neat hand. *We'll be in touch.*

CHAPTER 13

Imperial agents weren't the only ones with access to fast ships. A little gentle prodding convinced the captain of the *Mother Dawn* not only to provide Melantha a berth, but to change his schedule and sail with the next tide, close on the *Marid*'s wake. Which left her with nothing to do but wait, and fret, and dream.

She had spent a year crewing on a Ninayan ship—she was Charna then, a pleasant but short-lived identity. But that was long ago and far away and that woman was dead. Skills and knowledge remained, but she had no desire to wake ghosts. She spent the voyage in her cabin, away from salt and sky and the memories they might stir.

It didn't help. She still dreamed of the sea, of cold waves foaming against white stone cliffs, of the fog that drifted off Dian Bay. Some nights Adam stood beside her; some nights it was a man she'd betrayed in Yselin; some nights it was Brenna, the woman she had been, her long hair streaming in the wind, her face young and soft and sad. She never saw her mother in her dreams, but she heard her voice on the wind, telling her not to be a fool.

If only it were that easy.

The *Mother Dawn* reached Sherazad with the morning's flood tide, a day behind the *Marid*, and was immediately mired in a mess of other merchant ships awaiting customs inspection. The *Marid* had gone straight to dock—one advantage of being an imperial agent. Melantha had advantages of her own; she stepped from the shadows of her cabin into a gloomy dockside alley.

The reek of urine and dead fish made her grimace, and did nothing to help her stomach's uneasy sway. Something was wrong besides the stench—she felt it even before her feet touched solid ground. The shadows had the same unstable, abrasive touch they'd had in Ta'ashlan.

It didn't take long to learn what happened. Markets buzzed with the news, and old men discussed it in front of teashops, shaking their head at the state of the world. Fish still clogged the gutters, swarming with flies. No one wanted to touch them to clear the streets.

A cold knot of panic drew tight in Melantha's belly: The storm had never reached so far north before.

A dim stairwell took her from the hot, dusty street into a dark room and a different stink. Rats, this time, and the tang of pickling spices. A storage space above a shop, low-ceilinged and cramped. Light from one shuttered window striped the grimy floor. Her nose closed as she breathed in dust and stale air and she sneezed. All she wanted was a bath and a nap in a bed that didn't move. Instead she sat cross-legged on a filthy crate and began sifting through shadows.

An hour later a headache pierced both her temples, but she'd finally located Iskaldur. She thanked all the saints she didn't believe in that the necromancer was still in the city—losing her quarry would make the conversation with her mother that much more unpleasant.

Her breath came loud in the small space as she stretched. Sweat soaked her shirt and hair, and the morning's bustle had quieted with the rising heat. On the street a dog barked twice and fell silent. The building beneath her was empty and still.

The shop below was shuttered and locked, and from the look of the living quarters behind it no one had been there for days. The occupants weren't much for vanity—the only mirror she found was polished bronze, dusty now. It distorted her reflection but didn't hide the grime on her cheek, or the sweat-spiked horror of her hair.

"Mother," she said, laying her fingers against the metal until she felt the spell catch. Five smudges remained when she took her hand away. She stepped back, standing like a soldier at rest as she steeled herself for the conversation to come.

"Where have you been?" Nerium asked, cold and sharp. Her mother was always sharp, but this time Melantha heard the strain beneath it. "I've tried to reach you for days."

"I just arrived in Sherazad." Sea travel played havoc with scrying and magical communications—hard to pinpoint someone who was in constant motion.

"You might have told me your plans." It sounded like maternal concern, but Melantha knew better. Her mother scolded all her agents as if they were children out after curfew.

"I had no time. Iskaldur fled Kehribar and I followed." She swallowed, her mouth dry. "Corylus is dead."

"What happened?" Her mother's face was rippled and discolored in the mirror, but Melantha imagined her pinched frown perfectly.

"He tried to kill Iskaldur, on Ahmar's orders. He lost."

"Saints." Nerium swore primly, as if she were a devout matron and not a member of an organization with its fingers tangled in the purse strings of temples and kingdoms. "Do you have Iskaldur?"

"Not yet, but she's in Sherazad as well. An imperial agent came to Kehribar to collect her before I could make contact. What happened? Did the seals fail again?"

"Yes." Through blurred metal, she watched her mother scrub a weary hand across her face. "None of us expected it so soon, not even me." Nerium straightened. "This only makes your mission that much more urgent. I need Iskaldur here."

"She's guarded by an imperial spy. I can't simply steal her out from under his nose."

"Which agent?"

"Siddir Bashari."

Nerium swore again. "That means Asheris al Seth is likely behind this. You'll have even less luck stealing her from under his watch."

"What do you want me to do?"

"I don't care. Bring her here or convince her to come to us, only do it soon. Ahmar won't take the death of her agent well. We can expect another attempt on Iskaldur's life soon."

* * *

Melantha delayed long enough to scrub her face and hair under the house's tap, and to steal a shirt and pair of trousers not smeared with dust and rat droppings. With her face veiled against the dust and bowed to the sun, she made her way across the city to the Azure Lily.

Iskaldur was still at the courtyard table where Melantha had found her earlier. Warded as she was, the necromancer appeared as a grey blur through shadows. The obscuring fog crept toward her companions, but not enough to hide their faces: Bashari and Adam.

Melantha's breath hitched. When last she'd seen Adam he'd been cocky with youth, strong and lithe and beautiful in motion. She remembered his sharp-toothed smile and companionable silences. Now he was whittled to bone and sinew, his black hair cropped to stubble. In all her spying, she had yet to see him smile.

Memories welled up, one after the other, relentless. They had no right to sting so after thirteen years.

Adam had never been her goal. It was his friend and mentor she had seduced, a former mercenary who'd risen high in the confidences of the king of Celanor. Her affection for him had quickly become unfeigned, as had her friendship with Adam. His infatuation with her had been plain, but he never acted on it. She hadn't—Brenna hadn't—wanted to hurt him. Her time in Yselin had been the most complicated wirewalking she'd ever performed, and the closest she'd ever come to losing herself in a persona, or betraying her vows.

She'd wept when Brenna died, as she never had for any of her other selves.

She clenched her fists, mastering the urge to punch the nearest wall. *Get hold of yourself. Worry about the job.*

Adam hadn't stopped her from stealing from the vaults of the Eyrie—he wouldn't stop her now.

A long step through darkness deposited her in Bashari's suite, where the shadows were thickest. The room smelled of lilies and recent polishing, and the lingering amber and sandalwood of his perfume. She searched the room quickly out of habit, but Bashari was too long in the business to carry anything incriminating. She was tempted to rearrange his luggage just to keep him on guard, but this wasn't the time for games.

She checked Adam's room next, determined not to let sharp-edged memories keep her from her work. The bed was neat, most of the furnishings untouched. He had hardly any luggage.

You're stalling.

Shaking her head, she slipped sideways into Isyllt's chambers. And froze, half emerged from the wall. She wasn't alone.

Her breath caught, eased an instant later as she heard quiet snores. Iskaldur's apprentice lay curled amid pillows on the reed bed, nearly invisible through the gloom and bed hangings. Her eyelids twitched with dreams.

Pulse still sharp, Melantha eased into the room, steps whisper-soft on the tiles. She needed something to keep her on her toes, as muddled as she'd been lately.

She was staring at the warded pile of Iskaldur's luggage, wondering if she'd find anything of use in it, when a sharp crack splintered the stillness. Her throat closed around her pulse. A gunshot outside. She spun—

And came face-to-face with Moth, blinking in confusion and alarm as she struggled free of her blankets. Confusion gave way to shock as she saw Melantha.

"What—" Surprise only slowed Moth for an instant. She uncoiled, ripping the canopy from the bed as she leapt. Her teeth flashed as she lunged; her knife flashed brighter.

Melantha dodged and the blade gouged the plaster behind her instead of her flesh. She grabbed Moth's wrist, but instead of pulling back the girl lunged, sending both of them stumbling into the side table against the far wall. A bowl of lilies rattled, slopping water.

Moth struck again. Melantha twisted her wrist, bringing the girl to her knees with a hiss. The blade thumped against a carpet.

"No need for that," she said softly. "What if I'd been a maid?"

The girl stiffened at the sound of her voice. "You!" Moth elbowed her hard in the thigh. Meant for her knee, but it still hurt. Her grip loosened, and the girl pulled free, not bothering to turn as she slammed her weight backward into Melantha. Melantha grunted, breathless. She slid sideways into the table again; this time the bowl fell and shattered. The smell of water and dead flowers washed the room.

She fought hard and ugly, but Melantha had reach and training. After a grapple that left her jaw bruised and bleeding from nail wounds, she wrestled the girl to the ground and pinned her face-first into a cushion.

"I'm not here to hurt you," she said in Moth's ear, her voice rough. "Or your mistress. Stop fighting or I'll do worse."

The girl responded in badly accented and anatomically improbable Skarrish, but stopped struggling.

"You'll have to learn to curse in Assari," Melantha

said, stepping back. The mark of her hand rose angry and red on Moth's wrist—it would purple soon. The sight sickened her, until she felt the blood trickling down her neck, not to mention her aching leg. She wasn't quite brutalizing a helpless child.

Whatever lets you sleep at night.

Someone must have heard the struggle, she thought, but as she slowed her breathing and listened, the voices and running steps she heard were on the street outside. The gunshot had the neighbors distracted. Easing a curtain aside, she saw a crowd gathering, the rust-and-khaki uniforms of the city police pushing through. A trellised wall hid the rest of the scene.

"What happened?" Moth asked, and before Melantha could answer, "What do you want?"

"I don't know what's going on out there," she said. "I heard a shot." Her face throbbed with every word. A drop of blood splattered the tiles as she leaned forward, followed by another, heavier still. She wiped at her cheek, frowning at the quantity of crimson that stained her hand. It had only been a scratch...

She glanced back and met Moth's anger-dark eyes. Her stomach lurched. "Haematurge!"

The girl flinched at the word. Even as she dropped her gaze, one foot hooked a stray cushion and kicked it toward Melantha's face. She swatted the pillow aside, barely throwing up her other arm in time to block Moth's next clawing strike.

"Enough!"

Shadows roiled from the corners, cocooning the girl like a spider's web. Another wormed between her teeth when she tried to shout. Moth writhed against the bonds that stole her breath, slowly falling limp as syncope took hold. Tenebrous coils laid her carefully on the bed, and Melantha knelt to be sure she was breathing again.

As her hand settled on Moth's throat to feel her pulse, Melantha knew the leverage she needed.

The idea came like a fist in the stomach. "No," she whispered. "She's only a child."

Older than Melantha had been when her mother first chose to use her. She doubted Moth would appreciate being called a child. She would appreciate being used as bait even less.

But it was the only idea Melantha had, with no time to find a better one. Cursing under her breath, she searched the room for a pen and parchment.

CHAPTER 14

They left Sherazad before sunset. Isyllt spent an hour scrying for Moth while Adam searched the inn like a hound, but neither of them met with success. Adam found no trace of the woman in the halls or through the windows, though he said she'd been in all three of their rooms.

The way his voice deepened on that *she* promised a story to come.

After that fruitless hour Asheris swore they could delay no more. He bundled them into a carriage over Isyllt's protests and the innkeeper's hand-wringing apologies. Asheris put on a good act of being injured; he'd let Siddir fuss over him in public, cutting out the bullet—lead, for mage-killing—and dressing the wound, but the bandage was for show. Isyllt had watched a copper bullet melt from his flesh in Symir, as easily as she might draw out a splinter. That was the first time she'd realized he was more than a powerful mortal mage.

The rented carriage took them back to its stable, where Asheris dismissed the driver and hired extra mounts. The manager wasn't happy about letting his horses out unsupervised, but the gold Asheris pushed across the table—not to mention the imperial seal—soon changed his mind.

"We're not taking the river?" Siddir asked, clearly unhappy with the prospect.

"I took a ferry down. Our watchers may be waiting for us at the docks. Besides, it's slower upriver."

"So instead you'll kill the horses in the heat and leave us open to ambush on the road?"

"I would rather travel alone," Asheris said, a quiet warning in his voice. "The fewer strange eyes and tongues around us, the better."

Adam rode outguard while Siddir drove the carriage. Isyllt's back was swollen and mottled with bruises and her shoulder was likely sprained; she sat entombed in cushions to spare herself worse bruising. Assar's well-paved roads were scant balm for her aching flesh and pride, especially at the pace Asheris set.

"What's going on?" she demanded as daylight bled away and Sherazad faded to a dusty blur behind them. "Siddir wouldn't tell me what was so urgent that he had to pressgang me out of Kehribar. Someone was following me there, and tried to kill me—now I have the same reception here and my apprentice has been kidnapped." She winced at the sound of her voice; pain and worry left her waspish and the stifling warmth didn't help. "Not that I'm not glad to see you."

Asheris chuckled, his eyes glinting in the gloom. "I'm only ever shot when I'm with you. Don't think I haven't noticed."

"But you invited me anyway."

"I needed more excitement in my life," he said dryly.

Golden witchlight sparked between them, painting the walls with shadows. The air cooled as night came on but the coach held the heat of their bodies.

"I'm not sure where to start," he said after a moment of silence.

"I've heard of your warlord troubles."

Shadows exaggerated his frown. "They're the least of our concern. Or so I thought, until our sniper gave you Hamad's name."

"Who is this general who wants me dead?"

"Don't give him that title in the empress's presence, if you please. Samael Hamad was stripped of rank, and she grows tired of people forgetting. He was enough nuisance as a warlord—if he's taking orders now..."

"From this red lady?"

His jaw clenched. "If she is who I think, the trouble grows and grows." He leaned close. "Something's bothered me ever since Symir."

Isyllt nodded slowly. "Who was buying Rahal's smuggled diamonds?" The question had occurred to her more than once after she'd returned to Erisín.

"I'm starting to put some pieces together," he said. "Though I can't see the whole of it yet. I've heard whispers of a group called the quiet men."

Isyllt frowned. "I've never heard of them." Even as she said it a memory stirred, a dream of fish and shadows.

"Hardly anyone has, and most of the rumors are wild invention. There's truth behind them, though, I've convinced."

"What about this ghost wind?"

"It's . . . a storm. But calling it a storm is like calling the Archeon Ocean a puddle. It's a whirlwind of entropy. The touch of the void."

Their eyes met and Isyllt swallowed. The void she carried under her heart. They had both felt its touch in Sivahra. With it she had destroyed the enchantments that bound him to the emperor's service—and very nearly both of them as well.

"Is such weather common here?" She kept her voice light, but the idea chilled her through.

"No, thank every power. Most mortals thought it a myth, until it struck during Sebek. Even my people know little more." It took her a heartbeat to realize which people he meant. "And now it's struck twice in a month."

"What does the ghost wind have to do with these quiet men?"

"I don't know. And that troubles me a great deal."

They rode through the night, changing horses twice to maintain speed. The Assari didn't underestimate the danger of the desert—way stations and caravanserais lined imperial roads at regular intervals, providing water and fresh mounts and respite from the sun and parching wind.

Asheris took pity on them before dawn, and stopped to rest at one such serai. The square-walled courtyard was empty save for a sleepy stablemaster. Adam and Siddir flung their bedrolls down as soon as the horses were seen to, but Isyllt stopped them before they could follow.

"We've put this off long enough. It's time we got some answers from our friend." She stripped off her right glove. When she was sure the stablemaster was asleep once more, she led the others to the center of the courtyard.

The moon had set, and dawn was at least an hour away. The night was deep and still.

Her diamond flared as she summoned the brown man's ghost, bathing the gathered faces in milky light. Siddir's expression was pinched and unhappy, but he stood his ground. Adam looked tired but curious, and Asheris's dark face was smooth as a mask. A cold deeper than the desert night suffused the air.

The ghost was a washed-out shadow, all his living color faded to shades of blue and grey. His eyes narrowed as he scanned the night, marking the walls and the stars above. When he turned to Isyllt his lips curled in a smirk. She had to appreciate bravado that could withstand death and soul-binding.

"Good evening," she said with a smile. "I hope your stay hasn't been too unpleasant."

"The accommodations are rather spare, and the service nonexistent." His voice was rough and breathless; his death wound was a black blot on the side of his neck. "But I seem to have had a better time of it than you." He tilted his head toward her sling-bound arm and scabbed face.

"Someone else tried to kill me. He didn't have any more luck than you did."

The ghost shrugged. "They won't stop. Eventually that luck will change. All the spies and hired swords in Assar won't prevent that." He took in the three men with a contemptuous wave of his hand. Isyllt was sure much of his sardonicism came naturally, but she also knew a defense when she saw it.

"They?"

He snorted soundlessly. "I didn't follow you all the

way from Erisín for my own enjoyment, or the view. But you already know that."

As defenses went, his was an effective one. Isyllt forced herself not to bridle at his tone, to keep her own casual. "So tell me about your employers. You said *they*, not *we*."

"I did, didn't I? My oaths were only unto death."

"Then you can talk to me with a clear conscience."

The smirk returned. "I could, but I don't think I will. It's more fun to watch you scramble about in confusion."

"You'll tell me one way or another. Why not keep this polite?"

"Compulsion, you mean? You can torture me, if that's the sort of thing you enjoy, but I've probably had worse. And I don't think you can truly compel me without my name. Do I understand that bit of thaumaturgical theory properly?"

Isyllt's smile stiffened and slid away. "You do. And you're right—torture is pointless. Eternity in a soulstone, though..." She lifted her good shoulder in a shrug. "That might be enough to change your mind."

"It might. Why don't you leave me in there for a few dozen years and ask again?"

She took a careful breath through her nose. "I'm amazed you weren't murdered sooner."

The ghost chuckled; it sounded like a death rattle. "So am I, most days. And yet that bitch still took me by surprise." The words were wry, but Isyllt thought she heard real hurt buried beneath them. "I'm sorry she hasn't caught up with you yet—you two deserve each other."

Isyllt drew breath to reply, but Adam spoke into the silence first. "Brenna." She didn't recognize the name, but there was a weight of history in the flatness with which he said it.

The ghost turned, surprise flitting across his translucent features. Then he laughed, long and cold and hollow. The sound raised the hair on the back of Isyllt's neck. "Oh, Saints," he said at last. "Were you the one in Celanor, then? The one she was so miserable about? It doesn't matter. Whoever you thought she was, she isn't anymore. She never was. Stay away, or you'll end up like me." He lifted a hand to his neck and drew it away black. The stain faded from his fingers as he watched, and his hand clenched convulsively. All the bravado in the world couldn't stand against death.

He pulled away, fighting her summons. Isyllt let the diamond swallow him once more.

The darkness was thicker than ever in the absence of ghostlight. The four of them stepped apart at once, as if a bond had been broken. Isyllt worked her dry tongue against the roof of her mouth. Before she found her voice, Adam turned away, sand crunching under his boots.

She let him go too.

Adam and Siddir fell onto their beds and into the heavy sleep of the tired and pragmatic. Pain and fatigue dragged at Isyllt, but the lingering rush of magic kept her awake. After she gave up trying to work the kinks from her back, she sat by the well, skin rough with chill, watching the eastern sky grey with the coming dawn. The fading constellations were subtly different from those in Erisín, just enough to remind her how far she'd come.

"You'll be stiff as scorched leather if you sit there all night," Asheris said, standing behind her.

Isyllt turned, wincing as her neck proved him right. "Do you sleep at all?"

He offered her a hand and a wink. "The servants would talk if I didn't. Come on—the view is better from the walls."

They climbed the stone steps leading to serai's eastern watchtower. To the west, the swollen waters of the Ash rippled silver-black. The wind breathed damp against Isyllt's cheek, sweet after hours of sand and baked earth.

"It's so quiet," she said at last, releasing a breath she hadn't realized she held. An absence she'd felt in Sherazad was stronger here, without lights and noise to distract her, all the starker for having spoken with the dead. "Where are the spirits?"

Asheris turned his head, but not before she saw the sadness that passed like a shadow across his face. "Gone. Driven into the deep desert, or the mountains, or the jungles of Iseth."

"How? How can they ward so well?" She nearly said *you*—from the quirk of his mouth, Asheris noticed her hasty catch. "Erisín is hung with protections but still spirits get through. And the roads—" She shook her head at the futility of the idea.

"Selafai may have saints, but it doesn't have the Unconquered Sun."

"How can one more church make such a difference?"

"Not one more. One. *The* church. The empire embraces saints from all its kingdoms, but all fall under the banner of the one church. And the one church preaches the ascendancy of man. Every paean that rises from the towers is a ward, the peal of every bell. The force of tens of thousands of prayers is more than the little spirits can withstand."

"And the powerful spirits?"

He made a sound that wasn't a laugh. "The jinn, who might have been able to fight the church, withdrew into the desert instead, and built their own walls against outsiders. The ghuls retreated to Carathis in the mountains." He nodded east, where the serrated Teeth of Heaven chewed the sky. "The rakkash lost their tiger queen and scattered into the jungles. One by one all the spirit kingdoms fell or retreated or turned their backs on men. Only a few wanderers remain. And exiles like me."

She reached for his hand and once again the sharp heat of his magic bit her skin.

"What happened?" she asked, rubbing her fingers. "You weren't like this."

"No. I wasn't." He spread his arms and light like a false sunrise rose around him. *Otherwise*, Isyllt saw the winged, eagle-headed shape of the jinni hanging over him clearly. She turned away from his heat, the smell of smoke and incense. "I don't know what's happened to me. For the past decad and a half it's been harder and harder to keep control, to keep the fire inside the flesh. I hadn't meant to meet you in Sherazad at first, but once this started I had to leave the palace. If the truth were known, I would have nowhere to turn."

But turn he did nonetheless, casting a wistful glance to the west. Toward the darkness and the deep desert.

The next morning Isyllt cornered Adam as they broke camp, pressing a cup of sweet tea on him. He might have slept more than she had, but she couldn't tell it from the bruised circles under his eyes. Light slanted through the serai's high arched windows, picking out the dust in his cropped hair.

"You know the woman who took Moth. Tell me."

His mouth flattened, and she thought he would refuse tea and conversation. A moment later he accepted the cup and leaned against the rough stone wall behind him.

"Thirteen years ago. In Celanor. She was"—his throat worked as he sipped his tea—"my friend's lover. A mercenary, she said. A seamstress's daughter who decided she preferred knives to needles. Her story was—" He shook his head, the gesture heavy with regret and anger. "I can smell lies, but never from her. A year she stayed with my friend. I was certain she loved him." His voice strained, snagged on some submerged pain, then grew cool and clipped again. "It was all a ruse. She used him to gain access to the palace. When she'd stolen what she came for, she vanished."

"You're sure it's the same woman?"

"Her scent was all over the room."

"What did she steal in Celanor?"

"Gold and gems, as much as she could carry. My friend thought it was an ancient crown she was really after—a relic from the days of Archis, if the legends were true, full of diamonds. The Celanorans thought it was cursed."

Isyllt's fist clenched, the band of her ring cutting into her flesh. "I'm starting to think all diamonds are."

They kept up their pace for the next two days, changing horses as often as they could and eating as they went. Sleep was brief and heavy and Isyllt had no strength to spend on summoning. Siddir rode with her in the carriage to spare his injured leg—after a day of bumpy card games and dozing in the heat, both of them would rather have walked.

The landscape rolled by in a rust-red blur, veined with green around lakes and aqueducts. When the road rose, Isyllt saw the shining line of the Ash, swollen across the fields like a freshly fed snake. Houses and granaries draped its flanks.

"What is it?" she asked, after Siddir's brooding silence had lasted nearly an hour. "You've been on edge ever since we left Kehribar."

"It's... foolishness. And bad manners. But I remember when we first met. And now assassins, and the storm—"

Isyllt's mouth twisted. "You think I really am bad luck."

"I know better. Our troubles began before you arrived. Even before Asheris decided to send for you. The unrest in Symir certainly didn't spring from beneath your feet. All the same, these things seem to crystallize around you. Catalysis, alchemists call it."

She snorted. "*Catalyst* is a nicer term than *stormcrow*."

"The way *change* is a nicer word than *destruction*." His smile faded. "But it was you and Asheris in the heart of it, in Symir. And now you're together again." He shook his head. "I'm becoming as superstitious as my grandfather, but it seems an ill omen to me."

"The catalyst isn't consumed, remember. And Asheris is far more durable than I. We came out of Symir—we can come through your storm."

Isyllt was proud of the strength in her voice; she nearly believed herself. But she and Asheris hadn't been alone in

Symir. Another mage had stood with them when Mount Haroun broke its shackles and burned the jungles and villages. A young apprentice, who gave her life to save the city while Isyllt and Asheris were consumed by their own loyalties and conflicts.

And now, distracted by grief, she had lost another apprentice.

Not lost, she told herself. *Misplaced. I'll find her.*

There was little strength in this promise.

CHAPTER 15

Killing was so much easier than kidnapping.

By the time Melantha navigated shadows to one of Quietus's safe houses, her lungs burned and her bones ached with chill. Unconscious weight was no better than dead, and while Moth wasn't tall, she had enough growth to make carrying her awkward and slow.

The room, a hidden space inside a dockside warehouse, was stuffy with disuse and aromatic with the pickled fish stored on the other side of the wall. An oil lamp, a pallet on the floor, and a crate filled with emergency supplies were the only furnishings. Moth's eyes twitched when Melantha laid her on the bed, but she didn't wake. By the fitful lamplight her lips and fingernails were tinged blue, her bare arms rough with gooseflesh. Melantha tucked the single thin blanket around the girl and chafed her hands.

The lamp-flame warmed the narrow space quickly and Moth's color improved. Satisfied that the girl wouldn't die in her sleep, Melantha took a skin of stale-but-clean water and a roll of bandages from the crate and busied herself washing the scratches on her face until her nerves were steady again.

She didn't have time to waste. Iskaldur would search for the missing girl, and Moth should be well away from Sherazad before then. Not to mention the longer they stayed here, the longer it would take both of them to scrub the smell of fish pickle out of their hair. Her own skills couldn't get them out of the city quickly enough; she had only one means to accomplish that, no matter how loath she was to use it.

When her face had scabbed, she drew a deep breath and reached for shadows. Darkness parted and she spoke a name into the abyss. She felt the shift in awareness as it heard, a vast weight turning toward her.

The rift she'd opened stretched, peeling back on itself to disgorge Kash's gaunt shape. A smell like locusts filled the room; she preferred the pickle.

Sunlight revealed him as translucent, faded, a shadowy ghost. A ghastly shadow. Here in the darkness he was solid, sharp and gleaming as obsidian. His wings stretched to brush the sides of the room.

"You called, Arha?"

She stiffened at the name. "Nothing," the word meant in some dead desert language, or perhaps "devoured." The sounds rolled off Kash's tongue like the exhalation of a dying man.

"I need passage to Qais." She looked him in the eye—bird-like, he turned only one to her at a time. Her mother had trained her to never show fear, but his presence churned her stomach.

His beak gaped and snapped shut again. Ridiculous

to assign human emotions to a vulture's face, but she was sure of his mocking amusement as he regarded her.

Her memories of Kash were fractured and confused, like so much of her childhood. He hadn't always frightened her. Sometimes she thought he had been a guardian, a companion during her dangerous youthful escapades. But if that had ever been true, it had changed when she was twelve. The year her mother had given her to the abyss. She wasn't sure what had happened, but after that the jinni had nothing but scorn for her and threats and recriminations for her mother.

"I exist but to serve." His wings folded with his mocking bow. Not that she could blame him for hating Quietus—she at least had given her service willingly. "But who's this?" he asked as he straightened, his head swiveling toward Moth.

"She'll be our guest." She resisted the urge to stand between them, to shield the girl from Kash's dark, hungry stare. "No harm must come to her. Beyond that, she's none of your concern."

"All of Qais is my concern. Quietus has seen to that."

Melantha knelt, throwing Moth over her shoulder. Kash could have carried them both easily, but she had no desire to expose the girl to his touch. She grunted as she rose, knees and shoulders straining with the weight. Moth stirred and fell limp again.

"I don't have time to gossip. Please," she added. She'd seen how the Silent spoke to him—another reason she couldn't fault his vitriol. "May we go?"

He watched her for a moment with one sunken eye, then smirked. How a vulture could smirk, she wasn't sure.

"Since you ask so nicely." He extended one gnarled hand and she took it without flinching.

Together, they stepped into the abyss.

It was like her own trips through shadow, the way stepping into a shallow pool was like falling into an icy sea. There was no bottom to this darkness, no surface to break. The void was infinite—if she could survive the journey, she might find other worlds scattered in its depths. It thrilled and terrified her in equal measure.

Kash knew the path, though, a ferryman on a lightless sea. Darkness opened and they stepped into the courtyard before the Chanterie. Arid heat washed over them and Melantha sucked it down greedily. The broad rose-grey façade of the hall was as austere and imposing as ever, but a welcome sight after so much nothing. Neat rows of date palms rustled in the breeze. The scent of myrrh lingered under everything, like stepping into a temple. Or a tomb.

Moth's ribs swelled as she drew a frantic breath. Melantha winced; she must have woken during the journey. She bent to set the girl down, only to be toppled by a blow to the throat. She landed hard, eyes watering, heels scrabbling in the dust as she fought for breath. The helplessness of choking was worse than the pain.

Over her racing pulse, she heard Kash's harsh laughter.

Breath returned, slowly and painfully. Moth's blow had glanced off the side of her neck instead of crushing her windpipe. Give the girl a few years' growth and training and the outcome would be different. Melantha's hand tightened around the memory of the plumbata.

Her vision cleared to reveal Moth struggling in Kash's grip, her eyes wide and wild.

"I told you I don't mean to hurt you," Melantha croaked. "If you keep hitting me I might change my mind."

Moth's jaw worked, eyes sweeping the street. Melantha read the questions in her panic-dark gaze: *Where are we; who are you; what do you want?* She swallowed them all and stilled, shuddering at Kash's cold touch.

Melantha rose to her knees in front of the girl—out of range for a kick. "I will explain this, I promise you. But you have to stay calm and stop fighting. You won't win, and if you run we'll catch you. Do you understand?"

Moth's eyes flickered toward Kash and she nodded slowly.

"You're here as surety for your mistress. No one will hurt you. But if you fight, you'll be locked up—for your own safety. If you don't, we can keep this civil." She nearly said *pleasant*, but that was a worse lie than she was willing to voice.

Moth nodded again, but her eyes were sharp and narrow.

One half of the hall's great brassbound door swung open and Nerium emerged. Melantha caught Moth's startled blink: The white lady of Quietus was adept at looking harmless. Her pale robes were plain, the sleeves rolled as if she'd been working, her silver hair tousled. If not precisely grandmotherly, she looked the part of an academic, an underslept scholar-mage. Not someone who commanded assassins and kidnapped children.

Not someone who would throw her own daughter into a well of hungry spirits. Nearly thirty years had passed, and Melantha still hadn't reconciled herself to that.

Nerium's eyebrows arched as she studied the tableau

in the yard. Melantha rose, brushing dust off her trousers; despite everything, that quirked brow still made her feel like a truant child.

"What is this?" her mother asked.

"Your leverage. This is Iskaldur's apprentice."

"Kidnapping?" Nerium's lips pinched. "I need Iskaldur here willingly."

"You said whatever it takes. Besides—" She glanced away, cursing herself for it. "Iskaldur's bodyguard knows me. From a long time ago. He would never trust me if I spoke to them."

"Saints." Nerium shook her head. "It's done, I suppose. We'll make the best of it. Welcome to Qais, young lady," she said to Moth. Her eyes flicked from Moth's stony silence to the bruise rising on Melantha's throat. "I would prefer your stay not be a violent one."

"We've come to an understanding. Haven't we?" At her pointed glare, Moth nodded, but Melantha could see the plans spinning behind her eyes.

"Well then, let's get out of the heat." Nerium gestured toward the dormitory, and turned to lead the way.

Kash took it as a dismissal and released Moth, his dark shape unraveling on the breeze. The girl startled.

"You get used to it. Eventually." Melantha forced a smile she didn't feel. "Come on. Have you had breakfast?"

Despite her anger and suspicion, Moth was an adolescent, and Melantha had rarely known a child to refuse food. Sure enough, while the girl held her icy silence, she couldn't resist chilled water or bread and fruit. They ate in the kitchen—it was quiet and empty, the ovens cold. The

Chanterie's housekeeper and assorted servants baked and stocked the pantries twice a decad, and prepared the occasional elaborate meal, but for the most part the mages fended for themselves.

Moth and Melantha ate, but Nerium was pensive and distracted. The circles beneath her eyes were darker than usual and her hands trembled. She smelled of myrrh and honey and recent sorcery.

"What is it?" Melantha finally asked.

"The usual things. And—" She paused, making a show of considering. Melantha had befriended enough stray animals to understand: First they fed Moth and showed her little kindnesses; next they ignored her. Eventually she would grow used to their presence. Let her guard down.

"It's Khalil," her mother finally said. "He's not well. He hasn't been well for some time, of course, but now..." She shrugged. "I've sedated him. Rest is all I can give. It would be best if you leave him in peace," she added.

Melantha nodded, swallowing a mouthful of bread gone dry as ashes. Khalil had been her friend, her first combat instructor—kinder and freer with praise than any of her other teachers, including Nerium.

"I should return to my work," her mother said. "See our guest settled in, please."

Melantha's appetite had fled, but she waited for Moth to finish before leading the girl upstairs. As they climbed the second flight and entered a twist of hallways, Moth's curiosity finally overcame her silence.

"Is it always this empty?" she asked, flinching as the stillness broke.

"Not always, but for a long while now. We have other agents, but most work abroad. My mother and a few other mages live here, but no one has taken a new apprentice in years. Qais has guards and farmers, but they live elsewhere."

Slate-grey eyes glanced sideways. "We?"

"Quietus. And don't ask me why—the name is far older than I."

"It fits," Moth muttered.

The room Melantha chose had been her own once, decades ago. The choice discomfited her, but she also knew all the chamber's nooks and hiding places, and had long ago determined that it was free of secret passages. It had a window; denying the girl one would be the wiser choice, but also a cruel one. She hoped the drop from the third floor would give Moth pause.

The air was stale and heavy. Melantha stifled a sneeze as the draft stirred settled dust. "I'll send someone to clean," she promised apologetically. "And I'll find you clothes and such." She threw back the shutters, disturbing more dust. "When the servants come, you may be tempted to bash one over the head and run." Moth's cheeks darkened and she ripped her gaze away from a heavy lamp beside the bed. Melantha caught the girl's eye. "Don't. I may deserve your violence—they don't. Attack me as often as you like, but if you hurt anyone else I'll have you chained."

Another nod, this one slightly chagrined.

"Good. Rest, for now. I'll join you for dinner, if you don't mind the company."

"It won't work," Moth said as she turned to leave.

"What won't? Dinner?"

"You're using me as bait for Isyllt. It won't work." Her chin rose, shoulders squaring. "She doesn't want me. I'm useless as a bargaining chip. She won't come for me. So if you mean to kill me, do it now and have done."

Beneath the bravado, the words held a quiet, deep-buried hurt. Melantha might have feigned such, but she doubted Moth could. Her chest tightened—Moth believed it, believed herself unwanted, and turned her grief into armor to protect her mistress.

She hated Iskaldur in that instant, for inspiring such loyalty and pain. She hated herself even more.

"No one is going to kill you," she said. "And she will come."

She locked the door behind her.

Melantha meant to sleep after leaving Moth, but only managed to toss in the shuttered gloom. Her current room was a small chamber on the second floor, nearly empty. She kept books and clothes and stray keepsakes, but made few efforts toward coziness. She might always return to Qais, but she could pretend it wasn't home.

She tossed and twisted for an hour, marking time by the stripes of light creeping across the floor. Finally she rose and tugged her boots back on and went to disobey her mother.

The wing where Khalil lived was deathly silent. She remembered his tuneless whistling drifting through the halls, hearing him mutter to himself as he read—he had read to her when she was young, long after her mother stopped. If she pleaded enough, he would sometimes call up shadows to enact the fight scenes on her bedroom walls.

She once imagined doing the same for her own children, but had long since abandoned the idea; she could never bring a child here.

And now you have. Resolutions are such fragile things, aren't they?

Melantha raised her hand to knock on his closed door, but stopped before her knuckles fell. The door was warded, bound with spells. The kind any mage might use for privacy, but the tingle she felt was her mother's magic, not Khalil's.

She tapped on the frame beside the door, out of the spell's reach. No one answered. A furtive glance through shadow revealed nothing but darkness, and a single grey line of light through curtained windows. Unease soured her stomach—she stepped through the wall.

The room was stagnant—something he could never stand—and thick with salt and incense. As her eyes adjusted, she saw a thin form on the bed, behind the pale shroud of netting.

"Khalil?" Her whisper caught in her throat. "Mother said not to disturb you, but—"

No response, not even a snore. She clenched tingling hands. Had he died in his sleep? Nerium would have known. Wouldn't she?

Melantha crept first to the window, tugging one curtain aside. Shapes resolved in the gloom, familiar lines and unfamiliar: the same old desk and shelves full to bursting; a new chair; the bed had been moved away from the wall. At the floor at its foot rose stacks of... bricks?

"Khalil?" She drew back the hangings, her throat tight and dry. He couldn't be dead. She would smell it—

She touched the hand folded on his chest and let out a harsh breath of relief. Cool and dry and papery, but not cold. When she eased two fingers against the bone of his wrist, a faint pulse answered. But so weak, so slow.

"Khalil, wake up. It's me." He often lost track of her names and usually called her *child*—she loved him enough to abide it.

Once, when she was very young, she'd asked if Khalil was her father; her mother said no. Years later she realized the tightness around Nerium's eyes when she said it was one of her few tells. By then it was obvious that her mother would never tell her the truth, and she had decided it didn't matter—she loved Khalil regardless.

It still didn't matter. Kneeling beside him, his hand limp in hers, watching the faint rise and fall of his breast, nothing mattered but the pain in her chest. She loved him, and he was nearly gone.

She laid her head on the bed, only to recoil from the stench of myrrh. The sheets might have been soaked in it. In fact, she thought they had been. His robes, as well. Peering closer, she saw his usual gold earrings had been replaced with amber, and more chunks of resin were woven into his long white braid. His hands curled over a fist-size chunk of it. As always, she expected the stuff to dent at her touch, but it was hard and slick, neither warm nor cool. The bricks stacked by the bed weren't clay or stone, but rock salt.

Melantha backed away, scrubbing her hands on her trousers. She might be kamnur beneath all her shadow tricks, but she had studied as much thaumaturgy as any mage. Amber and salt and myrrh were preservatives—if she searched the bedclothes, she'd likely find honey as well.

She felt the shifting darkness that heralded Kash, but didn't look up until one clawed hand settled on her shoulder.

"Don't look," he said, drawing her gently around. "This is not for you." She couldn't tell if his care was mocking or not.

"This is my mother's work." She had to tilt her head to meet his gaze, all the more unsettling when he was close enough to embrace. "What is she doing?"

"I am forbidden to speak of it."

"Damn you!" She slapped his chest. "I've sworn the same vows she has! I need to know."

"Actually, you haven't." His second set of hands enfolded hers, pressing it to his hollow breast. Now the mockery was clear. She tried to pull away, but his grip was cold and unyielding as iron. "You swore to protect the order, its secrecy and its goals, with your life. *She* swore to keep the sleepers bound, to protect the world from them, no matter the cost. As for needing to know, I imagine that you do. But I am still forbidden to speak of it. And forbidden to let you intervene. Luckily, I wasn't ordered to report your intrusion. Not in so many words." He winked, an ashen membrane sliding sideways across his eye. "All the same, you should leave."

She tugged again and this time he released her. Her fingers tingled bloodlessly where he'd held them.

"This is madness."

"Is it?" His wings lifted in a shrug, all his usual caustic scorn returned. "The vagaries of the mortal mind are lost on me, I'm afraid. You're all mad to me."

Melantha fled, and his laughter chased her.

CHAPTER 16

In the dream, Isyllt fought her way through a crowded night market, pushed and elbowed by shoppers who looked past her as if she were a ghost. The pain of each shove against her bruised back indicated otherwise. The bazaar was packed wall-to-wall, and the roar of voices rose like a whirlwind.

Ahead she saw Moth through the forest of shoulders and arms and veiled faces, farther away with each glimpse. Isyllt called to her, but her voice was lost in the din of the storm. She tried to run but the press closed tighter around her; she reached for magic to force the crowd back, but her hands were bare and inside her was only a hollow place where her magic should be.

A merchant leaned across his table, exhorting her to buy a chicken. She ignored him, but he shook a black cockerel and a sudden rush of black feathers blinded her. Iridescent darkness sliced her face like glass knives and she stumbled and fell.

Feather-knives vanished, and she knelt alone and bleeding on a dusty street. The noise of the market re-

ceded behind her like the distant rush of the ocean. Moth watched her from an alley mouth, on the threshold of a greater shadow. A woman stood beside her, veiled all in black, one hand resting on Moth's shoulder.

Isyllt stood, shaky and aching, but the air held her like cold honey when she tried to step forward. Her voice locked tight in her throat.

The woman drew back her veil, revealing Kiril's face, cold and lifeless. Bloodless lips parted, but Moth's voice spoke from them.

"I don't love you."

Isyllt woke with a jolt, her stomach roiling with the juddering lurch of the carriage. Sweat soaked her shirt and stung in the healing scratches on her face. Her heart beat hard in her throat, and her chest ached with each breath.

Siddir leaned back against the far side of the coach, a pillow held before him like a shield. "Wake up," he said, in the cautious tones one might use on an animal or a madman.

She shuddered, shoving at the cushions that entombed her. The muscles in her back felt as if they'd been knotted and dried in the sun. "Sorry," she said at last, tongue thick and sticky in her mouth. "Dreams."

"I know." The words held a world of understanding. He passed her a water skin. "Drink. You can sweat to death even in the shade."

Whose faces did he see in dreams? What voices called to him? She nearly asked, but drank instead. The water was tepid, but it rinsed the salt-sour taste of sleep from her mouth and the clinging web of dreams from her mind.

Siddir drew back the curtains, letting in dust and warm afternoon light. "We're here."

Once Ta'ashlan was the Nahil Oasis, a shining green pool amidst the sweep of red sand and scrub, a gathering place for wild goats and jackals and the spirits who rode the desert winds. The green and wet drew men as well, who brought roads and walls and still more men. Now it was the largest city in Assar, home to the Lion Court and the Cathedral of the Sun, with five hundred thousand people packed within its walls. Merchants came from all across the empire to trade; pilgrims came for the blessings of the Illumined Chair; scholars and sorcerers came to study at the university. The Nahil was now a covered well, half forgotten in the center of the crumbling Garden Quarter, and the city's water ran through the great arching aqueducts and underground qanats that ran between the Nilufer and the Ash.

The carriage turned east onto the aqueduct road, a ribbon of dust unwinding behind it as it descended into the shallow Valley of Lions. Great sandstone arches stretched to either horizon, carrying water between the two rivers and beyond. Grass and trees grew in their shade, green with stolen moisture, vivid amid so much dry earth.

Isyllt sat beside Asheris on the driver's bench, squinting against the wind at the city below. She had known it was far older than Erisín, and far larger, but the width and breadth of its sprawl still impressed her. Buildings crowded together, brown and pale and square as sugar crystals. Domes and spires rose gleaming above the maze of streets—green and cerulean and white. Shouting over the rattle of hooves and wheels, Asheris pointed out landmarks: the palace's gold and crimson dome and green lawns; the university's latticed stone observatory tower; the cathedral, with its twin gold-chased spires—the Pillars of the Sun.

The sun sank behind them, throwing their shadow long against the stones of the road and paving the sky with carnelian and amber. Dusk washed the walls of Ta'ashlan not blue and violet, but a warm sepia red.

They neared the western gate when the first peal of a bell carried through the heavy air. Voices rose from distant temples, from houses, from guard stations along the wall. Thousands of voices lifting together, slow and sonorous as the sunset. The force of it washed over Isyllt, prickling her skin with its power.

Asheris hissed in pain, doubling over on the bench. The horses snorted and sidled at their driver's distress and the carriage tilted alarmingly to one side. Isyllt slid, clutching at the edge of her seat and the side rail. She heard a thump from inside the coach, followed by Siddir's muffled curse.

Heat rolled off Asheris in waves and she smelled scorching leather as she grabbed the lines. His white-knuckled grip didn't loosen; when she finally yanked them free, the straps came away smeared with blood and sweat and flaking char. The horses were no happier with the reins in her hands—she was an adequate rider at best, and had no experience with carriages. She thanked several saints when Adam drew his mount alongside the team, catching the left front horse's harness and drawing all four to a stamping, lather-slick halt.

"Asheris!" Isyllt grabbed his clenched fist, wincing as she leaned into his heat. She tried to tilt his face toward hers, but jerked away as a blister rose on her palm. The padded leather beneath them was crisping, the wood behind beginning to scorch. She reached for him again, only to be blinded as flaming wings burst free of his back. A horse screamed; Adam swore.

Warding herself against the heat, she grabbed the front of Asheris's robe in both hands and hauled, pushing him over the rail. The impact drew a breathless shout from him; it sounded like a raptor's shriek. She followed him over the side, jarring back and shoulder and ankles. And thank the Black Mother herself they were alone—she didn't know how she'd explain this to passersby. In a fair fight Asheris would outmatch her, but distracted as he was by pain and fire, she dragged and shoved him off the road and into the ditch.

"Asheris! Damn it, listen to me!" Straddling his chest, she slapped him once, hard and sharp. His eyes snapped open, but nothing human looked out at her, nothing sane. His skin scalded her, his sweat drenching both of them. Four burning wings beat frantically, searing grass and weeds. He shrieked again and a eagle's head rose from the man's like steam—its wicked beak snapped an inch from her ear, and Isyllt was just as happy not to know if it was solid.

The jinni would burn them both to ash to be free of its prison of flesh, and burn itself out in the process.

Spells of binding rose to her lips, harsh and clipped. If she could have reached the kit in her pocket she might have used salt and silver; without it she had only her will and long training, the cold strength of her diamond. She had bound dozens of ghosts and spirits, but nothing as powerful as a jinni.

Over the stench of nerves and sweat, dust and singing hair, she smelled cinnamon and clove and the turned-earth tang of patchouli.

The eagle receded into the man, sliding and twisting beneath dark skin. Asheris's burning gaze focused on her, and she'd never seen so much rage and hate on his face before. Not even when he'd tried to kill her.

"Enough!"

He surged beneath her, flinging her backward with inhuman strength. Tears of pain blinded her. She lay still, breathless, staring at the crystalline sunset sky, and waited for him to strike.

Instead he sobbed, crawling through the dirt and weeds to kneel at her side.

"I'm sorry," he whispered. His face was a mask of sweat and smeared dust, eyes flashing white.

"So am I," Isyllt muttered. "Haven't we done this already?"

He laughed, the sound tinged with hysteria, and helped her stand. They leaned against each other as they stumbled out of the ditch. The sky had cooled to slate and amethyst behind the towers of Ta'ashlan. The temple bells were silent.

Adam and Siddir stood on the edge of the road, watching the mages and each other simultaneously. Adam's hand was tight on his sword-hilt, and she caught the flash of Siddir's dagger as he sheathed it. The spy grimaced apologetically; Adam's expression didn't change.

"You're friends now?" he asked softly, offering her a hand. "I'm glad we're not that sort of friends."

She might have blushed, but her blood was busy throbbing in all her burns and bruises.

Asheris leaned against the side of the carriage. The horses snorted, calmer now but still sticky with foam. "I can't go in there like this. The songs—it feels like they're flaying me alive."

"You've lived there for years. What's happened now?"

"Ten years," he said, scrubbing a hand across his face. "Ten years like this. And I don't know." She'd never heard such despair in his voice, either. She preferred the rage. "Maybe I've finally run mad, as all demons must."

Isyllt felt Adam tense beside her, only the faintest shifting of weight to betray his surprise. She had never told him—Asheris was worn thin indeed to speak of it openly.

"I've known more mad demons than sane ones, but I'm not convinced it's an inescapable fate. In the meantime, though, I would prefer not to spend the night on the side of the road. If you try to burn the palace down, I'll stop you again."

Asheris's eyes narrowed, and sparks glowed in their depths. "I'll try to restrain myself then, lest I be subjected to further bindings."

They rode slowly to spare the horses; they rode in silence to spare themselves. The moon had risen pale and ghostly when they reached a narrow side gate into the palace, and Asheris had collected himself enough to get them quietly past the guards. Siddir vanished once they were inside.

Asheris led Isyllt and Adam across darkened lawns and paths lined with rustling date palms. She smelled gardens and kitchens and stables, glimpsed carven trellises and light glowing through keyhole windows, but they didn't pause long enough for her to appreciate the scenery or get her bearings. Granite glittered in dim lamplight as they passed through arching corridors and columned arcades. Distant laughter and conversation drifted through the halls.

Asheris cornered the first servant they passed, giving her a long set of instructions that sent her hurrying off in the direction they'd come. Another series of corridors and walkways led them to a dark wing that smelled of plaster and sawdust. From the depth of the silence, Isyllt guessed they were far from the central hub of the palace.

"Renovations," he said apologetically as they passed scaffolding and stacked lumber. "But at least you'll have privacy."

"And it's out of the way if more assassins come."

"That too."

He opened a door at the end of the hall and ushered them into a dark suite that smelled not of dust, but of long disuse. Stillness radiated from the plaster walls, the kind born of the absence of people.

"I must report to the empress," Asheris said, kindling a lamp. "Your luggage will be brought, and food. Wait here, please, until I come for you."

With her nodded agreement, he was gone.

Adam and Isyllt stood in the warm circle of light. After a moment Adam shrugged and found a second lamp, and began to inspect the rooms.

Wide and high-ceilinged: They would have been airy with the shutters open. The walls were pale plaster, the arching doors and windows crowned with stucco friezes. Blue-veined marble tiles covered the floor. The only furniture was a cedar wardrobe, a table with a single chair, and a low bed shrouded in netting. A smaller set of rooms adjoined the first, just as clean and empty.

The brief tour complete, Adam paused in the doorway. The lamp haloed his spiky hair in gold and painted his face with shadow. "What he said on the road... You knew."

"Yes."

"And you trust him, even so?"

"I do. And he trusts me even more to bring me here, knowing what I do."

Adam sighed. "Always secrets."

"You should have gone to the mountains," she said as he turned. She meant it to tease, but the words came out flat and bitter.

He paused, his broken-nosed profile against the light. "I should have. But I didn't."

His tone was not soft, precisely, or gentle, but it conjured a not-entirely-unpleasant fluttering sensation in the pit of her stomach. If she'd been less tired, perhaps, less filthy and reeking of horse and sweat—

"Rest," Adam said, a smile hooking one corner of his mouth. "I'll wake you if more assassins show up."

Isyllt woke to the smell of food and a soft *otherwise* touch. The food kept her from starting out of bed at the intrusion; killers rarely brought breakfast.

She couldn't remember falling asleep—she'd only lain down a moment to rest. The bed creaked as she stirred: a wooden frame and leather straps held the reed mattress off the floor. To let air circulate, she assumed, and to keep stray insects from crawling over one's toes.

The lamp still burned on the table, sharing the space now with a tray of food. Asheris sat in the chair, clean and freshly dressed, her luggage piled beside him.

She cocked an indignant eyebrow. "Watching me sleep?"

"Not long. I can't keep the food warm forever. Don't worry—you don't drool much."

She snorted, pushing herself up. She'd fallen asleep fully dressed, and now sand lined the creases in the sheets. More scraped inside her clothes and itched in her hair.

"I took the liberty of drawing a bath. I'll find you servants who aren't too squeamish of necromancers, but it may take more than a few hours' notice."

Her stomach growled at the smell of food, but a bath was the more pressing need. She felt better for the sleep—if she pushed herself hard enough she could sometimes escape the dreams. "What time is it?"

"Two hours before dawn."

A new lamp lit the bath chamber, warming creamy marble. The tub was wide and deep, set into the floor; towels and a robe lay folded neatly beside it. The water steamed, hotter than even royal plumbing could usually account for, and she suspected she had Asheris to thank for it.

A gilt-framed mirror stood in the corner of the dressing room and she flinched at the sight of uncovered glass. In Selafai, mirrors were doorways to the spirit world, and opportunistic spirits and ghosts waited on the other side. Vanity was dangerous without strong wards. In this spiritless place, the only thing waiting for her was her reflection, gaunt and bruised and filthy. That was danger enough.

But her nape prickled as she studied the glass, as if more than her own hollow eyes stared back at her. Paranoia, perhaps, but she'd be sure to cover the mirror. At least it didn't face the bathtub.

She climbed into the bath, sinking chin-deep and letting the nearly scalding heat soak into her abused muscles. When the water cooled, she ground soap and oils into her hair and skin, grimacing at the cloud of dirt and suds floating away. The water was cold by the time she felt properly clean, her fingers wrinkled. Burns and scoured scabs stung fiercely.

She emerged robed and toweled, leaving damp footprints on the tiles. The stone was cold underfoot—she'd have to buy rugs.

Asheris ceded the chair and rose to pace the room. Even the soft slap of bare feet carried through the chamber. Rugs, hangings, furniture: She started a list of things the room would need to feel less sepulchral. Assuming that she stayed, of course.

"What about Adam?" she asked, uncovering plates. She could hear him snoring in the other room. The food was still warm, despite her long bath. Pyromancy was a useful art. Maybe Moth could learn it.

Her jaw clenched to aching at the thought. *I'll find you*, she promised, but the vow felt weak and useless even as she made it.

"Let him sleep." Asheris unshuttered a window, letting in a draft that smelled of green and damp. "We can send for more food."

Her stomach snarled as she slathered harissa across a piece of bread, and saliva flooded her tongue. She tried to eat slowly, but her body was tired of starving. Whenever she paused, Asheris pressed something else on her—dates, cheese, slices of egg. By her third cup of tea her stomach was full to aching, and he finally let her push her plate aside.

"I don't know what to do," he said at last. He stood by the window again, a teacup cradled between broad brown hands. "Dawn is coming, and the prayers. What happened on the road...I can't risk that here." His voice lowered, and he closed the shutters one-handed. "And if you try to bind me, I'll fight. I can't help it."

"You know I hate it when we quarrel," she said dryly. Her left sleeve fell back, revealing the glossy band of scars on her wrist. Asheris glanced away, lips pressing pale at the corners.

She turned the problem over in her mind, hard and slick as a pearl. "There must be a cause. You don't have any other symptoms of madness, do you?"

"A certain sense of paranoia..."

She chuckled. "You live in a palace. They paint it into the walls. Let me look—we don't have any better ideas."

He set his untouched tea back on the table. "No, I suppose we don't. What do you need me to do?"

Isyllt stood, discarding her towel across the back of the chair. Her hair fell in a damp snarl down her back, hours of combing if she let it dry that way. She shook the sand from the bed with a snap of the sheets and motioned Asheris over.

"Lie down. This may be...intrusive. Try not to burn me, if you can."

He sat, swinging his legs onto the bed. His amber eyes were clear as he looked up at her. Human. "I trust you."

So did Moth, she thought bitterly. *And look how well that turned out.*

Focus on the problem at hand, she told herself, settling

cross-legged beside Asheris. She tugged the robe closed across her thighs and twisted her hair up to keep it from falling in both their faces. A memory rose: her hair sweeping across his bare chest. Her cheeks burned and she prayed the room was dim enough to hide her blush. In Symir he'd seduced her to distract from uncomfortable questions. Only a ploy, the sort any spy knew to watch for, but it had worked embarrassingly well.

Focus.

She laid a hand on his chest—mercifully clothed—and another on the curve of his brow. "This may tingle."

"I'm sure I've felt worse," he murmured. He still shivered like a fly-stung horse as the first tendrils of magic crept into his skin.

She'd never had an opportunity to examine a demon in such depth before. Arcanost scholars would give their teeth for a chance like this. Maybe the University of Ta'ashlan would accept a monograph.

Demon was a simplistic term, a catchall that meant any melding of flesh and spirit. Common wisdom held that such a mingling led to madness and hunger, usually for blood and flesh. Demons were abominations to be put down with salt and fire. Isyllt had seen her share of horrors: animated corpses, violent possessions, the vengeful fury of the dead. But she had also met demons like the blood-drinking vrykoloi who lived in Erisín's catacombs, who loved beauty and music and were no more mad or murderous than most of the living.

Demons like Asheris—trapped, two worlds and in between.

He was unlike anything she'd ever encountered. No death-echoes answered her questing magic, no hint of mortality. His heart beat strong and steady, speeding now with nerves. Closing her eyes, she felt the flame coiled amid meat and muscle, the heat of magic coursing with the blood in his veins. A whirlwind lay quiescent in his lungs. Inhuman fire tempering a mortal soul; flesh grounding a wild spirit.

It would have been beautiful, were it not his prison.

Entranced as she was by the alchemy inside him, she almost missed the foreign magic. It draped his skin like threads of silk, fine and nearly invisible. The touch of her power didn't stir it, but left her with the impression of fire and smoke, all but undetectable against the furnace of Asheris's own magic. Dark strands clung inside his lungs—whatever it was, he'd breathed it in.

Frowning, she reached deeper, digging ephemeral fingers under his skin. He convulsed at the intrusion, the fire of his heart flaring. The spell clung to her as she tugged, heat and stinging nettles. She yanked her hand away, shaking off the pain. Like a burr under a horse's saddle—a constant, inescapable irritation.

With it she smelled cinnamon and clove, smoke and fresh dirt. The same scent she'd caught on the road. Her nose wrinkled; she'd never be able to drink spiced tea again if this kept up.

"You've been cursed."

"What?"

She dug another skein of magic out of his flesh and held it between her hands like a cat's cradle. "Look."

The spell disintegrated quickly away from his skin. Within heartbeats the red-black glimmer faded, leaving only a faint smudge like ashes on her fingers, and the lingering scent of spice and incense.

Her vision focused on the solid world in time to see Asheris lever himself up on one arm, his mouth slacking and snapping shut again. A muscle jumped along his jaw, and sparks kindled in the depths of his eyes.

"You know who did this, I take it?"

"Ahmar." The priestess he'd spoken of on the road. "She put it in the temple incense, for everyone in the palace to breathe."

"But no one else in the palace has a second soul to prick into a rage. A pretty piece of sorcery."

"Can you undo it?"

"No," she said at last, peering closer. Not threads of magic but vines, sinking roots into his flesh, drawing nourishment from him as if he were soil and water. The deeper she looked, the more creeping tendrils she found. "It's powered by your magic. I can't attack it without attacking you. But—" She paused, squinting sideways at the lines of power. "I think I can dull it. Not a binding, but... a silence."

"Will it dull me too?"

"It may. Dawn is coming—do you have another solution?"

"I could burn the Pillars of the Sun to the ground," he muttered. "But I suppose that's impractical. All right. Do it."

It had been a long time since she'd had to improvise magic, she realized as she drew a deep breath and let it out. Too long. It was easy to fall back on a familiar set of spells—wards and bindings and knife-edged defenses—easy to make her power into a tool, locked into certain shapes. Useful, perhaps, but limiting. Boring.

She drew stillness from the walls, from the night air

trickling over the casement. She stole the chill from the stones, from the dew beading on the shutters. Numinous filaments shone between her fingers, fine as a spider's web. Isyllt held her breath as strand wove to strand, emptied her mind of everything save silence and shadows.

Her magic was rooted in death and decay. She would never heal, never warm, never conjure life. A limitation, but one that drove her to creative solutions. And, though she often forgot it in her dealings with ghosts, death held much of peace.

Spreading her hands, she exhaled. The web floated free, pale and shining, and drifted over Asheris. He drew a sharp breath, pulling the spell into him as it settled like frost on his skin. He shuddered, and she felt his skin roughen beneath the cloth of his robe.

Otherwise senses faded slowly, till Isyllt sat once more in shadows and faltering lamplight. Her hands tingled with the lingering thrill of spellcasting; her pulse beat hard and steady in her throat. Outside, larks and thrushes took up their dawn chorus.

"Do—" Asheris swallowed and began again. "Do you think it will work?"

"We'll find out." She climbed out of bed, staggering as blood returned to numb feet, and threw open the shutters. Beyond a trellis and a veil of trees, the sky pearled with the coming day.

They stood side by side, watching the leaves glow in the first orange light. With that vermilion kiss came the bells, and the glad prayers of the faithful, rejoicing for another night survived. Some mornings, Isyllt could see why that was worth praying for.

Asheris's throat worked as the music rolled over them,

and his eyes closed tight, creasing the delicate skin around the lids. Light gilded the tips of his lashes and warmed the mahogany planes of his face. Beads of sweat rose along his brow, glowing gold.

The song swelled to a crescendo and faded. Asheris slumped, steadying himself against the windowsill. Isyllt's chest ached with a breath she hadn't realized she held. She laid a hand on his shoulder and he leaned into the touch.

"Thank you," he whispered.

"I hate to spoil the moment with pragmatism, but it won't last. A few days, perhaps, but the curse will burn through the cure."

Asheris straightened, squaring broad shoulders. The light in his eyes was nothing preternatural, but a very human sort of venom. "Then we must deal quickly with this troublesome priest."

CHAPTER 17

Melantha dreamed of Khalil, sunken and cold, frozen like an insect in amber. She woke sick and desperate to flee Qais, but that wasn't an option. As an agent she had a great deal of autonomy, but cowardice ran counter to her oaths.

And having delivered Moth here, she couldn't abandon the girl. Instead, she set out to gain her trust.

At first it was simple things: taking meals together; granting her the freedom of the kitchens; providing new clothes. The only books in Selafaïn she could find were heavy thaumaturgical texts, but she offered them anyway; Moth didn't refuse.

On the second night, Moth tried to escape. She made it out of the Chanterie, only to be captured in the street by Salah's guards. Since she neither harmed the maid she'd slipped past nor attacked the guards, Melantha didn't speak of it.

On the fourth night, she tried the window. Melantha discovered her empty room at dawn, the shutters thrown wide. After a quarter hour of peering through shadows with growing concern, Melantha found the girl on the Chanterie's roof, crouching between the low battlement and an empty stone planter. By then the shadows were too thin to step through, so she climbed the inside stairs to the rooftop entrance.

The trapdoor was harder to open than she remembered—when sheets of sand cascaded through the gap, she understood why. Dust and grit and pigeon droppings piled in ankle-high drifts. Sweeping the roof had been a task for slow apprentices when she was a child, but Qais had long ago run out of apprentices.

Moth glared as Melantha climbed onto the roof, a flush rising in her cheeks. Melantha fought down a laugh.

"It's easier to climb up than down, isn't it?" From the narrowing of Moth's eyes, she hadn't quite dulled the bright edge of laughter from her voice. "I learned that the hard way, too."

She studied the wide expanse of roof, mazed with plant boxes full of dead earth. Even in her youth more of those had stood empty than not. "It must have been green up here once, and beautiful."

"What happened?" Moth asked, brushing with little effect at her dusty trousers.

Melantha shrugged. "Time. Time and apathy."

"How can you stand it here?" It was the most emotion she'd heard in Moth's voice since the girl stopped fighting.

"I can't. I hate it. But I endure because I have to, because I've sworn my service here, and Quietus's work must be done."

"Oh." Moth took a few hesitant steps closer. Closer to the hook. "What work?"

"Did you see the ghost wind that came to Sherazad?" The girl's wince was answer enough. "Quietus is sworn to keep the storm bound." She raised a hand to forestall Moth's sarcastic retort. "The seals are failing, faster every time we renew them. That's why my mother wants Iskaldur's help."

"So you kidnapped me." Moth's eyebrows rose.

Melantha didn't bother to hide her defensive shrug. "It was a bad idea. I panicked."

"Why?"

"That's not your concern." This was a familiar game—the fine balance of truth and secrets, just enough of each to engage the target and prick her curiosity, but not enough to ring false. "Come on. We're both sick of these walls. I can take you riding, if you'd like."

Moth started forward, then stopped and folded her arms across her chest. "You haven't even told me your name."

She blinked. "Melantha." Her tongue wasn't used to the name yet, even after six months' usage. It had sounded pretty when she chose it, but never quite took as a good name should.

Moth caught her hesitance. "Is that your real name?"

"No. Is Moth yours?"

The girl didn't answer, but Melantha thought she caught a wry hint of a smile, quickly hidden.

Qais's stables kept Tigras, short-backed desert ponies bred by the northern tribes. Not as elegant as their Resharan cousins, but with the same fire and stamina. Melantha avoided the stables more often than not—Brenna had loved horses the way Charna had loved the sea. The stablemaster cocked a curious brow as he saddled a dun mare and a grey, but offered no comment.

She'd guessed that a city rat like Moth would have little experience with horses, and the girl's seat proved her right. That was convenient for the moment, since she didn't relish the notion of a horse chase across the desert, but Moth's stiff spine and awkward knees made her wince. She would have to convince Nerium to let them visit a proper training stable.

She led them in a slow circuit around Qais, though the short narrow valley that enfolded the town and temple, and down the narrow pass that led out of the mountains to the erg. An unobstructed view of Al-Reshara would convince Moth not to flee more than any warnings Melantha might give. Only early morning, but already the heat-shimmer off the dunes blurred the distant horizon.

The ride was peaceful. Moth asked about the myrrh trees and the wells, but for the most part was content to study her surroundings in silence. Melantha was happy to be out of the oppressive weight of the Chanterie walls.

"The white lady," Moth said at last, as they started back to the stables. "Nerium? She's your mother?"

"Yes." They had met Nerium once or twice at meals, but had exchanged no more than a handful of words. Melantha had to bite her tongue every time to keep from demanding answers about Khalil.

"She's... distant."

Melantha laughed. "And harsh, and critical, and cold. To be fair, her work takes a great toll, but—" She shrugged, trying to seem careless. "We were never close." But that wasn't true, exactly. Her most distant memories were pleasant ones, when she and her mother had lived in

Anambra, by the sea. Nerium had always been exacting, but the chilly disappointment had come later, after they returned to Qais.

Moth snorted. "My mother would have sold me to a brothel when I was born, if any would have taken me. I don't have much to compare her with."

With Iskaldur's apprentice secured and the seals intact once more, Nerium concentrated on the necromancer. Scrying over such distance was taxing, but once she learned the trick to unraveling the other sorceress's wards she had a clear view. Al Seth was harder to see—his magic was a clever approximation of human craft, but the heat-shimmer that blurred him from her sight left the taste of the Fata in the back of her throat.

Scrying in such a way was like viewing a silent play. Voices were lost, but she read their lips and posture, the spaces between each companion. She'd used such skills every day in her youth, when she'd taken on names and lives like new cloaks. When she'd had the freedom of the world. For decades she'd had only the petty secrets and jealousies and endless numbing fatigue of Qais to observe.

The temptation to create her own narrative—to invent quarrels and loves and write her own lines for the silent puppets—was strong, but not one she could indulge in. She needed to understand Iskaldur if she was to court her to Quietus.

One thing she understood very well: The necromancer was lonely. She slept poorly and woke from unpleasant dreams. A finely drawn tension hung between her and her bodyguard, much akin to the tension she glimpsed between Bashari and al Seth. The strain of lovers, or merely the fragile web of secrets and alliances between spies?

As Iskaldur and her companions drew near Ta'ashlan, the pricking of Nerium's wards roused her from the distant vision. Not the seals on the oubliette, but the lesser charms she'd hung on Khalil's door. She let the sight of sunset over the City of Lions fade into the grey walls of her chamber and waited for the unpleasant conversation to come.

The light beyond her shutters cooled and dimmed and died before Shirin appeared at her door. By lamplight the librarian's face was sallow and drawn, her mouth a bloodless line.

"I've seen Khalil."

"I imagined you would, eventually. I thought about putting him in the basement, but all those stairs..." She lifted a hand as Shirin drew an outraged breath. "A bad joke. Spare me your righteous indignation, please, Shir. I know he deserves better—I cared for him as much as anyone."

"Then how can you do this? Entomb him alive!" The lamp-flame glittered in Shirin's eyes and threw her exaggerated shadow across the walls.

"He's asleep. At peace. It's more rest than any of us have had lately."

"He's your friend, Nerium! And you've turned him into—"

"Into a vessel, yes." Her knees cracked as she rose from her chair; she read Shirin's tension and spread her hands wide. Stories made mages' battles into epic things, thunder and lightning and earthshaking magic, bitter struggles till the dawn. The reality of two old women squabbling like schoolchildren would be embarrassing for everyone. And Nerium had no desire to fight when persuasion would serve. "We serve as we must. If there were a better option I swear I would use it, but there are too few of us."

"How can this be better than diamonds?"

"The diamonds merely imprison. Sleep and dreams will keep them quiescent. And the division between hosts lessens their power."

"And if it doesn't you've created demons worse than any false god or witch-king."

"I have considered that, yes." She abandoned her sardonicism and lifted a beseeching hand. "Don't you want to rest, Shir?"

Shirin looked away. "More than anything."

"That's why this will work. They're tired too, as tired of the fight as we are. Qais is slow death for all of us—I want to free our successors from that."

"You're mad," Shirin whispered, but the fight had gone out of her voice.

"I would hope madness would be easier," Nerium said. "Though that may be wishful thinking."

The librarian caught her eyes again, the last of her defiance sharpening her gaze. "You're willing to make this sacrifice as well?"

"I am. Have I ever shirked my duties?"

Shirin sighed. "No. Nor will I, if you're certain this will work. I'm worn through. Everything is dust to me—food, drink, even the books I love. I swore to give everything to Quietus, and I have."

"I know." Nerium laid a hand on the other woman's shoulder, felt the starkness of bone through thin flesh.

"We all have. All of us have, except—" She didn't finish the sentence, but saw the answer in Shirin's face.

"Ahmar will never accept this, her or Siavush."

"Don't worry about them. Ahmar underestimates us, both our strength and the depth of our sacrifice. She'll understand in the end."

Shirin caught her hand, her grip light and brittle as glass. "If you mean to do this, please do it soon. While I have the strength."

"Yes." She enfolded the other woman's hand in both of hers, squeezing as firmly as she dared. "Soon."

CHAPTER 18

Asheris left again after sunrise, once more bidding Isyllt to wait. Another meal arrived soon, carried by a nervous page who handed the tray to Adam and eyed Isyllt as though she were a wailing specter. Relieved of his burden, his hands clenched and unclenched nervously against his trousers until Adam tipped him and sent him away. Isyllt wondered if he'd boil the coin before he spent it.

"How long do you think he'll keep us mewed in here?" Adam asked as he uncovered plates.

Isyllt had no answer.

Asheris returned after the noon bells, carrying a small basket. "You have an audience with the empress. I'll take you there as soon as you're dressed."

Isyllt put down the comb she'd been wielding against her hair for the better part of an hour. "The dressing may prove a problem." She still wore her bathrobe—all the clothing in her luggage was too soiled to wear against clean skin, let alone for a royal audience.

"That's why I brought these." Asheris handed her the

basket, filled with pale cloth. "In Symir we might transgress, but not here. I'm sorry."

She lifted a fold of fabric: white silk, woven light as a whisper. The mortician's veil, worn by necromancers and funeral attendants alike—anyone who touched the dead for a living.

When she finished combing and plaiting her hair, Isyllt carried the hamper into the dressing room. Her reflection watched as she sorted through layers of cloth.

First came trousers and blouse of lightweight linen, followed by a raw silk robe that fell in heavy folds around her calves, shimmering with moonstone iridescence when she moved. The sleeves hung long and flaring, but could be cinched to her forearms with ties; very pretty, but she couldn't imagine performing an autopsy in it.

Next came the veil that wrapped her face and hair, leaving only her eyes exposed, and the robe's deep hood. Last, she drew on cotton gloves, hiding her ring. Her reflection stared back from the glass, stark and faceless. Like a ghost on an opera stage.

Jewelry was pointless when she was covered from head to heels, but Isyllt still took her coffer out of her luggage. The box was a tangle of garnets and opals and amethysts, stones too soft for mage-work. A ruby winked beneath a tangle of lesser gems—an unwelcome souvenir of her last job in Erisín. She sorted out the opals now, discarding hair clips and necklaces before finally selecting a pair of earrings, teardrops caged in white gold. No one would see them, but the weight was reassuring.

Asheris picked up a discarded necklet with a crooked smile; the opals had been his gift to her, years ago. "You'll have to oil them." The stones spat iridescent fire as he ran them through his fingers. "They'll chip in the heat otherwise. The desert isn't kind to fragile things."

Isyllt tried to smile, but it didn't fit. "Things like me?"

"Hardly. You're a diamond."

That drew a laugh. Her breath warmed the veil. "Cold and sharp?"

His fingers brushed her cheek, soft as kiss through silk. "Yes, but you'll weather anything." He returned the necklace to its box and offered her a hand. "Come on. Her Majesty is waiting."

She went before the empress in the Pomegranate Hall. A lesser audience chamber than the great apadana, Asheris explained, but impressive all the same. Her footsteps echoed as she approached the throne. Porphyry columns glittered in the sun; the slanting light threw their shadows stark and black across the white marble floor. The Indigo Guard, veiled and silent imperial bodyguards, were cool shadows on either side of the dais. In the center, framed by a chair of gilt and stained glass, sat the empress.

Assari poets and ambassadors called Samar al Seth the most beautiful woman in the world. As Isyllt stared at the woman glowing on the dais, she wondered if they were right. She knelt, turning her eyes to polished tiles, and waited. She felt the empress's measuring gaze; fabric rustled and soft footsteps moved toward her.

"Rise, Lady Iskaldur." Samar's voice was a low soprano, golden and clear. And, for the moment, emotionless.

Isyllt stood and lifted her eyes.

The glow was merely the afternoon light through high windows and gold powder sheening copper-brown skin.

The beauty beneath it was a human sort. Samar was a tall woman, long-limbed and heavy-hipped, her belly softened with age and childbirth. She wore burgundy silk, nearly the same shade as the porphyry columns, pleated and gathered beneath her breasts; gold and garnets gleamed at her throat and ears and amidst her henna-kissed curls. Long hazel eyes regarded Isyllt, smoky with kohl and powder.

"Please, remove your veil. Asheris speaks too highly of you for you to hide your face in my home."

Isyllt drew the cloth aside, willing her expression still. They were of a height, but Samar stood on the first step of the dais, making her tilt her head to meet the empress's gaze.

"You honor me, Your Majesty."

"I do." Samar winked, dark lashes brushing her cheek. "There will be talk." When she smiled, fine lines creased her face, like a statue coming to life. She and Asheris were only distant cousins, but Isyllt thought she saw a resemblance in that smile.

"Asheris tells me he's asked you here to help us with our...unusual weather. It's very kind of you to travel so far. Especially when your Crown has so often been at odds with Assar."

Isyllt inclined her head. "I no longer work for Selafai, Your Majesty."

"So I've heard. But I haven't yet heard the reason for the end of your service."

Isyllt couldn't keep her jaw from clenching, and wished she'd kept the veil on. She wanted to tell the truth: that she'd let the king die—let him be murdered—to try to save Kiril. Would have killed Mathiros herself to spare her master's life. But she'd failed in that as well. If she and Samar had been alone, she might have done so, just to see the empress's reaction. But a hall like this was doubtless full of stray eyes and ears.

"After my master's death, I wished for time away," she said instead. "And Nikos had people of his own. I'm here only as a friend of Asheris."

"And for that friendship I welcome you. He told me of the help you gave him in Symir. He's also requested that I appoint a court necromancer. I've been hesitant to do so, as it would unsettle the church and much of my court, but if you can help find a solution to the ghost wind, that would do much to sway opinions. I value good service over superstition."

Isyllt bowed her head to cover a grimace. Only kings and spymasters considered her sort of service good. Most simply called it deception and murder. "I shall make it my first priority," she lied.

Samar's lips quirked. "I understand you had some trouble in Kehribar, and in Sherazad."

"Kehribar was simply a misunderstanding. Sherazad—" She pressed her tongue against her teeth. But if Samar wanted perfect discretion, she should have granted Isyllt a private audience. "The trouble in Sherazad wasn't only mine."

"What do you mean?"

Isyllt paused, unfurling a cautious tendril of magic. Sure enough, besides the two guards on the dais, she sensed at least two other listeners, cunningly concealed behind panels in the wall.

"The assassin in Sherazad was aiming at me, Your Majesty, but my death was meant to undermine Asheris, and through him, you. I don't know if he's spoken of it yet, but Asheris has been cursed."

Samar's eyes narrowed. He had told her, Isyllt guessed, but only in private. "Cursed?"

"A wicked piece of sorcery, designed to drive him mad and eventually consume him altogether. Likely in a public sort of spectacle. We've dealt with the magic, but whoever cast it is very skilled, and may strike again." Best to provide a plausible cover story now, in case her countermeasures failed.

Samar's sculpted brows drew together. "Do you know who's responsible?"

"I'm afraid not. Being ignorant of your court and city, I have no suspects. If I met the person, though, I might recognize the magic."

"You'll inform me, of course, if you learn anything further."

"Of course."

"Already you prove your worth. You may encounter some...distance amongst the court and palace staff—I hope you will forgive it. Necromancers are rare here, and the white veil is off-putting to the devout. It will take some time for others to grow accustomed to your presence."

"I understand, Your Majesty."

"Then be welcome to Ta'ashlan, Lady Iskaldur, and to the Court of Lions."

After dinner that night, Asheris joined Samar in her study. The empress's desk was always crowded with matters needing her attention, but tonight an avalanche of parchment covered the wide ebony surface.

"There's something here we aren't seeing," Samar said, shaking a rolled map in Asheris's direction. "Something more than just the land. Ahmar wouldn't risk making an enemy of the Crown unless the result was worth more than a few setats of jungle, no matter how rich the soil."

A familiar knock on the hidden panel interrupted. The door swung open and Siddir emerged, a parchment tube tucked under one arm. All traces of sand and long travel had been scrubbed and oiled away; silk shimmered by lamplight, and his hair gleamed, long enough to curl again, the grey at his temples hidden beneath fresh dye. His smile gleamed brighter still.

"I found it." With a bow and a flourish, he handed the tube to Samar—the leather was scuffed and dented, one end sun-faded and grey with dust. "We weren't being paranoid enough. Not until I started thinking of your quiet men," he said, turning to Asheris.

"What do you mean?" Samar took the tube, but didn't yet uncap it.

"We thought that because there was nothing of interest on the surveys, the land itself wasn't the important piece of the equation. But what if the surveys were tampered with?"

Frowning, Samar twisted the cap off the tube. A roll of parchment slid into her hand, yellowed and delicate at the edges. The paper flaked as she unrolled it, and her frown deepened. "Where did you find this?"

"In Lord Jazra's personal library. His collection is eclectic, but so poorly cataloged he's forgotten half of it. I've used it before, when I didn't want the palace archivists paying attention to my research."

"You're saying that someone has altered records in the palace library, the royal archives, and the university."

"Once you accept the existence of conspiracies, these things become much more plausible."

Asheris walked around Samar's desk, leaning over her shoulder to see the parchment. It was a map, faded with age and ringed with tea-stains—the cartographer's mark on the lower corner dated it from 1163. It showed the southern half of Assar and the jungles of Iseth in detail. The legend explained symbols for resources scattered across the page—gold, silver, hardwood, rich soil—as well as dangers such as hostile tribes and spirits. Oraka, the land Ahmar was so eager to claim for the church, was full of trees and spirits, and one other symbol: diamonds. Asheris's indrawn breath hissed between his teeth.

Samar leaned back in her chair. "Why does the church want diamonds?"

"Not the church." Asheris straightened. "At least, I hope the whole church isn't involved. The quiet men."

"You keep mentioning that name," Samar said dryly. "Perhaps you'll eventually explain it."

"We never learned who was buying Rahal's smuggled diamonds. I think we finally have."

"Mages?"

"Who else would need so many stones? But I don't know why they want them so badly. Threatening you through me is...indelicate."

"And a threat they can only use once. If I give in, I'm theirs. But if I refuse, they must be prepared to expose you. Your necromancer has taken steps to lay out another story, but if they were bold enough to demand an examination—"

An exorcism. "Yes. I could deal with Ahmar, but she must be prepared for that. Someone else knows, and stands ready to accuse me if anything happens to the Asalar. And then the scandal will be even worse. I can't stay here."

Samar's eyes narrowed. "It seems you'll get your journey to the desert after all. Say nothing yet. I'll make a public announcement." She flipped through the collapsing stacks of papers till she found her calendar. "On the twenty-fourth. I can delay speaking to the church for three days."

Her voice lowered. "Find these quiet men and deal with them. I won't be backed into a corner like this."

Asheris bowed his head. "I have no desire to live under their threats either."

"Siddir—"

He bowed to the empress. "I'll stay, of course, Your Majesty. I'm always yours to command." A glance passed between them, fraught with something Asheris couldn't read. Samar lowered her eyes first.

"Never think I don't appreciate it," she said. "Either of you."

"What is it?" Asheris asked much later, lying in the darkness of his bedchamber. "There's something you're not telling me."

Siddir chuckled, breath warm against Asheris's shoulder. "There's always something I'm not telling you."

"Your secrets don't usually leave you so tense."

"Perhaps I'm unhappy that you spent our first night home with a foreign witch instead of me."

Asheris laughed, but something in Siddir's tone wasn't entirely in jest. "You're not really jealous, are you?"

"A little," Siddir finally admitted. "I know I can't be who you turn to for everything, of course. Still, one doesn't always like to be reminded."

They lay in silence, Asheris toying absently with Siddir's hair. The dusty pungency of walnut dye clung at his temples, not entirely hidden with clove oil. Beneath that, the bed smelled of sex and sweat and lingering perfume.

"Does it bother you?" Siddir asked, the words muffled against Asheris's shoulder.

"What?"

"That I'm aging and you're not. You'll look like this"—his fingertips traced a path from Asheris's collarbone to his navel, over muscled ribs and the flat planes of his stomach—"forever, and I'll wither."

"You all wither," Asheris said. "I see it every day. I see death watching me from the faces of everyone I meet."

Siddir bit him on the shoulder with a snort. "Try not to be so romantic, light of my eyes. I'm overwrought."

"You asked. And no, it doesn't bother me." Not yet, at least. "The problem will come when someone notices that I'm not aging." Asheris-the-man had been only twenty-nine at the time of the binding, in his prime, but that was ten years ago and even fortune and good breeding couldn't last forever. He had, he imagined, another year or so before his preservation became remarkable. Perhaps another handful before *remarkable* became *suspicious*. "Assuming Ahmar's machinations don't see me exiled in a decad."

"Assuming that, of course." That regretful undercurrent surfaced in Siddir's voice again.

Asheris rolled, propping himself on one elbow to look Siddir in the face. "Tell me what's bothering you."

The other man sighed. "I can't. I'm sorry. Not yet. In the meantime, you might as well distract me, while I'm still young enough to be of use to you." He cupped the back of Asheris's skull, drawing him down. With a sigh, Asheris relented.

* * *

Midnight found Isyllt sitting at the foot of her bed, a cup of wine warming between her palms. The Court of Lions didn't sleep so early, any more than the Azure Palace in Erisín had; the breeze carried distant music from the garden. The warm notes of an oud twined with a woman's soft voice, punctuated occasionally by tipsy laughter.

Of all the problems she'd anticipated in Assar, loneliness had not been one. She'd spent plenty of time by herself in Erisín when not working, but there had always been the option of companionship. Always the choice to leave her apartment and wander familiar streets, to idle in taverns and teashops if her own walls grew too stifling. Here she knew only three people, one of whom wouldn't admit to the acquaintance in public, and if she left the palace she would be shunned and stared at by the people in the city.

"What's wrong?" Adam asked, leaning in the doorway between their rooms.

"Nothing." But she realized as she blinked that her lashes were wet. "Feeling sorry for myself," she admitted with a rueful smile.

He stepped into the room. He'd come from the bath; moisture streaked his bare shoulders gold in the lamplight and his hair stuck up in black spikes. The shadows between his ribs were less stark than they had been; skin that had been slack a month ago was striated with muscle again. He paced the length of the floor and back again, bare feet slapping softly on tile.

"Any luck with Moth?"

Her mouth pinched. "No."

She'd spent hours scrying, collecting trinkets and stray hairs from Moth's luggage, anything to strengthen the magic. It didn't help; only darkness met her outstretched senses. Not the opposition of another mage, but simply *nothing*. The ghost in her ring swore he hadn't known of the kidnapping, and she almost believed him.

Once, in desperation, she tried a summoning of the dead, but no ghost answered. Relief warred with bitter frustration—even a terrible answer might be better than this blinding ignorance.

"She said she'd contact you." He hadn't spoken the kidnapper's name since that night in the desert.

"When? Where?" Her hand tightened on her cup, and she nearly flung the fine porcelain against the wall. "We've heard nothing, learned nothing. I feel so useless. Helpless."

Adam snorted. "When was the last time you were helpless?"

"Not since I was twelve."

"Me either." He stopped beside the bed, close enough that Isyllt felt his warmth. "But I felt it in Sherazad, after that storm. A despair like nothing I've ever known, even while I was locked in the Çirağan. It's not natural."

She thought of fish dying in the street, of Moth's tears, of the hollow emptiness in her chest. "No, it's not. But I don't know how to fight it."

The bed creaked as he sat. A handspan separated them. "No spells of cheerfulness?"

"My magic isn't the cheerful kind." She glanced at him from the corner of her eye, warmth that had nothing to do with wine rising in her cheeks. "But I can think of something we might try."

He chuckled, and she breathed in the laughter as she leaned close. His lips were cool at first, but warmed with the kiss. His hands settled on her shoulders, the right sliding down her left arm just in time to rescue the wine cup.

"Are you sure?" he asked, setting the cup out of harm's way.

"Do you mean, am I sober?" she said with a wry snort. Too sober. On the *Marid*, she had been thinking only of a night's distraction, an escape from dreams. Now a dozen doubts and questions chased their tails inside her head.

"That too. Are you?"

"Sober enough. Sure enough."

"Will you stay here?" she asked later, lying beside him in the dark. The party had finally ended and only crickets sang in the garden now. "When this is over?"

"I don't know." His fingers twined absently in her hair. "The desert is beautiful in its way, and I could find work. I've never been good at settling down, though. Even in palaces. Especially in palaces. What about you? Will you be a spy forever?"

"What else is there for me?"

"You could always become a mercenary."

Isyllt chuckled. "Some would say I already have." Her humor faded. "I don't know." Resting her cheek on Adam's chest, she studied the wide empty room. She could make a life here, even if it was a lonely one. What else did she have anywhere else?

She wished she could blame these doubts and fears on the ghost wind, but they were too familiar for that. "I don't know."

CHAPTER 19

News spread though the palace quickly, and through the streets of Ta'ashlan. The empress was holding a grand audience. Merchant families vied for invitations, while poor neighborhoods chose their most respected elders to attend and bring back news. Families of servants connived to sneak into the palace. Audiences like this meant free food and drink, as well as gossip and the occasional costly keepsake.

Isyllt spent the three days waiting and pacing. She would have left the palace, stares and whispers be damned, but Asheris kept her close. Despite her smothering boredom, she was forced to agree that crowded streets might not be the safest place. Though a bullet would have been more interesting than another day of studying the plaster.

The morning of the event, Asheris came with gifts: a new coat of figured silk, white on white, and a jeweled band to hold her veil in place. "You won't be in the crowd in the apadana tonight," he said with a rueful shrug, "but that's no reason not to look your best."

"I'm beginning to feel like an embarrassing mistress. Kept veiled and hidden away in opera boxes. You don't even take me to the opera."

He bowed apologetically. "It's been a dreary season. We're not missing much."

Her eyebrows lifted slowly. He was too dark to show a blush, but he had the grace to duck away from her gaze. "I'm sorry. This wasn't my intention when I brought you here."

"At least no one has tried to kill me in..." She counted on her fingers. "Nine days."

"Don't worry. We'll give them another chance."

She took his hand, pressing her narrow palm to his to listen to the resonance of magic beneath his skin. "How are you feeling?"

"Dawn was...unpleasant," he admitted. "But your spell holds. It will last through tomorrow—with any luck, we'll be gone from the palace by then." He pressed a kiss on her knuckles. "Be ready by Maghrevi. I'll come for you at the bells."

Adam lingered in the doorway after Asheris had gone, studying her with narrow eyes. "You care about him," he said at last, when she cocked an inquisitive eyebrow.

"Of course. We're friends." For all their honesty, the words slid too glibly off her tongue. "But that isn't what you mean, is it?" She sighed and sank onto the edge of the bed. "I know better. It's just—"

Adam's mouth tugged sideways, not quite a smile. "You don't know where to find nice men?"

Isyllt chuckled. "Or what I'd do with one if I did. It's easier, isn't it? Knowing there's something standing between you, something that isn't your fault?" Knowing that no matter how you loved someone, you would never come first in their affections. Never be what they needed.

Adam didn't answer, but meeting his tea-green eyes was like looking into a mirror. Isyllt was the first to glance away. "Are you coming with me tonight? We could find you something to wear—"

He pushed off the door frame, and a predatory look sharpened his face. "No. I have another idea."

Asheris found the empress in her dressing room that afternoon. She sent her maids away when he knocked, standing before her tall mirror in only a shift, her hair a wild cloud around her face. Fresh paint gleamed on her nails and she fanned her hands to dry them.

"Is everything ready?" she asked.

"All the extra security is prepared." The Indigo Guard and imperial soldiers were in charge of true security, the kind that stopped knives and bullets and malicious spells. Asheris had also made sure that a group of courtiers and senators were warned—in a vague way—of Ahmar's schemes against the empress. All of them were prepared to keep the Asalar away from the throne tonight, with conversation, feigned argument, or spilled drinks. He didn't trust the priestess not to make a scene if it would further her ends.

"Good. I sent a note to the temple, implying that I was inclined to be generous, and to arrange a meeting several days from now. That should give you time to be away from Ta'ashlan before she learns that my generosity is not what she expects."

"So you're really letting me go?" He'd half expected

some delay, some urgent need that would keep him in the palace.

"I'll make the announcement tonight." She turned away to inspect a tray of jewelry. "Which necklace?"

"The rubies," he said, glancing at her dress to confirm the choice. He picked up a collar dripping with ruby chips—all too tiny or infinitesimally flawed to be proper mage stones, but still a fortune's worth. And still capable of holding magic; he whispered a ward into them as he draped the necklace across Samar's collarbones, breathing in the henna and rosemary of her hair.

"Thank you." She drew a deep breath, shoulders squaring, and the gems threw crimson sparks. "I've made arrangements, supplies and such. You can leave in the morning, if you choose."

"Samar—" She was shutting him out, she and Siddir. It pricked him as sharply as Ahmar's curse. He glanced down at her stomach, soft and sloping beneath the thin fabric of her shift. If she had gained any weight, it could doubtless be attributed to too much lokum, but that wouldn't last. "What are you going to do?" he asked softly.

She winked, but her smile was strained. "You'll find out tonight. I hope you'll forgive me before you go."

"Forgive you? It was my idea. And you're protecting both of us by sending me away."

"That's not why." Her mouth twisted sideways and she brushed his hand, a touch and gone. "You'll see."

Asheris arrived as the sunset bells faded, resplendent in silk the color of rust. The petal-cut skirts of his long coat flared and glittered with every step, sewn with bits of turquoise and amethyst. Isyllt's opals and marcasites sparkled too, cold as frost beside his warm tones. Despite their eye-catching combination and the bustle of the palace, no one gave them a second glance as Asheris led her through the halls; his spell of obfuscation tingled against her skin.

They passed the great apadana through a servants' corridor, and Isyllt glimpsed a vast hypostyle, taller than the Pomegranate Hall, a blaze of chandeliers and pale marble. A crowd had already gathered, voices rising like a din of birds. Asheris didn't take her inside, but instead turned onto a narrow staircase and down another corridor.

"You can watch from here," he said, stopping beside a plain expanse of wall. She never saw the seams until he touched a concealed latch and a panel slid open. "It's not the opera, but court always has its share of melodrama."

The alcove was nearly the size of a theater box—a cheap one, at least. An elaborate soapstone carving screened the front, but if Isyllt stepped close she had a clear view of the room through the gaps.

Clerestory windows lined the room high above her—she wondered how they were cleaned, and how many servants fell to their deaths doing so. Friezes covered the walls, depictions of men and women in dozens of styles of dress. The various peoples of Assar, she guessed, all the nations subsumed by the empire. Flags hung from the ceiling as well, bright colors fluttering in the draft. She recognized only a few: the coiled red cobra on black of Khem, the golden bee on scarlet of Deshra, and the crimson-striped green of Sivahra. They reminded her of heads mounted on a hunter's wall.

Crimson drapes hung behind the throne—this chair was gold-chased alabaster with snarling lion heads on the arms. A pair of Indigo Guards lingered at the back of the dais, silent and unobtrusive as shadows amidst the rising noise.

"That," Asheris said, nodding toward the farthest corner, "is our priestess."

She followed his gaze to a tall, scarlet-robed woman, surrounded by what appeared to be priests of lesser rank. The priestess spoke quietly with her fellows, offering smiles like precious stones. Isyllt was glad to know the woman was scheming against the throne—she was far too gracious and serene to be innocent.

Asheris stayed for a quarter of an hour, pointing out various lords and senators and sharing gossip and anecdotes. The empress had no consort to sit beside her, but her closest advisors gathered directly below the dais. Among them was the Crown Princess Indihar, a girl nearly Moth's age—striking coppery hair and yellow silk made her a bright spot amidst the crowd.

When the hall had filled nearly to capacity, Asheris took his leave. "I'll come for you when the audience is over," he said. "If you see any assassins, feel free to stop them."

His timing was impeccable. Only moments after Isyllt watched him maneuver through the crowd to take his place in the front, a servant struck a heavy gong. When the third stroke faded, the audience fell silent as the empress emerged from a private door beside the dais.

Samar wore cream, a bright contrast to the crimson banners behind her. The cloud of her hair was twisted into loose, gold-bound knots that stood out from her face like rays from the sun, adding height and breadth to her frame. Bangles flashed on her wrists and rubies blazed across her throat. She wore no crown—she needed none. Every line of her spoke power and wealth and strength. When she spoke, her voice filled the great hall like clear water.

"Good evening. Senators, governors, people of Ta'ashlan, distinguished guests"—Samar gazed around the room, singling out a few with a glance or a nod while greeting the whole—"thank you for joining us, especially on such short notice. Tonight's address will be brief, but—I hope—worth your time.

"I know many of you are concerned with the ill-omened weather—the storm called the ghost wind. This storm has visited Assar before, though perhaps never twice in such a short time. I hope you all feel appropriately lucky." Polite laughter followed her sarcastic tone, but died quickly. "History tells us that the ghost wind, for all its horror and destruction, is a rare mystery. More terrible than the simooms, but elusive. We can find no record of its cause in all the archives. But what history cannot teach, we may discover for ourselves." Gold gleamed as she raised a hand. "Asheris."

Asheris stepped forward and knelt, the skirts of his coat flaring around him like a flower unfurling.

"You are my closest advisor." She spoke to him but pitched her voice for the entire hall. "Advisor, cousin, friend, and mage without peer. You understand, then, the weight of what I ask."

"I am yours to command, Majesty, to the ends of the earth."

"Hopefully not so far," she said dryly, "but perhaps close. Seek the ghost wind, into the deep desert or wherever the trail takes you. If you can stop it at the source, more glory to you, but I charge you to find the cause of this black storm and bring back the news. This devil wind has plagued Assar for centuries—if I can see it done, it will plague no future generations. Leave tomorrow, with soldiers and mages as you see fit. Any provisions we can provide are yours."

A cheer rose with Asheris, and courtiers clapped him on the shoulders as he retreated back into the crowd.

Samar lifted her hand again and a hundred voices fell silent. "But I didn't ask you here to speak only of the weather."

A curious mutter rippled and died.

"It has been, as many of you know, twelve years since I lost my beloved husband and child. My advisors and senators have urged me to wed since I took the throne, but I couldn't yet replace the memory of my family in my heart."

The mutter returned, louder, and was quashed again. Isyllt heard the rough susurrus of indrawn breath.

"Many candidates have been put before me," Samar continued. "Princes, amirs, generals, foreign nobles. Alliances have been offered, many of which would indeed be beneficial. For some time, however, I've felt the stirrings of affection such as I haven't known in years."

The crowd pressed forward with a sweeping rustle of silk.

"It is, as so many have told me, time for me to wed again, to strengthen the throne and the future of Assar. I can only beg you, my friends, to indulge me when I choose to temper politics with the desires of the heart."

She paused, letting heartbeats go by. Any longer and

the crowd might have screamed. Then Samar rose and walked to the edge of the dais, glowing in ivory and gold.

"Siddir Bashari."

The audience pulled back like a wave, leaving him alone on the shining floor. He too wore cream, shot with silver and chips of emerald. Hesitance slowed his stride as he moved toward the dais—or maybe that was only his limp. Black hair gleamed in the light of a hundred lamps as he knelt and bowed his head.

"You have been my friend for more years than I can count, long before I wore the crown. Your presence has soothed me in times of crisis and turmoil. When other duties have taken you from my side, I find myself restless in your absence."

A dark flush crept up Siddir's neck, though he kept his face calm.

"Would you do me the honor now of standing by me? Will you seal yourself to me before the throne and the Unconquered Sun, and take your place beside me as imperial consort?"

Siddir had known. His reaction was perfect: the flush, the silent opening and closing of his mouth, the way he wiped trembling hands on his coatskirts. Isyllt might have believed him as surprised as the audience, but for the way a dozen comments, a dozen silences and fitful glances came tumbling into place.

Isyllt swallowed and tore her gaze away from the spectacle to find Asheris. His face was stiff and still, brown skin draining grey; he hadn't known.

At last Siddir found his voice, and perhaps the catch therein was unfeigned. "Your Majesty— I never presumed—"

"No," Samar said with a smile. "You never presumed so much. I presume for both of us. Will you be my consort, Lord Bashari?"

"I—" He swallowed. "I will, Your Majesty."

The room rang with shouts. A few of outrage, and Isyllt was sure those were marked. Most, however, were happy cheers, as the theatricality of the scene swept them up.

"Then rise," Samar said into the fervor, extending both hands. "Rise and join me, and never kneel to me again."

Sunset prayers faded and shadows bled across the room. Adam waited.

He had no love for lights and crowds and noise, but it wasn't quiet that kept him here, sitting in the corner of Isyllt's room, draped in charms of silence and invisibility. All afternoon his neck had prickled with foreboding; something would happen tonight.

Part of it was only logic—if someone meant to sneak into their quarters to leave a message for Isyllt, this was the night to do it. But the greater part of his certainty sprang from intuition, the sort of hunch he'd learned long ago not to ignore. Tonight was his chance.

His chance at what, exactly? Justice for a crime thirteen years past? Revenge for his own heartache? Or just to learn the truth, to prove he wasn't going mad.

Lady of Ravens, he prayed, *at least give me that*. But the mercenary god—Saint Morrigan, they called her in places where gods had fallen from fashion—was hardly a deity who cared about truth. Revenge, perhaps; battlefield justice; sharp-edged mercy.

True night settled and still he waited, sword across his

lap, magic itching against his skin, toes curling inside his boots to keep the blood moving. What if he was wrong?

The first quiet footstep from the next room told him he wasn't.

Lightning seared his nerves, and only long practice kept his hands from going numb against his sword-hilt. He heard the whisper of a soft-soled boot, so light any distraction would have covered it, but he'd never heard the door or window open.

His vision tunneled as a slender shadow filled the doorway. His breath caught. Black cloth blended with the night, only a paler stripe of her face exposed. Her scent reached him as she stepped into the room, teasing, and it was all he could do to keep holding his breath.

Not precisely the same—no one would be after thirteen years. Brenna's familiar perfume—a heady blend of violet and bitter oranges he'd never forgotten—was gone, and the spices of a different diet soaked her skin. But the flesh and blood and female musk beneath—those hadn't changed.

She scanned the room as she moved, but her gaze didn't linger on him. He gave thanks to Isyllt and black-winged Morrigan in equal measure. Something pale flashed in Brenna's hand—not a blade, but a note. Instructions for Moth's return.

Thinking of the girl grounded him, eased the hot red bloodlust rising in his veins. He couldn't kill her. Not until they found Moth.

That didn't mean he had to be gentle.

When she reached the bed, he struck. Muscles clenched and uncoiled as he leapt, lifting his still-sheathed sword. The chair scraped and clattered behind him and Brenna swung around. His left hand opened as he moved; quartz clung to sweaty skin, then fell free. Another gift from Isyllt.

White witchlight filled the room. Adam expected it, but Brenna didn't. She froze, hissing, for just a heartbeat. Long enough for his weight to drive them both into the far wall, the wyrmskin scabbard catching her across the face.

Even off-guard, she was fast. She writhed out of his grip, an unseen blade tracing a line of fire across his side. But when they broke apart, he crouched between her and the door.

Moisture shone in the corners of her eyes. She dragged the scarf away from her mouth, smearing blood down her chin. An angry red line rose across her jaw and fresh blood welled from a split lip.

Her skin was darker, sun-bronzed instead of pale olive away from cloudy chill of Celanor. New creases lined her eyes. Not enough. She was his age, or so he'd thought, but he felt the thirteen years that had passed in all his scars and joints. He saw them on his face in the mirror. She looked scarcely older than she had been then—barely of an age with Isyllt.

He cursed himself for his hesitation even as he stared. She paused too, dark eyes widening.

"Adam." Her accent had changed, but the timbre of her voice was the same.

"Brenna."

That broke her inaction. She shook her head, streaking blood across her cheek. "Brenna is dead."

"Not yet." The scabbard slid to the floor as he brought his sword up.

She moved like quicksilver, rocking back and out of range. She ducked under his next swing, one hand darting toward the bed. He knew what was coming, but couldn't block the stinging snap of the sheet as she whipped it at his face.

Lady of Ravens, she was fast. Had he ever been that quick? His head turned, eyes watering, and she took the opening. A sharp blow in the ribs, a kick to his bad knee. He stumbled, fell, and she was on him like a hunting cat. Her knife was cold against his throat, but the metal warmed as she pressed it to his skin.

He still held his sword. She would kill him, but he might be able to take her—

"Is that what you want?" she asked. One knee dug into his stomach, forcing out his breath and grinding his back against the hard tiles. Blood from her first strike soaked through his shirt and into her trousers.

His lips peeled back from his teeth, a snarl tensing the cords of his throat. Skin parted, and warmth trickled down his neck. "Crows take you."

"Vultures, here." The pressure of the knife eased. "I don't want to kill you."

Focus, he told himself. *Remember what you're here for.*

"Where's Moth?"

She exhaled. "In Qais. She's safe. Tell Iskaldur to come to Qais, and she'll get the girl back." She chuckled humorlessly. "I'm sorry it turned out like this. It was meant to be more...graceful."

"Why?" He turned his head and spat. Sweat burned in the cut on his neck. "Why did you do it?" He didn't mean Moth; from her flinch, she knew it.

She leaned back, pulling the knife away. He could have taken the opening, but he wanted to hear her answer. Sadness washed across her face—he might have believed it, if he hadn't known exactly how well she lied.

"It was my job."

"Spy."

"Among other things."

Thief. Killer. Liar. But could he curse her with a straight face when a spy paid his bills? Could he say he hadn't done all those things himself?

She stood, cautious, knife at the ready. She was thinner than he remembered, and when her scarf fell back he saw she'd cut her hair.

He levered himself up, wincing as marble ground against bone. Blood smeared the tiles, seeping in dark lines along the seams; the servants wouldn't be happy. He returned his sword to its scabbard, moving slowly.

"Qais," Brenna—or whoever she was—said again; the name meant nothing to him. "Tell Iskaldur."

"Tell her yourself."

"A trade of hostages?" She smiled, then winced and touched her lip. "No thank you."

Adam stepped sideways, putting himself more firmly in front of the door. "You're not leaving." If he'd stayed at the Eyrie—if he hadn't been an infatuated coward—maybe things would have ended differently. Likely not, but the question still haunted him.

Her grin bared blood-filmed teeth. "Sorry to disappoint you."

He expected a feint, a rush. Instead she sheathed her knife and stepped back into the corner. The witchlit crystal had rolled under the toppled chair, casting its shadow long and black against the walls. One gloved hand reached for that shadow.

Reached into it.

The wall split open like a torn curtain, revealing darkness thicker than any night. Brenna shook her head as he gaped.

"Maybe I'll see you again," she said, stepping into that yawning black mouth. "It would be easier for everyone if I didn't."

The wind from the abyss chilled him to the bone and turned his bowels to ice water. But he couldn't let her escape so easily. He lunged, slipping in his own blood. The shadow portal was already closing around her.

Her teasing smile turned to shock as he followed her into darkness. "No!" She flung up a hand, but the rift sealed behind them, taking with it light and air.

Their fingers brushed, clenched, and then he was falling, blind and breathless, into nothing.

"Something's wrong," Isyllt said as they neared her rooms. Her magic reached, searching for Adam, but didn't find him. Instead she felt the angry buzz of recent violence and shed blood. She quickened her pace.

Her worry broke through Asheris's stony silence, at least—nothing else had. He lengthened his stride to keep up. "What is it?"

"I can't find Adam. But someone was here." Her hand lingered on the door, long enough to determine that her wards were still intact, including the weak point she'd manufactured to lure intruders. But someone else had been in the room. The door swung open and she smelled blood, and the acrid scent of nerves and sweat.

Witchlight glowed from her bedroom, casting stark shadows. Overturned furniture, sheets pulled off the bed. Rust-brown stains dried on the tiles, but not a great quantity. Her diamond was quiescent; no one had died here, or taken a mortal wound. She drew a grateful breath.

Two different people had bled here: one had fallen, leaving a smeared patch; the other had flung a line of droplets. From the way her magic lapped familiarly at the smear, she guessed that was Adam's. The drops were a stranger's—those she collected carefully on folded parchment and wrapped in silk. Footprints smudged the blood—mostly Adam's, but one narrower foot had left a track as well. The woman in black.

The footprints led toward a windowless corner and stopped.

"Is there a secret passage here you neglected to mention?" Isyllt asked, even as she unwound coils of magic into the wall; they found nothing but stone and timber and plaster. Her voice was even, taut. She wanted very badly to scream.

Asheris shook his head, amber gaze unfocusing as he studied the room *otherwise*. "They vanished. Not through the wall, though, even if that were possible. The heat simply stops."

Ghosts could sometimes walk through walls. Isyllt could do it herself, if she cast her soul free of its flesh. But it was always easier to pass through a door or window—that was their nature.

"Could they have stepped into the spirit world?" Dragging a living person through a mirror took immense power and skill, but she had seen it done. Through a wall, though...

"Perhaps," Asheris said, "but I find no trace of them in the Fata. The spirit world is worn so thin here that it would hardly be worth the effort. But a way was opened somewhere. Can you feel it?"

Isyllt pressed her hand to the cool plaster and closed her eyes. "Yes." Not magic, precisely. More like an absence of it. A chill snaked down her arm and echoed beneath her heart.

First Moth, now Adam. Her hands clenched, nails carving crescents into her palms. "I'm going to find these quiet men."

"Here's something." Asheris crouched beside the bed, fastidiously lifting his coatskirts away from the blood. When he straightened, he held a smeared and crumpled square of paper between two fingers.

The handwriting was the same as the first note. *Meet us in Qais.*

PART III

Come to Dust

CHAPTER 20

Isyllt slept badly, and was grateful when Asheris woke her. From her aching head and the weight of the stillness outside, however, it was earlier than she'd expected.

"I thought we were leaving at dawn," she said, rubbing grit from her lashes.

"So does everyone else."

"Right." She ground the heels of her hands against her eyes. "I should have become an academic."

She bathed and dressed hastily in the dark; her bags were already packed, the new white silks as well as her freshly laundered old clothes. She might have no need of them in the desert, but she didn't feel like leaving anything behind.

Horses waited for them, mounts and remounts and pack animals. More supplies than Isyllt had expected, until she remembered the wide desolation she'd seen from the road. Her mouth dried thinking about it.

She thought they would slip out without complications, until she saw a cloaked figure waiting by the narrow side gate. Asheris tensed, and Isyllt recognized the unshaven curve of Siddir's jaw in the lantern-light. Siddir drew his hood back, revealing the dark circles shadowing his eyes.

"I'm sorry," he said softly.

Isyllt felt the spell of silence enfold them, shutting out the tactfully incurious guards. She ought to be on the other side as well, but she stayed where she was, studying the toes of her boots.

"She spoke to my family first," Siddir continued. "Once my aunt and sister were involved . . . Well, it would have been that much more difficult to escape."

"When did you find out?" She flinched at the calm in Asheris's voice.

"Just before I left for Kehribar."

"You might have told me."

"I wanted to. I'd planned to, but then I learned of Jirair and the quiet men. If you were a target—"

"Then I was also a liability. Of course." Asheris laughed bitterly.

"I'm sorry," Siddir repeated.

"Don't be. If you weren't so competent, I never would have—"

Loved you.

Isyllt turned away, fists clenching.

"Don't worry," Asheris said, his voice easing. "I understand. We'll work it out somehow, when I return." Utterly reasonable, but she heard the lie. And if she could, Siddir must as well.

She looked up again when their embrace broke, schooling her face into a bland, pleasant mask. Siddir took her hand in both of his; his smile was crooked, ill fitting. "Take care of him."

"I'll do my best."

They left the Court of Lions in silence. Neither of them looked back.

They followed the aqueduct road to the river, where they spent the night waiting for the dawn ferry to carry them across the flooded breadth of the Ash. At a caravanserai on the other side they traded the horses for camels—tall, knobbly legged beasts with alarmingly peaked backs draped in brightly colored tack. Their long faces were bored and imperious, and they grumbled like rheumatic old men as they chewed their cud. Isyllt had read of them but never seen one close; books were poor preparation for the adventure of climbing into the saddle, or their rolling gait. Or the smell.

When their supplies were loaded on the new mounts, they took a moment to refill their water skins and consult the map. "Where is Qais?" Isyllt asked around a mouthful of fig.

"Here, somewhere." Asheris tapped an unmarked section of map. "On the edge of Al-Reshara, by the Sarcophagus Mountains. It's thought to be a ruin, like Hajar or Irim."

"Irim. You've mentioned it before."

"A dead city. Nearly a legend now. I'll tell you the story sometime."

They left the green banks of the Ash early that morning, riding through a narrow strip of scrubby brush and grassland. They passed painted dogs and grazing goats, some attended by goatherds, others roaming wild. Vultures traced lazy spirals across the sky.

Once they startled a terror bird, another creature Isyllt had only read of in bestiaries. As it rose from its meal of an unlucky goat, she was glad of the camel's height; the bird was taller than any man, with a wicked bone-snapping beak. It let out a startled *kweh* and unfurled clawed rust-red wings. The camels whistled angrily in turn. They eyed each other for a long moment before the bird decided they were no threat to its lunch.

The last green ended abruptly, giving way to flat red rock. Ahead, lost in the heat-shimmer, lay the desolate sprawl of Al-Reshara, the sand sea. Without the river's cooling influence, the west wind became the breath of a furnace. Isyllt had thought she understood the desert summer from the journey to Ta'ashlan. She realized now how wrong she'd been.

Heat bound her brow with iron, a heavy band slowly tightening. Asheris had shown her how to wrap her scarf into a turban, to retain moisture and keep her head from baking, but after an hour she was sure her skull would crack, letting her brains sizzle like eggs on a griddle. Her veil kept sand out of her teeth, but she envied the camels their heavy-lidded, long-lashed eyes. She pulled at her water skin while the wind dried her sweat before she could feel the damp.

They paused just after noon by the dubious shade of a scrubby acacia thicket. Asheris braved the sun to prepare a midday meal: tea and sweet sesame cakes for energy, olives and briny cheese to replenish lost salt. Isyllt shuddered at the first swallow of honeyed tea, and had to fight not to drain the cup at once. The heat left her with little appetite, though, and she shared half the cake with her camel.

The heat was too fierce for proper sleep, but she dozed against an acacia, heedless of the thorns. The horizon shimmered and bled, earth and sky melting into one simmering liquid. No wonder the Unconquered Sun reigned here; what else could rival that fury?

And that was only the first day.

They traveled early in the day and early at night, resting at noon and moonset. They rarely spoke; words dried and died on Isyllt's tongue, and silence was kinder. The rhythm lulled her into an uneasy slumber—creaking leather, the camels' deep breath, the whispering sibilance of sand. She grew accustomed to the camel's gait, to folding her legs around the wooden saddle, to the dry pungency of dung and sun-warmed wool. The heat was a revelation every day.

Asheris thrived. He kept his head covered to protect tender human skin, but every so often he raised his face to the blistering sun, drinking down its fire. He glowed with it. Once she woke from a doze to see his four burning wings unfolding behind him, but the vision vanished when she blinked.

"You said you'd tell me the story of Irim," she said on the third night, smearing camel grease on her cracked lips. She didn't like to use it in front of the camels, but the tent flaps were closed, saving her from their disapproving stares. Concern for dromedary sensibilities was probably a sign of incipient sun fever.

"I did." In the witchlit shadows of the tent, his face was leaner than usual, fierce and sharp-set. Only the desiccating heat, perhaps, but Isyllt imagined she could see his human façade burning away day by day. His brow creased for a moment, soothing again when he began to speak.

"Once, hundreds of years ago—before the warrior-queen Assar was even born, before men built churches to the Unconquered Sun—the Aal ruled the desert. Al-Reshara was smaller, then, surrounded by green, and the Aal girdled the sand with their cities: Hajar, Irim, Qais, Chât. Caravans traveled the length of the kingdom, laden with gold and incense—the Smoke Road, the route was called.

"The marvel of Aaliban, however, was not its wealth or armies or towered cities. Humans and spirits lived together there, if you can believe such heresy—trading, trysting, studying. Mortal and jinn scholars mapped the heavens, while the ghuls tunneled to the bones of the earth and rakkash physicians learned the intricacies of blood and bone and soul.

"It couldn't last, of course. No one is sure quite what happened, or whose fault it was. The humans blamed the jinn, and the jinn blamed the mortals in turn. Perhaps the ghuls or the rakkash remember better, but if so they don't speak of it.

"Wherever the fault lay, we do remember this: As they studied the stars, astronomers in Irim found something in the heavens, a wandering comet carrying a presence they'd never before encountered. They tried to communicate with it, and at last performed a summoning to draw the wanderer near.

"It worked."

"What happened?" Isyllt demanded, when Asheris fell silent for too long.

He shrugged, eyes glittering like citrines in the golden light. "They died. All right, all right!" He raised a placating hand as she threatened to throw the camel grease at him. "We don't know what that comet carried with it as it fell, but it was alien to us, and hungry.

"The weight of the falling sky leveled Irim, and turned the erg into the Sea of Glass. Mortals died by the thousands. Men and spirits both died when the hungry things—Al-Jodâ'im, they were later named—crawled out of the rubble. They were...the void incarnate. Cold, formless, killing with a touch. Where they went, entropy followed. According to the legend, they birthed the ghost wind. The destruction spreading from Irim threw all of Aaliban into chaos and destroyed the Smoke Road. Khemia remained fragmented and lawless for centuries, until Queen Assar came to power."

"And what happened to these things, Al-Jodâ'im?"

"Legend says they were finally bound, but the binding destroyed the last fragile peace between men and jinn. Jinn claim human perfidy, of course, and I'm sure mortals say the same of us. Either way, it's become a parable against contact between flesh and Fata."

"Is it true?"

"In part, at least, I think it must be. I've heard too many versions with the same heart."

Silence filled the tent, while the camels snored outside. Asheris stared for a time into the middle distance, while his witchlight danced in lazy spirals over his head.

"I had forgotten this story. I had forgotten so much—like a shroud drawn over my past. Ahmar's curse burned it away. I'll have to thank her before she dies."

The light vanished. "Rest," Asheris said, rising and opening the tent flap. Starlight kissed his skin with silver. "We go farther still tomorrow."

CHAPTER 21

Adam woke to heat and pain, red shadows and light. He winced at the brightness and closed his eyes, hoping he hadn't ended up in a Mortificant hell of fire and agony. He'd always hoped for a soothing afterlife. And he'd never imagined that death would feel like losing a fight—though now that he thought of it, that's exactly what it would be.

Blinking away tears, he looked again. The red shadow was rock—sandstone, streaked pink and grey. He sprawled in the dirt beneath a wind-polished ledge. A line of sun inched up his outstretched legs, scorching the black leather of his boots. His right hand still held his sword, white-knuckled and numb. His fingers cramped when he flexed them. The wrappings had carved raw lines in his palm.

Pain and light were gifts after the aching chill of the abyss. His sword was a better one.

"Lady of Ravens." He didn't realize he spoke until he began to cough. He swallowed phlegm and grimaced, licking chapped lips. The spasm reminded him of the slice across his ribs.

"No," a voice said. "Not ravens. I do appreciate carrion, though."

Not Brenna's voice. Not any human voice.

Adam drew his legs in, sighing at the absence of heat, and levered himself upright. A green-black scorpion the size of his hand skittered away from the movement, sending a shudder crawling the length of his body. He crouched under the low stone ceiling and waited out the pins-and-needles as fresh blood returned to his extremities.

"Where am I?" All he could see ahead was sunlight and dusty sky. He kept his eyes on the dirt, in case the scorpion returned.

"The middle of nowhere," the dry voice said. The voice of stone eroding in the wind, of bones crumbling to chalk; Adam's hackles lifted at the sound. "But no longer the middle of nothing, which is where I found you."

"Who are you?" He crawled out of the shade, pressing a hand to his wounded side. Dried blood plastered his shirt to his skin, flaking and tugging as he moved, but the scab held.

"I'm the one who saved your life. Not that you should thank me for that, since I've only brought you here."

Adam's joints creaked as he straightened. Late morning, closing on noon, and already the sun was a hammer. He stood on a rocky plateau strewn with boulders. Wind and time had carved them into fantastic shapes—arches and pedestals and hulking creatures balanced on spindly legs. Behind him sharp peaks rose against the sky; ahead, the red sand sea stretched toward the horizon. A deadly place—the kind that could kill a man in a day without water. But when he lifted his head to the wind he smelled moisture and cookfires. Someone survived here.

"Why bring me here?" He was alone on the cliff, except for the now-vanished scorpion. If bugs were talking to him, he'd lain in the sun longer than he'd thought.

"You were pointed this way already." The voice came from behind him, and he couldn't stop his startled twitch. "No, stay. You don't need to see me yet."

The shadow spreading at Adam's feet was larger than he could cast alone. He didn't turn, but his muscles twitched and leapt with the effort.

"You attacked little Arha. Bloodied her and made her cry and tried to give chase. That caught my interest."

Arha? Was that Brenna's true name. He kept the question to himself, along with the bitter disbelief that anything could make her cry. But even as he thought it, memory came like a razor stroke: Brenna, blood on her hands and face and unbound hair, weeping over a breech-birthed foal she couldn't save. Had that been a lie too?

"What do you want?" he asked his invisible companion, walking forward to be free of its shadow. The plateau ended yards from where he'd woken, giving way to a steep slope. In the valley below lay a city.

Adam lowered himself to the dirt to keep from being silhouetted against the sky. From his vantage the buildings looked like toys, the models generals used to plan troop movements. The streets were straight and wide, too neat to have grown naturally. Palm trees lined the avenues, shaded fountains and rectangular pools. Mudbrick houses clustered away from taller stone buildings, and on the far side a stunted orchard grew beside a pond. Nothing about it seemed natural, from the neat dimensions of the pond to the grand architecture in what seemed no bigger than a small desert village.

The smell of smoke was clearer now, and the sharp grassy scent of a stable. He saw movement in the distant orchard, but the streets were empty. Worse than empty—lonely, desolate. Haunted.

"Qais," he whispered.

"Yes." The voice was beside him again, once more staining him with its shadow. "The child Arha stole is held here, and this is where they mean to bring your necromancer."

"Why?"

The shadow croaked; it might have been a laugh or a curse. "That I am forbidden to say. And forbidden to stop. Bringing you here is all the leash I have to spare. So make the best of it, won't you?"

Adam turned in time to see a dark inhuman shape unravel on the breeze. Then he was alone with the wind and sun, and the scorpion watching him from amongst the stones.

He retreated to the shade for the remainder of the day, arranging a careful truce with the scorpion. He didn't know enough to make a plan, so he spent the hours resting, trying not to think about the moisture leaking out of his skin. Trying and failing not to think of Brenna.

He'd pitied Isyllt once; she could never be free of Kiril, even when the love brought her only pain. At least she'd loved a real man. The woman he'd thought he loved—and later hated—was nothing but a mask. A convenient disguise. But he still smelled her when he closed his eyes.

As dusk fell, a solitary lamplighter kindled the streetlights in the empty city. Adam had counted only a handful of people from his vigil on the cliff, and none of them lingered out of doors. He'd seen villages beset by bandits and demons act this way, but if a threat hid in the mountains, he neither saw nor smelled any trace of it.

When night settled heavy and silent between the walls of the canyon, he began his slow descent. The climb was steep and treacherous, and any incautious step sent rocks and scree hissing down the slope. If the denizens of Qais were so nervous, the hills would be warded and watched.

Disquiet filled him as he neared the valley floor. His ribs burned, and his bad knee ached more than the climb should warrant. He'd snuck into enemy camps before, but now misgivings plagued him with every step. This was suicide. He would die here, leaving Moth and Isyllt alone, and the mocking laughter of a woman who had never existed would follow him into the final darkness.

He'd felt this crushing despair before, he realized, when his hands were slick and shaking. This was the touch of the storm in Sherazad all over again. The ghost wind.

Was this its home? And if it was, what sort of fool was he to walk into it?

The sort who'd been paid for a month of service, and had four days left.

Scents drifted on the breeze: garlic and olive oil; hay and dung; the wetter stench of a human privy. The cloying bitterness of myrrh hung over everything, stronger than a street of temples—that must be what they harvested from the orchard. Human scents were fainter, and he caught no trace of Brenna or Moth.

Hugging the shadows, he prowled a circuit through the

city. Tracks and scent-trails wove paths through the dusty streets. Most led to one hulking central building. It had the look of a small fortress, all high walls and narrow shuttered windows. He saw no defenses, but who knew what magic it contained? No light burned in the windows, and the heavy brassbound doors were shut tight; the wood had been darkened by passing hands, the wide front steps worn in the centers. Crouching sphinxes flanked the entry—only decorative sentries, perhaps, but Adam resolved to avoid them just in case.

Another trail, faint but regular, led directly north from the palace, through a broad field of columns to a tall, stair-stepped building. He wasn't much for religion, but he knew a temple when he saw one. The sight of this one prickled his nape, though he couldn't decide why. At least it didn't have dried blood on the steps. One more place to avoid.

Moving west, he finally encountered light and noise, and another familiar structure: a barracks. Voices trickled from open windows, and occasional laughter. The sound drew him like a siren's lure. The first proof he'd had that Qais was peopled by anything but ghosts.

The next proof was a soft footstep behind him. Downwind. Cursing his distraction, Adam spun, to find himself facing the tip of a sword. Starlight silvered the razored edge, and gleamed in the eyes of the dark man on the other end.

"Good evening," the man said. His voice was dark as well, deep and rumbling in his broad chest. He had more than a handspan of height and reach on Adam, and perhaps three stone of heavy bone and muscle. His Assari was thick with an accent Adam didn't recognize. "You might have announced yourself at the foot of the hill. We do have wards, you know."

Melantha was still weeping when Kash arrived to return her to Qais. She expected questions and scathing jokes, but he carried out her tear-muffled request silently. The cold of between dried her tears.

She went to her own room before finding her mother. Once the blood was sponged away, a bit of paint and powder disguised her swelling lip. If her face was pale as mutton fat jade, well, such a long trip through the void was taxing. When her mask was in place, she went before Nerium and reported her mission successful.

Lies of omission were the second-easiest kind.

She had meant to visit Moth, but now she couldn't stand to face the girl. Instead she retrieved a bottle of wine from the pantry and locked the door of her room behind her. Sadly, holding her liquor was one of the many skills she'd learned over the years—one bottle was enough to warm her blood and melt her frozen tears, but not enough to grant the oblivion she craved.

Vallish mead, the kind Brenna and Ceinn and Adam had drunk together, or a good Celanoran whiskey: Those would get the job done.

Tears slicked her face and dripped off her chin. Wiping her eyes only made them swell faster. *It doesn't matter*, she told herself over and over again. *She's dead. She's dead and the nothing took her and now it's taken him too.*

Or maybe it hadn't. He'd followed her. She'd touched his hand, but couldn't hold on. But he might have fallen out again, back into the light—

Laughter ripped out of her in tearing sobs. "Keep

telling yourself that, *chara*. Believe it with all your heart and you'll make it true."

"You're dead," she spat, forcing the Celanoran lilt out of her voice. Her hands clenched white-knuckled around the empty bottle.

Keep telling yourself that too.

She imagined the arc the bottle would make if she threw it, the satisfying explosion of glass. Instead she opened her hands and let it fall. Glass clunked against the knotted silk rug without breaking. She tapped it with a boot as she rose, sending it skittering across the floor.

Another bottle. Maybe two. Anything to kill the voices. Let Melantha drown—she'd find a new name. A new life.

Take as many names as you like—her mother's voice followed her down the hall, as if Nerium walked beside her—*but this is your life.*

Maybe the first bottle had affected her more than she'd realized; standing in front of the kitchen pantry, she didn't hear the footsteps until they were nearly on her. She spun, a flick of her wrist dropping a blade into her hand.

"My lady." Salah, captain of Qais's guards, raised a placating hand. "I didn't mean to startle you."

"My fault for being distracted." She slipped the knife back into place, nonchalant as if she hadn't nearly gutted him. "Can I help you, Captain?"

"Yes, actually. I'd rather not disturb Lady Kerah. We've captured an intruder."

Sitting in the darkness of his newest cell, Adam tried to think of ways that this was better than the Çirağan. The guards were more pleasant, for one—the man who'd captured him had been quite civil, had even given him water. The quarters were cleaner, though that might not last. The climate was too dry for roaches.

Black humor was all that had kept him sane in the Çirağan, but the wretched miasma of this place soaked the stones and left no room for comedy. How did anyone live here without opening their veins?

This place is a prison for everyone. Some pretend not to see the walls.

Adam flinched from the hollow voice, but he was alone in the room. He sighed and laid his head on his knees. Going mad was one way to pass the time.

He drifted for a time, skirting the edges of sleep, afraid of what dreams waited for him. A change in the light roused him; someone stood outside the door. A key scraped in the rusted lock and light spilled in around a slender silhouette.

"Saints," Brenna whispered. "It is you."

Her eyes were red and raw, cheeks flushed, and the smell of wine filtered through her skin. Had the shadow been telling the truth?

It doesn't matter, he told himself as he stood.

"You know him?" the dark-skinned guard asked. A captain, Adam guessed, from the age and authority on his face, and the ease with which the other guards had deferred to him. A few of them lingered at the far end of the row of cells, pretending not to watch.

"I do. He has more lives than a cat, it seems. Let him go—I'll vouch for his good behavior." She cocked an eyebrow at Adam, daring him to argue. When the guard hesitated, she added, "And I'll explain this to my mother."

"As you wish." Relief flickered across his face, swiftly concealed. "What about his weapons?"

Brenna's eyes narrowed. "Keep those for now, but make sure they're cared for."

Adam frowned, but decided not to argue. *Think of Moth*, he told himself. *Think of the job.*

He followed her out of the guardhouse into the empty street. In the scant light spilling through the door, her eyes glittered as she glanced at him. "Are you going to hit me again?"

His hands tightened, but he kept them at his sides. "No."

"Good. Let's have a drink, then."

She led him into the main building—not past the guardian sphinxes, but through a side door—and through a maze-like twist of stairs and dark hallways. Even his night vision failed in a few black corners, but she moved with the ease of long familiarity.

"You live here?" he asked when they finally reached her rooms. They smelled like her, at least, her and wine; if he'd hoped for any revelations about her true identity, there were none to be found.

"I don't spend much time here. In Qais. Mostly I work abroad." She set a bottle of wine on a small desk and began to unscrew the cork.

"Like Celanor."

Her chin rose. "Among many other places." The wine opened with a pop.

"Where else?"

"Do you really want to know?"

He shrugged. "I'm curious."

She turned away, searching the shelves until she found

a second glass. "Ninaya, northern Assar, Iskar, Andemar—"

"So Andemar wasn't a lie, at least."

"Damn it, Adam." Glass thunked against wood. "It was my job. I remember some of your stories. Don't pretend your hands are clean."

"No. Never that." An apology was more than he could manage, so he held his tongue. She pressed a glass on him and he took it; she waved him toward a chair and he sat. Drinking was a bad idea while he was still dehydrated. He raised the cup anyway. The glass was swirled blue and green, imperfectly balanced and flawed with a dozen tiny bubbles. Pretty, in a magpie way. The wine was dark and dry and burned its way down.

"Brenna—"

She flinched. "Don't call me that. Brenna is dead. I thought you were dead too. How did you get here?"

He lifted one shoulder—the wrong one, he remembered, as the scab on his ribs pulled tight. "It's your magic trick. You tell me."

Her eyes narrowed, lips quirking. She knew, he guessed, about the shadow that had spoken to him on the cliffs, but that was no reason for him to volunteer information. She opened her mouth and shut it again with a frown. When she spoke, it was a different accusation than he'd expected. "You're hurt."

"Just a scratch. You used to be better than that."

"Hah! If I'd wanted you dead, you would be. Let me see."

He wasn't quite proud enough to let a wound fester rather than let her treat it. He stripped off his torn shirt and let her sponge away the blood and grime.

"What is this about?" he asked while she worked. "Kehribar, Moth..."

She discarded the dirty cloth. "Wait a moment—I need bandages." She stepped into a shadowed corner. Even anticipating it, Adam shuddered as she vanished into darkness. She returned a few moments later, from a different shadow this time, carrying folded bandages and jars. The smell of aloe rose from the first one she opened, the sharp blood-metal scent of copper from the next.

"The people I work for want Iskaldur," she said, each word carefully measured. "Her help, that is, not harm. I was sent to make contact. But when I saw you, I panicked." Her jaw tightened with the admission.

"So you kidnapped a child instead of talking?"

"You would have talked, instead of attacking me? It was a mistake," she continued, when he didn't meet her gaze. "But Moth is safe, and so are you—though following me into shadow was stupid, and by all rights you should be dead. Besides—" She nudged his arm away and smeared a cool, rust-red paste along the cut. "Iskaldur will be safer away from Ta'ashlan. The city is a stronghold for the people who want her dead. Be careful with this," she said, changing the subject as she wrapped his ribs. "Qais is... not healthy. Wounds don't always heal as they should."

"What is it? This place."

"It's—" She busied herself with the final knot. "Something very ancient sleeps here. Very dangerous. We—the people I work for—keep it bound."

"And that's why you want Isyllt."

She nodded. "Not that I understand the details. I'm just a spy."

He'd finished his wine while she worked—he set the cup aside before she could refill it. "What should I call you, if not Brenna?"

Her mouth twisted, and she rose and turned to the window. "I've been using Melantha lately, but it still doesn't fit. Like a pair of boots that never quite break in."

The shutters opened with a soft squeak, and cool night air filled the room. Adam hadn't realized how he stifled until the draft touched his face. The heat of the wine, of his wound, the scent of a woman who was friend and enemy and stranger all at once.

"What about a real name?"

"That's long gone." She threw a wry smile over her shoulder. "And I couldn't tell you anyway." She leaned her elbows on the casement and stared out the window. After a long silence, Adam joined her. The night was quiet, dust-faded. The stars ended at a ragged gash where mountains chewed the sky.

"Your hair—" His hand rose, nearly brushing the tousled curls at the nape of her neck. He stopped before he touched her.

"I could say the same to you." Her smile vanished. "The hair was Brenna's. That's how I killed her."

"You can't kill the past."

"Yes, I can." She turned to face him, catching his hand before he could draw it away. "I know because it haunts me."

She leaned against his chest, lifting her face to kiss him. He meant to pull away, but couldn't move. He wished he could blame her magic for that. He also wished he could remember the last time a woman had kissed him sober.

"I can't," he said when she drew back. His voice was rough and strained, and he shuddered like a stung horse.

"What's past is gone. You may hate me, but you still want me. And it helps—a little life to ward off the death in this place."

"The woman I wanted is dead. You said so yourself." But her scent tangled him, kindled heat in the pit of his stomach. Denying it was ridiculous, with her hips pressing against his.

"Does it matter in the dark?"

Yes. But her fingers caught in his hair, pulling his mouth to hers, and the word died unspoken. Beneath the wine, she tasted of blood and grief.

She filled the room with shadows and he was blind. His heart sped; fear did nothing to ease the pulse in his groin. She led him to her bed.

She wasn't the woman he had wanted. That woman had never existed. Brenna had been real to him, if a lie, but she had also been his friend's lover, and faithful within the confines of the lie. The woman who'd visited his dreams and clung to his waking thoughts the way strands of her hair sometimes clung to his sleeve—that woman only ever existed in his mind.

Brenna had been bright and dark and deadly, quicksilver with a blade and just as quick to laugh. It was her laughter that haunted him—her grin, her teasing eyes, her wry chuckles and the rich, raw croak of real humor. A laughing raven girl, and no wonder mercenaries fell at her feet.

The woman in his arms now—Melantha or whatever her true name was—was as sad as anyone he'd ever known. Desire warmed her scent, headier than wine, but no matter how she writhed and sighed at his touch, no matter how wild and strong she moved against him, pinning him to the bed and outpacing his rhythm till his control broke, there was a distance inside her he couldn't touch. When his breath returned he held her down in turn, using tongue and fingers until her climax rippled down the sleek muscles of her thighs. She clung to him, slick and gasping, bruising him with her grip, but even then there was something more she wanted that he couldn't name or give.

He would have given it in that moment if he could. He'd always been quick to lose his wits for women. But he couldn't, no more than he could have eased Isyllt's sorrow, or healed the hurt festering deep beneath Xinai's scars.

Was it easier, as Isyllt suggested, to know he couldn't? To know from the beginning that they would leave, and armor himself with that knowledge? He didn't think it was.

Nice women, Isyllt had said. He laughed, face pressed to the sweaty sheets, and his chest ached with the sound.

CHAPTER 22

Days melted one into another, till Isyllt could barely keep count. The journey wasn't a long one—Asheris estimated sixteen days of travel to the ruins of Irim, and perhaps twice that to Qais, if his maps were accurate—but the rolling waves of the erg was as timeless as the sea. And as beautiful, and as deadly.

Dunes rose and fell, fluted and ruffled by the wind, knife-edged on the leeward side. *Al-Reshara* meant "the red desert," but Isyllt found dozens of colors in the sand: rust, carnelian, ochre and honey and grey, glittering with flecks of quartz and green slivers of glass. The wind blew fine plumes of dust from their peaks, till the desert seemed to smoke and smolder.

Soon she could see the sharp peaks of the Sarcophagus Mountains in the distance, rising from the sand like the bones of some ancient giant, piercing the southwestern sky. Straight ahead lay nothing, only the liquid fire of the dune sea rolling to the horizon. And the sun with its molten unblinking eye. Unconquered. Conquering.

Many of the wells they passed were dry. Since Asheris

barely touched his share of the provisions they were in no danger, but every collapsing hole that had once held water twisted an unhappy knot in Isyllt's stomach. The desert was a killer without par, and in its vastness all her magic was only a tiny spark, so easily snuffed.

Despite the emptiness, sometimes at night her nape prickled with the sensation of watching eyes. Once, waking at dawn, she glimpsed a dark canine shape vanishing into the dunes.

"Jackals," Asheris said when she told him. "Friends, I think."

Asheris told more stories as they rode, stories of the Fata'im—some of sphinxes and ghuls, but most of Mazikeen, the jinn city of fire and glass where he had once dwelled. He spoke of their kings and councils and shining hosts, of their sacred Tree of Sirité, that blossomed into flame every hundred years and was fertilized by its own ashes. He told her of the eyrie of the rukh, where the jinn nursed the last egg of the giant birds, which might hatch a decade or a century or a millennium from now.

"Can you never go back?" she asked one day, as he brewed their midday tea. "What happened to you was hardly your choosing."

"No. But if I'd chosen to obey the Flames' injunctions, I would never have been captured. And while I don't know the truth of the break between men and the Fata'im, both sides have become equally immovable."

"We could stay here," he said that night, as they lay in the darkness outside the tent.

The moon had set and their campfire died, leaving no rivals for the stars. Isyllt had never seen a sky like this, the depthless black paved in jewels, ruby and topaz and brilliant diamonds. A dark ribbon bisected the firmament like a banner of smoke. The Mother of Heaven, Asheris named it, the great serpent who laid the first clutch of jinn eggs and breathed her fire into them.

"Here?"

"The desert. Leave men and their intrigues behind forever. Forget Qais and Ta'ashlan."

"You'd miss the theater."

It didn't earn the chuckle she'd hoped for, and she turned to watch him. Starlight filled his eyes and bathed his face. His beauty caught in her throat, and for a wild instant she would have agreed to anything. She held her breath until the foolish impulse suffocated. The dunes hissed softly around them, punctuated by the camels' snores.

"You're serious," she said at last. Sand rasped as she rolled over; despite her veils, grains caught in her hair and itched against her scalp.

"Why not? There's nothing for me there." He gestured to the east. "Nothing but heartache and eventual exile."

"Maybe not, but I don't believe you'd last long as a hermit. I know I wouldn't. And Qais has Moth and Adam—I can't abandon them."

"No, I suppose not. Human bonds are hard to break."

Isyllt shoved herself up. "Horseshit. Friendship is hardly a mortal foible. Not according to your stories. If it were you held prisoner on the other side of the desert, I wouldn't abandon you. You of all people should respect that."

He rose, more graceful on the shifting sand than she could ever hope to be. The fey light dimmed in his eyes, leaving the man she knew. "You're right. I'm sorry." He took her hand and kissed it, heedless of clinging dust. "We'll find your friends, I promise. I can always contemplate a hermitage after that."

She wished she thought he was joking.

The next day the sun poured fire and the wind only worsened the heat. Asheris kept his veil pulled tight, and more than once glanced unhappily toward their backtrail.

"What's wrong?" Isyllt asked. The wind stung her face; even veils and aloe and camel grease couldn't protect her from the sun. Her skin dried and lips cracked, and a few unguarded moments scattered throughout the day were enough to leave her nose pink and peeling and her eyelids tender. It wasn't yet noon—the desert always gave her something to look forward to.

"We're being followed. By something besides jackals."

She twisted in her saddle, sitting up straight and shielding her eyes. "Wouldn't we have seen them by now?"

Dust dulled the horizon, blurred the line between earth and sky. Her eyes tingled as she sharpened her sight, but she still saw nothing. Except a distant glint to the southeast that might have been sunlight on metal. She couldn't tell if it moved.

"Not if they rode through a wash. It's dangerous, but would keep them off the horizon. The ground hardens into reg closer to the mountains—desert pavement. It would lessen their dust. The desert tribes might travel so, but one of us should have sensed ordinary riders by now."

"The quiet men? Herding us to Qais?"

"Maybe. But Ahmar and your shadow from Kehribar seem to have different ends. Two different factions? A schism in the group? Since one of them wants you dead, this might not be the best time to find out."

"Maybe not. Can we outrun them?"

"If I knew where we were running, we might. Instead, I think I'll enliven their trip a little." He winked, and his magic crackled against Isyllt's skin. The wind rose with it. "Cover your eyes."

The wind strengthened, dimming the sky with dust—a smoky amber veil drawn across the sun. Isyllt drew her own veils over her face till she was all but blind, but still fine particles stung her eyes and crunched between her teeth. Once called, the wind took on a life of its own. They sped the camels to escape it, but the storm nipped at their heels even as it churned east.

"Something's wrong," Asheris said, raising his voice above the roar. "They're trying to turn the storm against me."

Isyllt was no weather witch, but as she stretched her senses toward the gale, she felt a second presence riding the wind, darker and colder than Asheris's familiar fiery magic. "Now what?"

"Now we try running."

The camels ran swiftly, surprisingly graceful on their long knobbly legs, but they couldn't outrun the sandstorm. The air grew thick and hot, earth and sky bleeding together, and the wind drew sparks from their clothes and the camels' hides. At last their mounts refused to go on and folded themselves to the ground, turning their backs to the wind and shutting their long-lashed eyes.

"They're wiser than we are," Asheris said, shoving Isyllt down into the shelter of her camel's leeward side. Dragging a tent from the saddle packs, he crouched beside her, draping the canvas over them and tucking it beneath their legs and the animals'. Fabric snapped in the wind, and sparks jumped and crackled like angry fireflies with every movement. The enclosed air was hotter than an oven; the camel's flesh behind her was cool in comparison.

They sat enfolded in pungent dromedary musk, broken by the occasional green whiff of cud. The sour, woolly smell had grown familiar over the past decad, very nearly comforting. The rush of the storm drowned even Isyllt's thoughts, lulling her toward sleep. But from under that din another sound grew: a low, fervent drumming.

"What is that noise?" Isyllt asked at last, wincing as her lips cracked on the words.

"Sand. I hope."

"What else would it be?"

"Stories tell of the zar, spirits of the wind who hold their revels during sandstorms. The sound of their drums is said to drive men mad with desire, till they leave their shelters and dance to their deaths in the sand. But by the time of my hatching, the jinn had seen no zar for decades." His eyes gleamed as he glanced at Isyllt. "You don't feel like dancing, do you?"

"You'll know the moment I do."

The drumming finally faded, with Isyllt's feet having done nothing more treacherous than fall asleep beneath her. The howl of the storm died to a sibilant whisper. As the tension finally began to bleed from her limbs, a deep chuffing breath shook the stillness.

The camel behind her startled, lowing in concern, and Isyllt toppled forward on her hands and knees. Asheris hissed, one hand closing on her arm.

"That wasn't sand," Isyllt whispered. "Or a jackal."

"No." His mouth compressed to a bloodless line. "I think it's time we were on our way."

Warm sand cascaded over them as they drew the canvas aside, sifting into Isyllt's shirt and boots. The air was a swirling orange cloud of unsettled dust, the sun a dull white disk overhead. Isyllt could barely see past her camel's nose as she clambered into the saddle.

The growl sounded again, an echoing cough. She couldn't tell what direction it came from, but it was much too close.

"It sounds like a lion," Asheris said, his voice low. "But... bigger."

Whatever prowled the dunes was no ordinary flesh-and-blood beast. Isyllt's nape prickled under sweaty hair, the familiar shiver that meant a powerful spirit was near. The camels, usually stoic and unflappable, shuddered with tension, eager to be away from the predator.

She thought they traveled west—hard to be certain, with the sun vanished behind clouds of sand. The camels shifted from their usual rolling walk to a bone-jarring canter, and then to a gallop. Not as fast as a horse could run, but their long legs devoured the distance. Isyllt set her teeth and clung to the saddle.

The beast kept pace. Once she glimpsed a sleek dark shadow loping beside them, but it vanished into the haze once more. Her camel veered away, gaining speed.

"It's herding us," she shouted to Asheris.

The smallest pack camel, also the lightest-burdened, took the lead. Soon only her tail was visible, crackling with sparks in the charged air. Asheris followed close behind, with Isyllt at his heels and the last two pack beasts at the rear. She expected their hunter to strike at the slowest camel. Instead it surged ahead to intercept the mare.

Isyllt saw it move, but had only a heartbeat to draw breath before flesh struck flesh. The camel screamed, shrill and lingering, and the smell of blood filled the air. Cursing, she tried to rein in her mount, but its momentum was too great. They avoided colliding with Asheris, but tangled in the thrashing legs of the wounded mare. Her camel shrieked and toppled, throwing Isyllt to the red-stained sand. Dazed and breathless, she rolled aside as its bulk came crashing after.

Dusty air billowed in the wake of a giant paw, retractable claws flashing inches from her eyes. Blood sprayed hot against her face and a camel screamed once more. Isyllt couldn't scream—her throat locked tight with terror, stomach twisting into an icy knot as predator musk washed over her.

Asheris's outflung arm knocked the rest of her breath away as he tackled her. Hands closed in her robe, dragging her away. "Run!"

Fire surged between them and the beast, singeing her lungs as she inhaled. The creature roared through the flames. The sound echoed through Isyllt's sternum and down her spine, filling her bowels with ice water. Instinct took hold, primal prey-fear, and she ran.

Glancing over her shoulder, she nearly ran straight into the shadow that loomed in front of her. She threw up her hands, scraping her palms on warm stone. A pillar, worn and pitted, rising from the dunes. They had reached the edge of a forest of broken columns.

"Climb," Asheris said, crouching and cupping his hands. "We won't outrun that."

To prove his point, the beast roared again and leapt, singeing its underbelly in the fire. Isyllt planted one boot in Asheris's hands and let him heave her upward. Her good hand closed on the lip of a crumbling architrave and she hung for an instant, cursing breathlessly. She hooked her other hand over the edge in an awkward two-fingered grip and pulled. One flailing foot found a toehold, then the other, and she scrambled up. Her nails splintered on stone, and the shoulder she'd hurt in Sherazad burned angrily once more. Clinging to the top on her belly, she looked down in time to shout helplessly as the lion-creature pounced on Asheris.

A blow from one shovel-size paw sent him sprawling, trailing blood across the ground. He sprang up and flung a handful of sand, which ignited as it struck the beast. The creature roared and swatted the sparks aside like gnats.

Isyllt dragged her belt knife free of its sheath, nearly disemboweling herself in the process. Not her demon-killing kukri—that, damn her own stupidity, was still hanging from her camel's saddle—but it would have to do. Steel didn't hold energy as well as silver, but the blade still glowed white as she poured magic into it. The metal would rust and shatter with sustained exposure, but she only needed it to last a moment.

The angle was bad and the set of her wrist even worse—Adam would have sighed to see it. All the same, she hit what she aimed at. The blade bounced off the monster's flank, but its snarl of pain assured her she'd drawn blood. Its right rear leg buckled as death-magic sank into preternatural flesh. The effect wouldn't last long from a slight wound, but an instant's distraction was all Asheris needed.

His wings burst free, incandescent in the gloom. Three powerful downbeats carried him to the top of the column beside Isyllt's, where he alit much more gracefully than she had.

"A manticore," he breathed. "I thought none were left in the desert."

Isyllt drew herself to her knees, shaking despite the heat. "What an opportunity for us, then. Can you fly us out of here?"

"I would love nothing more, but I'm afraid not." She couldn't see his face, but his voice was strained. "The manticore's tail isn't the only place it keeps its poison."

"How bad is it?"

"I'll recover, but the venom is in my blood. Wounds from the Fata'im last longer than ordinary injuries. It may take a few hours to heal."

"I'll try to keep my balance that long."

The manticore paced below them, growling and chuffing angrily, before it finally turned its attention back to the camels. Isyllt closed her eyes as their mounts bleated and wheezed and fell silent. The sound of ripping flesh that followed was almost an improvement.

The wind died and the dust settled, giving Isyllt her first clear view of the manticore. It had the body of a lion, but closer in size to a draft ox. Its head was neither cat nor man—maned in black, with saucer-size lantern eyes and a mouth thrice as wide as any human's. Blood-red hide glistened in the afternoon sun, and a scorpion's barbed tail arched behind it. Isyllt had only seen its like in illustrations, none of which had prepared her to be caught in its yellow stare.

The lull also let her study their surroundings. Columns rose from the sand like broken teeth. The desert had worn away their carvings, but a few ghostly engravings remained: stylized figures, some human, others winged and bestial. Here and there a ridge of wall broke the surface of the erg, suggesting a wide courtyard, and to the north she saw a shattered cupola. The sand itself glowed in the heavy amber light, strewn with glittering shards of glass, darkly iridescent as beetles' wings.

"The Sea of Glass?" Isyllt asked. Her dry tongue scraped over chapped lips and she spat metallic grit. The manticore's ears twitched at her voice, but it didn't lift its head from its meal of camel innards.

"Yes." Asheris's face was drawn and ashen. He kept his torn, bloody back turned away, but she had glimpsed the four deep rents in cloth and flesh; dark stains dried on the stone beneath him. "And these must be the ruins of Irim."

She had expected more from his stories, some sense of destruction or magic gone awry—Erisín was full of such places. Here, though, nothing pricked her outstretched senses. The ruin was silent, empty. Even the sounds of the manticore's meal and her own breath fading into the stillness echoing from Irim. A perfect desolation.

Isyllt shuddered as her awareness snapped back into her flesh. Too perfect. This place would erase her if she let it.

When it had licked the last scraps of camel from its face, the manticore rose and sauntered closer. Its shadow was red, thinner than those cast by the pillars; it would grow more solid with each kill, Isyllt guessed. Its pupils shrank to pinpricks in the light.

"I can reach you up there, you know." Its voice reverberated through its chest. *His* chest, Isyllt supposed, from the mane. He splayed one man-killing paw and chewed delicately at the webbing between his toes.

"I'm sure you can." She wasn't sure, but also wasn't about to antagonize him. Her pillar was twice her height—the manticore might be taller if he stretched.

"I'm full, you see, and neither of you looks especially tasty. But I wouldn't want you to think yourselves *safe*."

"Rest assured, the thought never crossed my mind." She'd pried a fist-size chunk of sandstone from the cracked architrave. It would be a ludicrous weapon against such a monster, but its weight steadied her.

"Although—" The manticore circled Asheris's perch, rubbing his massive head and shoulder against the stone; the pillar held, but sand sifted from its cracks. "I smell the fire in you. A taste of that might be worth a little effort. Why are you wearing that ridiculous ape-suit?"

Asheris lifted his head from his knees. "We all have our prisons. Our peoples have no quarrel, man-eater."

The manticore snorted, and a growl rumbled inside him. "I have no people, jinni. I have been trapped for centuries, and when I am allowed out to hunt and feed I find no trace of my kind on the wind." His segmented tail couldn't lash, but swayed menacingly over his back.

"We could help you search," Asheris said, "if you were to let us down."

The manticore chuffed again. "I don't trust bone-stealing mortal witches, nor anyone who hides in a man-suit. The wretched ape who holds my prison ordered me to slay you or trap you. Having done so, I wait for him.

If you tire of waiting, come down and I will eat you, but spare me your pleas and pathetic bargains."

With that, the beast threw himself down in the sand and closed his eyes.

The light deepened, as did Isyllt's thirst, and their shadows stretched farther across the sand. Perhaps two or three hours of daylight remained. The heat left her brittle and light-headed, detached from her own limbs as if she stared down at a broken doll. She felt the loss of the camels more keenly than anything, and would have wept if she'd had moisture to spare.

Despite Asheris's reassurances, he looked no better. Isyllt didn't relish the idea of a night spent perched like a wing-clipped bird, and neither did her bladder. She wasn't quite uncomfortable enough yet to brave the manticore, but that might happen soon.

The sight of their water skins tangled in the dead camels' tack mocked her. She'd been happy at first to realize the other three mounts had escaped; now all she could think of was the wealth of water in their packs, vanishing into the desert. She was considering increasingly ridiculous plans to reach the supplies—most involving daring acrobatics that she couldn't have managed at fifteen, with two good hands—when movement on the horizon distracted her.

A line of camels ambled toward them through the heat-shimmer, carrying a dozen riders. From the glitter of metal, Isyllt guessed them all armed. The manticore's ears twitched and his broad nostrils flared, but he only rolled over to follow a shifting stripe of sun.

Distance was deceptive in the desert. The riders vanished behind dunes and appeared again, constantly in motion but never seeming any nearer. By the time Isyllt heard their creaking harnesses and whuffing breath, she'd begun to think them an elaborate mirage.

They reined in a safe distance from the manticore, which lay still save for the sullen click of his tail. One man, apparently the leader, knelt his camel and dismounted. At his gesture, two others followed, reluctance showing in every stride. Behind them, a handful of men leveled rifles and waited. Isyllt recognized none of them, but from Asheris's sharp indrawn breath she guessed he did.

"What's this?" the leader asked, pulling his veil aside. The face below was weathered bronze, creased now in amusement. A patch hid his left eye—from the ridged scars trailing from brow to chin, Isyllt doubted anything remained beneath it. He wore a sword across his back, and a heavier scimitar hung from his saddle. "Pillar saints? I didn't know you were an ascetic, al Seth."

"And I never knew you were a lackey of the church."

"Don't be silly." He touched a rayed sun charm hanging against his breast. "I've always been a pious man. I was a loyal soldier, too. A pity your empress didn't understand that." His dark eye flickered toward Isyllt. "But who's your companion? We haven't been properly introduced."

"Where are my manners?" Asheris drawled. "Isyllt, this is Samael Hamad, formerly a general in the imperial army. Now a bandit and petty thief. And this is the Lady Iskaldur—you've tried to kill her once already."

Hamad swept a bow. "Don't make it sound so personal, al Seth. You know it's nothing of the sort."

"An interesting pet you have. A present from Ahmar?"

"Yes. Beautiful, isn't he?" He lifted his eye patch and something glittered in the hollow beneath his brow. Isyllt pressed her tongue against her teeth as she recognized the sharp-edged tingle of a diamond.

"Who knows how long he sat in Ahmar's jewelry box." Hamad tossed the diamond and caught it one-handed. The stone was a fine one—large as the iris of his missing eye and yellow as a citrine. "He was eager to stretch his legs."

The manticore didn't move, but Isyllt caught the flicker of his eyes as he tracked the stone's movement. A clever sorcerer could wield a stone without touching it; despite the powerful charms thrumming around Hamad's neck, she didn't think he was a mage. Not for the first time, she wished her magic had manifested in psychokinesis.

"Now that you've exercised your pet, are you going to leave us up here till we desiccate?" Isyllt asked. From the effort the words cost her, desiccation was already well under way.

Hamad smiled. "Actually, I planned to have my men shoot you down and feed you to the manticore."

She tilted her head wryly. "That is a more practical solution, yes." Her fingers tightened around the rock. She would only have one chance.

Hamad lifted his fist in a signal, the diamond still clenched in his palm. Asheris stirred, but Isyllt didn't watch him—instead she released a breath and a prayer and let her stone fly.

Her aim was true. Hamad shouted in pain as the rock struck his upraised fist. His fingers opened and the diamond traced a glittering arc through the air, vanishing into the glass-strewn sand. He dropped, rolled, and came to his feet with his sword drawn.

The manticore rose in a sinuous stretch. Muscles clenched along its blood-red sides as it began a slow *chuff-chuff-chuff*.

"Fire!" Hamad cried.

Fire answered. A wave of flame rolled across the sand, eclipsing the sunset sky. Isyllt gasped as its heat rolled over her. The thunder of guns carried through the crackling flames.

Her breath left in a rush as a hammerblow struck her left shoulder. She rocked back, and the world became a hot orange blur. Blinking, she looked down to see blood soaking the white cloth on her shoulder.

She reached, unthinking. Bone grated against bone and her vision washed white. Vertigo ripped the world out from under her—a heartbeat later she realized she was truly falling. Then she wasn't. She was no longer conscious either.

CHAPTER 23

Isyllt woke to the sound of teeth on bone.

She couldn't decide if the bones were hers or not; she didn't want to open her eyes to find out. The air stank of blood and burning, but the wind was cool against her skin. After a moment the growls and splintering crunch paused. Slow footsteps crunched the sand. The wind stopped, blocked by something large and warm.

"I know you're awake, bone-thief," the manticore said, hot charnel breath wafting across her face. "I hear your heart speeding." It must have been a conversational voice for him, but every word rumbled through Isyllt's bones. The vibration woke the pain in her left shoulder, and tears rinsed the grit from her eyes.

The manticore's face hung over hers, yellow eyes narrowed lazily. Whiskers flattened against his cheeks as he bared his teeth—more teeth than Isyllt had ever seen in one place, and she'd once dissected a shark. Her bladder cramped in terror before she realized he was smiling. A low rumbling chuckle shook his mane.

"I was going to eat you," he said casually, lowering his

head to his paws. She could taste his bloody breath. "Out of principle, you understand. But a pair of jackals came and asked me not to. They were very polite." He licked his paws with a barbed tongue as broad as Isyllt's face.

"As you said before, I doubt I'm very tasty." She wanted very badly to sit up, but the manticore's white claws flexed in the sand only a finger's length from her arm. His tail arched over his back, the poison tip gleaming in the starlight. "What about my friend?"

His nostrils flared. "Since when are jinn and witches friends?"

"For several years, in our case. I can't speak for others. Is he—"

"I didn't eat him, if that's what you're asking. The jackals were very insistent. And I'm full of foolish ape soldiers. They attacked me, you know, with their bullets and little steel fangs. It was charming."

Isyllt glanced at her shoulder. Turning her head woke fire across her sternum and crazed the blood dried across her chest and shoulder. Thinking of the wound too long left her queasy; she could feel the lead lingering in her flesh, poisoning her and weakening her magic. "I'm sorry I missed it. And Hamad?"

"I ate him first." His eyes narrowed, pupils flashing like embers. "If you search for the stone, not all the polite jackals in the desert will save you. Do you understand me?" His paw fell on her right hand, grinding it into the sand. Muscles flexed in his pads and one claw-tip pierced her skin. He could take her arm off at the shoulder before she could scream.

"The stone is yours," she said, voice steady. "I am in your debt, after all. Besides—I only bind my own kind."

He snorted, ruffling her tangled veils. "Witches. Vile creatures, all of you." The beast stood, stretching and shaking his mane. "And speaking of witches and debt...The one who bound me is likely bones and dust by now, in the manner of your kind. But should you find the one who gave me to those soldier apes, kill her. That will resolve the debt you owe me."

"I'll make every effort to do so."

With another derisive snort, he turned and loped into the darkness.

When he had vanished, Isyllt let out a heavy breath. Instantly she regretted it. She tried to inspect the wound, but turning her head was agony, and moving her right shoulder fanned the pain in the left. Her magic broke and died against the shards of lead when she tried to numb the wound. She would need a second set of hands to remove the bullet, and a bottle of strong whiskey.

"Asheris?" Her voice cracked on his name, and the effort not to cough nearly made her faint again. He didn't answer. Nothing answered, save the soft keening of the wind over broken stone.

The somnolence of Irim surrounded her, seeping into her skin. She wanted nothing more than to lie in the cooling sand and sleep. But dawn would bring the killing sun, and likely vultures. Would they be as polite as jackals?

Sit up, rig a sling, find Asheris: It was a good plan, soothing in its simplicity. Now she just needed the strength to implement it.

Before she gathered her resolve, a shiver spread across her skin. Magic was coming. Powerful magic. Something wrenched, a snag in the fabric of the world. The sensation echoed in her chest and she shuddered. The wind shifted, rushing past her toward the intrusion. Pain blinded her as she tried to look; through a blur of tears she saw a deeper black eclipse the stars. It vanished with a pop she felt instead of heard.

"Saints," a woman said, dry-voiced and sharp. "What happened?"

"A fight, it seems." If the woman's voice was dry, this was a drought. The hair on Isyllt's arms prickled—she knew that voice.

"Something ate these men," said a second woman. "Ate them and burned them, though maybe not in that order." Footsteps paused. "I found al Seth."

"Alive?" the first woman asked.

Isyllt held her breath in the pause that followed. "Yes. Saints only know how, with this many bullets in him. He's unconscious."

"Good. We'll need to restrain him before he wakes. Kash, you aren't to speak to him. What about Iskaldur?"

"Here."

Isyllt couldn't stop her flinch. The dry voice was right beside her, but she'd heard no one approach. She risked a glance through her lashes, but couldn't make sense of it. The shadow standing above her was tall and gaunt, but the head wasn't right, or the number of limbs. It chuckled once, a sound like gravel breaking, and she knew it saw through her feigned sleep.

"She only collected one bullet. There are no other survivors."

"Bring her. Gently, if you please. We can come back for their supplies—no point in leaving them for the vultures."

Cold hands slid beneath Isyllt's legs and shoulders. A moan scraped through her gritted teeth.

"Is she awake?" the first woman asked.

"I don't think so," the shadow—Kash?—lied. "She's lost too much blood and water for that."

Why did he lie for her? A memory rose, dream-faded. *We have so much in common.*

The wrenching magic came again. A sundering like she'd never felt before. A knife through the skin of the world. Cold bled from the wound, numbing her deeper than her magic ever could. It stole pain, stole thought, and left only darkness behind.

When the dark receded she was supine once more, on a bed instead of sand. A wet cloth wiped her face and throat, leaking rivulets of moisture that soaked into her hair and puddled in the hollows of her collarbones. Her mouth opened automatically as the water brushed her lips, desperate for any stray drops.

"Easy," a woman said. The woman from Irim. Beneath the white brilliance of witchlight, she was a grey-and-white blur. "Don't move—I haven't taken the bullet out yet."

That was all the caution Isyllt needed. "Where—" The word was an ugly croak, unrecognizable as speech.

"Here, chew this. Slowly." The woman pressed something against her lips. A bit of date, shockingly sweet.

Isyllt obeyed, careful not to bite her swollen tongue. Her shoulder objected to chewing as much as it did to breathing, coughing, and moving, but the relief of even the slightest moisture was stronger than the pain.

Water followed the fruit, a teasing trickle that was still

enough to make her choke. The woman held her good shoulder down when Isyllt would have lunged for the cup.

"Carefully," she cautioned. "Drinking too fast will make you retch."

"Thank you," Isyllt whispered after three proper mouthfuls. Her vision cleared enough to make out her rescuer—an older woman, white-haired and robed in white. Another necromancer? "Who are you?" The shape of the words felt strange, and she realized they were speaking Selafaïn.

"Nerium Kerah. You've come to Qais, though not as intact as I'd wished."

"Qais. Moth—"

"Is here, yes, and safe. And you're due an explanation for that, and an apology. But first I need to take this bullet out of you."

It seemed impractical to argue with that. "How bad is it?"

"The ball cracked the clavicle and lodged there. If it had turned down, it would likely have severed the artery here." She tapped the hollow below the bone, and Isyllt winced. "Once I remove the lead, setting the bone should be simple. Do you want to watch?"

Isyllt snorted. "Not particularly."

"Then close your eyes. This won't be pleasant."

"This would go better if you'd stop fighting me, you know," Kerah said later, as she wrapped Isyllt's shoulder to hold it straight. The movement tugged the neat black stitches tracing her clavicle.

Isyllt coughed and wished she hadn't. "I'm not fighting. I don't think I could."

"Not effectively, no. But I mean your magic."

Frowning, she closed her eyes and turned her attention inward. Sure enough, the other woman's magic lapped at her skin, spiraling toward the wound and the fracture below. She sensed no malice in it, but her own power responded automatically, trying to force the intruder out as it would an invading illness or infection. The confrontation itched and tingled unpleasantly—in her daze she'd mistaken it for the injury's natural discomfort.

"What are you doing?"

Kerah's eyebrow twitched again. She was very fair for a Khemian; from the shape of her cheeks and nose Isyllt guessed she had northern blood. Her hair was white and silver, cropped close to a square face. Age softened her throat and creased her skin her skin fragile as crepe, but she must have been striking once. No, Isyllt corrected herself as the woman's pale eyes met hers—she was still striking.

"I'm healing you, of course." The eyebrow climbed higher as Isyllt blinked. "I know they have healing mages in Erisín."

"Yes, but I mostly only saw anixeroi physicians." Her left hand twitched—an Arcanost healer had overseen that surgery, but provided no miracles. "I'm... resistant to healing magic."

"You're resistant to many things, I'm sure. It's instinct. And like any instinct, it can be overridden."

"Oh," Isyllt said cleverly.

Nerium snorted. "And the Arcanost calls itself the pinnacle of thaumaturgical education. If you can keep your magic from interfering with mine, the bone might heal in a few decads. Otherwise it will take months."

"I'll see what I can do."

Nerium turned to wash her hands, and Isyllt tugged her sheet higher over her chest. Her shirt had been cut away, and the thin linen bedding did little to ward off the chill. The room was high and wide, the door decorated with brass. The furniture was expensive, but everything but the bed and table holding Nerium's supplies was lightly filmed in dust. A breeze drifted over the casement, but a sluggish staleness lingered in the air. No one had lived here for a long time.

"Now what?" she asked, cradling a cup of water in her good hand.

"Now you rest. I'll send someone with food and clothes. And a bath," she added, eyeing the filthy, blood-stained ruin of Isyllt's shirt where it lay on the floor. "After that, you can see your friends."

A memory rose, Nerium's voice in the darkness: *Restrain him before he wakes*. Isyllt's jaw tightened. "Where is Asheris?"

"He's here as well. He was badly injured, but I imagine he'll mend. His kind tend to."

He'd shared his fears that Quietus knew his nature; having them confirmed was still unsettling.

"You said something about an explanation, as well."

"I did, didn't I?" Nerium's thin lips quirked. "That too, then."

CHAPTER 24

Despite her resolution to stay alert, Isyllt dozed after Nerium left. She woke when silent servants arrived with the promised food and water and clothing. Her own clothing, no less, though not all of it. Having seen the disemboweled camel, she wasn't inclined to complain; viscera stains weren't worth scrubbing. They dusted as well, and changed the bloodstained sheets and musty drapes. The stones felt old and silent, but Isyllt didn't realize just how old until she saw the antiquated plumbing. Bathwater was hauled in buckets to fill a copper tub. Grey water emptied down a narrow drain whose grate was blue with verdigris; other waste required a chamber pot. Hardly an ideal situation with only one arm.

At least she'd already learned to wash her hair one-handed.

Dressing was worse. Trousers she could manage, but the shirt defeated her. The sling looped both shoulders and knotted between them, holding her back straight and minimizing movement. Sleeves were right out. She settled on her last clean robe, draping it over her left shoulder. With that misery accomplished, she drained a cooling mug of willow bark tisane.

The only mirror was covered and she felt no telltale prickle against her wards—all the same, she felt herself observed. Finally she traced the sensation to a heavy shadow in the corner, a darkness that smelled of familiar bitter ashes.

"Who's there?" At her voice, the shadow vanished, leaving only natural dimness in its place.

"Charming," she muttered.

She ought to sit and rest, but agitation and curiosity drove her around the room, poking in drawers and peering out the window. A sound at the door distracted her from the desolate mountain view. Adam stood in the doorway and relief washed through her, cool and tingling.

"I leave you for a few days, and you've already broken something." A smile hooked his mouth, but his eyes were tight and troubled.

"Are you all right?"

"Better than you. I'm fine, and so is Moth."

She went to him, brushing light fingers against the side of his jaw to reassure herself that he was real. His eyes were bruised with lack of sleep, but she sensed no hurt in him. Except one—a fresh bruise on his throat, the familiar mark of human teeth. The scent of myrrh clung to him, as it seemed to cling to everything here, and under that, the jasmine and honeysuckle sweetness of a woman's perfume.

Her hand fell and her brows rose. "Tell me you came by that willingly."

A flush climbed his cheeks, and he didn't meet her eyes. "Yes. It was stupid, but it wasn't rape."

"Your Brenna?"

The flush darkened. "Not Brenna, and not mine. But yes."

She swallowed something snide. "I'm glad you're safe. I worried."

"I don't know about safe. This place is a tomb. Bren—*she*—says they want your help. But there's more than one agenda here—" He broke off, head cocking toward the hall at a sound she couldn't yet hear.

A whisper of footsteps approached, and Moth stopped outside the open door. Like Adam, she looked sound but ill slept—not, Isyllt hoped, for the same reasons. Her hair had grown long enough to curl in loose ringlets at her cheeks and brow, and the bronze tones in her face had deepened.

"You came," she said at last. Her eyes were dark, remote, her mouth an emotionless line.

"I came." Isyllt took a hesitant step closer. "Of course I came. I'm sorry it took so long." She knelt, jarring her shoulder; it left her looking up at Moth. "I'm sorry."

One corner of the girl's mouth quirked—whether in a smile or a flinch Isyllt couldn't say. "You're hurt. What happened?"

Isyllt eased the collar of her robe back with a grimace, baring the bandages and splint. "I was shot. Don't worry—they're all dead. I met a manticore, too. I'm sorry you missed that." She swallowed, humor drying in her mouth. "Have they treated you well?"

Moth snorted. "For a prisoner and bait, you mean? Yes. Melantha has been teaching me to ride." A crease formed and smoothed between her brows. "She's trying to turn me."

"Ah." Her tongue worked against the roof of her mouth until she could say the words lightly. "Is it working?"

Moth's chin lifted, her eyes unreadable. "I don't know yet."

Isyllt nodded. There was nothing else she could do. "Let me know when you decide. Until then—" She stood, hissing as the movement jarred her shoulder. "One of you help me with this damned sleeve. Then we find Asheris."

After navigating one dark and narrow corridor, Isyllt had no desire to play jinni-in-a-haystack through the whole building. Luckily Moth had seen guards carry Asheris in.

They found him in a windowless interior room, on the wrong side of a barred door. Adam threw back the bar while Isyllt stripped away a light web of wards, her stomach churning. If they'd hurt him— But the door swung open to reveal Asheris whole but half dressed, slumped on the edge of a bed with his head in his hands. He looked up with a weary smile.

"Oh, good. I was getting bored. Is this a rescue?"

"A relocation, at the very least. Are you hurt?"

"A bit sluggish still, but no worse. They were kind enough to take the bullets out while I was asleep." He nodded toward the bedside table, where a pile of misshapen lead balls gleamed greasy in the dim lamplight. His rent and bloody shirt lay beside him; when he stood, the skin of his chest and stomach was smooth and unscarred. "Lead isn't as painful to me. And you?"

She eased her collar back to show the bandage. "I'll mend, if not so quickly."

He glanced past her, to where Moth and Adam waited in the hall. "Your apprentice? Good—I'm glad we didn't come all this way for nothing." He brushed her good shoulder with his, a gentle touch to take the weary sting from the words.

"We're in Qais," she said while he inspected and subsequently abandoned his shirt. Four long lines ridged his back, pink and tender. "Even if we fought past the guards, we wouldn't get far. For the moment I'll settle for finding out hostess, and some answers."

They found Nerium in the library on the ground floor of Quietus's silent fortress-maze. The scent of parchment and leather and cedar breathed over them as the tall brass-studded doors swung open, mingling with the ever-present bitterness of myrrh. Shelves paneled the high walls from floor to ceiling, row upon row of books and cased scrolls. Isyllt whistled appreciatively. A pity, though, that such a collection was locked away in the middle of the desert.

Nerium stood before a tall window, its heavy curtains holding back the dawn. Two low stone tables lay beside her.

No, Isyllt realized as she drew closer. Coffins. Coffins made of red rock salt, the kind that would cost its weight in silver in Selafai. They had no lids, revealing the man and woman who lay within. But while magic prickled her skin as she looked down at their slack, time-worn faces, her ring held no chill. Not dead, merely sleeping, wrapped in enchantment like flies in spidersilk.

"Not your last guests, I hope," Isyllt said, burying her unease. Death and decay could never alarm her, but this unnatural sleep made her skin crawl.

"No. These are my colleagues. Fellow councillors of Quietus. Their sacrifice is the reason I've brought you here."

"You might have sent a letter, you know."

"I would have liked to, but one of our council opposes my summoning you, strongly enough to have you killed."

"Ahmar Asalar," Asheris said.

"Just so. I see she tipped her hand." Nerium's smile was tight and cold. "Because of our quarrel, I tried to have you brought here quietly." She acknowledged Moth with a wry tilt of her head. "You see how well that turned out. But you're here, and mostly whole, with only the loss of Ahmar's pet warlord to show for it."

"We're here," Isyllt agreed. "So tell us why."

"I'll show you. But it's not a sight for kamnuran or apprentices. If your friends would care to wait, or help themselves to breakfast..."

Moth frowned; Adam shrugged. "All right," Isyllt said.

Asheris didn't move from her side, and gave Nerium a chilly smile when she balked. His ruined robe hung open, baring his chest and flashing his scarred back, but his dignity was intact. "I am many things, lady, but *dim* is not one of them."

"Of course not," she said, with perfect aplomb. But it was to Isyllt that she looked, judging. Isyllt shifted closer to Asheris in answer. One ashen brow quirked acknowledgment. "Follow me, please."

She led them from the great hall and down a broad, dusty avenue. Dawn spread like a fresh bruise behind the eastern mountains and the morning was cool and still. As they passed through a neat orchard of columns, Isyllt blinked. The pillars were the same as the one she'd spent a day perched on, though in better repair. Ahead a familiar tower and cupola rose against the fading stars, and the courtyard walls formed the same angles: This was a mirror of lost Irim.

It was to that terraced tower that Nerium led them. As they climbed the worn red steps, an unquiet weight grew in Isyllt's chest and her neck prickled with a strengthening force of magic. She'd visited many places steeped in magic, whether it was the careful constant workings of the Arcanost, or the sour corruption of ancient spells gone wrong, but never had she felt anything like this.

At the top of the steps Isyllt drew up short. The door lay several strides ahead, but the air between might have been made of stone. When she looked *otherwise*, the power of the protective magic hung around the opening seared the backs of her eyes.

"The spells are keyed to our oaths," Nerium said, stepping forward. Magic blurred and distorted her face like heat-shimmer. "No one may enter the temple unless they're sworn to Quietus, or accompanied by a member."

Asheris pressed one palm against the ward. An orange spark flared, but like Isyllt he couldn't pass. Satisfied that they understood, Nerium took them each by the hand and led them through the caul.

The door opened onto yet another set of stairs—Isyllt lost count of steps after eighty, but her shoulder remembered every one. At the bottom of the narrow spiral, Nerium stopped, sweat glinting on her brow. Her conjured light couldn't reach the top.

"Do you know the story of Irim?" she asked, one hand resting on the latch of a red door. More rock salt, an unpleasant reminder of coffins.

"I've heard it," Isyllt said. "One version, at least." Asheris remained silent.

"This is the truth. We keep it, along with Irim's history.

Be careful inside, especially of your injury—they can exploit any weakness." The red door swung open.

The light was a wound, Isyllt thought as she stepped inside, a blasphemy against the power of the dark. A web of diamonds threw back shards of brilliance, sharp enough to cut. Behind the stones, black marble lined the walls and curving ceiling, swirled with grey and glittering sprays of gold, like the night sky.

"This—" She winced at the sound of her voice. "This is where Sivahra's diamonds went."

"And many more. For over a thousand years Quietus has bought and smuggled and stolen such stones, to keep the seals intact."

"Do you know the price of your seals in lives?"

"Better than you." By reflected witchlight Nerium's eyes were bright as mirrors, and as cold. "And I know the price we would pay if the seals fell."

"The ghost wind," Asheris whispered, his face transfigured with dread and awe. He hadn't left the doorway. "This is where it's born."

"Yes. Every lapse frees it. What you felt in Ta'ashlan and Sherazad were our failures here. They've learned to wear through the diamonds, you see, and they eat them faster and faster every time. Some of my colleagues would like to ignore this, and simply replace the stones whenever a flaw forms. If we did that, in a hundred years—or fifty, or twenty—the fortune of diamonds men have bled and died for would be as worthless as glass."

"What deserves such a prison?" Isyllt asked. She'd asked the same of Asheris once, when he still wore the collar imperial mages had used to enslave him. That had been a marvel of craftsmanship, magical and otherwise; it was a tattered thread compared with this room.

"Step closer and find out," Nerium said. "Carefully." She moved back to stand beside Asheris, gesturing Isyllt toward the well in the center of the room.

Isyllt's blood beat hard in her ears as she inched forward. The floor was flat and dry and stable, but the closer she drew to the pit, the more it seemed she balanced on tilting ice, and one wrong step would send her sliding. She stopped a single pace away from the edge—beyond the line of stone lay only empty black.

No. Not empty.

Under the rhythm of her pulse, a different music swelled. A low discordant wail, so soft at first that she thought she imagined it. The song rose and fell like a temple choir, one voice and a hundred. A song of loss and loneliness, of exile and longing. It scraped and shivered over her skin, aching in the roots of her teeth and driving a spike into her fractured clavicle. It would take her apart, muscle and bone, layer by layer, till all that remained was dust.

As the song rose, so too did the darkness in the oubliette. Black as ink, black as tar, black as a night without stars, welling past the lip of the pit and toward her boots. A delicate midnight coil, incongruously frail, licked curiously at her toe. A shudder racked her, clacking her teeth together.

"That's enough." Nerium's hand closed on her elbow, simultaneously holding her steady and pulling her back. "It's best to build a tolerance slowly."

Asheris walked behind Isyllt as they climbed the spiral stair, a reassuring warmth between her and the aching chill they left behind. By the time they reached the top she had stopped shaking, mostly. She stopped as the shroud of spells sealed behind them.

"What are they?" Her jaw ached with the effort from stilling her chattering teeth, and fresh blood oozed beneath her bandages.

"Look down," Nerium said.

In the morning light, Isyllt studied her boot. She'd bought them new only a month ago; the soles were scarcely worn. But where the darkness had touched her the leather was cracked and rotted, flaking away to expose the stocking beneath.

"Al-Jodâ'im. The Undoing. The greatest destructive force history has ever seen. The full extent of their devastation is lost to time and fallen kingdoms, but we know enough. Your people as well as mine."

That last she directed at Asheris, who nodded in reluctant agreement. "We know enough."

"What do you want from me?" Isyllt asked, dragging her gaze off her ruined boot.

"Haven't you guessed? You're an entropomancer, a vinculator—a specialist in our needs. I want you to join me, join Quietus. Help keep the world safe awhile longer."

CHAPTER 25

Nerium left them on the steps of the great hall. To let them consider, she said. Isyllt wasn't sure she could consider anything at the moment. Her thoughts chased themselves in frantic circles and eventually fell, exhausted. The weight of the journey settled heavy on her, compounded by the incessant ache in her shoulder. She sat on the broad steps, leaning against the plinth of a guardian criosphinx, and stared blankly.

The sun rode the crest of the mountains, casting long cool shadows through the streets. Sand eddied slowly in the breeze, glittering with flecks of quartz. How much sand in Al-Reshara was worn from the stones of long-dead kingdoms?

"You're thinking about it," Asheris said, settling beside her.

"How can I? How can I not? Do you believe her?"

"She believes herself." His hands hung between his knees; he scowled at the space between them. Isyllt waited for his silence to break.

"I won't dispute the danger of Al-Jodâ'im," he said at

last. "They destroyed spirits as well as men, and could not be reasoned with. The histories of Mazikeen and Carathis agree on this."

"But?"

"But what I felt in that room wasn't malice or rapacity or even spite. It was sadness. The deepest grief I've ever known."

"I felt it too. Does it balance? Their suffering, against the suffering of the world? A hundred Sivahri dead in those mines, to save a thousand here? Do the scales weigh even?"

"I don't know," he whispered. "I don't know." He stood, scrubbing his hands on his trousers, and walked away, vanishing into the empty streets of Qais.

Isyllt sat on the steps with the silent sphinx long after the sun cleared the spine of the Sarcophagi. Deliberating, she would have said, but in truth she dozed. A deliberate footstep roused her, when the doors opening at her back had not. She straightened, brushing a surreptitious hand across her mouth to make sure she wasn't drooling.

A slender, olive-skinned woman dressed all in black stood at the top of the steps, easing the heavy door shut.

"Lady Iskaldur." Her voice was soft and smoky. Short dark hair feathered against a square jaw and shaded her wide black eyes. She descended the stairs with the careless grace that came of strength and control, an alertness that spoke long training. A dangerous woman, and a beautiful one. Small wonder Adam had never forgotten her.

"You must be Melantha." Tact first, then the barb. "Adam told me about you."

The woman tilted her head in wry acknowledgment, leaning her hip against the opposite sphinx and folding her arms loosely beneath her chest. Nerium's daughter, Moth had said. The resemblance was clear in the line of cheek and jaw and the set of her eyes, though Melantha's features were softer.

"He told me hardly anything about you, but I've heard a great deal all the same. From Moth, and other sources."

Isyllt laughed. Point for point. "Yes, I've heard you seduced my apprentice and my bodyguard. Why are you here?" A wave of her hand encompassed dust and dry rock. "Many countries would pay passing well for skills like yours."

"My mother's told you what we do here. Don't you think that's more important than the schemes of kings and generals?"

"That's what I have to decide, isn't it? And somehow I don't imagine we'll be given camels and sent on our way with well wishes if I refuse."

"No. I don't imagine that you would. But understand, my mother is ruthless because she has to be." Melantha didn't glance away, nothing so telling, but her eyes glinted with subtle movement. "There's no room for mercy in their work."

"Their work. Not yours."

One black-clad shoulder rose and fell gracefully. "She is one of the Silent. I'm just an agent. A weapon." Her lips thinned on a smile.

"Like the man in Kehribar?"

"Yes. I was faster that day." Her voice held only blithe unconcern, but her fingers tightened around her elbows.

"He's with me, you know." Isyllt lifted her ring. "If

you had anything left to say." Antagonizing a woman who carried plumbatae was probably a bad idea, but she couldn't resist.

Melantha's eyebrows rose. "Not today. My mother will appreciate that, though—she likes to get as much use from her tools as she can." She straightened, arms falling to her sides. Her next smile was crooked. "But don't let our family bitterness sway you. Think about the offer."

"Do I have the freedom of the city, at least, or do you have snipers waiting if I stray too far?"

"You're safe within the canyon walls. Stray beyond them and you'll be collected. And there are more scorpions than snipers in the rocks."

Isyllt stayed well away from the canyon cliffs, instead settling by a shaded pool at the edge of the hypostyle. The ache in her shoulder curbed her desire to pace—the touch of Al-Jodâ'im had undone Nerium's soothing magic, and the willow bark as well. With the lead removed she could numb the pain, but the reminder of danger seemed apt.

The pool was peaceful, at least, if redolent of decay. The water mirrored the pillars and the high blue sky above, overlain with a lace of scum and moss and floating lilies. Midges droned across the surface, their feet pricking tiny ripples, but a chill teased from her ring kept them away from her skin.

Isyllt drew on the water's stillness, soothing her spiraling thoughts. As calm filled her, she felt again that watched sensation, separate from the constant low hum of magic that soaked the streets. This time she thought she knew the source.

If she was to consider Nerium's offer, she needed to hear more than one opinion.

"Kash. Is that your name? I feel you hovering in the shadows. Come out."

For a moment nothing answered. Then a slow chill gathered at her back and a longer shadow dimmed her reflection in the pool.

"They call me Kash. It's as close as mortal tongues can come. Conjure with it if you like. If you can."

The presence behind her reminded of a half-forgotten dream. A shadow, and dying fish, and her heart— Her pulse spread, threatening her hard-won peace. Kash chuckled, as if he sensed her unease. No doubt he did.

"It would be impolite to summon you on such short acquaintance. Nerium forbade you to speak to Asheris, but can you speak to me?" She tried to turn, but the cold weight at her back held her in place.

"I am speaking, aren't I?"

"Some prefer to have conversations face-to-face. I admit I'm one of them."

"I'm not handsome like your half-jinn friend."

"He would argue that *half*. And I'm not so shallow as to choose my companions for their looks."

He clucked sharply. "As you wish, necromancer. Look at Quietus's handiwork, then."

Turning around wedged a hot sliver into her wounded shoulder, but turn she did, tilting her head back and back again to see the tall shape behind her.

A vulture's head regarded her from atop a man's gaunt body, the profile of his flesh-tearing beak silhouetted against the sky. One sunken heavy-lidded eye glittered coldly. Where Asheris had four wings and two arms in his burning form, Kash had four arms and two vast wings, half mantled now. Instead of fire, he was made of smoke and shadow, ashes and falling dust.

"You were a jinni," she murmured, peering into the darkness where his heart should be. Perhaps a spark of that light and heat remained, but it was lost in the shifting haze.

Kash snapped his beak. "You said a conversation, not an examination. What do you want, witch?"

"I dreamed of you in Sherazad." She lowered her voice, in case more than one invisible listener haunted Qais. "It was a true dream, wasn't it?"

"I was there. I rode the ghost wind. I wanted to see this sorceress Nerium and her brethren were making such fuss over."

"Very flattering—right up until they tried to shoot me. You warned me away."

"But here you are."

Isyllt wrinkled her nose. "Yes, well. They were very persuasive. You, on the other hand, ripped my heart out."

His cold eye flared, a spark from buried embers. "I would rip the heart from every human mage I met, and stitch their cursed diamonds into their bloody flesh. But there is something of Al-Jodâ'im inside you, so perhaps we are cousins of a sort."

She touched her chest below the bindings of the splint. "A true kinship, or only a sympathetic one? Did mortals know entropomancy before Al-Jodâ'im came?"

"I don't know. The fall of Irim was long before my hatching. I knew only the segregation of the Fata." He made a harsh coughing sound. "The first mortals I met were Quietus."

"Tell me about them. Nerium told me her story, but I want another view. And please, will you sit? My neck hurts."

He crossed his long legs, furling his wings behind him. One pair of arms folded across his sunken chest and the other rested on his knees. In his dark, sharp-angled symmetry he looked like some ancient obsidian idol, a demon-god. His haunches didn't touch the earth, but hovered a few inches above it. Had this been what Irim was like—human and spirit sitting together, but without the bitter weight of history between them?

"I was, as you said, a jinni. Bright and beautiful and brash. Irim intrigued me since I was a fledgling, and I hunted the ruins for some trace of what had come before. One day I caught a scent on the wind, myrrh and magic, leading me south. I followed it here, and discovered Qais and its mages. And they discovered me.

"This was perhaps a century and a half ago, as the seasons reckon. Quietus had its council then as now, but in truth one man ruled them: Onotheras. He was powerful and brilliant and a little mad. He captured me at first out of simple practicality, so that I wouldn't tell anyone what I'd found. But once I was bound, he found another use for me.

"Quietus had bound Al-Jodâ'im, and siphoned from them to fuel their own entropomancy, but they had never found a way to harness the void. A few sturdier, foolhardier mortals attempted to scry the Undoing, but exposing humans to their touch resulted in... fewer humans." He lifted one wing in a shrug. "But with me bound, Onotheras made a new plan." His beaked face showed no emotion, but his harsh voice flattened, losing its sardonic cadence. "He cast me into the oubliette."

Isyllt drew a breath. She would have reached out to him, but she suspected any hint of pity would cost her the rest of the story. "What happened?"

"They consumed me, as they consume everything. But as they did, their song filled me and I understood them. They were travelers, crossing the void behind the stars in a barque of ice and rock and diamond. They traveled and they sang, to the stars, to the void, to themselves. But as they journeyed, another song reached them. It called to them, and in their curiosity they changed their course to answer."

"The song of Irim," Isyllt whispered, remembering Asheris's story.

"Yes. You know how that ended. They meant no harm, any more than the priests of Irim did, but the touch of the Undoing is destruction. The purest entropy. All they wanted was to go home, but they were lost, their vessel shattered and momentum spent. And when they tried to seek help from the humans who had called them—"

"Fewer humans."

"Just so. And from the destruction of Irim, Quietus rose, brimming over with self-sacrifice and righteous cause. They first wrestled Al-Jodâ'im into the scattered diamonds that fell with them; next they built the oubliette, and this mausoleum of a city to surround it."

"But what happened to you, in the pit? You weren't consumed."

His beak snapped. "Better if I had been, than to be left like this—dull and stained and foul." His wings flared, and the draft tasted of char. "I never knew why I survived. Perhaps Onotheras's controls worked, as he claimed. Perhaps Al-Jodâ'im have grown weak in their captivity, or an immortal soul is harder to digest than flesh." His eye pearled with the blink of a milky membrane. "Perhaps they took pity on me. They were never cruel, though they've learned enough of human brutality. I can't hate them for what they did. Onotheras, though, and his children—them I do."

"You said we could be allies. What do you want?"

"I want my freedom, and my vengeance. And if I could I would end their suffering." One wing pointed toward the temple, and Al-Jodâ'im. "Everyone in Qais feels their despair—it saturates the mortar and stone. But the humans would rather wallow in that misery than free their captives. I've dreamed of breaking the seals, of freeing the Undoing. I sometimes think it would be worth it, though it would mean the destruction of Mazikeen as well." He shrugged. "It's not as though the burning legion ever rode to my rescue. It's not as though they would take me back. Not like this." He spread hands and wings.

"If they were loosed, I think Al-Jodâ'im might swallow all the world eventually, and so be freed. It would be an end to suffering for everyone."

Isyllt swallowed, her mouth gone dry. "It would. I would prefer a less... absolute solution. If I could release you, I would. If I can, I will. But Nerium holds my friends' lives as surety. She wants me to join her. If I did, do you think she would let me free you?"

Kash laughed. "She would say so, I'm sure. She has before. And like before, she'll find a reason not to." His form shredded in the breeze. "If you want to hear another side to her story, ask her what happened to her daughter."

* * *

After her conversation with Kash, Isyllt found no more peace in Qais's empty streets and stagnant pools. She returned to the great hall, and found Adam waiting for her with a cold tray of breakfast.

"She wants me to stay," she said, staring at the food on her plate. "To join the order."

"I know. Bren—Melantha told me."

She stirred curried chickpeas without tasting them. A sheen of olive oil coated the spoon, and the smell of garlic and lemon wafted past her. She knew she needed food, but her appetite was cold and dead as the hearth. "What do you think?"

"I think you should eat that instead of playing with it, or I'll spoon it down you myself."

Isyllt snorted, but dutifully swallowed a mouthful, and followed it with a slice of paprika-dusted egg. "That's not what I meant."

Adam raked a hand through his hair; it was long enough to cling in disordered spikes. "This place is slow death. Or a very quick one, from some of the things Mel's said. But she swears that what they do is needful."

"The things they keep bound here might destroy the world. Or at least make things very unpleasant in Assar. There's always work that must be done, no matter how distasteful."

"I've done plenty of it. Is this worth it to you, binding yourself to this place?"

She stirred her beans again and chewed another spoonful before answering. "I don't know. In Ta'ashlan I would wear the white veil and watch people sign themselves against me. At least this is a more honest exile."

His brows pinched together. "Or we could get out of here. Go north and not worry about veils or prisons."

Isyllt laid down her spoon. Her last bite of egg tasted like paste, and every bone in her body ached, not just the broken one. "Would it really be any better there? I'm so tired, Adam. Tired of all of it."

"That's this place talking."

"Maybe so. That doesn't mean it isn't true. Don't worry," she added when his frown deepened. "I won't let you be trapped here too."

"Good." His chair scraped as he stood. "I don't like watching suicides. Especially pointless ones."

With Adam gone and Asheris not yet returned, Isyllt returned to the front step and its watchful sphinxes. The tattered shade of a palm tree protected her from the sun, and the warmth eased her aches and pains. She was scraped hollow, the worst she'd felt since the blood-sorceress Phaedra Severos had nearly exsanguinated her, since she'd woken in the hospital to the knowledge that Kiril was dead.

Would it be worth it to spend her life in solitary service here, if it meant never feeling another heart stutter and stop under her helpless hands? Her eyes ached with sleeplessness and tears she couldn't shed. The desert sun had baked all the moisture out of her—she had none left to waste.

Moth found her there, stewing in doubt and grief. The girl wore riding boots and a vest laced tight over her blouse; her hair was streaked dun with dust, and the smell of horse and sweat clung to her. She walked with a pained gait that spoke of stiffness and chafing, but her color was high and her eyes bright. Isyllt was glad to see her learning—horsemanship was one of the few things Kiril had neglected in her education.

Moth sat on the far side of the broad steps, wincing and shifting her weight. Isyllt waited for the inevitable question, but that wasn't what followed.

"I wasn't sure you'd come."

That penetrated her lassitude and stiffened her spine. "I would never have abandoned you. Although," she admitted wryly, "if Melantha hadn't left a note, I'm not sure what I would have done."

"I thought maybe it was Adam you came for."

"I wouldn't leave him either. But I meant it when I promised I'd take care of you. Mekaran would know if I failed." But she'd meant it when she swore her vows to the Crown too, and that hadn't kept her from breaking them. Nerium didn't know about those broken oaths—once a mage forswore magical vows, they found little trust with their fellows.

It took a moment to nerve herself to the next question. "Are you happier here?"

Moth frowned. "In Qais? No." Her voice lowered. "It's lonely, and I have bad dreams. But Melantha wants me. As an apprentice, I mean."

Isyllt bit back an automatic denial; she couldn't be certain it wasn't a lie. "Do you want her as a teacher?"

"She's the best I've seen with a knife. Better than Adam. And her shadow magic—" She picked at the stone between her knees. "I remind her of herself, I think. I can't decide if that's a good thing or not."

"You did the same for me," Isyllt admitted, "when we first met."

Moth shot her a narrow sideways glance. "When do I become myself, and not these shadows you cast on me?"

"I don't know. I'd like to say that's when you grow up, but I clung to Kiril's shadow long after. I hope you have better luck."

After she'd said it, she realized she hadn't flinched at his name. Maybe the wound was finally closing. Or maybe Qais made all other sufferings look small beside it.

"If you want to stay with Melantha, I understand."

"Just like that? You wouldn't fight for me? Or for Adam?"

Isyllt tried to hide a wince, but doubted she had. "You can't fight for someone's affections. I thought you could, once, but I was wrong. And if I kept you against your wishes, what kind of company would you be? Adam knows that."

Moth gave her another measuring look. "I thought maybe he loved her, at first. But I'm not sure. He looks so sad when she isn't watching."

"Love and sadness aren't exclusive." She smiled, but it was crooked. "You'll learn that."

The girl snorted. "Maybe I should have been a hijra after all. I thought I wanted choices, but choices just make you miserable, don't they?"

That night Melantha found Nerium in her private study, sitting at her desk with a pot of tea and a book. A familiar scene, but not quite right. A moment later she recognized the discrepancy: Nerium wasn't frowning. The book wasn't a thaumaturgical text or history, or missives from agents, but a slender volume of poetry. Aisha had been one of her mother's favorites since Melantha was a child, but she couldn't remember when she'd last seen Nerium reading for pleasure.

Melantha's mouth dried as she approached. Nerium had finally found a moment of peace, and she was sure to ruin it. She remembered Khalil entombed in salt and forced herself on.

Nerium looked up when her feet touched the rug beside the desk, folding a faded ribbon between the pages and raising an expectant brow. Melantha swallowed and bent her knees stiffly onto the carpet. *Say it*, all her collected voices urged. *Say it and be done*.

"Mother, I... I want out. If Iskaldur agrees—when she agrees—you won't need me anymore. Let me go." Familiar lines creased Nerium's brow, and she pressed on. "I'll keep my oaths of silence, I'll protect your secrets as I always have, but I can't keep doing this. It's been nearly thirty years—I want to be myself again."

Nerium tilted her head. "Do you even know who that is?"

"Please, Mother. Release me from my vows. I'm no use to you as a mage, and if your plan works you won't need me to steal secrets and stones."

"No," Nerium said slowly. "I suppose I won't." The lines around her mouth deepened. "If she agrees. And after I've taken her vows and the transference is complete. I need you here until it's finished, in case Iskaldur balks, or anything goes awry. After that..." She trailed off, frowning, and Melantha's pulse beat hard and fast in her throat. After a long moment, Nerium nodded.

"Thank you." Her vision blurred. On a wild, childish impulse she leaned forward and laid her head on her mother's knee. "Thank you."

Nerium flinched from the sudden contact, but didn't push her away. After a moment her hand landed on Melantha's hair, a trembling, uncertain caress.

"Save your thanks. Neither of our service is over yet."

CHAPTER 26

Lonely dreams chased Isyllt through the night and she woke with a stiff spine and a sharp ache in her shoulder. By the time she washed and dressed it was nearly noon, the sun high and hot in the flat dusty sky. Dust devils twisted in the streets outside; their dance was beautiful, but Isyllt had no wish to join them.

The Chanterie's corridors looked equally lifeless, but if she paused she could feel the patterns silent feet had worn. No visible track, neither scent nor sound, but a faint tingling hum inside her head. She nearly laughed—and she'd thought the Court of Lions lonely. Erisín had its share of empty places, but at least they were haunted.

She hadn't seen Asheris since the day before, nor spoken to Adam since yesterday's argument. With a curiosity bordering on desperation, she followed the trails. Where did the living go in Qais?

The first trail led to the library. It made a tempting refuge from heat and unhappy questions, but even the lure of strange books wasn't enough to ignore the two mages sleeping in salt coffins. If Isyllt did agree to stay, it would be contingent on Nerium moving her morbid experiments elsewhere.

The thought settled through her, becoming an unpleasant weight in her stomach—it was the first time she'd acknowledged that *if*, even to herself. She turned away from the library and the sleepers and chose another corridor.

This hall ended in a garden. The inner gate stood open and a damp green breeze sighed past her; her mouth watered at the sharp sweetness of water. Jujube trees and sprawling tamarisk shrubs grew inside the walled enclosure, beside wormwood and poison-pink oleanders. A fountain trickled lazily in the center, drawing scores of tiny brown birds.

Isyllt paused in the doorway, hearing familiar voices from the green shade. Metal flashed in the sun, followed by the *thunk* of steel striking wood. She hesitated only a heartbeat before wrapping herself in a concealing shadow and creeping forward.

"Keep your wrist stiff," Melantha said, "and your elbow higher. Follow through when you release. Again." Through a screen of branches, Isyllt saw her crouch to retrieve a blade, which she handed back to Moth.

"Right foot back," she said, correcting the girl's stance. "Elbow up."

The knife flashed again and stuck—hilt up and quivering—in a trellis post for a moment before falling to the grass. Moth cursed.

"Better." Melantha drew a knife of her own, holding the blade between thumb and forefinger. This one flipped end over end faster than Isyllt's eye could follow and sank deep into the wood. Moth cursed again, shaking her head.

"What about you?" Moth asked, turning her head. "Do you have any advice?"

A shadow below a sycamore tree stretched and resolved into Adam. "My advice is, hold on to your knife in a fight. That way you can use it more than once."

Melantha snorted. "And my way, you never have to get that close." She moved in a black blur, pivoting toward him to throw another blade. It stuck in the tree a handspan from his head. "You see?" the woman asked, turning back to Moth. "It saves scrubbing other people's blood out of your clothes. Go clean up—you'll just settle into bad habits if you keep trying today."

"Tomorrow?"

"Tomorrow," Melantha agreed, smiling. "If you keep improving, you can start aiming at Adam soon."

Moth laughed, short and bright. The sound was a knife all its own, twisting under Isyllt's sternum. She wished she could hate Melantha for it, but this was her own doing. Moth thrived under the attention, and she'd been too caught up in her own misery to give any.

Moth left the garden, passing an armspan from Isyllt. Her cheeks were flushed and damp, hair sweat-tousled, and grass clung to the knees of her trousers. Her brow wrinkled as she brushed the edge of Isyllt's obfuscation, but she walked on with only a heartbeat's hesitation.

Adam and Melantha lingered in the green shade. Isyllt knew that eavesdropping further would bring nothing but misery, but she didn't move.

"Feeling nostalgic?" Adam asked, tugging the knife out of the tree trunk. "It's been a long time since you threw knives at me." He hefted the blade lightly to check the balance, then tossed it in a slow tumbling arc. Melantha plucked it neatly out of the air.

"A long time, but you still don't flinch." She wiped the knife on her sleeve and sheathed it at her belt. "You still have the same frown when you're brooding too. What's wrong?"

That frown deepened. "I said something stupid to Isyllt yesterday." He shrugged, and leaf-shadows rippled across his face. "I was right, but I shouldn't have said it."

Melantha turned away to collect another fallen knife. "Do you love her?" she asked, too casually.

Adam laughed humorlessly. "Lady of Ravens, I hope not. But...she's not a bad partner. For a spy." Isyllt's hands tightened on her folded arms and she bit back a retort.

Melantha's shoulders rose and fell with her breath. Adam stood beside her, not quite touching. "Now it's my turn to ask you what's wrong."

"I'm leaving," Melantha said. "I spoke to my mother. When this is over, I'll go. Far away from Qais." Her breath caught as she turned to face him. "Come with me."

Isyllt's chest hitched, and the cost of keeping silent made her jaw tighten and throat ache. She had witnessed far more intimate conversations than this, but none that had made her stomach churn so much.

"We'll be mercenaries," Melantha continued, before Adam could speak. "It'll be—" She swallowed. "It won't be like the old days. It will be different. Something new. I'm tired of this life—I need to start over."

Adam laid a hand on her shoulder. "How many times have you started over already?"

"I've lost count." Her chin lifted. "I have to get it right eventually, don't I?"

Isyllt turned away, her nails carving hot crescents into her upper arms. She couldn't stand to hear his answer; she'd learn it soon enough either way. Her bad shoulder clipped the doorway as she retreated and a single hiss of pain escaped. She fled into the darkness of the Chanterie before she could be discovered.

That afternoon, the heavy silence was broken by a clatter of voices and dishes in the kitchen. Qais rarely saw guests, and any new face was cause for a proper meal. Soon the halls smelled of oils and spices, fresh bread and roasting meat. The scents and noise and occasional laughter lifted the oppressive gloom—by the time dinner was laid out that evening, even Nerium was nearly smiling.

Asheris returned from his wandering with no more peace than he'd taken with him. The soothing power of sun and wind faded in the shadow of the prison-temple. The smell of roasting garlic lured him into the dining room, however, a reminder that he'd neglected his flesh for days, and still felt the wounds the manticore had dealt him.

The food was excellent: spiced tomato soup and stewed chickpeas, followed by tajines of mutton with nuts and fig sauce and platters of pearled couscous and vegetables. Asheris tasted every dish, but could never wholly banish the bitter aftertaste of myrrh. However well they fed him, he was a prisoner here.

Food couldn't cure everything, though. The meal was strained and awkward, full of shifting tensions and things loudly unspoken. He traded barbed pleasantries with

Nerium, while Isyllt held to chilly tact. Adam and Nerium's daughter sat together, hardly speaking, and Isyllt looked everywhere but at Adam, despite his attempts to catch her eye. The apprentice Moth rolled her eyes so often that the necromancer finally kicked her ankle under the table. Asheris would have laughed, had not Ahmar's curse burned against him like a coat of nettles.

After custard and the last bottle of wine, Melantha and Moth retreated. With one last inscrutable glance at Isyllt, Adam followed, leaving Asheris alone with the sorcerers. He would have fled as well, but Nerium invited Isyllt into the study, and Isyllt took his arm as she acquiesced.

The room was nothing like cozy, but less sepulchral than the rest of the Chanterie. Statues and paintings lined the walls, engravings and friezes and parchment—styles from all across Khemia and the north as well, and some he recognized from university texts as civilizations long vanished. So much wealth and knowledge here, locked away from the world. To keep them safe, he supposed, but that was the reason the mad emperor Altair had given for walling his wife and children in a tower.

He accepted Nerium's offered brandy, though he longed to fling the glass into the fire. It was a rare luxury, costly to import from Erebos, and a childish gesture would accomplish little. But it would burn prettily.

Isyllt and Nerium spoke of magic and travel, carefully avoiding the subject that hung between them like an odor everyone was too polite to mention. Though well versed in politic conversation, Asheris couldn't bring himself to join in. It was difficult for him to become intoxicated, but he might have managed it tonight. The women's voices were too sharp, the room too bright and slightly distorted, as though he watched through a crystal lens. Something jagged and ugly crouched in his throat, waiting for a chance to strike.

He remembered his conversation with Isyllt in the desert, and wondered if he should have chosen selfishness over friendship after all.

He was young for a jinni—only seventy years had passed since his fire-opal egg hatched in a glass-walled rookery. His friendships among jinn had been shallow, childish things. Little wonder he was foolhardy enough to disregard the prohibitions against the world of flesh and seek out men. Asheris-the-man had been more mature by human reckoning, but still reckless and curious. Years of slavery had tempered them both. If that incautious young jinni had realized how much he would miss his home—

Asheris threw back a swallow of brandy. Grief was a blade transfixing his chest, and he would be damned a dozen times over before he would weep in front of Nerium. He collected himself in time to hear Ahmar's name. Not a pleasant topic, but one that let him focus his wine-soaked wits.

"Why the church?" he interjected. If he was trapped here, he might as well learn something. "Why not put your people on the Lion Throne instead?"

"There were attempts," Nerium said, wry as ever. "But the duties of kings and emperors too easily oppose the goals of Quietus. We want the empire strong—order against chaos—but it's better for all involved if whoever wears the crown doesn't know we exist. Which doesn't mean we haven't sought out candidates who would be...amenable to suggestion."

"Like Rahal."

"Yes. As for the church"—she shrugged—"we built it."

Asheris stiffened, sloshing brandy over the rim of his glass. Isyllt leaned forward and spoke before he could. "You what?"

Nerium chuckled. "I shouldn't say *we*, I suppose. I may be old, but not as old as that. But yes, Quietus helped shape the sun church. My predecessors feared that the ancient spirit-worshipping tribes would turn their faith to Al-Jodâ'im, and that would put an end to the seals. When Aaliyah and her sun cult began preaching, the Silent Council decided the Unconquered Sun would serve their purposes. Light and order and separation from the Fata were exactly what they needed. So they supplied the sun-worshippers and taught them warded prayers. We've had members close to the Illumined Chair for centuries."

She spoke casually, but Asheris marked the cool glitter of her eyes as she watched him. She spoke of secrets that would never leave Qais. His hands tightened around his glass, aching with the effort not to shatter it. Not to incinerate the room, to burn Qais to the ground. He wasn't tipsy enough to think he could succeed.

Isyllt changed the subject, trying to ease the tension, but Asheris excused himself quickly. She glimpsed some of the misery beneath his careful mask, and wondered if she should follow. But a moment alone with Nerium was an opportunity she meant to take advantage of.

"I have a question."

Nerium's mouth quirked. "And I imagine I should dread it. You've spoken to Kash."

"I have." Isyllt rolled the brandy's burnt-sugar heat

across her tongue. "He told me to ask what happened to your daughter."

"He would." Nerium sighed. "I should be glad he didn't tell you himself. But for all his spite, I doubt he could make the story any worse."

"Is this Melantha, or another?"

The woman blinked. "That is her name now, isn't it? She's had so many I forget them. But yes. I only have one child." She lifted her glass, staring into it before she drank. "Kash told you, I suppose, about his capture."

"About Onotheras, yes."

The woman nodded. "Onotheras was my grandfather. I wasn't alive yet. By the time I was born, Kash had been a prisoner for fifty years. My father had learned to use him as a weapon, and I would be taught in turn. But when I was a child he was merely a curiosity. A pet monster, and something like a friend.

"I spent years as an agent abroad. My daughter—Melantha, if you prefer—was born in Anambra during my assignment there. We of Quietus learned the hard way that the presence of Al-Jodâ'im can lead to complications in birth. When she was ten years old, my father died, and I returned to take my place on the council.

"After I returned, I became…closer to Kash. Though I now controlled his bonds, he was still my childhood friend. The other mages shunned him, but we were comfortable together. He begged me for his freedom, and I wanted very much to grant it." She smiled ruefully. "There is little true happiness in Qais—I was still young and foolish enough to wish for some. But despite my wishing, to release him would have been a loss to Quietus, and a potential danger. My oaths forbade that.

"Kash's time in the oubliette had bonded him with Al-Jodâ'im. Through him, we could harness their powers, the void itself, but his service would always be under duress. If we could repeat the experiment with a human, someone willing and loyal to us, the possibilities might be limitless. If I could replace Kash with a better tool, I could free him with no danger to my vows."

"Not yourself?" Isyllt said, cocking an eyebrow.

Nerium's lips thinned. "No. And not for cowardice—not entirely. I'm a healer. It's a rare talent to grow in Qais. It also means my magic runs counter to entropomancy. I can't control the nothing that is Al-Jodâ'im, only oppose it. The odds were poor that I'd survive the process.

"By that time Melantha was twelve, and close to Kash the way I was in my youth. It had become obvious that she was kamnur. For a child raised by mages, this was naturally a disappointment."

To whom? Isyllt drowned the question with a swallow of liquor.

"I didn't lie to her, nor did I disguise the danger. Twelve is old enough to take our most preliminary vows, and those vows can't be made on pretenses or half-truths. And while other members might have undergone the attempt for gain and glory, none of them would have supported freeing Kash. It was, I thought, the best choice."

"To feed your own child to the abyss."

Nerium's lip curled. "If she had been someone else's child, would that make it better? Don't think it was an easy decision, or a heartless one."

Isyllt lifted her glass, but it was empty. "What happened?"

"We made the attempt. I duplicated my grandfather's

precautions, and added more of my own. With Kash's help we had more chance of success than any other experiment Quietus had undertaken." Her eyes closed, lids thin and fragile. "I put my daughter in the pit." She swallowed and continued. "Even knowing what was to come, it was... hard. She only screamed once, but that made the silence all the worse. The timing was key—too long an exposure and she would die; too short and we would accomplish nothing."

"Since I spoke to her at dinner, I can only assume you didn't leave her in too long." The image of Melantha deflating like an overcooked pastry made Isyllt bite her tongue against untimely laughter.

Nerium closed her eyes again, longer this time. "I flinched. I pulled her out too soon. Oh, it changed her, in striking ways. But not the ways we wanted. I didn't dare try again. And that meant that I couldn't release Kash. He never forgave me for that."

"It seems Melantha did. Enough to stay, at least."

"The oubliette... took so much from her. As much as it gave, if not more. She recovered, but I'm not sure she understood how much it devoured. I've earned other resentments since."

She smiled bitterly and threw back the last of her drink. Her eyes met Isyllt's as she lowered the glass. "Think me heartless if you wish. I'm sure I deserve it. But I want you to understand the things I've done for Quietus. You know what it's like to sacrifice for vows, don't you?"

"I do." It wasn't precisely a lie. She had watched Kiril sacrifice so many things for his, even if she had been unwilling to do the same in the end. "But there are things I won't sacrifice. If I choose to join you, Adam and Moth won't be bound by my vows. Or Asheris."

Nerium cocked an eyebrow at the challenge in her voice, but nodded. "The mercenary, no. You might wish to reconsider about the girl. We've grown lax in recruiting new members—another complacency we can ill afford." Her focus drifted for a moment, then snapped back to Isyllt. "Your companions may leave if they choose. But if they won't take our vows they can never return, or leave with knowledge of what we keep here."

"Even Asheris? You won't cloud his memory so easily."

"Of course," Nerium said, only a heartbeat too quickly. "We know as many of his secrets as he knows of ours, after all."

Isyllt pressed her tongue against her teeth to hold back a challenge; it would help no one right now. "Why me?" she asked instead. "Out of all the mages in Khemia, why look to me for this?"

"You first came to our attention after Sivahra. Many of my colleagues were furious to lose so many years of effort there, but I chose to take it as a sign. I'd already seen the hastening trend of failure in the seals, but no one was ready to listen. Losing such a rich source of diamonds was the perfect excuse for me to begin making other plans. As for you—as I said before, as a vinculator and entropomancer, you were exactly the sort of mage we needed. And, I admit, I had a less noble reason as well.

"Many years ago, our supply of apprentices had already begun to dwindle. Since it was clear that Melantha couldn't take my place, I began searching elsewhere. I'd trained in Selafai long ago, and knew the Arcanost taught the skills we sought. So I went to Erisín hoping to recruit a bright young talent."

To let them smother here.

"I spoke to your master," Nerium continued, "hoping to find him sympathetic."

Isyllt rolled her empty cup between her palms. "He wasn't, I take it."

"He might have been, if I could have told him the truth. But without understanding my true purpose, he saw only a foreign agent trying to recruit Selafaïn mages for her own ends. My welcome in Erisín was very short."

"So you would recruit me now out of spite?"

One cheek creased with her smile. "At my age, you learn to take whatever satisfactions you can find. Even petty ones."

Nerium set aside her cup, and humor with it, and leaned forward. Despite herself—and her shoulder—Isyllt swayed closer in turn. The force of the woman's gaze was hard to ignore; if she hadn't chosen to cloister herself, she could have commanded armies. Nations.

"What we do here is beyond nations," Nerium said, as if she saw the thought inside Isyllt's skull. "Beyond kings and emperors, priests and spymasters. I can offer you wealth—we have vaults of it—but no chance to spend it. I can offer you glory, but only a handful will ever hear of it. You'll have a place of honor in histories no one will read. But most of all, I offer you purpose. An end to doubt and wandering."

It wasn't a thing so hard to guess, especially if she'd been watching, or listening to Isyllt's conversations. All the same, it felt as though Nerium stripped away her armor to see the weaknesses beneath it. Isyllt leaned back, cursing herself for the tell.

"Can you offer me untroubled sleep?" She'd meant to be defiant, but the question came out soft and pleading.

"Oh, child." Nerium's voice gentled, and her eyes were bright and sad. "No one can give you that, except you. And it's a rare gift indeed." Then she smiled, sharp and dry once more. "Live as long as I have and you won't need as much rest. But you're young, and should go to yours. Think on what I've said. All of it."

"I will." That, at least, was a promise she could keep.

CHAPTER 27

After her conversation with Nerium, sleep seemed an unlikely prospect. So Isyllt was still awake, staring at the ceiling as if only her attention kept it from falling, when Asheris knocked hours later.

"I realized," he said with a grimace, "that I was never given a room without a bar on the wrong side of the door. May I stay with you?"

"Of course." It would be a welcome distraction from wondering—and knowing—where Adam slept. "Normally I'd warn you that I kick in my sleep, but I can't move at all with this damned splint."

Asheris shed his robe and shirt—intact ones salvaged from their luggage—and ducked behind the sandalwood screen to wash. The lines of his back and shoulders were stiff and unhappy, even more so than after dinner.

Isyllt sat up to make room on the bed, squaring her back against the wall. Her shoulders, like her left hand, were something she took too much for granted.

"What's wrong?" she asked. The wood-and-leather

frame creaked softly as he sat. "Besides the dozen obvious things."

He gave a bitter laugh. "Only those." He turned to meet her gaze; his own eyes were dark and raw. "I can't stay here. The walls, the secrets, a thousand years of injustice piled one against the other—it's too much. But how do I go back to Ta'ashlan and keep these secrets, knowing they're killing the Fata? Knowing that mortal kingdoms are built on the suffering of spirits?"

"I don't know." She reached for his shoulder, meaning to offer comfort, but he recoiled from her touch. Her diamond glittered on her outstretched hand.

"I'm sorry," he said after a moment, his fear-blackened eyes turning amber again. "It isn't you. It isn't even this." He gestured to her ring.

"I know. It's this place." She leaned forward slowly, painfully, letting him see the motion before she pressed her lips against the curve of his ear. Muscles tensed and jumped beneath his skin, but he kept still. "I also know," she breathed, "that there is nowhere here where we aren't watched, or overheard. So be careful what you admit out loud." She kissed his cheek, tasting salt and lingering soap, and pulled away.

His defenses rose piece by piece, till he was calm and unflappable as ever. "You're right. Of course you're right. The atmosphere in this place makes me melodramatic—imagine setting a play here. And speaking of which, a production of *The Rain Queen* is scheduled to start soon in Ta'ashlan. How much longer will you consider Lady Kerah's offer?"

"I'll have a decision for her soon. If I can ever sleep on it."

* * *

But sleep didn't come. She lay beside Asheris, each wandering in their own dark thoughts, as dawn crept toward them inch by inch.

It hadn't yet caught them when a chill drew Isyllt upright. Not the draft over the casement, nor the cold of her ring that signaled death, but an unpleasant hollow sensation behind her sternum. The splinter of void that lived in her. Something, she guessed, had stirred Al-Jodâ'im.

Beside her, Asheris opened his eyes. "What's wrong?"

"I'm not sure, but something is. Shall we get into trouble?"

He grinned. "If they didn't mean us to, they surely would have provided more entertainment."

They met Adam and Melantha on the steps—neither of them looked well rested either. Moth trailed behind, still fumbling with her shirt-buttons.

"What's happening?" Isyllt and Moth asked on the same breath.

"Trouble in the temple," Melantha said, frowning. "My mother's there." Her vision blurred, looking elsewhere. "So is Kash." She bolted the steps two at a time, leaving Isyllt and the others to scurry after.

As Melantha neared the top of the temple stairs and the wards there, Isyllt quickened her pace. "Wait!" Her shoulder burned, and every bouncing step felt like a saw cutting through her clavicle. "We can't go in without you."

"You don't need to. This is Quietus business, whatever's happened."

Isyllt caught her eye—hard to look commanding when she was gasping like a landed fish. "If a mage is in trouble down there, you'll need me."

Melantha wasted only a heartbeat debating it before she reached through the barrier and grabbed Isyllt's sleeve. With her tug Isyllt stumbled through and across the dark threshold.

The discordant music of Al-Jodâ'im swelled to meet them as they plunged down the spiral stair. Even ancient spirits didn't like being woken in the dead hours of night. Beneath it, Isyllt felt a raw jagged rage that she recognized as Kash.

Isyllt stumbled into Melantha as the other woman drew up short at the red salt door. Over her shoulder she saw Kash, his wings a black storm as he threw himself at Nerium. The mage stood against the onslaught, her wards a shining web between them, but sweat glistened on her brow. As Isyllt watched, she retreated a single step. One step closer to the oubliette.

Melantha hesitated, reluctant to break Nerium's concentration. Isyllt ducked past her into the chamber. Magic raged like a whirlwind, buffeting her back into the doorway.

"You want to know about Quietus? About Nerium?" Kash's voice was a spike between her brows. "I'll show you."

Images unfolded behind her eyes, straining the sutures of her skull: Nerium alone in the room, unraveling the spells around a single diamond with a surgeon's precision; the storm that sprang up as that stone failed, gyring across the desert to strike at Ta'ashlan. She saw plants and animals fall in its path, felt the hearts and minds of men fail as it swept through the city. Saw a woman weeping over a black-and-gold drift of dead bees. Heard a young girl scream as darkness closed around her.

Watched Nerium's eyes glisten with tears that never fell as she built an old man's coffin. Felt the chains that bound Kash every day, hobbling wings and will, felt the hate and misery that grew in the scorched field where his heart had been.

Over the barrage of visions, Kash spoke. "No amount of death or misery will sway her, not even her own. Any mercy she ever knew has turned to salt and ashes. She'll never let you go, and she'll destroy your jinni for the secrets he's learned. You know it."

"I know," Isyllt whispered. The taste of copper coated her tongue as she spoke; her nose was bleeding.

"Stand with me and we can end it now. Now while she's weak."

Nerium didn't speak, but her eyes met Isyllt's. A muscle leapt in her jaw, the cords of her neck taut with strain. She offered no denials, no pleas.

Melantha caught Isyllt's arm. A knife was in her other hand, but she made no move to strike. "If my mother falls, the seals will fall. Are you prepared to release this darkness on Assar?"

Was it worth it? That was the question any spy had to answer. Kill a king to stop a war. Kill a friend to keep your cover. Let a city burn to undermine an empire. Bind the dead to spare the living. Drive spirits from their ancient homes so that mankind could thrive. Was it worth it?

She had thought so once. Before the vampire Spider, who lied and murdered to help his people just as she had killed and deceived for hers. Before Asheris, who lived among humans who would revile him rather than be alone. If Al-Jodâ'im suffered in secret to keep all of Khemia from chaos, didn't the scales balance? If spirits withered while Assar grew strong, was that her problem?

Even if it was, unleashing the ghost wind on the world might be vengeance, but it would only bring more suffering.

There was no solution without betrayal and pain. No choice that wasn't lined with misery. But she'd long since reconciled herself to painful choices, and she had to choose now. And if it ended in her death—well, what wouldn't? She hadn't known many spies old enough to collect pensions.

Isyllt shrugged off Melantha's hand and stepped forward. Nerium's nose was bleeding, too, and her shoulders sagged under the force of Kash's attack. Sparks bled from her wards.

Kash's attention shifted at Isyllt's approach, split between the two mages. She tasted his exultation as she reached for him.

And felt the white-hot lash of his rage as her diamond flared, and her voice rang with words of binding.

Nerium's voice cracked as she joined the chant, then grew strong. Kash shrieked in fury at the doubled assault. Light flared in a hundred diamonds, shredding his shadow skin. With one last raptor cry, he unraveled, banished once more beyond the temple seals.

Nerium gasped and fell to one knee. "Thank you," she wheezed. "I know better than to drop my guard around him, but I was distracted—" She shook her head at the excuse; sparks crackled in her short hair. Her eyebrows rose as she looked up at Isyllt. "I wasn't certain you'd intervene on my behalf."

"I wasn't either, at first." She held out a hand and helped the older woman to her feet. "But now that I have,

I've made up my mind." The splint kept her shoulders square already, so she raised her chin for emphasis. "I'll swear your oaths. I'll join Quietus."

She and Nerium emerged from the darkness of the oubliette together, and descended the steps side by side. They said nothing, but Isyllt's choice hung between them like a banner. Adam cursed and turned away, avoiding her eyes. Asheris's face drained dull and stiff as a mask. Moth only watched, her slate-colored eyes flat and unreadable as their stone.

She spoke her vows on the temple steps, by the rising light of dawn. She swore to serve the Silent Council, to keep the secrets of Qais, and above all to keep Al-Jodâ'im bound no matter what the cost. She swore it on her magic and her life and on the black diamond ring she had yielded to Nerium. She had sworn her oath to the Crown on the same stone ten years ago. Kiril had received her vows that day, while the king and crown prince of Selafai looked on.

Today Melantha and Moth bore witness. Asheris and Adam walked away, unable and unwilling to take part. Isyllt was just as glad—it was easier to speak the words without them watching. Easier to swear herself to dust and loneliness, to commit herself to a prison even as she became its warden.

She made herself hollow, and let the words fill her, drawing strength from Nerium's voice. No glib lies would satisfy these vows, so she made herself a mirror for the other woman's grim conviction. The trick was not to feign innocence, but to find true belief. And not to lose yourself in it before the end.

When the oath was spoken and Nerium had sworn her support in turn, Isyllt took back her ring. It hung loose on her finger; the desert had whittled her down. She thought it would hurt, to repurpose the stone Kiril had given her—that day had been the proudest of her life. Now she felt nothing. That was for the best.

When it was over and done, Isyllt returned to her room alone. She slept.

CHAPTER 28

With sleep came dreams.

She lay not in her bed but on a red salt table, motionless and aware. Nerium bent over her, opening her chest with a shining scalpel while Kash stood by like a midwife's attendant, ready to receive her dripping heart when Nerium cut it free.

"She won't need this," Nerium said, and now Qais was replaced by an examination theater in the Arcanost, the seats filled by a faceless crowd. "What should we replace it with?"

"This," said Moth, standing beside the coffin-table. Blood smeared her smock and clung in a flaking line across her nose. She held the black diamond ring. "This is all she needs."

"Very good. Yes." Nerium took the ring with one bloody hand and fit it into Isyllt's gaping chest. "Would you care to do the stitching?"

Light shattered off the tip of Moth's needle.

She woke before the first stitch. Normally such a dream would leave her breathless and sweating, but she was calm now. Her heart beat slow and soft. The surgery must have been a success.

And thinking of Moth, bloodstained and beringed, she knew what she had to do.

Isyllt went downstairs in the afternoon, after another awkward one-armed bath, and joined Nerium for tea. The other woman looked happier than Isyllt had seen before—nothing effusive, but her eyes were brighter and less strained, the crisp tones of her voice less caustic.

She had known this woman for three days, she realized with a start. The timeless air of Qais made it feel much longer.

"Now what?" she asked, blowing on the surface of her tea. The dry air stole even the moisture of steam, making it too easy to burn a careless tongue.

"Now..." Nerium tilted her cup, as if reading their future in the leaves. "It won't be long before Ahmar realizes what's happened. As fond as I've been of antagonizing her, I don't look forward to that confrontation. But it will have to come before we can continue our work here. I'll need your help." If the admission pained her, she hid it well—or perhaps it was merely a command. "And," she added, sliding a plate of cakes across the table, "I need you strong. Eat. Rest. I'll look at your shoulder again tomorrow and see if I can't speed the healing."

"I am tired," Isyllt admitted. Denying that would be ridiculous; she'd seen her face in the mirror. The desert and sleepless nights had left her hollow-eyed and hollow-cheeked, a sunburned death's head.

"Rest," Nerium said again. "You'll need all your wits

and strength if we have to face Ahmar, not to mention Al-Jodâ'im."

"I will." She took a dutiful bite of pastry, though honey and poppy seeds felt like scorched earth in her mouth.

She spent the rest of the evening in her room, lying with her eyes closed and pretending to nap, building a spell layer by careful layer. She emerged after dinner, drained but clearheaded.

Adam and Asheris were nowhere to be found. That was still for the best, but as the numbness wore off their avoidance pained her. Moth, however, was in her room, and opened the door at Isyllt's knock.

"Are you happy," Moth asked, "now that you've chosen? I wasn't sure you would."

"Not happy, no." That much was perfectly true. "But I think I made the right decision." Of that she was nowhere as sure, but she'd find out soon enough. "I have something for you." She took a silk-wrapped ring from her pocket: a pigeon's blood ruby, cushion-cut and set in white gold. It sat like a bloodstain on the white handkerchief, a reminder of her dream.

Moth swallowed. "This was *hers*."

Phaedra Severos, she meant. The haematurge's sorcerous plague had nearly killed Moth, along with dozens of others in Erisín.

"It was. It deserves to be worn again." She hesitated. "We never spoke of it, but I know... the flavor of your magic. You could be a strong haematurge some day, with proper teaching."

"I'm nowhere close to deserving a stone like this."

Isyllt smiled crookedly. "That's because I've been a

horrible teacher. You'll grow into it." She pressed the ring onto Moth's palm and folded the girl's fingers around it.

"There's something in here," Moth said, frowning.

"A present." She winked. "You just have to learn how to open it."

Moth's frown deepened. "You're saying good-bye."

Despite all her careful emptiness, pain still slivered between her ribs. "I don't want to. Please believe that. But I would rather not leave it unsaid, just in case. You're bright and clever and resourceful—you'll do well no matter where you end up. I haven't been half of what you deserve, and I hope you can forgive me for that."

The crease between the girl's brows eased. "You have been a lousy teacher, and not much fun to be around. But I asked you for choices and for change, and I can't say you haven't delivered." Her mouth hooked sideways. "Next time I'll know to ask for choices that aren't terrible."

Isyllt turned away before her face could betray her. "Anyone who offers you that is a liar."

Isyllt lay awake after midnight, stretching out her senses—quietly, carefully, light as a thief. She touched Moth, still awake, and brushed across Melantha, sleeping fitfully. She wanted to linger as she found Adam, wanted to say something, but there was nothing to say, and it would only make things worse. Next she felt Nerium, and held her metaphorical breath against discovery; the sorceress slept as well, if only lightly, and Isyllt hurried on. She found the sleepers in the library, and a guard dozing at his post at the side door. Of Asheris there was no sign, and she couldn't extend herself past the walls of the Chanterie.

Hours later, she wrapped herself in robes and silence and slunk out of her room. The hour of the wolf, this was called in Selafai; the Assari felt the same, though here it was the jackal. The hall was dark and still, and nothing stirred as she crept down the corridors and out an unwatched door.

She breathed in dust and myrrh, reaching out once more. Asheris had passed this way some time ago; the familiar warmth of his magic cooled in the night, a faint trail nearly gone. Swallowing a curse at the delay, she followed it north.

"Where are you skulking, witch?" Kash's voice came from behind her, but she didn't startle; she'd been expecting him. "Oh, forgive me. Where are you skulking, *mistress*?" His voice was vitriol, burning to the bone.

"Is it skulking if this is home? I'm looking for Asheris—have you seen him?"

"I see everything in Qais."

Isyllt sighed as he fell silent. "Will you tell me where he is, please?"

"Spare me your courtesy." His beak snapped, and she wondered how he made the sound so scathing. "You made your loyalties plain. Your jinni feels the same way."

"Where is he?"

"Near the boundary of Qais." He tilted his head northward. "And very close to crossing it."

An indrawn breath hissed between her teeth. "Stop him!"

"So sorry, mistress, but Lady Kerah hasn't yet rescinded her orders."

"You don't have to speak with him, damn you, just don't let him leave!"

"I'm already damned, and if you think I'll stop another jinni from fleeing this place, you're a fool. You may command me, oathsworn, but I can fight you long enough to buy him time."

"Damn you both," she spat. "Your fiery hearts have burned up your brains. Take me to him, Kash." She made his name a lash, sharpening it with will and magic. He flinched, and an angry spark woke in his dull dead eyes. "Now!"

"As you wish." One hand closed on her wrist like a steel band and yanked her forward into nothing.

It was the same rending of the world that had brought them to Qais, but this time he wasn't gentle. She gasped and choked as blackness flooded her lungs. If he let go she would drown in shadows. But his grip held and the void spat them out again. Kash released her as though her skin fouled him and she fell to her knees on stony ground. As her vision stopped spinning, she recognized the narrow pass that led from Qais's valley back to the endless waste of Al-Reshara.

"Isyllt?"

Asheris knelt beside her. He reached out, but didn't touch her. Since he was reaching for her left shoulder, she didn't complain.

"Don't," she wheezed, her lungs still aching. "Don't you dare run away."

"I told you I couldn't stay here." He touched her now, helping her stand, but his grip was as cool and distant as his eyes. "Especially now. You're my friend, Isyllt, one of the dearest I've had. Let me remember you that way. Not like this."

Her hands ached, clenched at her sides to stop her from

shaking him till he rattled. "Did flesh dull your wits, or have you always been this stupid? I need your help, damn you. I'm going into the oubliette tonight. You're the only one strong enough to go with me and have a chance in hell of bringing me out again if I fall. And no matter what you and Adam seem to think, this isn't my way of committing suicide."

His mouth opened and closed again, and Isyllt spun away with an exasperated curse. "I've sworn the vows, Kash, and I can command you, but I don't want to. So please, please, *please*, take us to the thrice-damned oubliette."

His bald head swiveled, regarding her from each eye in turn. Both eyes pearled as he blinked. "Yes, mistress." Kash took her arm again, and she barely had time to catch Asheris's sleeve and pull him after. They emerged on the top of the temple stairs. All of Qais spread out around them, dark and silent.

"This is as far as I can take you," Kash said, gesturing to the warded door. "I am forbidden the oubliette unless Nerium herself summons me. You may command me, but she holds my prison. You're free to enter, but if you tamper with anything I'll know, and so will she. If that were to happen, you would have very little time." He vanished—to spare himself knowledge that he would be forced to divulge.

Isyllt lifted a finger to forestall Asheris's questions and took his hand again. Nerves scalded her cheeks as she stepped forward. The wards licked at her, tasting her magic, tasting the oaths she had sworn, and parted for her. The door beyond was unlocked. She called no light till it was safely shut behind them, and then only a pinprick.

"What are you doing?" Asheris asked as they descended the stair. A whisper, but the sound rose like a wave through the well.

"Going into the oubliette. It's Nerium's idea. She wants to bond a mage to Al-Jodâ'im, a human mind to command the power of the void."

He recoiled. "Abomination."

"Maybe, but it's clever. If any human can survive it. She seems to think I can."

"As a demon? As something twisted like Kash?" He caught her shoulder as they reached the bottom and turned her to face him. "Isyllt, is this really what you want?"

She grinned; in the mirror of his eyes she looked like a demon already. "I wanted a purpose. This wasn't exactly what I had in mind, but it will have to do."

Even the smallest witchlight was enough to ignite the diamonds set in the walls. Walking into the round room was like floating in the night sky, close enough to touch the firmament. The sight caught in Isyllt's throat—so much beauty wasted on a prison.

"This is a very bad idea," Asheris said.

"I know. That's why I need you here." She leaned close to kiss his cheek. "If this fails, it may fail spectacularly. Be ready to run, just in case."

"What about the others?"

"Moth will know what to do." If she'd solved the riddle-spell on the ring in time, and understood the message inside. If she knew how to use it. Isyllt rarely bothered to pray, but she prayed now: *Black Mother, keep them safe.*

Praying for her own safety would be ridiculous, under the circumstances.

"Isyllt—"

He reached for her but she turned away, turned toward the pit. She didn't look back or slow her stride as she stepped over the edge.

If she fell and broke her leg—

She didn't fall.

She fell forever.

The nothing cradled her, drew her down into a black embrace. Its song slid inside her, under her skin and through bone, crawling between the seams of her skull and echoing inside her head. She was too small to hold it—it would shatter her.

The song wove pictures in the darkness, dressed her in alien memories. She saw Al-Jodâ'im, sailing the seas between stars, at home in the frozen abyss. She was them. Stars sang in voices of fire and crystal; the dust of dead worlds whispered in sidereal winds; hollow drumbeats tolled the failing hearts of suns. And Al-Jodâ'im sang to them all, and to one another, a dozen voices and one.

Then came the other song, an insistent whisper pulling them in, dragging them from their course. Pulling them down. Then the fall, into heat and light and screaming. A harsh, hot place trapped in form and flesh, and that welcoming song became shrieks and curses. The creatures who had summoned them fled, dissolving at every desperate touch. The weight of the world crushed them and their craft was shattered, their home far from reach.

Next came the chains, frail form-bound shapes standing against them, binding them with stone and spell, caging them in darkness. And the darkness was soothing after the fury of the world, but it was still a prison, and they wept within its walls for all they had lost.

She watched the failed experiments of Quietus, mages lost for knowledge and control. She saw too the experiments that hadn't failed: how the quiet men siphoned entropy out of the oubliette to fuel their own magic and keep themselves strong, even as that entropy crept into all their workings and soured their hearts. All around her brighter shadows fluttered in the dark—bits and pieces of all the mortals and spirits consumed throughout the centuries. Kash was here, and a child whose name had been forgotten, and a hundred others, all trapped within these narrow walls.

The darkness dissolved her; she became nothing. Nerium was right—with the right timing, the right strength and will and understanding, she could rise from the pit changed, inhumanly strong. But that would do nothing but repeat the sins of the past for another thousand years.

Isyllt tried to speak, but her strength leached away too fast and her voice failed. At least it was a painless death. Like falling asleep in the snow…

The cold retreated, driven back by warmth and light. Burning wings enfolded her, holding her up even as the icy touch of the void shredded them. "If you're going to do something, do it now. We'll have company soon."

Asheris's voice was sweet and rich as honey, and the sound drew her back from the edge of consciousness. She laughed as her fading focus returned.

"I'm here to free you," she said to the void. "You've been bound long enough. Come with me, and I'll show you the way out."

Her vow constricted like a chain of ice around her throat and heart. For an instant she thought the oath was too strong, and the breaking of it would kill her. Then, like ice, the links cracked and fell away. As with lying and murder and so many other things, treachery came easier the second time.

Darkness filled her, more than she could ever contain. It bled from her eyes, her mouth, her fingertips. It lifted her out of the pit and set her on the edge, Asheris at her side.

She saw the lines of power carved into the walls, the channels through which magic flowed. She saw the weak points, and where to strike. Sharing her eyes, Al-Jodâ'im saw into the crystal depths of the diamonds, to the tiny flaws no human could perceive.

A hundred diamonds exploded at once. Asheris's wings enfolded them both, shielding them from the spray of razor shards. The red salt door fell from its hinges and shattered; the impact rippled through the floor, shaking the stones beneath their feet.

The floor shook again, throwing them sideways. Deep cracks crazed the marble ceiling, raining grit. Somewhere overhead, the building groaned.

"I think you were overzealous," Asheris muttered.

"Maybe so." The words spilled power from her lips like black vomit. The edge of the pit collapsed. She clapped one hand over her mouth in surprise, but couldn't stop the wild laugh that followed. Stone dissolved like wet paper.

"This isn't the tomb I'd have wished for myself," Asheris said, catching a melon-size chunk of ceiling that would have split his skull.

"It won't be." This time her words rent the air itself, opening the shadow-ways. "Come on."

They stepped between darknesses, emerging on top of the temple in time to see the observatory tower shear and topple, crashing to the ground with an earsplitting roar. The floor continued to shake; with inhuman senses, Isyllt felt the spiral stair eroding beneath them. Asheris held her close and carried them aloft as the entire rooftop gave way.

Melantha's dreams turned tense and frantic before she woke, dreams of racing after faceless figures, desperate to reach them before something terrible happened. A hand on her shoulder pulled her free, and she lashed out blind and breathless. Adam blocked the clumsy blow and caught her wrist before she could strike again.

"Easy," he murmured. "It's a dream."

"No," she said, fighting for breath. The ringing in her head wasn't only nerves. Sheets tangled her legs as she tried to get out of bed. "Something's wrong. In the temple." Twice in two nights was too much—something was badly wrong.

The floor jolted as she stood, flinging her down again. Hands and knees scraped on the stones, and her teeth clacked as tremors shook the room. Glass rattled off a shelf and shattered. The crash drowned Adam's curses. As the ringing in her ears dimmed, she heard a distant rumble of stone.

"Saints," she muttered, scrambling for her clothes. Cloth snagged painfully on her bloody knees.

"What was that?" Adam asked as he grabbed his sword belt.

"Nothing good."

She shouted for Nerium as she flung open her door, but it was Moth she collided with in the corridor.

"It's Isyllt," the girl gasped, steadying herself on the still-shivering wall. "She went into the oubliette." Something glittered on her hand—a ruby Melantha had never seen before.

"She told you?" *And you didn't warn us?* She stopped the question in time—she knew better than to think she'd won Moth's loyalty yet.

"She left me a message." Her ringed hand clenched. "I only found it when—"

Another tremor shook the hall, throwing them all sideways. The Chanterie groaned around them as they ran; shelves ripped from the walls and furniture toppled. As they reached the ground floor, Melantha heard a splintering roar from the library. Her throat clenched as she thought of Khalil sleeping there, but there was no time to rescue him.

Guards and servants shouted, scrambling into the street. In the hypostyle a pillar tilted and fell, then another, and another, like a row of children's blocks. All of Qais shook like a tabletop under a pounding fist.

"Lady!" She turned to see Salah bolting toward her, dust rising from his steps. "What's happened?"

"I don't know. Get as many to safety as you can." If there was any safety to be found. "Wait," she called as he turned to obey. "My mother?"

"She ran for the temple." He vanished into the chaos before she could ask more, shouting commands to his men.

The temple that was collapsing as she watched.

She reached for shadows, thinking to bypass the toppling pillars, but the darkness split with a howl that knocked her backward. Only Adam's hasty catch saved her from falling in the street. The wind from the void scraped over her like sharkskin; the effort to seal the rift left her shaking.

"Stay here," she said, forcing her trembling knees to still.

In response, the lintel cracked, raining chunks of sandstone onto the Chanterie steps. Moth yelped as a stray shard caught her brow.

"I don't think so," Adam said.

"That's it!" Moth wiped her forehead, smearing blood. Pink light crackled across her fingers. "There's something else in here besides the message, but I couldn't work the spell."

Before Melantha could react, the girl darted close and plucked a knife from her belt. Her arm rose to block a strike, but that wasn't Moth's intention. Instead she brought the blade down the outside of her own left wrist. Blood trickled into her palm and dripped between her fingers. At its touch, the ruby blazed with hot red light, and a shining veil of power rose around them.

"What is that?" Adam asked.

"A ward. Isyllt left it for me to find. She must have known—"

Another chunk of masonry crashed down, but the shield held. As she watched the city collapse around them, Melantha couldn't find any gratitude for Iskaldur's foresight.

"I have to get to the temple," she said to Moth.

Magelight sparked in the girl's eyes. "I know. So let's go."

They dodged falling pillars and teetering walls. Somewhere along the way Moth had sliced her other wrist;

blood streaked her face and rained from her fingers, faster than the shallow wound should allow. The more she bled, the brighter the protective spell burned.

As they cleared the hypostyle, Melantha drew up short, breath abandoning her lungs. The ghost wind poured screaming from the fractured temple, stronger than she had ever seen it. But instead of grief and despair, this storm howled in exultation, fierce and free.

At the base of the temple steps, in the shadow of the maelstrom, Nerium and Kash struggled. The jinni fought with savage desperation, but he was still weak from last night's defeat. Nerium flung him away, crushing him to the ground with a word.

Melantha moved to join her, but paused as Iskaldur and Asheris descended from the storm, held aloft on flaming wings.

"What have you done?" Nerium shouted over the roar of falling masonry. Her nightdress was smeared with dirt and sweat, and blood trickled from a shallow cut on her cheek. Power crackled at her fingertips.

"It's over." Iskaldur's voice rang with inhuman strength. Another column split and fell. She gestured to the ruined temple and corrosion flew from her fingers to splinter the steps. Her hair writhed around a death-white face, floating in the draft of the void.

Melantha's chest hitched as she understood: Iskaldur had succeeded where she had failed so many years ago. She had become the void.

"It's over," the necromancer said again. Her voice was nearly human this time.

Nerium's face was grey and streaked with tears. Melantha couldn't remember when she'd last seen her mother cry. "I thought you understood. All we've done, all the sacrifices—"

"I do understand. That's why I did it. No one ever needs to make those sacrifices again. This has gone on too long, Nerium."

"Look up, you fool! Look at what you've unleashed."

Iskaldur lifted her head to the storm, jaw gaping as if she only just noticed the widening spiral.

Now, Melantha thought. *While she's distracted.* Her fist clenched around a knife. Demons could still die. And if she couldn't kill the necromancer, at least she could distract her for Nerium. It might be the last chance she had—

To do what, she asked herself. To make her mother proud?

She coiled to strike, but fell instead as Adam hooked her legs and tugged them out from under her. She lunged up, spitting sand, and he caught her knife-arm and twisted.

"No," he said, his voice as gentle as his grip wasn't. "I can't let you do that. I have to trust her."

"Trust?" She spat the word in his face. "Trust that?"

Asheris's shout drew their attention in time to see Nerium strike, magic a killing blade in her hand. The jinni threw himself in front of Iskaldur, wings flaring.

Kash got there first.

"It's over," he said, all the malice drained from his voice. Four gaunt arms held Nerium close and his killing beak brushed her cheek, soft as a kiss. "It's done, Nerium. Now we can both be free. Now you can rest."

His wings flared, obsidian feathers slicing open the night. He fell backward, Nerium cradled against his chest. The void took them both.

"No!" Melantha flung Adam aside, ripping open the night as she dove.

A storm raged beneath the skin of the world. The tempest caught her, spun her, sucked her down. Blind and breathless, she fought the current, reaching frantically for her mother. Instead familiar cold fingers closed on her wrist, steadying her amid the whirlpool.

"It's done, Arha," Kash whispered. Instead of spite or mockery, his voice was soft and tired. "Let her go. You're free now."

Free. The word was hollow, just as she was. She'd said she wanted out, but without Quietus what was she? An empty shell, full of ghosts and other people's memories.

"Are you going to kill me, too?" It would be easier if he did. How many times could she kill herself and start over? She felt like salted earth inside.

"No," Kash said. "I have something else for you. Talia."

"What?" The sound echoed in her head like a forgotten dream.

"Talia. That was the name your mother gave you, the name you lost to the void. It can be yours again, if you want it."

"What do I do with it?"

She felt his shrug. "Whatever you like."

He let go, and she fell through shadow and out the other side, to collapse weeping onto the sands of Qais.

Asheris sighed as Kash and Nerium vanished, his wings slowly furling. "It's done," he repeated.

Isyllt shook her head. "No." Her hard-won control slipped, and the denial opened a gash across his cheek.

They both flinched and she turned away, hugging herself as if that could contain the destruction. "Not yet. Al-Jodâ'im didn't deserve what happened to them, but the world doesn't deserve this. They don't want to be here—it hurts them, even as they destroy us. I have to send them home."

She understood in that heartbeat how to do it. And something else, too. She turned back to Asheris, and the voice that strained her throat to bursting was not her own.

"We can set you free, jinni." Her hands rose like a puppet's to cradle his face. Ahmar's curse disintegrated at the touch, wiped away as easily as a spiderweb. Darkness rose from her skin like smoke, and the fire in his blood flared to meet it. ***"You are trapped as we were. We can take apart your prison as you did ours, till only the fire remains. You would be as you were once more."***

"Free." Wonder and disbelief transfigured his face, lit his eyes like flame within crystal.

"You can go home."

His hands closed over Isyllt's as if in prayer, and his eyes sagged shut. When they opened again their light was fiercer, sharper, and so very sad.

"Thank you. More than I can ever say. But no."

"What?" Isyllt reclaimed her voice, shoving Al-Jodâ'im aside even as she questioned the wisdom of interrupting cosmic powers. "What do you mean, *no*?"

"I can go home to Mazikeen, hide behind shining walls, while the Fata bleeds dry. Or I can fight. I thought I was trapped between two worlds—what if I can be a bridge instead?" He gave her a lopsided smile. "And you were right—I would miss the theater."

"Very well," said the Undoing, returning Isyllt's mental equivalent of a rude elbow. ***"We have learned something of sacrifice in that pit, for good or ill. We've learned about vengeance too, and enemies. So we can give you another gift instead."***

Isyllt felt that gift leave her, disappearing into the roiling storm above their heads. Her awareness followed, and for an instant she saw through the eyes of the storm. It spiraled across the desert, spinning faster and faster. The black wind swept toward the northern coast, where its daughter-storms would founder ships and douse the flames of lighthouses. It swirled west to the mountains of Ninaya to wake avalanches on their shoulders. In the shining city of Mazikeen, jinn drew back in horror as their glass-walled towers fissured and leaves fell from the Tree of Sirité, and to the south little spirits cowered as the gale shook the jungle canopy.

But it was east that the Undoing flew, east to Ta'ashlan. Darkness broke in a wave over the City of Lions, and a thousand screams rose and were snuffed. Men and women fell in the streets, and those indoors fell to their knees and prayed. In the imperial palace, the empress collapsed on her balcony, clutching her stomach as the wind brushed past. But the storm gathered thickest over the great cathedral. One of the Pillars of the Sun split and crashed into the street below, destroying a line of buildings with its rubble. On the Illumined Chair, an old woman's heart burst as she cried out to her god. And in the apiary, her hands sticky with honey and pollen, Ahmar Asalar looked up in horror and awe as the full force of the Undoing descended on her. And fell, dying, amid the ruin of her hives.

With a whiplash shock, Isyllt's awareness returned to

her own flesh. The enormity of what she'd unleashed washed over her, sharp as a razor whose kiss wasn't felt till blood flowed. Before she could try to understand, Al-Jodâ'im's attention turned back to her.

"Home."

"Home," Isyllt whispered. Her wild elation drained, leaving fatigue in its wake. Not the smothering oppression of the ghost wind, but the strain of sleepless nights and more magic than fragile flesh could bear.

"How?" asked Asheris. "How can you return them there?" He gestured upward, to the stars lost behind the storm.

Kash and the ghost wind had shown her the first night in Sherazad, but she only now understood. "The void touches everything. I have a piece of it inside me. I am the gate—I just have to open it."

Asheris frowned. "That doesn't sound pleasant."

Isyllt smiled, but it felt like a grimace. "I won't feel a thing," she lied.

She lay down in the sand of ruined Qais and rose again into the Fata, shrugging off her flesh like a cloak. She looked down at her body, gaunt and wasted, white robes stained ochre with dust. A spent husk with neither soul nor spirits animating it. Asheris stood beside her, his eagle's head hanging like a burning mask over his human face. He spoke, but the roar of the storm swallowed the words. His fire was a spark against the seething darkness of Al-Jodâ'im. The Undoing drowned all of Qais, filled the valley like ink in a bowl.

Isyllt knelt beside herself, flexing ghostly hands. Both hands were whole here, freed from crippled meat, and she had use of her shoulder again. She wondered if she'd live to use the real one again, but it was too late for that to matter.

She plunged her two good hands into her breast, through skin and meat and bone. Muscle throbbed in her grip, slippery as a dying fish. She ripped her heart free.

Light sprayed from the wound like blood, a hemorrhage of magic. The hollow black diamond Kash had shown her glistened between her fingers, pulsing like a living thing. She dug her thumbs into the groove between ventricles and it came apart like a scored pomegranate. Instead of pith and seeds it held stars, and all the darkness between them.

"There," Isyllt said. She felt the word on her lips, but couldn't hear it. Her living heart faltered at this violation, and her ghostly form shuddered with every beat. "That's your door. Go."

An icy touch brushed her cheek in benediction. Then the wind from her sundered heart caught them, drawing them in. The void calling its children home.

Like water down a drain, darkness spiraled into the rift, faster and faster. Isyllt screamed as the maelstrom rushed past her, or thought she did; the void took that too. The current spun her, filling her with black and cold.

You may come with us, if you wish.

It was an offer no other mage might ever receive. For a wild instant she even considered it. But a voice spoke her name, calling her back to her failing flesh.

Good luck, she wished them as she fell.

The darkness that swallowed her was the ordinary kind.

CHAPTER 29

She wasn't dead. She could tell because she hurt.

Isyllt opened her eyes to neither stars nor ceiling, but striped cloth. The air smelled of wool and smoke and desert night. She tried to roll over and remembered the splint halfway through the motion. With a croak that should have been a curse, she fell back on the blankets.

"Here." Adam slipped a hand under her good shoulder and helped her sit. When she had her balance, he held a cup to her lips. The water was tepid and tasted of leather, a welcome change from the sour film of sleep that coated her teeth. Half the liquid trickled down her chin, but that was all right; she needed a bath.

When he took the cup away, Isyllt scrubbed her face with her sleeve. "The world is still standing, I take it?"

Adam shrugged, crouching beside her. Firelight trickled through the open tent flap, painting his face with shadows. "Most of it, anyway. There's less of Qais than there was. Part of the hall collapsed in the aftershock—that's why we're sleeping out here."

"Is everyone all right?" The question sounded ridiculous given voice.

"The mages in the library died, but I don't think they were all right to begin with. Moth was exhausted after that spellcasting, but she'll be fine. Brenna— She's used to starting over." For once he didn't correct the name.

"Asheris?"

"He's out there somewhere." He gestured beyond the tent. "We've taken turns looking after you, but he's restless."

"How long has it been?"

"This is the third night. You woke a few times before, but not for very long. This is the first you've been coherent."

"I don't remember," she admitted, wiping her face again. Her head was still full of Al-Jodâ'im and their song. "But I do remember you calling me, at the end. When I was fading."

He looked away, staring at the slice of night framed by the tent flap. "You hired me to look after you. Even when you do stupid things."

"Your contract ended over a decad ago, by my count."

He snorted. "I'll bill you."

Isyllt laughed, and something lodged in her chest snapped and fell away. "Help me up. My legs will atrophy if I lie here any longer."

The night was deep and still, well past midnight from the stars. Two tents were pitched by the canyon walls, between the ruins of Qais and the path leading to Al-Reshara. It was toward the ruin that Isyllt walked, stretching cramped limbs.

The starlight was enough for mage-trained eyes to see

the rubble of the temple, and the gap-toothed hypostyle beyond. Past the columns, the Chanterie was a blacker bulk in the darkness, its silhouette uneven now. No lights burned throughout the empty city.

"What happened to the people?" Isyllt asked softly, respectful of the weight of silence. "The guards and servants."

"Most have already gone. Melantha sent them away. It's a long trek to anywhere worth going, but between the myrrh and the money in Quietus's coffers, I think they'll be all right. A few are still here. Waiting to be sure we don't break anything else. Do you think anything will ever grow here?"

Isyllt drew a deep breath, tasting the night. Old magic remained thick in the air, and would for a long time to come, but the sense of hopelessness and loss was already fading. "Eventually."

They stood in the dark for a time, listening to the gentle whistle of the wind through the canyon walls.

"Are you going with her?" Isyllt finally asked. She'd thought she was too tired and scraped clean to care, but as soon as the words left her mouth she knew that wasn't true.

"Does that mean you didn't spy on all our conversations?" Adam exhaled sharply. "No. I'm not. I thought about it, but..." He shrugged. "The poison has drained, and I'm glad of it, but that doesn't mean we're good for each other. Maybe I'll look for nice women from now on."

"Let me know how that works for you."

Adam chuckled. "Come on. You're going to fall over soon."

She couldn't argue with that. Her knees quavered and

only the splint—filthy and itching by now—kept her spine straight. She followed him back to camp, but shook her head when he held the tent flap open.

"I need air." And the stars. Their song was fading, but she could still hear the faint crystal chime of constellations.

"Watch out for scorpions."

They settled by the dying fire, leaning against a boulder still warm from the sun. Isyllt closed her eyes and listened to the starlight and wind, the crackling of embers and Adam's soft breath. It was lonely in the way of empty places, but peaceful now with the prison destroyed and prisoners freed. For the first time in decads, she didn't dread sleeping.

Adam's indrawn breath roused her from the edge of a doze. "You swore their oaths," he said quietly.

She smiled into the dark. "I lied. I am a spy, after all." Her smile faded. It wasn't something to take lightly—if it were ever known that she was twice forsworn, she would be anathema to mages across two continents. She worked her dry tongue against the roof of her mouth before she spoke.

"I'm tired of being a spy. I was considering becoming a mercenary. What do you think?"

He was silent long enough for her throat to tighten. "You might survive it," he finally said. "If you start eating more."

"I'd need a partner. Someone who wouldn't get me killed. Who'd keep me from doing stupid things."

"You would." She risked a glance from the corner of her eye; his eyes glittered, but bloody firelight shadows hid his face. "But I'm not sure anyone can do that."

Isyllt laughed. "No, probably not."

Another silence. Embers cracked and hissed as the fire dimmed. "There's usually work in the north, in the mountains."

"Mountains." She rolled the word over her tongue. "It's a long way out of the desert, though."

"It is. So try to get some rest."

As he had a dozen times that night, Asheris paced a circuit at the edge of Al-Reshara, his boots wearing grooves in the dusty reg. When the stars wheeled into Ishâ, the quarter between midnight and dawn, he sank cross-legged onto the cooling ground. For the third time that night, he conjured flame.

He didn't bother collecting twigs or dung, but called the fire from the stones. The flames leapt and sparked, fueled by agitation as well as magic; he had called to Siddir every night since the fall of Qais, but with no answer.

This time, however, he felt the spell catch on the other side, and both his hearts leapt. Siddir's face wasn't the relief he'd hoped: grey and drawn, eyes sunken and bruised. As their gazes met through the fire, a sick feeling curdled in Asheris's stomach.

"What happened?"

Siddir laughed, raw and harsh. "You mean to tell me you don't know?" When Asheris shook his head, he laughed again. "The ghost wind happened. Three nights ago. It came like a wave out of a clear sky, right over the city. I thought it meant you were dead. Or that you did it yourself."

The final words of Al-Jodâ'im rang in his head. "It wasn't my doing. I had— I had a warning, but I didn't understand it until now. How many dead?"

"Hundreds, I imagine. They're still combing the rubble. The cathedral was destroyed—Ahmar is dead, and Mehridad, not to mention all the other unlucky priests and novices and supplicants." He shook his head. "I would have killed her myself for threatening you, but not like this." Siddir looked up, hazel eyes sharp through the distortion of heat-shimmer. "Do you swear you didn't cause this?"

"I—" Asheris inhaled the taste of char and burning sand. "I can't. I didn't mean to, but I helped free the ghost wind." If he'd taken the freedom Al-Jodâ'im offered in the first place, there would have been no need for their vengeance. He forced the thought away, before it poisoned him.

"Helped?" Siddir's eyebrow rose. "Helped Isyllt? I should have known."

"The wind is gone now, forever. She sent it back where it came from."

"Samar will be glad to hear that, at least." He winced at the empress's name, and Asheris frowned.

"What is it?"

Siddir glanced away, scrubbing a hand across his face. "She was outside when the storm struck. She'll be all right," he added, before Asheris could form a reply. "The baby too, we think. There was bleeding. It was touch-and-go for a while. And now the physicians know, and a few servants. Which means everyone will, soon. She . . . admitted that it's mine." His mouth twisted. "Are you coming back for the wedding?"

Asheris swallowed. "I don't think that would be wise, under the circumstances."

"No one blames you. Not yet. Someone will think of it

eventually, but I'm sure you can come up with a story of a terrible battle and how it nearly killed you."

His nails scored his palms as he tried to answer; his throat was as dry as the ground beneath him. But he'd had days to consider this, and to convince himself it was the best plan. "I'm not coming back. Not yet. This ruse was nearly spent, and there are things I have to do. You have my blessings, though, if they mean anything."

"Not as much as it would mean to have you." Silence grew between them, and for a moment Asheris thought Siddir would break the connection. Instead the other man leaned forward, voice lowering. "I could follow you. If you wanted that. Not right away—Samar needs me, and the city is in chaos—but eventually. It wouldn't be the first time I've faked my death and snuck out of town." He said it with a wry grin, but his voice was rough, burred with something raw and earnest.

Asheris reached, unthinking, but his fingers touched fire instead of flesh. A dozen replies caught and died before he found one he could speak aloud.

"Don't. Not because I don't want you to," he added quickly. "But because I mean to come back to Ta'ashlan eventually. I mean to change things. And when I do it wouldn't hurt to have the imperial consort on my side. Besides, I'm going into the desert. You'd be bored sick of it within a decad. Tell Samar I'm sorry."

"Don't be too long away." Siddir raised long brown fingers to his temple, where dye covered greying hair. "Some of us don't have forever."

Asheris's throat closed around all the things he wanted to say, all the things they'd never told each other. To say them now would sound too much like a farewell. "I won't," he said instead, and made the words a promise. He raised his hand once more, a phantom caress.

The fire died, and he was alone again. He swallowed the taste of salt.

From across the desert, deep into the glittering erg, came a high chittering cry. Another answered, and fell silent. Wild spirits, the kind he hadn't seen or heard since he left Symir.

Asheris swallowed again, and this time he tasted hope as well as dust.

Isyllt returned to her tent at dawn and woke hours later to find Moth watching her. The girl passed a skin of water and bowl of boiled grain and fruit, and waited for Isyllt to eat and drink.

"Are you all right?" Isyllt asked at last, setting down the empty dish.

"Fine. I mean," she added with a shrug, "I will be." A bruise darkened on her forehead, and fresh cuts scabbed on each wrist; she rubbed one absently now. Her face was pale beneath the desert tan, and the ruby gleamed on her left hand. She tingled against Isyllt's *otherwise* senses, stronger than she ever had before. "I've never used so much magic at once before. I had barely solved your puzzle before you did... whatever it was you did."

"You did well."

Moth glanced away, color rising in her cheeks.

"What will you do now?" Isyllt asked.

The girl frowned, twisting the ring. "I've been wondering that myself. I think... I think I want to go with Melantha. Or whatever she's going to call herself now. She doesn't have anyone. And she reminds me of me."

Her eyes flickered, a quick glint of humor. "I want to see all the places she's told me about."

Isyllt swallowed. "If that's what you want. I know you can take care of yourself. But if you ever need me—"

Moth smiled, quick and gone. "I'm glad you didn't get yourself killed."

"So am I," Isyllt said, and surprised herself with how much she meant it.

That afternoon Isyllt managed a clumsy bath, and Adam helped her wrap her shoulder in a fresh splint. All of Nerium's healing had been undone by Al-Jodâ'im; a stitch had torn free, and the flesh around the rest was warm and proud. She didn't need to worry about infection, but it would scar. Next time she injured herself, she'd have to remember to do it somewhere besides her left arm.

Clean and dressed once more in white, she followed Moth's directions and went searching for Melantha. She found the woman sitting on the Chanterie steps between the sphinxes, rubble strewn about her feet. The great brassbound doors hung crooked on their hinges, and fissures crazed the tall red walls.

Melantha looked up when Isyllt stopped in front of her. Her eyes were bruised and red. Something in her face was different, though Isyllt couldn't say what. She looked older. Quieter inside. Perhaps it was only the weariness of grief.

"I'm sorry about your mother," Isyllt said. "She believed in what she did. I wish I could have known her without her vows.

Melantha laughed, a sound like breaking bones. "So do I."

"Take care of Moth."

Isyllt watched a retort rise to the woman's lips, watched her swallow it back. "I will. You take care of Adam."

She could have left it at that—should have, no doubt—but as she turned away, a perverse impulse caught her. She paused, casting a last glance over her shoulder. "Before I forget, I'll let you say your good-byes." Her ring flickered, and the air chilled as the brown man's ghost materialized beside her.

"Why am I not surprised to see what's happened while I was gone?" His voice was hollow and death-faded, but acerbic as ever.

Isyllt lengthened her stride, before a knife found its way to her back.

Isyllt woke during the hour of the jackal, and couldn't sleep again. Finally she rose and tugged on her boots, moving quietly to keep from waking Adam. In the other tent, Asheris seemed to sleep as well, or was lost in his thoughts. The night was peaceful, broken only by the distant yipping of jackals, but a heavy weight settled in her chest.

She climbed the ruined temple carefully, testing every step. Her magic told her all the entropomantic power in the building had faded, but that wouldn't save her if a load-bearing structure gave way. None did, however, and she reached the top unscathed.

The highest tier where tower and inner stairs had stood was now a pit half filled with broken masonry, like a collapsed well. No one would reach the oubliette and its buried fortune again without a team of architects.

The stars moved while she stood there. Their light glinted on the black diamond as she turned her ring between her fingers. The dull cabochon shape was lusterless without ghostlight, hollow and weightless without its burden of souls. The stone was near to priceless, the dearest gift she'd ever received and a reminder of the man she'd loved for half her life. A bitter reminder now, but that might ease with time.

It was also a prison, and the mark of a station she'd lost and oaths she'd broken. And she was sick to death of diamonds. Sick of prisons.

Black diamond and white gold glittered as the ring fell, clinking softly as it bounced and rolled. With one last spark, it vanished into a crevice beyond her reach. Her right hand clenched at her side, naked and cold. Her stomach cramped and she sank to her knees on the stone, eyes blurring as she fought the urge to crawl after it.

She held herself still until the worst scald of regret passed. It would scar, but it would heal. If she told herself that often enough, one day it might be true.

On the valley floor, Adam and Asheris had risen and were breaking camp. Isyllt scrubbed the last tears off her cheeks and went to join them. Hours remained until dawn, but they had a long way still to go.

ACKNOWLEDGMENTS

As always, I owe a huge debt of gratitude to Elizabeth Bear, Jodi Meadows, Celia Marsh, Liz Bourke, and everyone in the drowwzoo chat. They've helped me through four novels now, and deserve medals. And of course my husband, Steven, who's lived with me through all four of those books. I would also like to thank the Partners in Climb, all my Internet friends, Jennifer Jackson, DongWon Song, and everyone at Orbit who gives me such beautiful covers.

I owe an additional thanks to Marq de Villiers and Sheila Hirtle for their book *Sahara: A Natural History*. My descriptions of Al-Reshara would be much poorer without their detailed research and graceful prose.

Thank you!

DRAMATIS PERSONAE

Adam—a mercenary, Isyllt's bodyguard
Ahmar Asalar—priestess of the Unconquered Sun, and a member of Quietus
Ahmet Sahin—spymaster of Kehribar
Al-Jodâ'im—the Undoing, ancient spirits bound by Quietus
Asheris al Seth—an Assari mage, also a jinni
Corylus—an agent of Quietus
Isyllt Iskaldur—necromancer and sometime spy
Kash—a jinni, bound by Quietus
Khalil Ramadi—a member of Quietus
Melantha—an assassin with a past (several of them, in fact)
Moth—Isyllt's apprentice, formerly named Dahlia
Nerium Kerah—Melantha's mother, a member of Quietus
Raisa—a ghul
Samar al Seth—empress of Assar
Shirin Asfaron—a member of Quietus
Siavush al Naranj—a member of Quietus
Siddir Bashari—an Assari nobleman and spy

APPENDIX

Calendars and Time

Selafai and the Assari Empire both use 365-day calendars, divided into twelve 30-day months. Months are in turn divided into ten-day decads. The extra five days are considered dead days, or demon days, and not counted on calendars. No business is conducted on these days, and births and deaths will be recorded on the first day of the next month; many women choose to induce labor in the preceding days rather than risk an ill-omened child.

The Assari calendar reckons years *Sal Emperaturi*, from the combining of the kingdoms Khem and Deshra by Queen Assar. The year begins with the flooding of the Rivers Ash and Nilufer. Months are Sebek, Kebeshet, Anuket, Tauret, Hathor, Selket, Nebethet, Seker, Reharakes, Khensu, Imhetep, and Sekhmet. Days of the decad (called a mudat in Assari) are Ahit, Ithanit, Talath, Arbat, Khamsat, Sitath, Sabath, Tamanit, Tisath, and Ashrat.

In 727 SE the Assari Empire invaded the western kingdom of Elissar. Elissar's royal house, led by Embria Selaphaïs, escaped across the sea and settled on the northern continent. Six years later the refugees founded the kingdom of Selafai, and capital New Tanaïs. They established a new calendar, reckoned *Ab urbe condita* but otherwise styled after the Assari. Selafaïn years end with the winter solstice, beginning again after the five dead days, six months and five days after the Assari New Year. Selafaïn months are Ganymedos, Narkisos, Apollon, Sephone, Io, Janus, Merkare, Sirius, Kybelis, Pallas, Lamia, and Hekate. Days of the decad are Kalliope, Klio, Erata, Euterpis, Melpomene, Polyhymnis, Terpsichora, Thalis, Uranis, and Mnemosin.

Selafaïns measure twenty-four-hour days beginning at sunrise. Time is marked in eight three-hour increments known as terces. The day begins with the first terce, dawn, also called the hour of tenderness. The second is morning, the hour of virtue; then noon, the hour of reason; afternoon, the hour of patience; evening, the hour of restraint; night, the hour of comfort (also known as the hour of pleasure or of excess); midnight, the hour of regret; and predawn, the hour of release.

The Assari divide their days into four six-hour quarters, roughly coinciding with liturgical services: Fajir, or dawn; Zhur, the zenith; Maghrevi, dusk; and Ishâ, the nadir.

extras

meet the author

AMANDA DOWNUM was born in Virginia and has since spent time in Indonesia, Micronesia, Missouri, and Arizona. In 1990 she was sucked into the gravity well of Texas and has not yet escaped. She graduated from the University of North Texas with a degree in English literature, and has spent the last ten years working in a succession of libraries and bookstores; she is very fond of alphabetizing. She currently lives near Austin in a house with a spooky attic, which she shares with her long-suffering husband and fluctuating numbers of animals and half-finished novels. She spends her spare time making jewelry and falling off perfectly good rocks. To learn more about the author, visit www.amandadownum.com.

introducing

If you enjoyed THE KINGDOMS OF DUST,

look out for

THE HUNDRED THOUSAND KINGDOMS

By N. K. Jemisin

Yeine Darr is an outcast from the barbarian north. But when her mother dies under mysterious circumstances, she is summoned to the majestic city of Sky. There, to her shock, Yeine is named an heiress to the king. But the throne of the Hundred Thousand Kingdoms is not easily won, and Yeine is thrust into a vicious power struggle.

I am not as I once was. They have done this to me, broken me open and torn out my heart. I do not know who I am anymore.

I must try to remember.

* * *

My people tell stories of the night I was born. They say my mother crossed her legs in the middle of labor and fought with all her strength not to release me into the world. I was born anyhow, of course; nature cannot be denied. Yet it does not surprise me that she tried.

My mother was an heiress of the Arameri. There was a ball for the lesser nobility—the sort of thing that happens once a decade as a backhanded sop to their self-esteem. My father dared ask my mother to dance; she deigned to consent. I have often wondered what he said and did that night to make her fall in love with him so powerfully, for she eventually abdicated her position to be with him. It is the stuff of great tales, yes? Very romantic. In the tales, such a couple lives happily ever after. The tales do not say what happens when the most powerful family in the world is offended in the process.

But I forget myself. Who was I, again? Ah, yes.

My name is Yeine. In my people's way I am Yeine dau she Kinneth tai wer Somem kanna Darre, which means that I am the daughter of Kinneth, and that my tribe within the Darre people is called Somem. Tribes mean little to us these days, though before the Gods' War they were more important.

I am nineteen years old. I also am, or was, the chieftain of my people, called *ennu*. In the Arameri way, which is the way of the Amn race from whom they originated, I am the Baroness Yeine Darr.

One month after my mother died, I received a message from my grandfather Dekarta Arameri, inviting me to visit the family seat. Because one does not refuse an invitation from the Arameri, I set forth. It took the better part of three months to travel from the High North continent to Senm, across the Repentance Sea. Despite Darr's relative poverty, I traveled in style the whole way, first by palanquin and ocean vessel, and finally by chauffeured horse-coach. This was not my choice. The Darre Warriors' Council, which rather desperately hoped that I might restore us to the Arameri's good graces, thought that this extravagance would help. It is well known that Amn respect displays of wealth.

Thus arrayed, I arrived at my destination on the cusp of the winter solstice. And as the driver stopped the coach on a hill outside the city, ostensibly to water the horses but more likely because he was a local and liked to watch foreigners gawk, I got my first glimpse of the Hundred Thousand Kingdoms' heart.

There is a rose that is famous in High North. (This is not a digression.) It is called the altarskirt rose. Not only do its petals unfold in a radiance of pearled white, but frequently it grows an incomplete secondary flower about the base of its stem. In its most prized form, the altarskirt grows a layer of overlarge petals that drape the ground. The two bloom in tandem, seedbearing head and skirt, glory above and below.

This was the city called Sky. On the ground, sprawling over a small mountain or an oversize hill: a circle of high walls, mounting tiers of buildings, all resplendent in white, per Arameri decree. Above the city, smaller but brighter, the pearl of its tiers occasionally obscured by scuds of cloud, was the palace—also called Sky, and perhaps more deserving of the name. I knew the column was there, the impossibly thin column that supported such a massive structure, but from that distance I couldn't see it. Palace floated above city, linked in spirit, both so unearthly in their beauty that I held my breath at the sight.

The altarskirt rose is priceless because of the difficulty of producing it. The most famous lines are heavily inbred; it originated as a deformity that some savvy breeder deemed useful. The primary flower's scent, sweet to us, is apparently repugnant to insects; these roses must be pollinated by hand. The secondary flower saps nutrients crucial for the plant's fertility. Seeds are rare, and for every one that grows into a perfect altarskirt, ten others become plants that must be destroyed for their hideousness.

At the gates of Sky (the palace) I was turned away, though not for the reasons I'd expected. My grandfather was not present, it seemed. He had left instructions in the event of my arrival.

Sky is the Arameri's home; business is never done there. This is because, officially, they do not rule the world. The Nobles' Consortium does, with the benevolent assistance of the Order of Itempas. The Consortium meets in the Salon, a huge, stately building—white-walled, of course—that sits among a cluster of official buildings at the foot of the palace. It is very impressive, and would be more so if it did not sit squarely in Sky's elegant shadow.

I went inside and announced myself to the Consortium staff, whereupon they all looked very surprised, though politely so. One of them—a very junior aide, I gathered—was dispatched to escort me to the central chamber, where the day's session was well under way.

As a lesser noble, I had always been welcome to attend a Consortium gathering, but there had never seemed any point. Besides the expense and months of travel time required to attend, Darr was simply too small, poor, and ill-favored to have any clout, even without my mother's abdication adding to our collective stain. Most of High North is regarded as a backwater, and only the largest nations there have enough prestige or money to make their voices heard among our noble peers. So I was not surprised to find that the seat reserved for me on the Consortium floor—in a shadowed area, behind a pillar—was currently occupied by an excess delegate from one of the Senm-continent nations. It would be terribly rude, the aide stammered anxiously, to dislodge this man, who was elderly and had bad knees. Perhaps I would not mind standing? Since I had just spent many long hours cramped in a carriage, I was happy to agree.

So the aide positioned me at the side of the Consortium floor, where I actually had a good view of the goings-on. The Consortium chamber was magnificently apportioned, with white marble and rich, dark wood that had probably come from Darr's forests in better days. The nobles—three hundred or so in total—sat in comfortable chairs on the chamber's floor or along elevated tiers above. Aides, pages, and scribes occupied the periphery with me, ready to fetch documents or run errands as needed. At the head of the chamber, the Consortium Overseer stood atop an elaborate podium, pointing to members as they indicated a desire to speak. Apparently there was a dispute over water rights in a desert somewhere; five countries were involved. None of the conversation's participants spoke out of turn; no tempers were lost; there were no snide comments or veiled insults. It was all very orderly and polite, despite the size of the gathering and the fact that most of those present were accustomed to speaking however they pleased among their own people.

One reason for this extraordinary good behavior stood on a plinth behind the Overseer's podium: a life-size statue of the Skyfather in one of His most famous poses, the Appeal to Mortal Reason. Hard to speak out of turn under that stern gaze. But more repressive, I suspected, was the stern gaze of the man who sat behind the Overseer in an elevated box. I could not see him well from where I stood, but he was elderly, richly dressed, and flanked by a younger blond man and a dark-haired woman, as well as a handful of retainers.

It did not take much to guess this man's identity, though he wore no crown, had no visible guards, and neither he nor anyone in his entourage spoke throughout the meeting.

"Hello, Grandfather," I murmured to myself, and smiled at him across the chamber, though I knew he could not see me. The pages and scribes gave me the oddest looks for the rest of the afternoon.

I knelt before my grandfather with my head bowed, hearing titters of laughter.

No, wait.

There were three gods once.

Only three, I mean. Now there are dozens, perhaps hundreds. They breed like rabbits. But once there were only three, most powerful and glorious of all: the god of day, the god of night, and the goddess of twilight and dawn. Or light and darkness and the shades between. Or order, chaos, and balance. None of that is important because one of them died, the other might as well have, and the last is the only one who matters anymore.

The Arameri get their power from this remaining god. He is called the Skyfather, Bright Itempas, and the ancestors of the Arameri were His most devoted priests. He rewarded them by giving them a weapon so mighty that no army could stand against it. They used this weapon—weapons, really—to make themselves rulers of the world.

That's better. Now.

I knelt before my grandfather with my head bowed and my knife laid on the floor.

We were in Sky, having transferred there following the Consortium session, via the magic of the Vertical Gate. Immediately upon arrival I had been summoned to my grandfather's audience chamber, which felt much like a throne room. The chamber was roughly circular because circles are sacred to Itempas. The vaulted ceiling made the members of the court look taller—unnecessarily, since Amn are a tall people compared to my own. Tall and pale and endlessly poised, like statues of human beings rather than real flesh and blood.

"Most high Lord Arameri," I said. "I am honored to be in your presence."

I had heard titters of laughter when I entered the room. Now they sounded again, muffled by hands and kerchiefs and fans. I was reminded of bird flocks roosting in a forest canopy.

Before me sat Dekarta Arameri, uncrowned king of the world. He was old; perhaps the oldest man I have ever seen, though Amn usually live longer than my people, so this was not surprising. His thin hair had gone completely white, and he was so gaunt and stooped that the elevated stone chair on which he sat—it was never called a throne—seemed to swallow him whole.

"Granddaughter," he said, and the titters stopped. The silence was heavy enough to hold in my hand. He was head of the Arameri family, and his word was law. No one had expected him to acknowledge me as kin, least of all myself.

"Stand," he said. "Let me have a look at you."

I did, reclaiming my knife since no one had taken it. There was more silence. I am not very interesting to look at. It might have been different if I had gotten the traits of my two peoples in a better combination—Amn height with Darre curves, perhaps, or thick straight Darre hair colored Amn-pale. I have Amn eyes: faded green in color, more unnerving than pretty. Otherwise, I am short and flat and brown as forestwood, and my hair is a curled mess. Because I find it unmanageable otherwise, I wear it short. I am sometimes mistaken for a boy.

As the silence wore on, I saw Dekarta frown. There was an odd sort of marking on his forehead, I noticed: a perfect circle of black, as if someone had dipped a coin in ink and pressed it to his flesh. On either side of this was a thick chevron, bracketing the circle.

"You look nothing like her," he said at last. "But I suppose that is just as well. Viraine?"

This last was directed at a man who stood among the courtiers closest to the throne. For an instant I thought he was another elder, then I realized my error: though his hair was stark white, he was only somewhere in his fourth decade. He, too, bore a forehead mark, though his was less elaborate than Dekarta's: just the black circle.

"She's not hopeless," he said, folding his arms. "Nothing to be done about her looks; I doubt even makeup will help. But put her in civilized attire and she can convey…nobility, at least." His eyes narrowed, taking me apart by degrees. My best Darren clothing, a long vest of white civvetfur and calf-length leggings, earned me a sigh. (I had gotten the odd look for this outfit at the Salon, but I hadn't realized it was *that* bad.) He examined my face so long that I wondered if I should show my teeth.

Instead he smiled, showing his. "Her mother has trained her. Look how she shows no fear or resentment, even now."

"She will do, then," said Dekarta.

"Do for what, Grandfather?" I asked. The weight in the room grew heavier, expectant, though he had already named me granddaughter. There was a certain risk involved in my daring to address him the same familiar way, of course—powerful men are touchy over odd things. But my mother had indeed trained me well, and I knew it was worth the risk to establish myself in the court's eyes.

Dekarta Arameri's face did not change; I could not read it. "For my heir, Granddaughter. I intend to name you to that position today."

The silence turned to stone as hard as my grandfather's chair.

I thought he might be joking, but no one laughed. That was what made me believe him at last: the utter shock and horror on the faces of the courtiers as they stared at their lord. Except the one called Viraine. He watched me.

It came to me that some response was expected.

"You already have heirs," I said.

"Not as diplomatic as she could be," Viraine said in a dry tone.

Dekarta ignored this. "It is true, there are two other candidates," he said to me. "My niece and nephew, Scimina and Relad. Your cousins, once removed."

I had heard of them, of course; everyone had. Rumor constantly made one or the other heir, though no one knew for certain which. *Both* was something that had not occurred to me.

"If I may suggest, Grandfather," I said carefully, though it was impossible to be careful in this conversation, "I would make two heirs too many."

It was the eyes that made Dekarta seem so old, I would realize much later. I had no idea what color they had originally been; age had bleached and filmed them to near-white. There were lifetimes in those eyes, none of them happy.

"Indeed," he said. "But just enough for an interesting competition, I think."

"I don't understand, Grandfather."

He lifted his hand in a gesture that would have been graceful, once. Now his hand shook badly. "It is very simple. I have named three heirs. One of you will actually manage to succeed me. The other two will doubtless kill each other or be killed by the victor. As for which lives, and which die—" He shrugged. "That is for you to decide."

My mother had taught me never to show fear, but emotions will not be stilled so easily. I began to sweat. I have been the target of an assassination attempt only once in my life—the benefit of being heir to such a tiny, impoverished nation. No one wanted my job. But now there would be two others who did. Lord Relad and Lady Scimina were wealthy and powerful beyond my wildest dreams. They had spent their whole lives striving against each other toward the goal of ruling the world. And here came I, unknown, with no resources and few friends, into the fray.

"There will be no decision," I said. To my credit, my voice did not shake. "And no contest. They will kill me at once and turn their attention back to each other."

"That is possible," said my grandfather.

I could think of nothing to say that would save me. He was insane; that was obvious. Why else turn rulership of the world into a contest prize? If he died tomorrow, Relad and Scimina would rip the earth asunder between them. The killing might not end for decades. And for all he knew, I was an idiot. If by some impossible chance I managed to gain the throne, I could plunge the Hundred Thousand Kingdoms into a spiral of mismanagement and suffering. He had to know that.

One cannot argue with madness. But sometimes, with luck and the Skyfather's blessing, one can understand it. "Why?"

He nodded as if he had expected my question. "Your mother deprived me of an heir when she left our family. You will pay her debt."

"She is four months in the grave," I snapped. "Do you honestly want revenge against a dead woman?"

"This has nothing to do with revenge, Granddaughter. It is a matter of duty." He made a gesture with his left hand, and another courtier detached himself from the throng. Unlike the first man—indeed, unlike most of the courtiers whose faces I could see—the mark on this man's forehead was a downturned half-moon, like an exaggerated frown. He knelt before the dais that held Dekarta's chair, his waist-length red braid falling over one shoulder to curl on the floor.

"I cannot hope that your mother has taught you duty," Dekarta said to me over this man's back. "She abandoned hers to dally with her sweet-tongued savage. I allowed this—an indulgence I have often regretted. So I will assuage that regret by bringing you back into the fold, Granddaughter. Whether you live or die is irrelevant. You are Arameri, and like all of us, you will serve."

Then he waved to the red-haired man. "Prepare her as best you can."

There was nothing more. The red-haired man rose and came to me, murmuring that I should follow him. I did. Thus ended my first meeting with my grandfather, and thus began my first day as an Arameri. It was not the worst of the days to come.

THE INNOCENT MAGE

Kingmaker, Kingbreaker: Book One

Karen Miller

A debut fantasy adventure that grabs you from the first page and never lets go.

Being a fisherman like his father isn't a bad life, but it's not the one that Asher wants. Despite his humble roots, Asher has grand dreams. And they call him to Dorana, home of princes, beggars...and the warrior mages who have protected the kingdom for generations.

Little does Asher know, however, that his arrival in the city is being closely watched by members of the Circle, people dedicated to preserving an ancient magic.

Asher might have come to the city to make his fortune, but he will find his destiny.

"Talk about making a splash debut!"
– *Romantic Times Book Review* (starred)

"Miller's prose is earnest and engaging, and h[er] complex story accelerates nicely toward a brutal cliffhanger finale."
— *Publishers Weekly*

A MADNESS OF ANGELS

Kate Griffin

For Matthew Swift, today is not like any other day. It is the day on which he returns to life.

Two years after his untimely death, Matthew Swift finds himself breathing once again, lying in bed in his London home.

Except that it's no longer his bed, or his home. And the last time this sorcerer was seen alive, an unknown assailant had gouged a hole so deep in his chest that his death was irrefutable...despite his body never being found.

He doesn't have long to mull over his resurrection though, or the changes that have been wrought upon him. His only concern now is vengeance. Vengeance upon his monstrous killer and vengeance upon the one who brought him back.

"London's magic has seldom if ever been brought to life so electrifyingly and convincingly."

– Mike Carey

"Griffin's novel mixes fantasy and reality into a plot that brings to mind Neil Gaiman's *Neverwhere*."

— *Romantic Times Book Reviews*

"Griffin's lush prose and chatty dialogue... create a wonderful ambiance..."

— *Publishers Weekly*

THE MAGICIAN'S APPRENTICE

Trudi Canavan

In the remote village of Mandryn, Tessia serves as assistant to her father, the village Healer. Her mother would rather she found a husband. But her life is about to take a very unexpected turn.

When the advances of a visiting Sachakan mage get violent, Tessia unconsciously taps unknown reserves of magic to defend herself. Lord Dakon, the local magician, takes Tessia under his wing as an apprentice.

The hours are long and the work arduous, but soon an exciting new world opens up to her. There are fine clothes and servants – and, to Tessia's delight – regular trips to the great city of Imardin.

However, Tessia is about to discover that her magical gifts bring with them a great deal of responsibility. For a storm is approaching that threatens to tear her world apart.

"A wonderfully and meticulously detailed world, and an edge-of-the-seat plot, this book is a must for lovers of good fantasy."

— Jennifer Fallon

"Her magical world is brilliantly conceived."

— *Romantic Times*

THE PRODIGAL MAGE

Fisherman's Children: Book One

Karen Miller

Many years have passed since the last Mage War. It has been a time of great change. But not all changes are for the best, and Asher's world is in peril once more.

The weather magic that keeps Lur safe is failing. Among the sorcerers, only Asher has the skill to mend the antique weather map that governs the seasons, keeping the land from being crushed by natural forces. Yet, when Asher risks his life to meddle with these dangerous magics, the crisis is merely delayed, not averted.

Asher's son Rafel inherited his father's talents, but he has been forbidden to use them. With Lur facing devastation, however, he may be its only hope.

"Ms. Miller is wonderfully talented in building her worlds and in filling them with well-developed characters that are believable in their thoughts and actions."

— Darquereviews.com